The Extraordinarily Ordinary Life of Cassandra Jones

Walker Wildcats Year 2

The Extraordinarily Ordinary Life of Cassandra Jones

Walker Wildcats Year 2

Episode 1: Creature Comforts
Episode 2: Supreme Talent
Episode 3: Camping Blues
Episode 4: Holding It Together
Episode 5: Birthday Goals
Episode 6: Coming of Age
Episode 7: Endings

Tamara Hart Heiner

Paperback edition
ISBN 10: 0-9890888-6-3
ISBN 13: 978-0-9890888-6-2

Also by Tamara Hart Heiner:
The Extraordinarily Ordinary Life of Cassandra Jones
Walker Wildcats Year 1 (Tamark Books 2016)

Perilous (WiDo Publishing 2010)
Altercation (WiDo Publishing 2012)
Deliverer (Tamark Books 2014)
Priceless (WiDo Publishing 2016)

Inevitable (Tamark Books 2013)
Lay Me Down (Tamark Books 2016)

Tornado Warning (Dancing Lemur Press 2014)

TABLE OF CONTENTS

Episode 1: Creature Comforts

CHAPTER ONE

Homecoming

"Home!"

Cassandra Jones stopped just inside the entryway of her parents' plantation-style house and dropped her suitcase. After a week in the arid heat of the Arizona desert, she welcomed the comfort of the sticky Arkansas humidity, even if it made her long dark hair sticky and her glasses kept sliding down her face. This was home to her, even though they'd only moved here a year ago.

Besides, she and her younger sister Emily had Girls Club Camp in a week. She'd get to see her best friend Riley for the first time since fifth grade let out for the summer. That was more exciting than flying across the country without her parents, or spending a week feeding apples to her grandparents' sheep.

"Put your suitcase in your room," her dad said, coming in behind her with Emily's bag. Her two sisters and brother followed. Cassie picked her bag up and went to the room she shared with Emily.

It was just as messy as she remembered it. Her parents had taken down the bunk bed, and now Cassie and Emily had two twin beds filling up the space in their tiny bedroom. Scattered everywhere between the beds and on every exposed square of carpet were clothes, toys, books, and old homework papers. Cassie wrinkled her nose. She'd kind of hoped her mom would clean their room while they were gone.

"Ugh, I have to pee again!" Dumping her stuff on the bed, Cassie raced to the bathroom. It had started in Arizona, this crazy need to pee all the time, along with an odd burning feeling every time she tried. Last night and this morning, she'd had to use the bathroom more times than she could count.

From the toilet, she listened to everyone getting settled in the house around her. Someone said something about the kitten, and Cassie wobbled on the toilet, wanting to see how the baby cat was doing. But she hadn't peed yet. Giving up, she washed her hands and left the bathroom.

"Kids," her mom shouted from the kitchen, "unpack your bags, then come help me with dinner."

"Sure," Cassie shouted back. She saw Annette, her four-year-old sister, outside on the deck, playing with the cats. Cassie opened the back door and slipped out also. She'd unpack in a little bit.

The baby cat had gotten bigger, hardly even a kitten anymore. Cassie played with him until the sight of her dad bringing in colorful plastic bags attracted her attention. "What's that? Groceries?" She followed her father into the kitchen.

"Fireworks." Mr. Jones set the bags on the table and grinned behind his mustache. "It's the fourth of July. I thought we'd get started."

Scott, her younger brother, joined Cassie at the table.

"Fireworks!"

"They're for after dinner," Mr. Jones said, shooing them away. "We have to wait for it to get dark."

Mrs. Jones handed Cassie a stack of plates to set out. When everyone sat down to eat, her mom smiled wearily at her four children.

"It's nice to have you home again."

"It's nice to *be* home," Cassie said, enjoying her mom's rice and chicken far more than her any meal she'd had in the past week.

The sky finally darkened enough for fireworks around nine o'clock. Cassie followed her dad out in her flip-flops, joining her siblings as they lit sparklers, cheering and hooting in the front yard.

Mr. Jones looked at Cassie. "Will you turn on the floodlights? It's a bit dark out here."

The switch to the flood lights was in the garage, just around the corner. "Sure," Cassie said, moving across the driveway. She stepped into the pitch black ground between the driveway and the side door. Locked. She gave the handle one more good twist just to be sure. "It's locked," she called to her dad. "I'll have to go in the house and do it." She took a step toward the driveway and winced when a branch poked her in the side of the foot. "Ow," she grumbled.

Her dad had out the Black Cats firecrackers now and barely glanced at her when she came back to the front porch.

"I have to go inside," she repeated, in case he hadn't heard her. "It's locked."

"That's fine," he said. "We'll be here. Tell your mom we're waiting for her."

Cassie made a face as she opened the front door. Her foot stung where the branch had pricked her. "Mom!" she called. "Dad's waiting for you."

Her mom poked her head out of the kitchen, her short, curly hair proofing around her face and adding to her frazzled look. "No one's been helping me clean up, so he'll just have to wait."

Cassie heard the chastisement but brushed it off, determined not to be guilted into cleaning. "I stepped on a branch, and it poked my foot." The stinging had turned into a definite throbbing now.

Mrs. Jones came into the entryway and looked at Cassie's foot, irritation marking her features. "Cassandra, put shoes on! We don't go outside in flip-flops!"

Cassie hurried to her bedroom and plopped onto the floor. Outside, she could hear her dad and brother lighting more fireworks. The shrill whistles echoed around the house, and she wished she were still outside. Her mom's voice joined the foray, yelling about something.

A moment later Emily entered the bedroom too. "I don't see why we can't wear flip-flops," she grumbled, coming in behind Cassie. She quickly slipped some tennis shoes on over her bare feet.

Cassie winced as she pulled off her flip-flop, then cradled her left foot in her hands. She bent her head over it, long dark brown hair falling around her face. "My foot really hurts."

"Humph." Emily just grunted and left the room.

Abandoning her tennis shoes, Cassie went for the clogs in the back of the closet. Her foot hurt too much to put on a shoe that would cover it completely. She got the clogs on but cringed with each step. She hobbled down the hall to the entryway, where her mom stood waiting for her.

"Come on," Mrs. Jones said, glancing out the window toward the rest of the family. "We're the only ones not out there."

Each step felt like a knife digging into Cassie's foot. She sat down and clutched her foot to her chest. "Mom, it really hurts."

Mrs. Jones rolled her eyes and heaved a sigh. "Cassie, honestly."

Now even her ankle throbbed. Cassie bit her lower lip, fighting tears. "Really, Mom. It really hurts."

"Take your shoe off."

Cassie gripped the end of the clog and pulled, but it was stuck. She tugged harder, trying not to yelp at the pain. She finally grasped the shoe and yanked it off.

Her foot, which minutes before had looked perfectly normal, had now swollen up so that a large round welt sat on top of her toes.

Her mom uttered a gasp. "What happened?"

Cassie shook her head, a tear escaping her eyes and trailing off the tip of her nose. "I don't know. I was just walking around the driveway to turn on the lights, and I stepped on something. I thought it was a stick. It stung me."

Mrs. Jones knelt in front of Cassie. She took her foot in her hands, and Cassie cried out.

"Shh," her mom murmured. "I'm looking for a wound."

Cassie tried not to cry as her mom tenderly turned her leg over and examined her insole.

"I see a few pin pricks right here. Could be from a stick that poked you. Come on, let's get you to the couch." Her mom put her arms around Cassie and helped her walk to the living room.

CHAPTER TWO

Intervention

The pain was worse now, coursing up her leg in waves. Cassie couldn't stop the tears, though she tried to slow them down by taking deep breaths.

Mrs. Jones stepped outside. "Jim," she said, "we have to stop. Cassie got hurt."

"Tell her to shake it off and come do fireworks with us."

"Jim." A warning note entered her mom's voice. "You need to come in here."

He must have heard it too, because he came back in without further argument. The other kids followed, and Cassie lowered her eyes to hide her tears.

Her dad examined her foot in silence, not bending to touch her. "What happened?"

"She stepped on something," her mom said, shoving a hand through her short brown hair in a nervous gesture. "She thought it was a stick."

"It's all big," Scott said, leaning over to stare at her foot.

"Get back!" Cassie snapped, wishing they'd all go away. She began crying in earnest now, not able to cope with the knives of agony slicing up and down her leg.

"I'll get the neighbors. They might know what it is." Mr. Jones walked out of the house.

"Emily, take everyone else to your room," Mrs. Jones said. Emily herded the younger children away, and Mrs. Jones sat by Cassie, taking her hand. "How bad is it, honey?"

"Really bad," Cassie sobbed. She couldn't think through it. Fire seemed to be dancing around her foot, over her skin, under her skin, boiling her blood. She squeezed her mom's hand and cried.

Mr. Jones finally came back in with Mr. Peterson, their neighbor, and his two oldest daughters. Mr. Peterson was a true Ozarkie, with a long, bristly gray beard, overalls, and a baseball cap on his head. The Petersons lived in a large log cabin at the bottom of the hill that he'd built with his own two hands.

"Get ice," Mr. Peterson told the older daughter. She hurried to the kitchen. He turned to the younger one. "Take care of the smaller children." She left to find Emily and the others. Mr. Peterson faced Mrs. Jones now. "She been bit or stung by something. Can' say fer sure what." He picked up her foot, and Cassie screamed.

The older daughter reappeared with a bowl of ice. "Here." She handed it to Mrs. Jones, who placed it on top of Cassie's foot.

Cassie jerked away from it. "No, no, no!" she cried. "It hurts, it hurts, it hurts!"

"What is it? What got her?" Mrs. Jones asked, her voice wobbly.

"Could be scorpion. Maybe snakebite. You need to get her to the hospital."

"You take her," Mr. Jones said. "I'll stay here with the

8

other children."

"You both go," Mr. Peterson said. "The girls and I will watch them."

Mrs. Jones was already grabbing her purse and the car keys. "Carry her to the car, Jim."

Cassie felt her dad's arms go around her, lifting her from the couch with a small grunt. "Thank you," he said to their neighbor.

From their seven-acre, plantation-style house in the heart of the Ozark mountains, the nearest hospital was only a fifteen-minute drive. But for Cassie, who felt like her leg had tripled in size and turned into a fire pit, the drive took an eternity. She sobbed into her hands and bit her knuckles to stifle the pain. "It hurts, it hurts, it hurts," she moaned over and over again, the chant becoming something of a mantra.

"Listen to you," her mom said, leaning over the seat and trying to laugh. "You sound so silly."

The humor was completely lost on Cassie. She just bit her knuckle harder and cried some more.

Mr. Jones stopped at the ER long enough to get a wheelchair, and then he parked the car while Mrs. Jones wheeled Cassie inside.

Cassie calmed down a little bit in the hospital. Her foot still burned and had grown heavy as lead. She tried to move it and couldn't. Her body began to shake, and her teeth chattered.

"Are you cold?" Mrs. Jones asked, moving Cassie to a corner once she'd signed them in.

Cassie shook her head, but her whole body trembled. Even her good leg bounced up and down.

And then she felt something else. That small burning

urge that had become far too frequent the last couple of days. "I need to pee," she gasped out.

Her mom stroked her hair. "Okay, honey. We'll get you to a bathroom as soon as we get checked in.

The waiting room was full. A man with his head wrapped in a bandage leaned over his knees, hands around his forehead. A baby cried in a woman's arms. A bleeding man on a stretcher flew past them, moaning as the paramedics ran him through the waiting room. Cassie kept glancing at the clock. Five minutes. Ten minutes. Her dad came in, scanning the room until he saw them.

"You haven't been seen yet?" he asked, his face a mask of annoyance.

"Not yet."

A nurse poked her head out the sign-in window. "Cassandra Jones?"

Finally. Her mom wheeled her over and quickly explained the situation. The whole time, Cassie didn't stop shaking. She clamped her teeth together to stop the chattering, but her jaw shook instead.

"Let's get her back to a room and take a look," a man in white scrubs said behind the window. He had a friendly face, young, with curly brown hair. "Looks like she's in shock."

Cassie tugged on her mom's arm as they wheeled her away. "Bathroom, Mom."

"Doctor," her mom said, stopping him as he directed them to a small room, "she needs to use the bathroom."

"Oh, I'm just a nurse. We'll get right on that. Let's put her on this bed first."

The room looked more like what she might expect at a doctor's office than a hospital. It had a small bed with a white cloth on it, a counter, and several containers full of cotton balls, swabs, bandages, and the like. The nurse and her mom lifted her onto the bed, and Cassie's stomach churned. She swallowed hard.

"I'll be right back with a doctor," the man said.

Cassie's mom wrapped her arms around her shoulders, but suddenly Cassie's insides revolted. She snapped forward and vomited all over the ground. She cried again, the tears rolling down her face as she dry heaved.

"Go find the doctor, Jim," her mom snapped at her dad, who stood helplessly in the corner of the room. He hurried out of the room, and Mrs. Jones grabbed a paper cup. She filled it with water from the sink. She rinsed off Cassie's face, using paper towels she found on the counter. "It's okay. It's okay," she soothed.

Cassie started to respond, but instead she leaned over and puked again. A warmth trickled out between her legs. In spite of the pain in her foot and the unrest in her stomach, shame crept up her face. Eleven years old, and she'd wet herself. "Mom," she whispered as her mother wiped her mouth down again, "I just peed my pants."

"It's okay. It's okay, sweetheart."

Cassie's chest heaved, and her shoulders shook.

"Okay," the nurse said, coming back in. "The doctor will be in here—"

Mrs. Jones jumped to her feet and went around the bed. "I told you she needed to use the bathroom! Do you know how embarrassing it is for a eleven-year-old girl to have an accident here in front of you male nurses and doctors?" Her face was red, her eyes glistening as she shook her finger in the young man's face. "You should have taken her to the bathroom when I first told you to!"

"I-I'm sorry, Ma'am," he stuttered, his own face flushing. "I'm very sorry. Let me help clean this up."

"No! You get out! I want a female nurse in here!"

"Yes, Ma'am."

Cassie actually felt sorry for him as he hurried away, but her thoughts didn't dwell on him for long. The pain in her leg was growing, traveling up to her knee cap, making her feel stiff and tired.

CHAPTER THREE

In Case of Emergency

In the next moment, the small room erupted with activity. Two nurses came in.

"Cassandra," one said, "we're moving you to another room. We're going to change your clothes. Just relax."

Before she could really think about what they were saying, the nurses were hauling off her shirt and pants. They shoved them all in a plastic bag, including her wet underwear. Next, a paper-thin gown went around her waist, her arms thrust inside the little sleeves. They tied up the back and laid her down on a stretcher.

"Mom!" she called, panicking. "Mom?"

"I'm here." Her mother took her hand, her face pinched with worry.

Then they were moving. Cassie stared at the overhead lights as they rolled by, door frames flashing in and out of her line of sight before they turned a corner and stepped into an elevator. Then they were going down.

They'd barely stepped past the automatic doors when Cassie said, "I'm going to throw up!"

Arms steadied her, lifting her, turning her, and she made

the cleanest vomit pile possible on the floor beside the gurney.

They laid her back down and rolled forward again, finally coming to a stop in another room. This one had machines that beeped and long poles with bags full of liquid. Cassie lost track of the people as voices lolled around her head.

"Measure the circumference of the leg."

"Search for a vein on her forearm."

Someone grabbed her arm, poked it, and then a band wrapped around it. She felt the jab of a needle, but the pain didn't even register in her body.

"No go on the arm. Her veins are rolling."

"Try the other arm."

"The leg is swelling too quickly. We need to administer antivenin. If the swelling goes past her knee, we risk cutting off circulation and losing the leg."

The same cold swab on her other arm was followed by another quick jab. "No go. Rolling."

"Doing a skin test."

"Try her foot."

"Got a vein!"

"Start the drip!"

There was another jab in her foot. Cassie's body convulsed, and her eyes rolled around in her head. Her stomach started up its familiar churning. Before she could warn anyone, the involuntary spasm hit her. She jerked upward and vomited all over her legs and the personnel at her feet. Something tugged on her right foot, and a slender plastic tube danced in front of her face.

"Clean her up!"

"She just yanked the IV right out of her foot. Blew the vein."

"Find another one!"

Cassie stared at the lights over her head as firm hands pushed her back down. The lights waved and blurred and then disappeared. She heard her dad's voice, felt his hands on her head, but the room went black.

~

"Cassandra."

Someone shook her shoulder, and Cassie awoke with a shudder. She opened her eyes and tried to focus on the blurry image silhouetted against the light. Somewhere close by, a machine kept up a steady beeping rhythm. She blinked and widened her eyes, but without her glasses, she couldn't make out the face leaning over her.

She turned her head and saw white bars around her bed, holding her in. She swallowed, her pulse quickening. Behind her, the machine began beeping faster.

"It's okay," the woman said. "I'm a nurse. I'm just here to take your blood."

Cassie realized then that she was in the hospital. "Where are my parents?" Had they left her here alone?

She pointed across the room. "Your dad's on the couch sleeping."

"Daddy," Cassie called. "Daddy, wake up."

A lump in the corner moved, and her father's figure lifted in the darkened room. "I'm here, Cassie," he said in a groggy voice.

"They're going to take my blood." She couldn't stifle the fear in her voice. She wanted him to tell them to go away, to not do this to her.

"It's all right."

"It'll be okay." The woman leaned closer, and Cassie smelled her flowery shampoo.

"You should have just let me sleep." She winced when the needle bit into her arm.

"I couldn't take the chance of you waking up and jerking the needle out."

Cassie just bit her lip, trying not to cry.

"All done." The woman put the vial of blood on a cart. "Go back to sleep. We'll do this again in a few hours."

Cassie exhaled, letting out a breath she didn't know she'd been holding. She spotted her glasses next to her head, on a small tray. Cassie picked them up and noticed a small glowing light attached to her finger. She wiggled her finger, and the machine beeped in time with her movements. An IV dangled from a vein on her other hand. Putting her glasses on, she spotted a clock under the television. Just after four in the morning.

Television. That meant there was a remote control close by, right? She sat up, and something pulled on her chest. She looked down her hospital gown to see several round stickers with cords coming out of them stuck to her chest. "I look like E.T.," she said with a laugh. She glanced toward her father to see if he'd heard, but apparently drawing her blood hadn't woken him up the way it had her. He lay on the couch, snoring lightly.

Cassie pointed the remote control at the TV and turned it on. She watched reruns of *Lassie* for twenty minutes before her eyes finally grew heavy and she went back to sleep.

A little after seven, the nurse woke her again. Cassie knew because as soon as her eyes opened, she focused on the clock across the room. She groaned when she saw the needle.

"Just let me sleep!" she said.

"This'll be quick. And then we'll bring you your breakfast."

"Daddy," Cassie called, determined not to bear this pain alone.

He awoke with a grunt. "What?"

"We're taking her blood again," the nurse said, eternal patience in her voice.

"Oh. Okay."

Cassie wished he'd come over and hold her hand, but he didn't. She gritted her teeth together and looked the other way.

"All done. Breakfast will be here in a minute."

She wanted to ask what it was but didn't dare. She wasn't sure she could eat.

That turned out to be a good thing when, a moment later, the nurse came in with her breakfast: a cup full of a chalky brown liquid.

"This is breakfast?" Cassie stared at it, wanting very much for it to taste like chocolate milk but doubting it would.

"You can only have liquids, honey. If you want some juice, we can get you that too."

Juice sounded good. "Do you have apple?"

"Sure." The nurse left the cup of chalk on the tray and disappeared.

"How are you?" Mr. Jones asked, stretching before coming to sit in the chair by her.

"What happened?" Cassie asked. Her images of last night were disjointed, blurred. She knew from the IV on her hand that they'd eventually succeeded in getting one in, but she didn't remember it.

"A little boy came in earlier yesterday with a snake bite. His symptoms matched yours, and he'd seen the snake. So they treated you for a copperhead bite."

Copperhead. Cassie tested the word out in her mind. She'd heard of that kind of snake before, but she'd never seen one. She wasn't too familiar with it. "It's poisonous?"

"Yes. There's an antidote, but unfortunately, you're allergic." He gripped her hand and turned it so her palm faced upward. "Here's where they tried it." He ran his fingers over a red rash on the inside of her forearm.

"Oh. So then what?"

"We prayed. They just had to wait. The poison has to drain from your body on its own."

"How long will that take?"

"Well, you seem a lot better. You're not vomiting anymore. We're pretty sure you're on the upside. But you're still in the ICU, so, we're taking it easy."

"ICU?"

"Intensive Care Unit."

Cassie tried to internalize his words. She remembered something else, something about her leg— "Am I going to lose my leg?"

He gave a brief smile. "You're a very luck girl, Cassie. The swelling went all the way to your knee and stopped. If it had gone past, we were at risk of it cutting off your blood circulation. But that didn't happen."

She looked toward her legs now, hidden under the blankets. "Can I see my foot?"

He patted her hand. "Not now. Your mom will be here soon. I know she'll want to take a look. Oh, and to top it off, you had a bladder infection."

"A what?" Cassie squeaked.

"A bladder infection. I don't know if you noticed having to use the bathroom more, but that would be why."

Cassie's face burned at talking about this with her father, but she had noticed. "Oh." That probably explained why it hurt when she peed.

CHAPTER FOUR
Rest and Relaxation

Mrs. Jones arrived with Emily a little after eight in the morning, when visiting hours started. She brought balloons and coloring books from Annette, which Cassie usually had no interest in but was excited for now. The television repeated the same shows over and over again. Mr. Jones gave Cassie a kiss goodbye and left for work.

"Smile, sweetheart," Mrs. Jones said, aiming the cell phone at Cassie's face.

Cassie smiled, holding up her E.T. finger.

The camera flashed, and immediately all the machines in Cassie's room went off.

"What—what did I do?" her mom gasped.

Three nurses streamed in, their expressions intense and worried. Cassie looked at them blankly, and they rushed over, sticking a thermometer in her ear and a blood pressure cuff on her arm.

"It's my fault," Mrs. Jones stammered. "I took a picture —"

They stopped their movements and gaped at her.

"You took a photograph?" one asked.

"You can't do that in here," another said. "This is secure equipment. You'll have to delete that photo."

"Didn't they give you a handout about phones at the desk?" the other asked.

"I'm sorry," her mom stuttered, blushing. "I haven't looked at it yet."

The third nurse waved a hand and gave Mrs. Jones a sympathetic smile. "It's all right. Just don't do it again. Consider yourself lucky for that one photo." She tucked her stethoscope away. "Looks like you're fine here, Cassandra."

Her mom and sister sat in stunned silence for a moment after the nurses filed out.

"Well. That was interesting," Mrs. Jones said. She put her camera away. "Guess we won't document this visit."

"Can we see the leg?" Emily asked, her brown eyes wide. "Can you see where the snake bit you?"

"I haven't seen it yet," Cassie admitted. "Daddy wouldn't let me look."

"That's because it grosses your dad out," Mrs. Jones said. "Let's take a look."

Cassie leaned forward and watched as her mom peeled back the bedsheets. Her thigh looked perfectly normal, and her knee only slightly rounded. But past the knee, her whole calf swelled up like an elephant's leg. Her ankle vanished in the swollen flesh, and the skin of her foot had bubbled up like a bowling ball, swallowing her toes. Pen marks dotted her leg where the hospital staff had measured the circumference.

"Oh, wow," Emily murmured.

Cassie could only stare at it. How was it possible this leg would ever go back to normal?

"Too bad we can't take a picture of it," her mom said.

"What about Girls Club Camp?" She worked hard to blink back the tears before they could fall. "I was so looking forward to seeing Riley again."

"Cassie. Don't worry about that right now. Let's worry about you getting better, okay?"

Easier said than done. Now all she could think about was how she'd miss the sleep away camp, her first chance to ever go to one. She tucked the worry away in the back of her mind. Her mom was right. If she wanted to go, she had to get better.

Someone knocked on the door frame, and the same nurse who had been kind to Mrs. Jones about the camera incident came in.

"Sorry for the confusion earlier," she said. "We just have to be careful. We've had people sue, you know, odd things happen. I'm Mabel, by the way." She flashed a badge from the lanyard around her neck.

"Of course." Mrs. Jones nodded. "How's Cassie looking? Do we have a time-frame here?"

"Really hard to say. But her vitals looks great. I expect we'll be able to move her to pediatrics later today."

Cassie sipped at her apple juice. "When do I get real food?"

"When we move you to pediatrics."

"What's that?"

"It's the kids' floor. You'll meet lots of other children in here once we get up there."

Cassie perked up at the thought of not being so alone. "Is there a bathroom? I really need to go."

"Oh, honey, we can take care of that right now." The nurse bent over, and Cassie waited for her to unfold a wheelchair. Instead, she produced a small, u-shaped bowl. "Here, I'm going to help lift you."

Cassie had no idea what that bowl was for until the nurse stuck in under her backside. Then she gasped in astonishment. "I'm supposed to pee in here?"

"It's quite all right, sweetheart. We're used to it."

Her face burned. She couldn't look at her mom or sister.

"We'll step outside," Mrs. Jones said. She took Emily's hand and pulled her into the hallway.

"Go ahead," Mabel whispered.

Cassie nodded and told herself to pee. She willed it to happen, but being stared at seemed to stop up her bladder. Finally she managed to get out a trickle.

"Good girl," Mabel said. But she didn't leave Cassie's side.

"You're going to move this thing, right?" She didn't want to sit on this bowl any longer than she had to.

"You don't have anything else?"

"No, I'm done."

"Are you sure?"

What did she mean? Cassie tried to pee again, but there was nothing left. "Yeah."

"Well, you let me know when you need to go number two, okay?"

Number two. So that's what she meant. Cassie exhaled. Being examined by medical staff for every bodily function would take getting used to. Now that she thought about it. . . . "I do kind of need to do that."

"Go ahead, sweetie. That's why I haven't moved the pan."

It took a moment, but then Mabel's meaning slammed into Cassie. "I'm not pooping in this bowl."

"Well, you have to."

"I'm not. I'll wait till I get to the bathroom."

"We can't take you to a bathroom. You're bedridden. You can't go up to the pediatric unit until you've had a bowel movement."

The argument didn't sway her. The ICU seemed awfully comfortable. "I'm not doing it."

"All right." Mabel finally removed the bowl and left the room.

"Well, how did that go?" Mrs. Jones asked, sweeping back inside.

Cassie told her.

"You wouldn't go in the bedpan?" her mom asked, furrowing her brow.

"I went pee."

Emily laughed. "I wouldn't do it, either."

Eventually Mrs. Jones took Emily home. Mabel came back in with another nurse, and both of them tried to convince Cassie to go in the bedpan. She wouldn't. When Mrs. Jones returned, they cornered her.

"She needs to have a bowel movement. If she doesn't, all the toxins in her waste will start to disperse throughout her body. They could make her really sick."

Mrs. Jones approached Cassie with a worried look on her face. "Honey, I know you don't want to, but you need to use the bedpan."

As if Cassie hadn't heard everything they'd said. "Take me to a toilet. There's a wheelchair." Why were they being so difficult? It couldn't be that hard.

Mabel exhaled, blowing a piece of hair out of her face. "Cassandra, it's really not that bad."

"I won't do it."

CHAPTER FIVE

Toilet Troubles

Mrs. Jones leaned over and muttered to Mabel, "She can be very stubborn."

"I have an idea." The other nurse left the room, and Mabel wrung her hands together. When the nurse returned, she carried a toilet seat attached to long legs.

"A bedside commode!" Mabel brightened. "The doctor said it would be all right for you to try using it. Here you go, Cassie."

Cassie examined the portable commode sitting next to her bed. There was no water in it and it didn't flush, but it had toilet paper, and at least she wouldn't feel like she was sitting in her own poop. "Okay."

Her mom and the nurses helped her turn sideways and slide from the bed to the toilet. The moment her foot left the support of the bed, gravity pulled it downward, clanging it against the commode legs. Cassie inhaled to keep from crying out from the pain. She focused on the seat, ignoring the throbbing weight coming from her heavy, misshapen leg. It distracted her from the staring eyes.

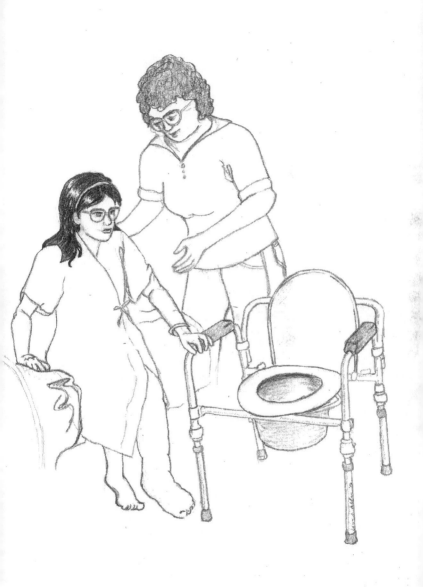

Mabel squeezed her shoulder. "We'll just pull this curtain and everyone else can go on the other side, but I need to stay in case you need me. Okay?"

"Okay," Cassie murmured.

Everyone looked satisfied when she finished. They helped her slide back into bed, but Cassie couldn't lift her leg up. She could feel the muscles straining, trying to respond to her commands, but the leg was too heavy.

"I can't get it up," she said. Would she always need help to use the bathroom?

She explained her fears to her mom after the nurses got her settled on the bed and left the room.

"Let's try something," Mrs. Jones said. "Leave your leg on the bed and turn sideways. Don't let your leg fall." They practiced sliding Cassie on and off the commode without moving her leg, and then Cassie did it herself several times until she felt comfortable.

"Thanks, Mom," she said, relieved. Gaining back at least that much freedom rejuvenated her spirits.

Her mom left around two o'clock to be with the other kids, leaving Cassie alone for three hours until her dad arrived from work. She colored, watched TV, and wished she had a book to read.

Mabel came in around four. "Guess what, Cassie? We're moving you to the pediatric floor!"

Cassie looked up from her coloring. "That's great! Will I be able to walk around?"

"Not yet. But there are other kids there. You'll see them."

Mabel unhooked the finger monitor, the chest stickers, and took out the IV. Cassie flexed her hand, glad to have the tube of dripping liquid gone. Mabel moved her into the wheelchair while Cassie gathered up her things.

"Will my dad be able to find me?" she asked.

"We'll make sure he knows where you are." Mabel wheeled Cassie into the elevator and pressed Floor Four.

"What about the other boy bit by a copperhead?" Cassie asked. "Is he still here?"

"Yes, he is. He'll just be a few doors down from you."

Cassie couldn't wait to meet him and tell him she'd been bit too.

Mabel helped her set up her stuff in the pediatric unit, then rang the floor nurse. A handsome black man came in, sporting a full head of curly hair and a small goatee.

"Zack, this is Cassandra," Mabel said. "She was bit by a snake also. I'm leaving her in your care. She'll need a bedside commode."

"Hi, Cassandra!" he boomed, flashing a big smile and holding out a hand. Cassie took it and smiled back. "I'll get what you need." He left the room.

Mabel gave Cassie a hug. "You get better. It was a pleasure to meet you."

Cassie didn't realize until that moment that Mabel wouldn't be her nurse anymore. "Are you leaving?"

"The ICU is my unit. But Zack will take good care of you, I promise."

The goodbye was over before Cassie could get emotional. Then Zack was back, a bedside commode slung over one arm.

"Anything else I can get for you, Cassandra?" he asked, setting it by her bed. "Will you need help with that?"

"No, I got it," she said, embarrassed he would even ask. "I did want to meet the other little boy bit by a snake. Can you take me to see him?"

"Let me see if he's awake. If he is, I'll wheel you over."

Zack returned a few minutes later. This time, a little boy shuffled in behind him, one leg bandaged up.

"This is Kevin," Zack said. "Kevin, this is Cassandra. She wanted to meet you."

He was just a little guy, seven or eight years old. "You can walk!" Cassie said, lighting up.

"Kevin was bit on his leg," Zack said. "So he was able to walk quicker than you will, Cassie."

"You were bit by a snake too?" Kevin asked.

"Yeah. I guess I stepped on it when I was walking outside in flip-flops. What about you?"

"It was under my bed. We were playing hide and seek and I crawled under there. It bit me. But we killed it."

"It was in your house?" Cassie stared at him in horror.

"Yeah. But we leave the front door open so the dogs can come in and out."

Still, the very idea of such a creature invading her personal space . . . Cassie shuddered.

"I'm taking Kevin back," Zack said.

"Come visit anytime," Cassie said, already feeling lonely as they moved toward her door. "When I can walk I'll come visit!"

~

Mr. Jones arrived just as Zack brought dinner in. Cassie's stomach roared in anticipation when she realized it wasn't juice or a chalky drink. She lifted the lid off the food tray and breathed in the aroma of instant potatoes and pot roast, never so happy to see solid food.

"How are you doing, Cass?" Mr. Jones gave her a kiss and settled in the chair next to her bed.

"Much better." Cassie dug into her dinner. "I get real food again."

Zack measured her leg while she ate. "Her swelling's gone down. Things are looking good."

"I'll be able to walk soon," she added around a mouthful of food.

"Soon," Zack agreed. "Not today."

That didn't surprise her, though it was disappointing. "When?"

"We'll check your swelling in the morning."

Cassie didn't sleep well. At least they weren't checking her blood every few hours, but after doing nothing but lay in bed all day, she had a hard time feeling tired. She watched late-night shows and cartoons until the early morning hours.

In the morning, after she'd had her vitals checked, she insisted on trying to walk. Mr. Jones and Zack carefully lowered her to the ground. She sucked in a breath, her foot still impossibly heavy. She tried to hold it up, to hover it above the surface before gingerly putting it down, but she didn't have enough control over it. It slammed into the linoleum floor, and she choked back a gasp.

"Not yet," Zack said, picking her up and putting her back into bed. "The swelling has to go down more. Maybe tomorrow."

The day passed in absolute monotony. The only highlight came when Kevin shuffled into her room to say hi. Cassie gave him a sheet to color, and he sat by her bed with her.

"There are other kids here," he said. "Tom is in the room next to yours."

"What's wrong with Tom?" she asked.

"He fell out of a car. Broke a lot of bones. His leg is screwed into the bed."

Cassie couldn't even picture that. She decided as soon as she could walk, she'd have to go see Tom. "Who else?"

"There's Maggie. She just came yesterday."

"What happened to her?"

"Her appendix burst. They did a surgery on her. She's fine now. I see her in the game room."

"There's a game room?" Why hadn't Cassie heard about this before now?

"Yeah. It's got some movies, video games, a few board games. Lots of kids hang out there."

"Wow." That did it. She had to be able to walk tomorrow. She couldn't stay in bed another day.

~

Cassie watched Zack measure her leg in the morning.

"How's the swelling?" she asked.

"It's looking better." He eyed her as he put away his instruments. "You want to try walking again?"

She nodded. This time, she was determined to do it no matter how much it hurt.

Mr. Jones had already left for work, so Zack helped her out of bed by himself. She tried to control the swing of her foot as gravity pulled it toward the floor. She managed to slow it right before it hit. Holding her breath, she let her foot touch the ground.

"Careful," Zack murmured.

She straightened up, putting more weight on it. Oh, it hurt. Stabs of burning pain flashed up her calf. She gritted her teeth and forced a grin. "I can do this."

"Really?" Zack backed away, examining her uncertainly.

"Yeah." She hoped he would leave soon. She didn't know how long she could hold this fake grin. "Thanks for your help."

She stayed where she was, grinning like an idiot, as Zack left the room. Then she grabbed the bed and leaned against it, letting out a gasp.

"Oh," she moaned. That hurt. But she was out of bed.

Steeling herself, Cassie began a slow shuffle out of the room. She kept to the edges, leaning against the wall and putting as little weight on her foot as possible.

She didn't make it to Kevin's room. By the time she reached the hallway, beads of sweat had popped out on her head, and she was panting. She made it to the next room over and dropped into an empty chair, breathing heavily and wishing she could lift her leg off the ground.

"Hey."

Cassie hadn't paid any attention to the room resident on the bed until he spoke to her. The TV was on, and the noise of the cartoon characters had distracted her from anyone else in the room. Now she turned her head and started at what she saw.

A boy lay there, about the same age as Kevin. His right arm and leg were in a cast. The left leg, on the other hand, was in a sling hanging from the bed. In the middle of the sling, right through his knee, was a fat bolt, like the kind used to close a hotel door at the top. Bloody tissues surrounded the knee on either side of the bolt.

"Hi," Cassie said, remembering now what Kevin had told her. "Sorry to barge in like this."

"That's okay. I'm Tom. What room are you in?"

"Right next to you. I'm your neighbor. Cassie."

"What are you in for?"

"I got bit by a snake." She eyed his knee. "Does that hurt?"

"Sometimes. When they clean it. I fell out of a car."

32

Cassie nodded. "That's so crazy."

"Want to play a game?" Tom nodded at the table. "I have some card games."

Cassie hated card games. She never understood the rules and always lost. "That's okay. I just need to catch my breath."

He looked at her foot. "Maybe you shouldn't be walking yet."

What did he know? She scowled at him. "I'm taking it slow."

"Okay." He turned back to watching TV, and she felt bad.

"I'm going to see Kevin. But I'll come back later."

"Sure." He faced her again. "My birthday's tomorrow. My family's having a party. You should come by."

A birthday party. In the hospital. A lump formed in her throat. "How long have you been here?" She noticed then all the cards in the room, the balloons, some half-floating, others hanging limply around the bed, and a myriad of drawings taped to the walls.

"Two months. I'm doing a lot better now."

Two months in the hospital. Cassie shuddered. She'd been here three days and couldn't wait to leave. "Yeah, I'll come by tomorrow."

"See ya."

"See ya," she echoed, forcing herself out of her chair. She grabbed the wall again and made her way out the door.

In the hallway, she paused. She could continue on to Kevin's room and make the lengthy, painful trek back to her room after. Or she could just go the few steps to her room now and try again tomorrow.

She turned toward her room.

CHAPTER SIX

Professional Walker

"Look at this leg." Zack grinned at her as a doctor she didn't know prodded and poked her and wrote down a few things in her chart. "Your foot already looks better."

It did. Cassie could see her toes again, and even some ankle definition.

"How was walking yesterday?" Zack asked.

The doctor looked up, raising her eyebrows. "You've already walked on this?"

"A little," Cassie said. "I got tired yesterday. I just went to Tom's room."

Zack nodded and squeezed her shoulder. "Good thinking to come in and rest when you got tired."

Cassie smiled, not about to admit how hard walking had been for her.

"That's good," the doctor said. "Everything is looking great. You should be able to walk around on it easier today. Tomorrow you can leave, if all continues this way. We'll get you some crutches when you are discharged." She handed Cassie a paper cup of water and the usual giant pills, or horse pills, as Zack called them. "Take your meds. Wash them down with extra water."

She did as expected, excitement mounting in her chest. Girls Club Camp started Sunday. If she got out of the hospital on Friday, surely that gave her enough time to go to camp.

Cassie knew her mom would come by soon, but she was anxious to try walking again. She was surprised at how much easier it was to slide her legs off the bed today. She put her feet on the ground and took a few ginger steps. Definitely painful, but not nearly as hard as the day before.

She crept out the door and over to Tom's room. It looked busy. Several kids played with toys around Tom's bed, and a fat man sat overflowing in the chair Cassie had sat in the day before. More balloons and streamers decorated the room.

She didn't want to stay, but she poked her head in. "Happy birthday, Tom!" she called, waving.

He turned his head toward her. There were purple circles under his eyes, and he didn't look all that excited. "Thank you," he said.

Not sure what else to do, Cassie stepped out and continued to Kevin's room.

"You're up!" Kevin was, too, and heading for the door. "I'm going to the game room. Want to come?"

"Yes," Cassie said, though her leg was already throbbing. She was very curious about this room.

It wasn't much bigger than a living room, and just down the hall from their rooms. A movie played on the big screen, and two kids sat in front of a video game console, controllers in their hands. Kevin pulled out a box of checkers and sat at one of the low tables. "Want to play?"

"Sure." Cassie sat across from him. She watched other

kids shuffle in and out. A girl with short hair and glasses came in, putting one foot in front of the other in slow, halting steps. She dragged an IV pole behind her, and a woman followed.

"That's Maggie," Kevin said, making his first move. "She's the one who had her appendix out."

"Oh," Cassie said. Maggie's face was pale and tense, as if every step caused her pain. Cassie hoped she never had to have her appendix out.

Kevin won the first game. He set up to play again and said, "I should be leaving today."

"Really?" She felt a stab of jealousy. "But we got here the same day. And I don't get to leave until tomorrow."

He shrugged. "Maybe I healed faster."

She mulled over that, wondering why he would heal faster than her. Was it because of the antivenin? It was the only thing she could think of.

After the third game, she felt sleepy. "I'm going back to my room to rest."

"It's the medicine they give you," Kevin said with a knowing nod. "It makes you tired."

Maybe so. She was really too tired to consider arguing with him right now. Or consider not taking the meds. "Okay. Come say bye before you leave."

"I will."

~

Her dad's laugh carried in from the hallway. "Thanks, Rich. I appreciate you doing that."

Cassie's eyes popped open. She stared up at the fluorescent light panel overhead, and then sat up straight in bed. "It's Friday," she breathed. "Today I get to go home." Unable to keep the grin from spreading across her face, she pulled herself out of bed and crept toward her father's voice.

He stood in the hallway just outside her room, talking with Rich, an older gentleman from church.

"Well, there she is," Rich said, spotting her. "The survivor herself."

"Hi," Cassie said, giddy with glee to be leaving this boring place.

Mr. Jones patted her head. "I'll be right back, Cass." He wandered over to the nurses' station.

"How are you feeling today?" Rich asked. He gave her an easy grin. Rich was like a grandfather to all the kids, usually with candy in his pockets and a teasing smile.

"Great!" She leaned against the wall behind her. "I'm going home today."

"Oh, really?" He arched an eyebrow. "How do you know?"

"They said I get to go home on Friday."

"Well, honey, it's not Friday. It's Thursday."

"No, it's not." Cassie shook her head and giggled at him. "It's Friday."

He laughed. "It's Thursday."

"No." She knew how he liked to tease. "It's Friday."

"No, it's Thursday."

Cassie just laughed. "You're so funny." She turned around and hobbled back into the room.

Mr. Jones came in and sat down in the chair as Cassie tried to gather up her pile of get-well cards. "When do we go?" she asked.

He glanced up from the remote to the television and laughed. "I thought Rich was joking when he said you thought it was Friday. Today's only Thursday, Cassie."

"It is?" Her spirits fell. "But yesterday was Thursday."

"You took a really long nap." His face was sympathetic, but his eyes sparkled with humor. "You must've woken up and thought it was the next day."

Had she done that? Cassie couldn't believe it. She sighed and crawled back into bed. "I'll just go to sleep again until tomorrow." She closed her eyes and tried to sleep, willing her body back into the hypnotic trance that would carry her into the next day.

Nothing happened. Her heart pounded with painful anticipation of leaving the hospital, not accepting that she'd be here one more day.

She heard Kevin's shuffling footsteps moments before he said, "Hi, is Cassie here?"

"Yes, but I think she's trying to sleep," her dad said from beside the bed.

Cassie's eyes snapped open. "No, I'm just laying here." She sat up. "Hi, Kevin."

His hand bobbed at his side in a wave. He wasn't in his hospital gown anymore, but normal clothing. "Just came to say bye. I'm leaving."

A mixture of envy and sadness flooded her. "Bye, Kevin. Thanks for keeping me company."

"Hope you get better soon."

"Who was that?" Mr. Jones asked.

"Kevin," Cassie said. "The little boy bit by a snake."

"Oh, that's right. Well, he was bit just a few hours before you. Which means you're next!"

"Yeah." Cassie grabbed the remote control and heaved a sigh. Tomorrow could not come soon enough. Not even her books were interesting anymore.

As much as she looked forward to her moment of

leaving, when it finally came the next morning, it seemed extremely anticlimactic. The nurses gave her some crutches, which weren't as easy to get around on as they looked. They rubbed her armpits, and Cassie winced with every step forward. The only person she had to say goodbye to was Tom, so she crutched her way to his room while her mom packed up all the cards and things.

She knocked on the open door frame and poked her head in. "Tom?"

The only response was a whimper. Stepping in, Cassie saw he had two nurses with him. They both worked around his leg, cleaning the wound where the screw connected him to the bed. Cassie stood there, awkward and uncertain, feeling like the intruder to an intimate scene. "I just wanted to say bye."

A small sob escaped Tom's lips, and he turned his head to face the opposite wall. Cassie's heart clenched. She wished she could help him somehow. She maneuvered her way out of the room and back to hers.

"Did you say goodbye to your friends?" Her mom picked up the small box of belongings and shoved a hand through her short, curly brown hair. She flashed Cassie a smile.

"Yeah." Cassie leaned on the crutches, taking the weight off her foot. It already throbbed, and she hated to say that she wanted to lie down again. "I'm so ready to get out of here."

"Then let's go."

"Cassie."

She turned around as Zack came in pushing an empty wheelchair, a big grin on his face. "Hi, Zack," she said.

"Look at you, up and about. All ready to go home. Come

39

sit down. You get one last ride out of here."

Did he know her foot hurt? She cast him a grateful look and slid into the wheelchair, holding her crutches across her lap. "Oh, Mom," she said, thinking of something else, "am I still going to be able to go to Girls Club Camp?" She held her breath, waiting in expectation for the answer. The last time she'd asked, her mom had said not to worry about that right now. But camp started in two days, and if she wasn't going, she wanted to know.

"Yes, Cassie," Mrs. Jones said. "The doctor cleared you for camp. And the camp nurse already knows the situation. But we're going to need to talk about it so you don't overdo it, okay?"

"Sure," Cassie said, though at that moment she probably would have agreed to anything. She resisted the urge to clap her hands. Camp would be so much fun. And her best friend Riley would be there!

CHAPTER SEVEN

Sleep Away

On Sunday after church, Mrs. Jones drove Cassie and Emily out to their very first sleep away camp, Camp Splendor. Though Cassie had been looking forward to going to Girls Club Camp for months, she wasn't excited about her younger sister coming along. But, as her mom stated quite clearly, it wasn't up to her.

"Besides, I think you'll be glad she's there," her mom added as she got in line behind dozens of other cars on the winding forest road. A big wooden sign, half camouflaged by the vines and long branches around it, read, "Camp Splendor." "She can take care of you."

"Yeah!" Emily said perkily.

Cassie just rolled her eyes and looked out the window. Even though she was on crutches, she didn't want everyone to think she was an invalid.

They finally pulled through the line of cars and stopped by a pavilion. Several vehicles were backed up to it with their trunks open, and parents and girls hauled out sleeping bags and suitcases. Behind the pavilion, in a neat circle, were half a dozen platform tents. The platforms were supported by stilts and were several feet off the ground. Long canvas walls had been tied up, leaving the interior of the tents open to the outside air.

Oh, this looked fun.

Emily hopped out of the car. Impatient, Cassie worked her seatbelt. Mrs. Jones opened the door and handed her her crutches. At the same time, Cassie spotted her best friend Riley, loading her things into a tent.

"Riley!" she called.

Riley turned around, her short hair spinning with her. At first she just looked at Cassie as if she didn't know her, then she smiled and waved. "Hi, Cassie!" She took a step in Cassie's direction just as Cassie placed her crutches on the ground. Riley halted.

Cassie bit her lower lip in concentration. The rocky, uneven terrain beneath her wasn't exactly crutches-friendly.

"Can you do this?" Mrs. Jones murmured.

Not doing this wasn't even an option. "Of course." Still, the stiff rubber bit into her armpits, and she hoped she could sit down soon. "Which tent is mine?"

Tennis shoes came to a stop under her nose, and Cassie lifted her face to find Riley gaping at her.

"What happened to you?" she asked.

"I was bit by a snake," Cassie answered, somewhat proudly. How many people could say that?

"I don't think they'll let you be here on crutches." Riley's voice took on that haughty, know-it-all attitude Cassie recognized a little too well.

"They already said I could."

"Uh-oh," an adult voice said. Cassie and her mom swiveled as a woman in khaki shorts, t-shirt, and bandanna over her hair approached. "Crutches? That's going to be a problem."

Cassie looked at the woman, a feeling of panic and alarm flooding up from her stomach. "But," she said, swallowing past a painful lump in her throat, "they said I could come." They had to let her stay. She'd been looking forward to camp all summer. Cassie turned to her mother, desperate for reassurance.

Mrs. Jones set her mouth in a straight line. "It won't be a problem. I already spoke to the camp director and the camp nurse."

The woman furrowed her brow and gestured to the woodsy area around them. "We're in the middle of the

woods. She can't possibly keep up. We can't carry her. I just don't see how she can be a part of this."

"And who are you?" Mrs. Jones asked.

"I'm the counselor over this unit."

Her mom jutted her chin out. "The camp nurse said she'd pick her up and drive her to meals and activities. She can still participate. She just can't run."

"Or walk, or swim." One eyebrow lifted on the counselor's face. "There's isn't much she can do."

Cassie felt her face growing hot, and she knew she was about to cry. They weren't going to let her stay.

"We'll help her," Emily said, stepping up to Cassie.

"Yeah," Riley joined in. "We'll be her buddies. We'll stay with her."

Mrs. Jones hauled out Cassie's suitcase and met the counselor's eyes. "Which tent is Cassie's? And what was your name again?"

The counselor hesitated, and then backed down. Maybe she realized she didn't get to call the shots here. "We all have camp names. I'm Rainbow. Cassie's in tent two, right over there." She pointed to one of the platform structures. "I'm just going to radio the camp director. Excuse me."

"You do that," Mrs. Jones muttered. She plastered on a smile. "Come on, Cassie. Time to hobble down to your tent."

Maneuvering the rocks and twigs was harder than it looked. By the time Cassie reached the tent, she had her doubts about her ability to be here, also. Her mom finished laying the sleeping bag over the mattress and looked up. "Emily's in your tent with you."

"Me, too," Riley said, sitting on the bed across from her. "I made sure we were in the same tent."

Feet pounded up the wooden steps, and Rainbow ducked her head inside. "Well, I just spoke to the camp nurse. She's very kindly agreeing to shuttle Cassie around whenever we go outside our campground. But that's the only exception we're making. She has to work and clean just like the other girls."

From the tone of her voice, Rainbow didn't approve of this decision. But Cassie just flashed her brightest smile, not about to complain. "Thank you so much! I can't even tell you how excited I am to be here! And I'll pull my weight, I'll do what I have to!"

Rainbow nodded. "Finish up here. We'll be going to dinner soon, and the nurse will be here for you in just a minute."

"Girls, I'm leaving." Mrs. Jones kissed and hugged both Emily and Cassie. "Cassie, I'm only an hour away. If you decide you want to come home, just have them call me."

"It's hard out here," Riley said. "I came last year. I bet you'll want to go home."

Cassie kept her bright smile on her face. She knew no matter how hard it got, she wasn't going home. "Thanks, Mom."

As soon as Mrs. Jones left, Riley hauled her suitcase out from under her bed. "Look at all my snacks," she said, tossing it open.

Cookies and candies and bags of chips filled up almost the entire bag.

"Wow!" Emily breathed.

Cassie felt a flash of envy, and her stomach rumbled. She hadn't brought any snacks. "That's nice," she said. She knew better than to expect Riley to share. She often showed up at Girls Club with extra candy and food, which

45

she used to bribe the other girls.

Riley opened up one of the bags of cookies.

"Can I have one?" Emily asked, holding out a hand.

Riley looked at her, all while nibbling on a chocolate-chip cookie. "Sure." She handed one over.

Cassie leaned forward. "Can I too?"

"No." Riley put the bag away. "You haven't been nice to me."

"What?" Cassie exclaimed. "When was I not nice to you?"

Riley shrugged. "If you're nice, you'll get one."

Whatever. Cassie turned away from her and pretended to search for something important in her suitcase. She didn't want one anyway.

The rumbling engine echoed around the campsite several minutes before a big white truck parked next to the pavilion.

"That's your ride, Cassandra!" Rainbow called from another tent, where she helped the girls rearrange their beds. "Take a buddy!"

"Want to come with me?" Cassie asked Riley.

Riley glanced around and wrinkled her nose. "No. I've already made some friends here. I want to hang out with them."

Cassie felt a stab of betrayal. Riley had told Mrs. Jones that she'd help out. "Okay, then." Who else? She didn't know anyone here.

"I'll be your buddy." Emily came over, handing Cassie her crutches. "Come on."

Only her sister wanted to be her buddy. She was feeling less wanted by the minute.

Two girls carrying logs to the fire pit passed her and

Emily as they hiked up to the pavilion.

"What happened to your leg?" one asked, stopping in front of them.

"I got bit by a snake," Cassie said, a little sheepishly.

"What?" gasped the other girl. "Was it poisonous?"

Cassie nodded. "I spent a week in the hospital. Just got out two days ago."

The two girls' eyes went wide as saucers. "No way," the first one breathed. "That's so awful. Like, the worst thing ever. I'm Tiffany, by the way."

"I'm Alicia," the other added.

"I'm Cassie. This is my sister Emily."

"Can we see the bite?" Tiffany asked, edging closer.

"Maybe later," Cassie said. "We have to ride with the camp nurse to dinner now."

"Oh, right." The two girls nodded in understanding.

"It's a long hike to the mess hall," Alicia said.

"We'll see you in a few minutes, then," Cassie said.

"Yeah." Tiffany waved as they continued on to the fire pit. "Save us a seat. I want to hear all about it!"

A flicker of warmth grew in Cassie's chest. She might not have had any other friends, but it wouldn't take long to make some.

CHAPTER EIGHT
Foot and Oh

Cassie and Emily arrived first at the mess hall, thanks to the camp nurse. They picked a table and waited for the other girls. Campers began to arrive in groups, each accompanied by a leader, but Cassie didn't recognize them. She knew there were several campsites at Camp Splendor. There had to be a least a hundred girls here this week.

Finally she spotted Rainbow leading the way, a line of girls behind her. Tiffany saw their table first, and her face brightened. Even though she was a smaller girl, short with petite features, she had an enigmatic energy that brought the room's focus on her. She tugged on Alicia's hand, then pulled her out of line and hauled her toward the table. To Cassie's surprise, four other girls followed.

"Hi," Tiffany said, pulling out a chair and sitting down. "I hope you don't mind if we brought some friends. Everyone wants to meet you."

"Oh! No, of course," Cassie said, surprised but pleasantly flattered. "I'd love to meet your friends."

Tiffany tossed her pigtails over her shoulder and smiled around the table. "This is Cassie. She's the one who was bit by the snake."

Cassie pushed her glasses up on her nose and responded to everyone's cheerful greetings. Out of the corner of her eye, she saw Riley walk past their table and pause for a moment before continuing on.

She could sit here, Cassie thought. There was room. But Riley didn't ask, so Cassie didn't offer.

After dinner, all the campers gathered around the stone fireplace and sang songs. The leaders led them through the verses several times, and by the time everyone stood up to head back to the campsite, she felt like she could easily sing along to those songs again.

Rainbow nodded at Cassie. "We'll see you back at camp."

"Thanks."

Cassie and Emily left the mess hall and waited for the nurse to arrive in her white pickup truck again. A mosquito buzzed around Cassie's ear, and she swatted at it.

"What do you think so far?" Emily asked. "Is it fun?"

It hadn't been long enough to tell. "Yeah. Everyone seems pretty nice. And I like the music."

"Yeah, that's fun."

They drifted into silence, and the nurse's truck pulled up, kicking gravel and clouds of dirt behind it.

"Come on in, girls," she called through the open window.

They arrived at the campsite before the others had finished the hike through the woods. Cassie and Emily arranged their things better around the tent, though they couldn't really unpack. There was no place to put anything.

Cassie heard the other campers approaching long before they arrived. They were singing, or chanting, or something, and the mingled tones of a dozen voices carried through the trees. She watched with anticipation, her heart in her throat, wishing she could join them. They burst out of the forest, a flurry of waving arms and bobbing heads.

"So there must be a trail through the woods that goes straight to the mess hall," Emily said from beside her. "Since we didn't pass them on the road."

Cassie nodded. "Must be." And of course she couldn't go on it. Not with these crutches. But if she could just walk. . . .

She stood up on the platform, carefully putting her weight on both feet. Stabs of shooting pain rushed up her calf, and she sucked in a breath. Slowly, she pushed her left foot flat on the ground.

"What are you doing?" Emily whispered.

"I just want to walk," Cassie replied.

"Cassie, hi!" Tiffany broke away from the group of girls and marched over to their tent. "Oh, I didn't know you can walk on it."

"She can't yet," Emily said.

"But I'm trying." Cassie shot a glare at her sister. If she could convince the other girls she could walk, maybe Rainbow would let her go on the trail with them. Just once.

"Can I see your foot?" Tiffany asked in a loud whisper. Her eyes went wide with anticipation.

"Sure." Cassie shrugged and sat back down. "It doesn't look so bad anymore."

Holding onto the pole in the middle of the tent, Tiffany whipped her head around and shouted, "Alicia! She's going to show me her snake bite!"

Alicia wasn't the only one who came running. A smile tugged at the corner of Cassie's mouth as most of the girls from the unit crowded into her tent.

"It's a lot better now," Cassie said, keeping her eyes averted. She started unraveling the gauze around her foot. The girls let out a collective gasp at the swollen, slightly purplish foot. Even Cassie admired its ugliness.

"It doesn't look that bad," Riley said.

Cassie glanced up at her. She leaned against the tent pole, her arms crossed over her chest, a scowl on her face. Cassie nodded. "Yeah. You should have seen it in the hospital. It was awful. The swelling went all the way to my knee." She lowered her voice, getting carried away with the story. "They almost had to amputate my leg."

Tiffany sat down in the middle of the tent. "Tell us everything. The whole story."

Cassie launched into it, starting at the beginning with doing fireworks.

She didn't fail to notice Riley push away from the pole and leave the tent.

~

"Girls!" Rainbow called. "Everyone gather at the pavilion! We're going to go over a few rules!"

Only a few campers remained in Cassie and Emily's tent. They stood up now, waiting for Cassie to get her crutches under her arms before trotting down the steps.

"You are so brave to have gone through that," Alicia said, lingering at Cassie's side.

"Thanks," Cassie said. She certainly hadn't tried to be brave. She didn't have a choice, really. She just had to endure it.

Rainbow was already talking by the time Cassie and

Alicia reached the pavilion. " . . .the buddy system. So don't ever go anywhere alone. And if you see someone without a buddy, make them join you and your buddy."

"Even to the bathroom?" someone called out.

"Even to the bathroom," Rainbow confirmed. "Even if that means waking your buddy up in the middle of the night to go to the outhouse. Your buddy will love you for that."

Several groans followed this, as well as some titters of laughter.

"Outhouse?" Cassie said, glancing around the pavilion. Maybe she'd heard wrong. Certainly they had bathrooms here.

Riley turned around and arched an eyebrow. "You mean you haven't seen them yet? They're the only bathrooms at Camp Splendor. We all have to use them."

"There are two outhouses, behind tents three and six. Make sure you close the door when you're done, or the girls in those tents won't be too happy!"

More laughter. Cassie checked her tent. Number two. Whew.

"The showers are communal and are behind the pavilion. You'll have time for that before breakfast. Please shower and brush your teeth every day! After breakfast is pool time and outdoor activities, and then quiet time. That's when you can take a nap or write letters home or to your boyfriends." Rainbow made kissy noises. "Oh, and one last thing. No food in your tents. It attracts the wild animals. So if you have any, bring it up here." She pushed a large plastic tub to the center of the pavilion. "I'll lock it up, and when you want it, you can have it. Any questions?"

Cassie couldn't think of any. No one else raised their hands.

"Then go get ready for bed and lights out, girls! I recommend leaving your tent flaps up unless it rains because it gets hot! I'll be here if you need me!"

Cassie changed into her pajamas in her tent, keeping her eyes focused on herself and hoping Emily and Riley were too. She didn't like changing in front of people.

Riley's suitcase fell open with a slap, and she pulled out a bag of chips.

"You're going to turn that food in, right?" Cassie said.

"No." Riley wrinkled her nose at her. "It's mine. I'll eat it when I want."

"But what about the animals?" Emily chimed in.

"That's not really true. You'll see. Besides, if you don't tell Rainbow I have it, I'll share it with you."

Cassie exchanged a look with Emily and shrugged. The animals would go through Riley's stuff, not hers. "Sure." She held her hand out. "Chips, please."

Riley glared, but she offered the bag to Cassie. Emily grabbed a handful too.

Cassie grinned as she crunched on the salty morsels. This arrangement might work out after all.

CHAPTER NINE

Ted

While Cassie enjoyed most things at camp, there were a few very big downfalls.

Like the bugs. She was certain crickets were hopping over her face in the night. And when she woke up, bug bites covered every inch of her exposed skin. After four days, her arms reminded her of cheetah fur, with lots of spots everywhere.

And the heat. She couldn't get in the pool because she couldn't get her foot wet yet, so Cassie hovered with one side of her body draped in the water, the other side stretched out across the hot pavement. Sweat dripped down her face, and she resisted the urge to drink from the pool.

And some of the counselors, who seemed to think Cassie was making up her foot condition to get special treatment, made things difficult for her. They rolled their eyes when she spoke, casting knowing glances at Rainbow.

But the worst thing of all, the very worst, was the outhouses. The bugs loved the stinky out buildings, and Cassie crossed her eyes and pinched her nose every time she went inside, not wanting to think about the spiders in the seat beneath her or crawling on the ceiling above her. She missed the bedside commode at the hospital. She hated that Emily had to take her crutches and hold the door for her because she couldn't just walk in and use the toilet herself.

So it was with some relief that Cassie realized during lunch she needed to use the bathroom. The flushing toilets were just up the stairs from the mess hall, a climb she would gladly make. She waited until everyone finished eating and started to gather around the fireplace for singing time, then she turned to Alicia.

"I really need to pee. Will you be my buddy?"

"Of course," Alicia said, brightening. She stood up, her body tall and lanky next to Cassie. She held the crutches steady so Cassie could get herself arranged.

They went out the front door and headed for the stairs leading up to the bathrooms. Cassie had just put her crutches on the first step and started to swing her body upward when an adult voice called out to them.

"Girls. Where are you going?"

Cassie stopped and swiveled her head as the counselor came over. She didn't know her name, but Cassie had seen her, with her head of poofy blond hair and huge collection of tie-dyed shirts. "We're going to the bathroom," Cassie said, though she suspected this information was self-explanatory.

"The flushing toilets are for staff-only." The counselor folded her arms across her ample chest.

"Where am I supposed to go, then?" Cassie asked. Surely this woman didn't really expect her to hold it.

The counselor focused on Alicia. "Take her behind the

mess hall. We put toilet paper in the woods for anyone who needs to go."

Cassie's jaw dropped. She had seen girls climbing down the steep hill to the trees out back, but she hadn't realized what they were doing.

Alicia scrunched up her nose. "She's on crutches."

The counselor shrugged. "If she needs to go that bad, she'll make it."

Cassie was tempted to completely ignore the order and continue up to the flushing toilets. But the counselor hadn't moved. She looked at Alicia, who shrugged.

"I guess we better go," the other girl said.

Cassie felt the sweat gather along her forehead as she slowly maneuvered each crutch to the inclining ground in front of her.

"Careful," Alicia said, a hand on Cassie's elbow to steady her. Or grab her if she lost her balance and fell.

Cassie shot a glance forward and groaned. The forest edge looked so far away.

"We'll get there," Alicia said. "One step at a time."

Cassie crutched on, trying not to pitch into the grass with each downward swing. Her clammy palms trembled, making the crutches even wobblier. It took all her strength to keep moving the wooden pegs ahead.

Finally they broke through the edge of the forest, and Cassie breathed a sigh of relief.

"Ew," Alicia said.

A quick glance around showed why. Small piles of excrement and toilet paper littered the forest floor in front of them.

"Ugh," Cassie said. "This is sick." It was far worse than the outhouses, actually.

"Um. Do you need help?"

Cassie looked down at her hands, keeping herself up and mobilized by holding onto her crutches. She'd have to put her crutches down to do this. But she couldn't stand without them. Was she expected to hop around or sit down?

"No." Cassie swiveled around and crutched out of the woods. "I'll wait till we get to the outhouses."

"Are you sure?" Alicia asked, trailing behind her.

"One-hundred percent."

The nurse's truck was waiting in front of the mess hall when Cassie and Alicia returned. Cassie hobbled over as fast as she could and climbed inside, Alicia right behind her.

"You've got to take me back to camp," Cassie said, sitting down on the seat and squeezing her legs together.

"Are you okay?" the nurse asked.

"I've got to pee," she admitted, her face warming. "I can't do it in the woods and they won't let me use the bathroom up here. So I need the outhouse. Quickly."

The nurse frowned, the freckles under her clear blue eyes crinkling up. "They won't let you use the bathroom here?"

"She tried," Alicia said. "One of the counselors made us hike into the woods."

The nurse huffed, her face turning pink. "That's ridiculous. I'll take you to the sickroom, Cassie. You can use the bathroom there. Anytime."

"Really?" Cassie exhaled with relief. Maybe from now on she only had to hold it until meal time.

Too bad there was only one more day of camp.

By the time she and Alicia (who also used the indoor bathroom) made it back to the campsite, all the other girls were there. It was quiet time, and Cassie climbed into her bed and pulled out her notebook paper.

"What took you so long?" Riley asked, chewing on a licorice.

"Long story," Cassie said, reluctant to share it with her. Sometimes Riley was nice, but mostly she seemed annoyed with Cassie. She was right about the critters, at least. Nothing had tried to sneak into their tent.

"Did you get hurt?" Emily asked.

Cassie shook her head. "No. I needed to use the bathroom. So Alicia and I hiked down below the mess hall, but it was too hard to go while holding on to my crutches." Saying it out loud, Cassie realized how ridiculous the situation had been. How could anyone expect a girl on crutches to use the bathroom in the woods? "So the nurse took me to her lodging and let me use the bathroom there."

"Oh, good," Emily said. "That was nice."

"She shouldn't have done that," Riley exploded, pieces of red licorice flecking her lips. "No campers are allowed in the adult bathrooms."

"It was the sickroom, Riley," Cassie said. "Sick campers are allowed to go there. I'm practically sick."

"If you're so sick, you shouldn't be here!" Riley jumped up, her face red with anger. "You should have to follow the same rules as everyone else!" With that, she stomped out of the tent.

"Don't listen to her," Emily said, rolling her eyes. "She'll be back soon."

But Riley didn't come back, except to grab her sleeping bag and pillow and leave again.

"I guess she's sleeping somewhere else," Cassie said, her chest aching in spite of her anger.

"We should tell Rainbow she has a secret stash of food here," Emily said.

Cassie considered that, then shook her head. "Then she'd have a reason to be mad at me."

"We should eat her food, at least."

Cassie laughed. "She probably won't notice if we eat a little bit."

Tiffany sat down next to Cassie during evening crafts. While Cassie tried to form the intricate knots to her friendship bracelet, Tiffany said, "So it's our last night and all, and Alicia and I really wanted to hang out with you. Do you think your tent mates would mind if we had a slumber party in your tent?"

Riley would mind. Cassie knew in an instant that she wouldn't be happy about it. But then she remembered something else, and she smiled. "My sister won't care at all. And Riley already decided to stay in another tent tonight. So you and Alicia can sleep in our tent, no problem."

"Great!" Tiffany gave her a hug. "We'll have so much fun. Alicia's mom always sends her tons of food, and we keep forgetting to go up to the pavilion and get it. So we can stay up all night eating junk and telling stories!"

Cassie's heart lifted. "That will be great!"

It ended up being six girls in all, tossing down sleeping bags and squeezing onto the cots in the tent. They tried to tell ghost stories, shining flashlights on their faces while they munched on skittles and peanut brittle, but Emily kept giggling or shrieking, and the stories always dissolved in laughter. Then their voices dropped to low whispers and they talked about boys and kissing. Cassie was only eleven and had never kissed a boy, but Alicia, who was thirteen, had already kissed one. Part of Cassie was embarrassed to listen to the experience, but another part of her was insanely curious.

Someday, she'd kiss a boy. She had no idea who. What would it be like?

~

The morning came way too soon. Cassie buried her head in her sleeping bag at the sound of Rainbow's voice yelling through the campsite. She poked her head back out, the outside air nipping at her face. It would be hot and muggy later, but right now, it was chilly. She reached a hand up and felt around her head until she found her glasses. Then she slipped them on, bringing the world into focus.

Stretched out on Riley's bed, Tiffany groaned. "We stayed up too late." One foot dangled over the side of the cot above Alicia's sleeping bag.

"Yeah." Alicia poked Tiffany's bare foot. "Your fault."

"But it was fun." Cassie pulled the rest of the way out of her sleeping bag, and the other girls roused themselves also.

"Bathroom buddy!" one of them called.

Cassie watched them head to the outhouse. She didn't intend to use it again. She'd use the toilet in the sickroom, and after that, she'd be home.

The tent slowly emptied until it was just Emily and Cassie. She rolled up her sleeping bag and sorted her suitcase. The nurse's truck pulled up to the pavilion.

"Buddy?" Cassie asked her sister.

"Sure."

Emily slowed down so Cassie could hobble along beside her. Although she'd spent all week practicing walking, Cassie still couldn't put weight on her foot for very long.

She watched the rest of the girls line up at the trailhead. Maybe next year.

"Hey, Cassie."

She turned her head to see Riley approaching. The skin around her eyes was swollen, and her face had a pinched, tired look.

Cassie hesitated. Had Riley come to yell at her? Did she know Cassie and Emily had eaten her cookies? "What?"

"Can I be your buddy to breakfast?"

Cassie lifted her eyebrows. She hadn't expected that. She glanced at Emily, who shrugged.

"Yeah, sure, I guess," Cassie said.

"I'll see you there," Emily said, running off to join the line.

It was the first time Riley had been Cassie's buddy all week. They climbed into the nurse's truck, and Cassie kept sneaking glances at Riley.

"Are you okay?" she finally asked.

Riley sniffed, and her eyes glimmered. "You hurt my feelings last night."

Cassie worked hard to keep her mouth from falling open. "I did?"

"You had a slumber party with half the girls in our unit and didn't invite me."

"You're the one who stormed out."

"But you're supposed to be my best friend. And you've hardly talked to me all week."

Cassie wasn't about to let Riley twist this and put the blame on her. "I came to camp because of you. I thought we'd hang out all week. But you never wanted to."

"That's because you had all your new friends all the time. You didn't even notice me." Riley pressed her lips together and lifted her chin.

Cassie didn't even know what to say. Was Riley right? Had she ignored her? What good would it do to argue the point? "I thought we'd spend more time together, too. But you were always rude to me."

"Yeah, well." Riley averted her eyes and picked at the hem of her shorts. She shrugged. "Sorry."

That was it. But Cassie suspected that was all she'd get. "It's okay."

They arrived at the mess hall, and Riley helped her out of the truck. "So can we sit together at breakfast?"

"Sure."

But Cassie realized, once they'd sat down to eat and Riley was back to acting fun and friendly again, that she'd lied. It wasn't okay.

Episode 2: Supreme Talent

CHAPTER TEN

Concerta

Emily Jones burst into the bedroom she shared with her sister Cassandra. Emily's face was flushed with excitement. "How do I look?" she asked, giving a full spin so Cassie could admire her flower-printed dress.

"Fine," Cassie said. She pushed past her sister, still moving gingerly on her healing foot. At least she didn't need crutches anymore. Last month she'd been bit by a snake, and she could finally get around on her own now. The swelling had disappeared completely, though the snakebite changed the shape of her foot. Where before the bone of her big toe had jutted outward, now the foot was completely straight. No curvatures or anything unique.

"Mom!" she shouted across the hall. "Do I really have to go?"

Emily had started piano lessons over the summer, and tonight was her first recital. Cassie couldn't think of anything more boring.

"Get dressed, Cassie!" her mom shouted back.

Cassie heaved a sigh. She tried one last question. "Can I wear pants, at least?"

"As long as they're clean!"

Clean. That she could do.

Twenty minutes later the entire Jones family piled out of the car and entered the small studio. Cassie found a seat near the back and surreptitiously opened her paperback novel. Absorbed in the plot of the book, she didn't hear anything around her until the notes of a high soprano rang out across the room.

Cassie lifted her eyes from the book, her breath catching. There, standing in front of the room, was a girl her age, blond hair pulled back from her face in ringlets. The ethereal notes coming from her mouth penetrated Cassie's ears, and all she could do was stare. A warm longing grew in her chest, wrapping around Cassie's torso. She wanted to do that. She wanted to sing.

Cassie waited until everyone had finished congratulating Emily before she sidled up to her mother.

"What did you think of Emily's piano performance?" Mrs. Jones asked, wrapping an arm around Cassie's shoulders.

"It was great," Cassie said, though she couldn't even recall it. "What was the singing?"

"Oh, Emily's teacher teaches voice and piano," her mom answered, checking her watch. "Everyone performs together. Are you ready to go?"

Voice lessons. Cassie had never heard of such a thing. She grabbed her mom's arm as she started to walk away. "You mean they teach you how to sing?"

"Sure, just like they do piano."

"I want to do it." The words flew out of her mouth before she could second-guess herself. But as soon as she'd spoken, Cassie felt certain. "I want to take voice lessons."

Mrs. Jones hesitated. "You do? What about clarinet?"

Clarinet. Cassie hadn't even touched it since the school talent show last spring. "Well, Daddy already said he's not going to do the school band this year." Last year, Mr. Jones directed a band for the older grades at Walker Elementary. It had been a lot of fun, but a lot of work on his part. "I think I'm a better singer, anyway."

"I'll talk to Ms. Malcolm about it and we'll see." Mrs. Jones patted her hand. "Find your younger siblings and get everyone into the car."

~

In the end, Mr. Jones agreed to let Cassie take voice lessons only if she practiced every day. If she quit trying, the lessons would stop.

"I'll never stop," Cassie promised. "I love to sing."

"Then I'll talk to Ms. Malcolm and sign you up for September."

A week before school started, Mrs. Jones came home with their school supplies and class lists.

"Cassie, you're in Ms. Timber's sixth grade class," she said, handing her a new backpack stuffed with essential things like folders and tissue.

"Great." Cassie didn't really know much about the sixth grade teachers, so any would have been fine with her. "Any one of my friends in my class?" She held her breath, anxious for the answer.

"Riley's not in your class." Mrs. Jones watched Cassie's reaction, but Cassie just shrugged. They hadn't spoken since the last day of camp.

"That's okay. Anyone else?"

"Andrea."

"Oh!" Cassie's eleventh birthday had almost been a total

flop. Riley hadn't told her she wasn't coming, but at the last minute, Andrea and Betsy came, saving the day. "I like Andrea."

"Yes, me too, she seems like a nice girl. And Emmett, too."

"Oh, good!" Emmett helped introduce Cassie to the Science Olympiad program. He'd always been very nice to her.

"I'm sure you know some of the other kids, but I didn't write down all the names."

"That's all right." Cassie wasn't the new girl anymore, and she marveled at how different it felt. Last year, she'd been terrified to step into the school building where she knew not a single soul (other than her sister and brother). This year, she knew that most of the kids would be familiar to her. She wasn't afraid at all. In fact, she was quite excited.

She laid out a pretty red dress with black polka dots for the first day of school and planned how she would do her hair. She crawled into bed early, determined to get a good night's sleep. But sleep wouldn't come. She tossed and turned, heart hammering out with anticipation every time she thought about class. It almost felt like Christmas.

When her alarm went off in the morning, it took her a full two seconds to remember why she was getting up so early. Then she jumped out of bed and ran to the bathroom to do her hair before Emily could get there.

Mrs. Jones was up, something that only occurred on special occasions. Usually Cassie was in charge of getting all the kids fed and out to the bus on time.

"Mom, I need to use the bathroom," Emily whined from the hallway.

"Hurry up, Casandra," her mother said. "You need to get breakfast."

Cassie tugged on the rubber band she'd put around half her hair. She knew how she wanted this to look, and it wasn't working. "Fine," she sighed, yanking it all back out.

She kept shoving a hand through her thick dark hair while she ate her cereal, unhappy with the way the strands fell around her face. She had to get it out of the way. As soon as she was done eating, she ran back into the bathroom and began trying to pull it up again. Little bumps of hair popped up on top whenever she pulled it tight, and Cassie yanked it out three times.

"Cassie!" her mom shouted. "I see the bus coming up the hill! You need to go now!"

"Ugh!" With a cry of frustration, Cassie shoved a clip through the side of her hair and ran into the living room. The front door was wide open, as everyone else had already left for the bus. Panicking, Cassie grabbed her backpack and flew after her siblings.

She spotted the bus at the top of the hill, its yellow lights blinking, the red stop sign out on the side to indicate the door was open. The stop sign started to close, folding into the side of the bus.

"I'm coming!" Cassie shrieked, pumping her legs harder. She burst around the front of the bus, and the doors opened again.

"You're lucky I waited," Rhonda the bus driver said, the black eye-liner thick around her eyes. She paused just until Cassie got to the top of the steps before closing the doors.

Cassie looked around for a familiar face, wondering who to sit by. She spotted her friend Betsy and hurried to her seat.

"Hi!" Betsy greeted her with a hug. Her round face wore a huge, excited smile. "How was your summer?"

Between going to Arizona for a week, spending a week in the hospital, and a week of Girls Club camp, the summer had been one huge adventure after the other. "It was great," Cassie said, opting for the shorter version. "How was yours?"

"Awesome!" Betsy launched into a description of her cousin's house in southern Arkansas where she'd spent most of her summer. Cassie nodded along, taking several deep breaths and waiting for her heart to calm down after the run up to the bus.

The first day of school jitters returned in full force when the bus came to a stop in the drop-off zone at Walker Elementary. Cassie shouldered her backpack and pushed her hair behind her ears. She stood up straight and pulled her shoulders back as she walked down the steps, imagining that she looked like the mature, sophisticate sixth grader she was. They ruled the school now. They were the big kids. Finally, the ones on top.

Her heart pounded nervously when she stepped through the double doors and turned left for the sixth grade hall. She trekked through the familiar fifth grade corridors, ignoring the groups of younger kids shrieking and hugging and sharing stories.

Outside the sixth grade classrooms were similar huddles, but Cassie didn't stop to see if she knew anyone. She wanted to get her stuff put away and find her seat. Only once seated would she be able to relax again.

She found Ms. Timber's class and walked inside. She wasn't the only one with this idea. Though quieter in here, a handful of students had already put their backpacks away and sat on each other's desks, talking. Cassie went behind the wall of cubbies, searching for her name. *Howard, Hall, Jeffrey, Jones.* There she was. She dropped her backpack onto the hook and stepped around the wall.

Before she could look for her desk, Andrea spotted her. "Hi, Cassie!" she said, waving. Like Cassie, Andrea wore glasses, though hers were round wire-frames. Her blue eyes blinked from behind them, and her auburn hair fell in frizzy waves.

"Hi!" Cassie hurried over to her, and they hugged.

"I missed you!" Andrea said. "You should come over to my house sometime."

"That would be fun!" Cassie lived so far out in the country, though. She knew it wasn't easy for her mom to fit car rides into her schedule. They came into town frequently for groceries and church and the post office, and her mom usually tried to combine the trips so they weren't driving into Springdale all the time.

"Hey, Cassie," a boy said.

Cassie swiveled her head, not recognizing the voice. Her eyes widened at the sight of Miles, the boy who helped her with her airplane class at Science Olympiad last year. They weren't in the same fifth grade class, and she hadn't talked to him since then. Now her stomach did a somersault. Miles still wore his glasses, but he'd gotten taller over the summer, and his brown eyes crinkled in the corners when he smiled at her.

"Miles!" she said. "You're in my class!" Inwardly, she kicked herself for stating the obvious.

"Or you're in my class," he replied, still smiling.

"What? Oh, right. Yeah." Cassie smiled and nodded, not understanding why she suddenly felt flustered.

The bell rang in the hallway, and the kids began to filter into the classroom. Cassie found her desk and sat down, trying to bring her thoughts back to concentrate on the first day of school.

Ms. Timber stepped in last, her red hair cropped closely to her head. "Welcome to sixth grade, class!" she said, and was immediately greeted by cheers and excited calls. "We're going to work hard this year, but I can promise you this: it will be the best year of your schooling so far."

Cassie glanced around the room while her teacher gave a pep talk. She knew the kids next to her by name, but not very well. She spotted Danelle at another table and turned away before the other girl caught her looking. Danelle had been her first friend when Cassie moved to Arkansas, but the friendship didn't last long. Danelle had changed over the summer, too. She'd gotten thinner and taller, and her lips sported dark red lipstick. Cassie cast her eyes down at her polka dot red dress, suddenly feeling very juvenile with her glasses and hair clip.

"So please pull out a notebook," Ms. Timber said, catching Cassie's attention again. "And begin your first day's journaling. Whatever comes to mind, feel free to write. Remember I will read these, and sometimes I'll even comment on them."

Cassie hadn't heard all of the explanation, but she got the gist of it. Suddenly eager to sort out her thoughts, she found a green notebook. Ms. Timber set a timer, and Cassie chose her red ink pen. It was her favorite to write with.

"The first day of school," she wrote. *"It's not what I expected. I was so excited to see my friends again, but now I feel insecure. I realize I don't really have a best friend anymore. Danelle and I used to be best friends, and then it was me and*

Riley, but I don't think Riley's actually been a very good friend to me. So I'm not really sure what to expect anymore. And Miles — " She stopped, remembering that the teacher would read these. Deep down inside her gut, she felt a stirring of something when she pictured the way Miles had smiled at her. But she couldn't write that. She couldn't even think about it. She scratched out the last two words.

"I hope to be a better student this year and get good grades. And make new friends." There. It might be generic, but it was true.

CHAPTER ELEVEN
School Daze

Even little Annette was in school this year. She didn't stop talking about kindergarten and all the fun she had the whole walk from the bus stop to the house. She kept up her chatter right into the kitchen, where Cassie grabbed an apple and went downstairs to find her mom.

"How was the first day of school?" Mrs. Jones asked. She didn't look up from her sewing machine, her fingers carefully pushing and pulling on the fabric while her foot made the motor whirl.

Cassie sat down on the floor and bit into her apple. "Weird. I think everyone changed over the summer."

"Well, you did too."

"How?" Cassie didn't see any differences. She'd grown a little and wore bigger clothes, but that was it. Same glasses. Same hair.

"You're more mature. More confident."

She took another bite. "More confident?"

"Sure. Did you talk to Riley today?"

Cassie shrugged. "She's in Ms. Roxi's class."

"So you didn't see her?"

"I saw her."

"Did you talk?"

"She said hi." Actually Riley had seemed rather excited to see her.

"That's what I mean, Cassie. Last year you let Riley walk all over you. This year you're stronger."

"I didn't let her walk all over me," Cassie protested.

"Yes, you did. And you still thought of her as your best friend. Now you know you deserve someone who treats you with respect."

Cassie considered that as she ate the last bite of her apple. "Yeah, maybe." She stood up, holding the core in one hand. "I have to make a collage about myself for homework."

"Sweep the kitchen and feed the animals first, and take out the trash if it needs it."

Last year her only job had been unloading the dishes. She wished she had that one again. "All right."

"And send the other kids down, will you? I want to know how school was for everyone."

"Okay."

~

Cassie stayed up late working on her collage. She found some poster board in her dad's office. She glued a picture of herself to the middle and then found other pictures to show the things she enjoyed. She pasted them around her portrait and attached string with thumbtacks between herself and her hobbies. Singing. The animals. Reading. Camping.

She admired it for a moment when she finished, and then collapsed into bed, exhausted.

"How's Ms. Timber?" Betsy asked as soon as Cassie sat

down next to her on the bus. "I heard she's really strict."

Cassie shrugged. "I thought she seemed nice. She's a teacher. They're all kind of strict." And a little cranky, and sometimes funny. It was like they came from the same mold, all the way down to their short hair. "What about Ms. Roxi?"

"Oh, she's really nice. Mostly we just played games and got to know each other yesterday. She didn't even give us homework."

"We had homework." Cassie yawned, remembering how late she'd stayed up. "But it was fun. We had to make collages that tell about ourselves. Then we'll share them with each other. I guess that's Ms. Timber's version of a getting-to-know-you game."

"Oh, cool!" Betsy tossed her straight brown hair over one shoulder. "Can I see yours?"

"Sure." Cassie pulled her backpack into her lap, eager to show off her collage. She froze when she realized there was no poster board in front of her. She pushed to her knees and turned around, checking the seat behind her, but she knew it was a hopeless endeavor. The poster board had to be by the front door, right where she'd put it down so she could loop her arms into her backpack. "I left it at home." She swallowed hard and blinked back tears.

"Oh, Cassie!" Betsy exclaimed. "I'm so sorry! Can you call your mom? Maybe she can bring it to you."

Cassie's eyes burned, and she couldn't keep the tears from overflowing down her cheeks. It was only the second day of school. What would Ms. Timber think of her?

As soon as the bus parked, Cassie ran to the office. Hoping her eyes weren't too red and trying to sound composed, she asked the secretary, "Can I use the phone? I need to call my mom."

"Sure," the woman said, pushing it across the counter toward Cassie. "Are you sick? Do you need to see the nurse?"

Cassie shook her head. She didn't feel like explaining.

The phone rang four times before going to voicemail. Cassie hung up and tried again, just in case her mom was in the bathroom and hadn't been able to get to the phone in time. The answering machine picked up again. Swallowing hard, she put the phone back in the cradle.

Her mom wasn't home. She must have gone somewhere.

"Are you all right, hon?" the secretary asked.

"Yes," Cassie answered, blinking rapidly to keep the tears at bay. It didn't work. Instead, she lowered her head and hurried out of the office. There was nothing to do now but face her teacher.

She wanted to talk to Ms. Timber without the audience of all of her peers. It was bad enough that people noticed her as she scurried through the hall, head down, but at least no one tried to talk to her. She stepped into the classroom, only to find Ms. Timber wasn't in there.

But other students were. Her classmates already showed off their poster boards, laughing over their pictures and drawings.

Cassie hurried behind the wall of cubbies and waited. Ms. Timber had to come in soon.

Andrea came back, giggling with Kendra Melendez. They both spotted Cassie hiding by the backpacks.

"What are you doing back here?" Andrea asked. At the same time, she must have noticed Cassie's face. "What's wrong?" Both girls stepped closer.

Cassie put her hands over her eyes. "Nothing. I'm fine."

Andrea whispered something to Kendra, and Kendra's black loafers backed away from the wall. Andrea put an arm around Cassie's shoulders.

"It's just me now," she said. "Tell me what's wrong."

Cassie burst into tears, crying hard now. "It's my homework. I forgot it."

"You mean your self-collage?"

Cassie nodded.

"You forgot to do it?"

"No!" That was the worst part. "I stayed up late working on it. I forgot to bring it!"

"It's okay," Andrea said, rubbing Cassie's shoulder. "We can call your mom. I'm sure she'll bring it."

"I already tried. She didn't answer. I don't think she's home."

"It's all right." Andrea hugged her. "Ms. Timber will understand."

Cassie didn't think she would. Only the second day of school, and Cassie was making a bad impression. Ms. Timber would think she was one of those lazy kids who didn't care about their grades.

"Let me get you a tissue." Andrea disappeared into the classroom and returned with a handful of soft white paper. "Clean your face. The bell's about to ring. Come sit down. Tell Ms. Timber what happened."

"Thank you," Cassie whispered, taking her glasses off and wiping her eyes.

The bell rang, and she followed Andrea back into the classroom. Most of the kids coming in were too busy chatting or putting away their things to notice her. She avoided the gazes of the few that did give her a second look, and nobody asked any questions.

"All right," Ms. Timber said, coming in and clapping her hands to silence them. "Take out your journaling folder. This is how you start each day."

Cassie pulled out her notebook and pen, but all she could do was stare at the paper and will herself not to cry again. No words came to her. She uncapped the pen and wrote the date across the top, and then, *I forgot my homework.* She could think of nothing else to say, so she just sat there staring at her paper for the fifteen minutes. She didn't dare go talk to Ms. Timber right now, not when the room was so quiet. Everyone would overhear their conversation.

CHAPTER TWELVE
Bad Start

"Okay, put away your journals," Ms. Timber said, calling attention back to the front of the classroom. "Before we get onto our English assignment, please bring your self-collages up to my desk."

Every student in the classroom stood up, tucking their collage under an arm or securing it in both hands, and walked to the front of the room. Cassie waited a moment, then joined the line, holding her hands together and hoping they didn't look too inconspicuous in their emptiness. Andrea laid her collage on the pile and gave Cassie a sympathetic look as she passed.

Cassie held her breath. The line dwindled, and finally she was the last one. She stepped up to the desk and leaned over. "Ms. Timber," she said, "I forgot to bring my homework."

Ms. Timber looked up from the grade book on her desk. She lifted a brow over her brown eyes. "You forgot to bring it? Or you didn't do it?"

The tears welled in her eyes again. This was exactly what she'd been afraid of. Ms. Timber didn't know her. She didn't know anything about Cassie's character, or her work ethic. "I did it. I just forgot to bring it."

Ms. Timber closed her grade book and pulled a small white square of paper from a drawer. "Well, that's too bad. You're in sixth grade now. Even if we do something wrong on accident, we have to pay the consequences. It's Cassandra, right?"

"Yes," Cassie whispered. Behind her, the room seemed to have gotten very quiet. She didn't dare turn around, but she feared all of her classmates were watching her.

Ms. Timber filled out the little slip of paper and handed it to Cassie. "You'll spend recess in the classroom, making a new collage."

Cassie stared at the slip of paper, not reaching for it. Not once in the past three years had she missed recess as a punishment. "I don't want to start a new collage. I like the

one I did last night."

"But you didn't bring it. And it's due today. So you'll have to make a new one."

She hadn't thought she had any more tears left to cry, but she felt the sting again. "Okay," she whispered, taking the paper. *Don't cry, don't cry, don't cry,* she told herself. She kept her chin up and went back to her desk, closing her fist around the offending paper.

"All right, class, if you'll pull out your English reader," Ms. Timber called.

Cassie did as instructed. Once she was sure the class was focused on the teacher and not on her, she pressed her forehead into the palm of her hand and let the tears drip silently onto her desk.

~

"Are you okay?" Andrea asked Cassie as they stood in line for lunch. "Did you get in trouble?"

"I have to miss recess. And make a new collage." Cassie couldn't meet Andrea's gaze, or she knew she'd cry.

Andrea gave her arm a squeeze. "Want to sit with me at lunch?"

"Yeah." Cassie gave her a grateful smile. "That would be nice."

Recess was after lunch. Cassie handed her white slip to the teacher on duty, and then went back to the classroom to start her new collage. Ms. Timber was in there, but all she did was tell Cassie where the art supplies were. The only things Cassie had to work with were a stupid sheet of paper and colored pencils. Still, she drew an image of herself in the middle of the paper. She remembered what she'd put on her collage, but she scowled at her drawing. The pencil artwork didn't look anything like her. It was more of a representation than a likeness.

Ms. Timber stood up from her desk. "Keep working, Cassandra. I'll be right back." She walked out of the room, her heels clicking smartly on the linoleum.

Cassie sighed and started to draw her other activities.

"Hey."

She looked up as a voice spoke from the doorway. A tingle ran down her spine when she saw Miles. He stepped into the classroom, his brown hair standing up a bit more than it had been this morning. He pushed his glasses up on his nose and approached her.

"Ms. Timber isn't in here," Cassie said, her hands moving to cover the embarrassing drawing. "She'll be right back."

He pulled up a chair and sat down in front of her desk. "I came to see you, actually. What happened? Are you okay?"

Cassie looked down, her cheeks warming. "I forgot my homework. So I had to miss recess."

"Really?" He sounded shocked. "On the second day of school? That seems so harsh."

Cassie nodded, feeling the hot sting of tears pricking her eyes again. "And now I have to make this stupid version of my collage." She gestured at the pencil drawings on her paper.

"Let me see."

Cassie hesitated, then slowly uncovered the paper. Miles took the end of it and pulled it to him.

"Hmm," he said, cocking his head as he studied it. "I can see what you mean. Is this Cousin It?" He pointed to the drawing in the middle and lifted his eyes, winking at Cassie. She felt a smile pull at her lips and shook her head.

"Oh." He nodded. "I didn't see the glasses. Is it you?"

She gave a little laugh. "Probably."

"Okay, so drawing's not your strong point." He pointed at the drawing of her cat. "I can tell you like bats."

Cassie laughed out loud now. "It's a cat."

"Are you sure? So maybe it's not a bat. But it kind of looks like a monkey. Check out this tail."

She laughed again and gave him a small shove on his shoulder. Instantly she jerked her hand back, feeling scalded. She hadn't meant to touch him. What if he was offended?

But he didn't seem to even notice. He took her pencil and added wings to her cat. "There. Now it's a bat." He pushed back his chair and smiled. "Just bring your real one tomorrow. She just needs to get to know you better."

With that, he walked out of the classroom, leaving Cassie holding her pencil between two hands and staring after him. Not like Miles knew her that well, either. So he'd spent a few minutes with her building paper airplanes last year. But somehow, he did know her.

~

Cassie went straight to the classroom when she got off the bus the next morning. This time, she was in luck. Ms. Timber was at the white board, drawing some sort of graph. A few students sat at their desks or by the cubbies, but the classroom was mostly empty.

"I brought my real collage," she said, holding up her poster board. She hadn't made any changes to it last night. She didn't want Ms. Timber to think she'd lied about having it done. "Can we use this one instead of the paper one I made yesterday?" The awful, slightly hilarious paper where one of her pets was a bat with a long tail. "I'm sorry

I forgot it. I promise I don't usually do things like that."

Ms. Timber put down her dry erase marker and picked up the collage. "This looks very nice, Cassandra." She met Cassie's eyes, studying her very carefully. "I'll make an exception this time. I'll let you use this one as your homework and your presentation. But next time, you won't get a second chance. You need to bring your homework to school every day."

Cassie nodded, standing a little straighter. "I understand." She put her collage behind the teacher's desk and turned around. She spotted Miles as he came in, talking to another boy from her class. She flashed him a smile, and he grinned back at her.

CHAPTER THIRTEEN

Kick Shot

Last year in fifth grade, Cassandra Jones had spent every recess on the swings. She and her best friend from Texas used to try and see who could swing the highest, and when Cassie moved to Arkansas, it gave her some comfort to continue the tradition.

This year, swinging had lost its appeal.

Riley Isabel asked Cassie to swing today, and she had no real reason to say no. From the highest vantage point on the upward swing, Cassie watched the boys playing soccer out on the field. She'd never played a sport, but the way they maneuvered the ball with their feet, and sometimes their heads and bodies, inspired her.

Riley was saying something about Girls Club, which would start next week. Ever since camp last summer, Cassie felt like she and Riley hadn't really been connected. Her words stirred up a feeling of impatience within Cassie. Cassie interrupted her.

"Let's go play soccer," she said.

"What?" Riley was on the upward motion of the swing, her short blond hair flying around her face, and they passed each other.

Cassie waited till she got to the bottom and then hopped off the swings. "Let's go play soccer!" she called up.

Riley crinkled her nose and didn't jump off. "That's a boys' game."

"No, it's not. Girls can play too."

"Do you see any girls out there?"

Cassie looked toward the field and had to admit she couldn't. But that didn't mean anything. "Come on, it'll be fun."

"You don't even know how."

"I'll learn. Come on."

Still Riley didn't hop off. "I don't want to."

End of story. If Riley didn't want to, she wouldn't do it. Cassie shrugged. "Fine. I'll do it by myself."

Mrs. Jones said Cassie had changed over the summer. She said Cassie was more mature, more confident, more able to stand up for herself. Maybe her mom was right. Last year she would've gotten back on the swing and forgotten about it.

She crossed the short distance to the field and joined a huddle of boys watching. "Can I play?"

As one, they turned to face her. Some of them were short, others tall, some skinny, some muscular, some leaning toward the fatter side. But all of them wore the same expression: confusion.

"Can I play?" she repeated.

Finally one of the bigger boys spoke up. He crossed his arms over his chest. "We're all waiting our turn to play. Besides, we don't play with girls."

"Well, that's not fair," Cassie said. "Girls like to play, too."

"Then get a bunch of girls together and form your own team."

That kind of made sense. She turned and walked away, disappointed at the rejection but also slightly relieved. Playing with boys who already knew the rules was more intimidating than she'd first expected. She went back to the swings.

"Change your mind?" Riley asked.

Cassie shrugged like it was no big deal. "They didn't really need me." But she couldn't tear her eyes from the field.

Which was probably why when she jumped off the swings after recess, she didn't even notice her glasses flying off until she crunched them under foot.

Cassie cringed at the sound. "Oh, no."

"What?" Riley stood in front of her, eyes scanning Cassie, looking for evidence of bodily injury.

"My glasses." Cassie grimaced as she knelt and picked up the crooked turquoise frames. "I stepped on them."

"Your mom's going to kill you!" Riley said.

Cassie pulled her long, dark brown hair over her shoulder and twisted it anxiously. "I know."

~

There was no hiding the fact that Cassie had broken her glasses. She couldn't patch them with tape or try to balance them on her nose. Instead, she stayed in her room reading until her mom yelled at her to come out and do her chores.

Cassie lowered her head as she pulled up the trash bag, hoping her hair covered her face.

"I need you to help me set the table, Cassie," her mom said just as Cassie hefted the trash bag over one shoulder.

"Okay," Cassie said. She turned her head to the side.

"Cassie?"

She braced herself. This was it.

"Why aren't you wearing your glasses?"

A lie popped into her head. She could say they were in her room.

But then her mom would tell her to go and get them.

So she could say she left them at school. And her mom would ask for them every day, until eventually . . .

No. It was easier just to tell the truth.

"They broke," she said with a loud exhale. "When I jumped off the swings they fell off. I stepped on them."

Her mom's dark brown eyes narrowed. "On purpose?"

"No!" Cassie protested. "I loved those glasses!"

Mrs. Jones pinched the bridge of her nose and sighed. "Our insurance only covers one pair a year, Cassie. You'll have to help pay for the next one."

Cassie nodded, images of her tiny allowance dwindling away. "Okay." What else could she say? It was, after all, her fault they were broken. She dragged the trash out, deciding this wasn't the best moment to bring up her desires to play soccer.

Instead, she waited until everyone had a serving of rice and chicken on their plates before bringing the subject up.

"Can I play soccer?"

Her dad stopped moving with his forkful of rice almost to his mouth. "Soccer?"

"A sport?" Her mom furrowed her brow, looking confused. "But you're so into music. We just started you with voice lessons. Your first lesson's next week."

"I love singing. But I want to do something else. Can't I do two things?"

"She needs it, she's getting fat," Scott, her rude and

obnoxious seven-year-old brother, said.

"No, I'm not!" Cassie protested. She wrapped her arms around her torso just in case.

"I think it's a great idea," Mr. Jones said, finally taking his bite and leaning back in the chair. "What do you know about soccer?"

"Not much," she admitted. "You have to kick the ball into the goal and can't use your hands." How hard could it be?

"I want to play," Emily said.

"Of course you do," Cassie said. "You always copy me."

"No I don't!" she protested.

"That's enough." Mr. Jones held up a hand to stave off the arguing. "If one of you does soccer, all of you can. What a great family activity."

Cassie exhaled, some of her excitement deflating. "Can't there be something I do by myself?"

"That's selfish," her mom said. "Why should you get to say who's allowed to do what activity?"

Cassie scowled at the chastisement.

"Yay, I love soccer!" Annette said.

Scott shrugged. "Might be fun."

"Keep in mind," Mr. Jones said, "it's not a free ride for anyone. I'll put you in soccer, but you have to work at it. Really put in the time to practice and make yourself better. I'm not paying for something you don't dedicate yourself to. That goes for all of you." He gave a steely look to each one of his children.

"I suppose it will be good for them," Mrs. Jones agreed, rather reluctantly. "But it will be more time—practices, games—and with four of them. . . ."

"We'll make it work. I'll help out." Mr. Jones smiled

across the table at her.

"Hmm," her mom said. "We'll see." She turned her eyes to her plate and took a bite of rice.

Mr. Jones called Cassie down to his office before bed. She already wore her pajamas, a long t-shirt and shorts.

"Did you get your homework done?" he asked her.

"Yes," she said, braiding her long brown hair. Maybe tomorrow it would have a pleat in it.

"Get your chores done?"

"Yes." Why was he asking all these questions? Usually only her mom cared what she got done.

"Look." He swiveled the computer screen so she could see it. "This is the online registration for soccer. We've already missed the deadline for the fall season, but I can sign you up for spring. Do you want me to?"

"We missed fall?" Her hopes fell. "But I really wanted to play now. When does the spring start?"

"The middle of February."

February! That was so far away. "Isn't there any way I can start sooner?"

Her father tapped his chin with one finger. "Tell you what. I'll register you for the spring. Then I'll call your coach and see if you can come to practice just once, just so you can meet the team. They keep the same team for fall and spring, for the most part."

Cassie considered that for a moment, then gave a nod. It wouldn't be the same as playing for the next two months, but at least she'd get to show her face. Everyone would know she'd be on their team in the spring. "Yeah. Yeah, that sounds great."

~

The following Wednesday before Cassie's first voice

lesson, Mrs. Jones took her to pick up her new glasses. The beautiful turquoise and polka-dotted frames Cassie had so loved were no longer available. Instead, she'd chosen a pink one that Mrs. Jones said accented her olive skin.

She didn't feel accented. She felt eight years old instead of eleven.

But her focus quickly drifted elsewhere when Mrs. Jones pulled up to the music studio.

"Good luck, sweetie!" her mom said.

"Thanks," Cassie barely managed to whisper. Her legs trembled as she let herself out of the car. What if Ms. Malcolm didn't like her or thought she didn't have a good voice?

"Come on in," Ms. Malcolm said when Cassie knocked on the studio door. The small room held a black piano, several bookshelves, and a mirror. Cassie scooted inside and set her backpack down.

"All right," Ms. Malcolm said. Her dark brown hair coiffed around her head, held firmly in place with what Cassie could only imagine was an entire can of hair spray. Bright red lipstick stained her pale face. "Put your shoulders back. Let's hear you sing a scale on ah."

Cassie took a deep breath and looked at her reflection. The pink glasses hung out on her nose, an unfamiliar accessory. "Ah-ah-ah—"

"Stop," Ms. Malcolm interrupted. "Look how you're standing."

Cassie glanced down at her clasped hands, her feet together.

"You'll never get the proper breath support that way. One foot should always be in front of the other for good balance. Hands at your side."

Cassie unclasped her hands and shuffled her feet.

"Now look at my mouth. It's not an 'aa,' it's an 'ah.' See? Try again."

Heart pattering in her throat, Cassie took a deep breath. "Ah-ah-ah-ah-ah—"

"Let's practice your breath support," Ms. Malcolm said, her fingers dropping on the piano keys. "Your tone is all breathy. Take a deep breath in through your nose, feeling your diaphragm widen." Ms. Malcolm demonstrated. "You try."

Cassie inhaled, and Ms. Malcolm shook her head.

"No, you're still breathing with your chest. You should feel your belly expand. Watch."

Cassie watched Ms. Malcolm as she lifted her hand, brought her chin up, and breathed in noisily. Cassie swallowed. She'd had no idea that everything she did was wrong.

"Now. Let's try again."

~

"How was your first lesson?" Mrs. Jones asked cheerfully as Cassie piled back into the van afterward.

Cassie's head throbbed, and her throat clenched as if she fought tears. But no way would she admit that to her mother. "It was great. Ms. Malcolm said I have a wonderful voice."

"Of course you do." Mrs. Jones beamed at her. "I'm so proud of you."

Cassie nodded and looked out the window. If only Ms. Malcolm had said that to her.

CHAPTER FOURTEEN

Rivals

"My dad signed me up for soccer," Cassie told Andrea as they walked to recess together after lunch. They'd eaten lunch together every day for the past week, but this was the first time they'd gone to recess together.

"Wow, soccer!" Andrea's eyes grew big. "That's so cool."

"I know. Have you ever played any sports?"

"No." Andrea shook her head. "I might try to do cheerleading when we go to junior high."

Cassie wasn't exactly sure what that was. "Okay. Cool."

They reached the playground behind the building. "Do you like to swing?" Cassie asked, wandering that direction out of habit.

Andrea shrugged. "Sometimes. We could just walk around the playground and pick flowers. See, there's a pretty purple one."

"Sure."

Andrea bent to pick up the flower. "Hey, what are you doing tomorrow?"

"Nothing." Cassie couldn't think of anything she ever did on Fridays. Her life wasn't exactly exciting.

"She's coming over to my house."

Cassie and Andrea both turned to see Riley approaching. Riley stepped between them, effectively blocking Andrea from the conversation.

"I waited for you at the swings," she said. "Why didn't you come?"

"I get tired of swinging sometimes," Cassie said. "So we're picking flowers."

Riley lowered her gaze to the small purple blossoms around their feet. "More like, weeding."

Cassie looked at Andrea over Riley's head and rolled her eyes. Andrea smiled.

"Since when am I coming to your house?" Cassie asked, bringing the conversation back to what Riley had said.

Riley lifted her chin. "I asked my mom last night. She said you could come over."

"That's too bad," Andrea said. "I was going to invite you to spend the night."

"Really?" Cassie said. No one had invited her over to their house except Riley in the whole year they'd lived here.

"But you can't," Riley said. "She's spending the night at my house. And then we're going to the mall to get matching outfits."

Cassie's head spun. This was the first she'd heard of these plans. "Does my mom know?"

"My mom's going to call her." Riley hooked an arm through Cassie's. "We're going to go swing now. Bye, Andrea."

"Bye," Andrea said, lifting an eyebrow. "I'll call you, Cassie. You can come over sometime next week."

"Okay," Cassie said. She waved at Andrea and allowed

Riley to pull her away.

~

Cassie burst through the front door after school. "Mom?" she called, checking the kitchen. No Mom. "Mom? Mom?" She ran downstairs and checked the office. Not there, either. "Mo-om!"

"In my room, Cassie!"

She ran down the hall to her mother's room. Her mom sat behind five baskets full of clean laundry as she folded a towel.

"Mom," she said, trying to catch her breath. "Did Riley's mom call you?"

Mrs. Jones frowned at her. "No. Why?"

Cassie exhaled, her chest deflating. Riley couldn't have lied about the whole thing. Did she? "She said she was going to call so I could spend the night tomorrow."

"Well, I guess that's fine, if your homework is done."

"But she hasn't called."

"Then call her."

Cassie stomped back to kitchen. She had Riley's number memorized, even though they hadn't spoken on the phone in weeks.

"Hello?" Riley answered.

"Hey, it's me," Cassie said.

"Oh, hey!" Riley said, perking up.

Cassie continued without giving her a chance to say anything else. "I just asked my mom about tomorrow. She doesn't know anything about it."

"Oh. Let me ask my mom."

"Ask your mom? You said she already said yes!" Cassie exploded.

"No, I said I know she'll say yes. Hang on."

Cassie fumed on her end of the phone and tried to listen in on Riley's conversation, but all she heard were muffled noises. Finally Riley came back to the phone.

"It's all arranged. She'll pick us up from school tomorrow. Your mom can bring your stuff over later, or we can pick it up on the way home."

The annoyance went out of Cassie in a big rush. "Really?" This was a real invite? She was actually going to spend the night somewhere?

"Yep. After school we'll go to the mall. Just like I said." Now her tone sounded triumphant.

"Okay," Cassie said. "I'll go pack my stuff."

~

Margaret, Riley's mom, picked both girls up in the car line on Friday.

"Hi, Ms. Isabel," Cassie said, climbing into the back of the van. Riley sat in the passenger seat.

"Hi, Cassie. Are you girls hungry? Should we get a snack?"

"Yes!" Riley said. She leaned over the seat to talk to Cassie. "We always go to Sonic and get the corn dogs. They're so good."

Cassie knew Sonic was a fast food place, but that was all she knew about it. She'd never been there. Her family didn't really do fast food very often. "That sounds great." Anything did, really. She was so hungry.

They got corn dogs and sodas from Sonic and then drove over to the mall.

"Did you bring money?" Riley asked.

"Yeah." Cassie unzipped her backpack and revealed twenty dollars, all that her mom had allowed her to keep after buying the new glasses. "I brought all my money."

"That's not very much."

Cassie frowned and put it back. "What are we going to buy?"

"Well, matching outfits, right? But with twenty dollars you won't be able to get much."

"Oh." Cassie didn't buy her own clothes, and they didn't shop at the mall. Her clothes usually came from Walmart or Target.

"Didn't you ask your mom for money?"

"No. Why would I do that?"

"So you could buy stuff!"

"Riley." Ms. Isabel parked the car. "You're being rude. Besides, you have more than enough. If you see something you want to buy, just buy an extra for Cassie."

"But it's my money!"

"But who gave it to you?"

Riley pressed her lips together. "Fine."

They stepped through the double doors, and Cassie whispered to Riley, "You don't have to buy me anything."

"I know."

Ms. Isabel followed behind while Riley led the way to different clothing stores. Cassie watched her try on shirts and jeans and skirts, coming out of the dressing room every few minutes to model a new outfit. Ms. Isabel ooed over every single one.

"Aren't you going to try anything?" Riley asked.

Not if she didn't have to. But Cassie thumbed through the racks of clothing, trying to look interested. Trying to be interested. "This shirt's kind of cute," she said.

"Try it on," Riley said, exchanging one outfit for another and returning to the dressing room.

Cassie didn't really think it was cute. "Okay."

She stepped into the dressing room, changed her shirt, and changed back. When she stepped out, Riley was waiting for her.

"Well, where is it?" she asked.

"Here." Cassie held the shirt up.

"Didn't you try it on?"

"Yeah."

"Why didn't you come out?"

Cassie blinked at her. "You wanted to see it?"

Riley rolled her eyes. "That's kind of the whole point."

"Oh." Cassie tried to wrap her mind around this concept. They were trying on clothes so they could show each other what they looked like in those clothes?

Riley heaved a sigh. "Never mind. Are you going to get it?"

"No." Cassie put the shirt back on the rack.

"Then let's go."

"What about you?" Cassie resisted Riley's pull. "Aren't you going to get the clothes you tried on?"

Riley shrugged. "No. They were just for fun."

Cassie revised her mental understanding of clothes shopping: try on clothes you don't intend to buy, show them off, then put them back.

She'd rather read a book.

Speaking of which . . . "Can we stop by the bookstore while we're here?" Cassie asked.

"If we have time," Riley said. "Oh, I love that store!" She ushered Cassie into a different clothing store.

While Riley tried on a pair of jeans, Cassie glanced at the price tag of one of the shirts. "Forty dollars! Yikes!" she muttered, dropping the sleeve before she ripped it or smudged it with her finger oils.

"I want these pants," Riley told her mom, and Cassie watched as Ms. Isabel paid for the jeans that cost more than a hundred dollars.

Crapola.

"Anything you like in here?" Riley asked.

Cassie shook her head.

She followed Riley's lead down the corridor. A sparkle caught her eye, and Cassie drew up short. In the middle of the corridor was a jewelry kiosk. Jewelry was one of Cassie's weaknesses. She'd changed her style a bit from last year, when her favorite was bright and colorful, long necklaces and unusual earrings. Now her favorite necklaces were on skinny gold and silver chains with dainty charms on the end. The only problem was, she only had one like that.

"Oh, stop, stop!" Cassie exclaimed, pulling Riley to a halt next to her.

"See something you like?" asked the teenage girl sitting on a stool behind the kiosk.

"Can I see that one?" Cassie pointed to a gold chain with a pink and gold butterfly on it.

"Sure." The girl undid the lock and pulled it out for Cassie to see.

"It's beautiful," Cassie murmured, awed by the delicate wings of the golden insect. She flipped it over and her heart sank. The little necklace was sixty dollars. "It's too much," she said with a sigh.

"What's your budget?" the girl asked, accepting the necklace from Cassie.

"Twenty dollars." Cassie's cheeks burned as she realized how cheap she must sound.

But the girl only smiled. "Come on over to this side."

Cassie and Riley followed her to the other side of the kiosk.

"See all these?" She waved her hand over a row of necklaces and rings. "They're all thirty dollars or less. Just ask, and I'll check the price on any you're interested in."

"Cassie!" Riley said, immediately excited. "Look at this one!"

"Which one?" Cassie wondered what could have caught Riley's attention. She didn't even wear jewelry.

"The best friend one! Look, it's a heart broken in half! We could each wear one half!"

"Oh." Cassie had seen those kinds of necklaces before and always wished she had a best friend to give the other half to. But she wasn't sure if Riley was that friend.

"Let's get that one. How much is it?" Riley asked the girl.

"The one with the pink gem in it is twenty-five. But this one here, it just has a sterling silver overlay. It's only fifteen."

"That's perfect!" Riley exclaimed. "Let's buy it, Cassie!"

Cassie hesitated. If she bought that, she'd only have five dollars left. But if she didn't, how would she explain to Riley what she was feeling?

"That's so beautiful," Ms. Isabel said from behind them. "What a nice way to represent your friendship. Though you girls are more like sisters than friends." She beamed at them.

Cassie felt trapped. "Okay," she said. "I'll take that one."

Riley twitched with anticipation as the girl pulled out the necklace. Cassie handed over her twenty, and the two chains with the broken heart dropped into her hand. Riley snatched up the first piece.

"Let's put them on right now."

Cassie watched Riley put on the piece that said "best." It hung nicely from her neck, and Cassie pushed away her trepidation. Maybe the necklaces meant something good would come of their friendship. Maybe it would be better than last year. Cassie put hers on, latching it behind her neck.

"Oh, you two! Let me take a picture." Ms. Isabel had her phone out, ready to snap a photo.

Riley slung an arm around Cassie's shoulder, and Cassie remembered to smile before it flashed.

CHAPTER FIFTEEN

Soccer Knocks

Andrea slipped Cassie a note during journaling on Monday morning.

How was your weekend?

Great! Cassie wrote back. *Yours?*

Boring. But my mom said you can come over after school this week. Want to tomorrow?

Yes! Then Cassie remembered something, and she quickly added, *But tomorrow I have Girls Club. Maybe Wednesday?*

Right around that time, Ms. Timber started walking around the desks and watching the kids while they journaled. Andrea hid the note, and Cassie finished writing about her weekend.

"Wednesday should be fine," Andrea said, finding Cassie during morning recess. "I don't have anything going on after school."

Cassie joined her as she began her walk around the play yard. "I'll talk to my mom and have her call you. What's your phone number?"

"I'll write it down for you. Hey, how was Riley's?"

Cassie shrugged. "It was good. We had fun." She didn't want to tell Andrea about the best friend necklaces, for some reason. "Today's my first day of soccer."

"Oh, that's right! Are you nervous?"

"Yeah."

Andrea took her hand and squeezed it. "Don't worry. You'll be amazing."

They finished their loop around the play yard and approached the school again. Miles stood with a couple of boys by the sidewalk.

"Hi, Miles," Cassie blurted, then felt her face burn. Why had she done that?

He glanced over at them and smiled. "Hi, Cassie. Hi Andrea."

"Hi, Miles," Andrea echoed. She exchanged a smile with Cassie as they started on a second loop. "He's so nice, isn't he?"

"Yeah," Cassie agreed. "So nice."

~

After dinner, Cassie's dad drove her to the local junior high to meet her soccer team. She wore a t-shirt and basketball shorts, and a pair of shin guards with cleats.

"You better like this sport," her mom had warned her after buying the shoes and equipment. "I'm not spending this money on you just so you can change your mind."

"I'm going to love it," Cassie had replied.

Now, in the front seat of the car next to her dad and feeling oddly dressed, Cassie wasn't so sure.

Mr. Jones parked the car in front of the field. A few kids were already out there, running around and kicking the ball.

"This is their first practice," her dad said. "They're just

getting to know each other too."

Cassie nodded. These kids had probably been playing together for years, though. She doubted anyone was just now starting.

Her dad got out, and she followed.

"Hi," he said, approaching the only other adult on the field. They shook hands. "I'm Jim Jones. This is my daughter, Cassie."

"Oh, yes." The tall red-headed coach turned his attention to Cassie. "You're the one who didn't register in time for the fall season, right?"

She nodded.

"Well, we'll be happy to have you practice with us if you want. I'd let you play at the games, but others might complain, since you haven't paid for the season. If you want a practice schedule, just let me know."

"Thanks," Cassie said.

"I'm Coach Price, by the way."

"Cassie, I'll just watch from the side." Mr. Jones went back to the wooden fence and leaned on it. Cassie wished he'd leave. Playing in front of him made her nervous.

"Wait, is she on our team?"

She turned, recognizing the voice but not able to place it. Oh, Connor. Her heart sank a little. The big blond kid had been in her dad's band last year, and he pretty much ignored Cassie except to make fun of her.

"She can't play soccer," Connor continued.

"Says who?" A girl joined them now, and she kicked at Connor's foot with her skinny leg. Her sandy blond hair was in a messy ponytail, but she still managed to look cute. "You've never seen her try." She waved at Cassie. "I'm Erica. I go to Elmdale."

"Hi," Cassie said, glad for a friendly face. She didn't knew where Elmdale was, but she knew it was another elementary school.

"She's too fat to play," Connor said. "I bet she can't even run." He put his hands on his chest and mimicked someone gasping for breath.

Erica rolled her eyes. "Connor, you're such a jerk."

Cassie clenched her jaw and fought a sudden onslaught of tears. "It's this shirt," she said. She glanced down at the t-shirt. Was it too tight? What about her outfit made her look fat?

"Cassie's on our team, but she won't join us till next spring," Coach Price said. "She's here today to practice with us and get to know everyone."

"How many years have you been playing?" another boy asked.

"I haven't," Cassie said, more anxious by the second. "This is my first time."

Connor snorted. "She's a newbie, on top of everything else?"

"Connor," Coach Price said in a warning tone. "You're not being very friendly."

"I'm just saying what everyone is thinking."

"Five laps, Connor. Now!"

Grumbling and shaking his head, Connor took off down the field.

"All right, everyone. Let's line up and do some drills!"

First they did dribbling, which was basically pushing the ball down the field with the inside of the feet. Or it should have been, but it became painfully obvious that Cassie had no skill with this. Each time she touched the ball with her foot, she shot it down the field and had to chase after it.

Everyone else had dribbled to the goal and back several times before she made it there.

"You'll get it," Coach Price said, coming over to demonstrate. "Just make smaller moves. That's it."

Cassie tried to control the ball, but all she managed was to nudge it.

"Keep trying. It's coming along." He jogged off to check on the other kids.

Cassie wiped at sweat dripping down her forehead and tried not to pant. The hot September sun beat down on her. This was much harder than she expected.

Coach blew his whistle. "Water break!"

They all hurried back to their bottles of water. Cassie's legs quivered as she chugged hers.

"Next up, grab a partner," Coach said. "We'll practice passing."

Instantly the team of thirteen kids paired off, leaving Cassie alone.

"Let's see . . ." Coach Price said. "Landon, you partner with me. Connor, you're with Nicole. Erica, partner with Cassie."

They rearranged without complaining too much, and Erica led Cassie to a spot away from everyone else.

"Okay, so remember what you just did with the dribbling?"

Cassie nodded.

"So do that again, but this time, you get to be stronger. You're trying to get the ball to me."

"Okay," Cassie said, confident she could kick it harder.

She could. But apparently not to her partner.

Erica chased the ball down and sent it back to Cassie with a direct kick each time.

"How long have you been playing?" Cassie asked, trying to control the direction the ball went.

"Since I was seven. I love it."

"Holy cow," was all she could say. She was definitely behind.

Coach finally blew his whistle. Cassie tried to jog over to join her teammates but ended up walking. She stopped to breathe as soon as she joined the huddle, propping her hands on her knees and bending over.

"Great job, team," Coach said. "I know it's been a few months since we played, and we have some new members, but I see a good hustle out there. We're going to be an awesome group this year."

The team greeted his words with excited exclamations.

"Give me two laps up the hill and then you're done. Go team!"

"Go team!" everyone except Cassie shouted. And then they took off across the field, racing for a small hill at the other end.

Cassie stopped mid-pant, eyes following them. Crapola. They weren't done?

She made it one lap. Almost. By the time she started back down the hall, her side hurt, and breath wheezed in and out of her lungs. She wanted to press her hands to her chest just like Connor had done when making fun of her, but no way would she do that. Instead she half-walked, half-limped back to her water bottle.

Even though she'd only done one lap, she wasn't even the first one done. She avoided her teammates' eyes and guzzled her water, then dumped it over her head and neck. Her dad was talking to Coach Price, and Cassie walked over, a bit reluctant to interrupt.

"Well, what did you think?" Coach Price asked, turning to her when she reached them.

Cassie did her best to smile. "It was fun. I have a lot to learn."

"You'll get there. Come practice with us a few more times this season."

Mr. Jones waved and headed for the car. "Sure appreciate you letting her come out."

"You bet."

Cassie drank the rest of her water and climbed into the van next to her dad.

"Was it all you hoped it would be?" he asked, looking over his shoulder as he backed the car out of the parking space.

"It was harder than I expected. I didn't have much control of the ball." The worst part, though, was the running.

"Did you want me to get the practicing schedule?"

She hesitated, then shook her head. "Not yet. I want to build up my stamina first. Start running a bit."

"That's a great idea. You could get up every morning before school and go for a fifteen-minute jog. Want me to go with you?"

"Yeah, I'll do that. But I want to go by myself."

"I'll wake you up tomorrow morning at six."

"Tomorrow?" Her eyes widened, startled.

"There's no reason to wait another day."

Her mind searched for an excuse, but she found none. "Okay," she said, giving up.

CHAPTER SIXTEEN

Little Runner Girl

When her dad woke her up at six the next morning, Cassie wanted to change her mind. She wanted to tell her dad that she'd lost interest in soccer. Then she remembered her mom's threat and somehow pulled herself out of bed. If she couldn't quit, she needed to improve. She didn't want to be the slowest kid on the team in the spring.

Pioneer, the dog they'd gotten last year when they moved into the new house, joined Cassie as she jogged. He seemed to think this was a game, created for his enjoyment. He barked and wagged his tail, then ran ahead of her and crouched down, waiting for her to catch up.

Her side began to cramp up, and Cassie slowed her pace. Her neck ached from holding her head up and bouncing up and down. Lifting each leg felt like lifting a sack full of lead. The run became a walk, and Cassie turned back toward home. It had to have been fifteen minutes by now.

She stepped into the dark and silent entryway and looked for the microwave time in the dining room. 6:07 a.m. What? That wasn't possible. Cassie hadn't left the house until a little after six. Surely she'd run for more than five minutes . . . had it only been five minutes?

She held a hand to her side and went into the kitchen for water. Little muscle spasms sent flickers of pain and heat through her calves and thighs. Running was brutal. She couldn't do this again.

Her dad came down the hall around six-twenty. "Cassie?" he called.

"In here," she answered, getting down a bag of cereal from the pantry shelf.

He stepped into the kitchen, finishing up the knot on his tie. "How was your run?"

"Really hard," she admitted, though she didn't mention that she only lasted five minutes.

"It will get better. Running is really good for you. I'm proud of you." He picked up his briefcase from the dining room. "I'm off to work. Wake everyone up and help them to the bus, just like always."

"Okay," Cassie said, pleased with his praise and at the same time feeling guilty that she hadn't run as much as he thought she had. Oh well. She'd do better tomorrow.

~

Girls club met after school today, the first time this school year. Riley waited for Cassie after class so they could walk to the cafeteria together.

"I haven't missed Trisha," Riley said, referring to the assistant club leader.

"Me neither," Cassie said. She'd had an altercation with Trisha at the beginning of the school year last year, and even though neither of them ever brought it up again, it was always, always in the back of her mind.

"Maybe she'll be nicer this year," Riley said.

"Maybe," Cassie said, though she doubted it. The stocky

woman was cranky and snappy. Her daughter Jaiden was petite and friendly, a complete opposite. She was also fiercely loyal. Cassie had to be very careful about what she said, because Jaiden reported back to Trisha. Cassie knew better than to even trust Jaiden. She changed the subject. "I went to soccer practice yesterday."

"Were you any good at it?"

For some reason, the question bothered Cassie, and she reacted defensively. "Of course. I still have a lot to learn, but I've got some natural talent."

"Oh."

Was it Cassie's imagination, or did Riley seem disappointed?

The conversation slid to a halt when they entered the cafeteria. Cassie immediately brightened when she saw the familiar group of girls she'd gotten to know so well last year. "Hi, Janice! Maureen! Leigh Ann!" All of them had different groups of people they hung out with during the day. At Girls Club, there was only each other.

"Hi, Cassie, Riley!" The girls all hugged and exchanged stories before the leaders arrived.

Trisha and Margaret, the other leader and Maureen's mother, entered the cafeteria at about the same time.

"Welcome to another year!" Trisha said, her voice booming in the nearly empty cafeteria. "We have some big plans for the next coming months. First off: a campout."

"Oo, when?" Janice asked.

"I love campouts!" Riley said.

"Not me," Ciera said, wrinkling her nose. "All those bugs." She tossed her shoulder-length hair behind her.

"Our campout's at the end of this month," Trisha said, ignoring their comments. "Just when the weather starts to get cooler."

"Where are we going?" Leigh Ann asked. Cassie was glad she did, because she wanted to know, but she never asked questions or made comments when Trisha was talking.

"Camp Splendor."

Now Cassie cheered with Riley. They'd spent a week at Camp Splendor over the summer, except Cassie had been on crutches. She couldn't wait to explore the campsite without them.

"Okay, so let's divide into two groups and start planning. Ms. Hemming will take one group, and I'll take the other."

Cassie followed Riley to Ms. Hemming's group. There was never any question but the two of them would stay with Margaret whenever they could.

~

"Cassandra!"

Cassie jerked awake Wednesday morning when her father called her name. "What? Am I late?" She sat up and reached for her alarm clock, a shot of adrenaline warming her system.

"No, Cassie," her dad said. "It's time for your jog."

She lay back down and blinked in the darkness at the ceiling. Jog? Then she remembered. She wanted to be a better runner for soccer.

Right now, that seemed like a horrible idea.

"Are you coming?"

She didn't want to. She heaved a sigh and tossed her legs over the side of her bed. "Yeah."

Her dad disappeared back into his room. Cassie threw on a pair of shorts and a t-shirt, then stepped into the hallway. Pioneer padded his way to the her side. She rubbed his head while she slipped on her tennis shoes. She made sure the lights were on outside and left the house. The air nipped at her bare arms and she shivered. Pioneer kept time with her as she broke into a jog. Today she should be able to do more than yesterday, at least.

She reached the same spot in the road and bent over, gasping and holding her side. She had almost reached the bus stop at the top of the street. Cassie gritted her teeth and forced herself to run farther. She got two more paces when her legs refused to lift for one more step. Shrugging it off, she turned around and walked home.

The first thing she did in the house was check the time. Her heart sank. She'd only been out there seven minutes. She'd thought for sure that with the walking, she would take more time. "I don't want to do this anymore, Pioneer," she whispered to the dog, and got herself a drink of water.

Her dad came into the kitchen ten minutes later and spotted her by the refrigerator. "How was your jog?"

"Great," Cassie lied. "I think I'm getting faster."

"Good for you, Cass. How far did you get this time?"

What would be a logical distance and still believable? "I just ran to the bus stop and home twice."

"Really? You ran the whole time?"

He sounded a little suspicious, so Cassie shook her head. "No. I walked some of it."

"Hmm. Tomorrow you should see if you can do that three times in fifteen minutes."

"Yeah," Cassie said. He walked away, and her mind raced. By tomorrow, she needed to have an excuse not to do this.

~

"Don't forget you're going to Andrea's after school today," Mrs. Jones reminded Cassie in the morning. "Here's a note for your teacher."

"Thank you," Cassie said, taking the note from her mom.

"You won't be there long," Mrs. Jones added with a yawn. "You have voice tonight." She glanced around at everyone as they slipped on their backpacks, gave a wave, and went back to bed.

Andrea's mom picked both her and Cassie up after school in her white four-door car. Cassie fidgeted excitedly. All day she'd been afraid something would happen and she wouldn't be able to go to Andrea's house. Riley hadn't spoken to her since lunch, when Cassie mentioned that she was going to Andrea's.

They drove down the street, turned left, and went up a long driveway with a brick house at the end of it.

"You live so close to the school!" Cassie said. She had been here once before, to pick Andrea up for Cassie's eleventh birthday party. But Cassie had been so emotional that day she hadn't really paid attention to where they were going.

"Yep." Andrea pushed on her glasses and hopped out of the car. "But my mom won't let me walk to school."

"Too dangerous," Mrs. Wall said, locking the car once they were all out. "You can't trust people anymore. Where do you live, Cassie?"

"Out in the country," Cassie said. "I ride the bus. It takes like an hour to get to school."

"I would love to ride the bus!" Andrea said. She grabbed Cassie's hand. "Come on! I'll show you my room."

They ran through the kitchen, a living room, and down the hall to Andrea's room. She had a huge white vanity and a large pink bed inside. The closet door was open, revealing colorful clothes and a messy array of shoes.

"I love your room!" Cassie exclaimed. What would it be like not to share with her sister? And such a big bed!

"Look at these." Andrea opened a drawer on the vanity and pulled out a set of rollers. "Someday when you spend the night we'll put your hair in curlers. It would look so pretty."

Cassie nodded. "My mom did that to my hair last year. I loved it. But it took forever."

"That's why we'll do it sometime when you stay over."

"Girls." Ms. Wall poked her head in. "Get your homework done before you play."

"We don't have any," Andrea said.

"Just reading," Cassie said.

"Then both of you read for twenty minutes." Ms. Wall picked up a timer from Andrea's vanity. She turned the dial and set it back down.

"Yes, Mom." Andrea sat down on her bed, pulling her book from her backpack.

Cassie did the same. Normally she loved to read, but today, she just wanted to talk with Andrea.

The timer buzzed, and Andrea snapped her book shut. "Let's go outside on the trampoline!"

Cassie followed, marveling at Andrea's nonstop buzz of energy. She tried to keep up, but Andrea jumped circles around her. Finally Andrea collapsed on the elastic black screen, laughing and gasping for air. Cassie sat across from her.

"So," Andrea said, taking another deep breath. "Tell me a secret."

"Secret? I don't know any secrets."

"I'll tell you one. Can't tell anyone. Cross your heart."

Cassie ran her fingers over her chest in a cross sign. "Promise."

Andrea leaned forward and lowered her voice. "I heard that Cara Barnes kissed Jay Miller on the bus."

Cassie gasped. Cara was a beautiful, skinny blond who already had to wear a bra. "But she's so quiet."

Andrea shook her head. "You never know with people. She's only quiet because she thinks she's better than us."

Cassie couldn't confirm or contradict that. She'd never said two words to Cara.

"Your turn," Andrea said.

Cassie wracked her brain, searching for a secret. "I don't like running."

Andrea laughed out loud. "That's not a very good secret. Okay, how about this: who do you like?"

"Like?"

"You know." Andrea waved a hand. "What boy? Who would you like to kiss?"

Oh. The heat rushed to Cassie's cheeks and she looked down, but the tingling sensation in her belly made her feel warm and gooey inside.

"Ha! There is someone!" Andrea crowed. "Who?"

"What about you?" Cassie challenged, lifting her chin. "Who do you like?"

"Connor Lane," Andrea said without hesitation.

"Connor? But he's—" *such a jerk.* The words died before they left her lips. She couldn't say that to Andrea, not if Andrea liked him.

"He's what?" Andrea asked.

Cassie swallowed back her misgivings. "He's on my soccer team."

Andrea's eyes widened, her eyebrows lifting. "Really? Maybe I should join soccer!"

They laughed for a moment, and then Andrea grew serious. "No, but really. Your turn. Who do you like?"

Cassie licked her lips, noting how dry her mouth felt. "Promise you won't tell anyone?"

Andrea made the same cross sign over her heart. "Promise."

Cassie's voice dropped low enough to be a whisper. "Miles."

Andrea sucked in a breath. "Miles? Miles Hansen?"

Cassie nodded. She dropped her eyes.

"Oh, Cassie! He's so sweet! You guys would look so cute together!"

Cassie raised her eyes, a slow smile creeping over her face. "You think so?"

Andrea squeezed her arm and giggled. "Yes!"

By the time Mrs. Jones showed up to get Cassie two hours later, her daughter had been transformed under two layers of eyeshadow, thick mascara, and bright red lipstick. Andrea and Cassie stood on the front porch giggling while their mothers talked.

"I think they had fun," Mrs. Wall said. "I made them do their homework first."

"Thank you so much for letting Cassie play. I know she misses her friends in Texas sometimes."

"Well, she and Andrea can play anytime."

Andrea pulled on Cassie's hand. "Did you hear that?"

"Yes!"

They hugged, and then Mrs. Jones said, "Come on, Cassie!"

"See you in school tomorrow!" Cassie called.

"I'll see you and Miles!" Andrea called back.

Cassie waved to shush her, then glanced at her mom to see if she'd noticed. She thought she saw the corners of her mother's mouth turn up, but if Mrs. Jones heard, she didn't say anything.

CHAPTER SEVENTEEN
Ambassador

Cassie heard her alarm clock go off at six o'clock in the morning, but she ignored it. Twitching her arm just enough to hit the snooze button, she buried her head under her pillow, determined to go back to bed.

Until she heard her father's footsteps coming down the hall. She sat up and poked her head out the bedroom door before he could open it. "I'm up," she whispered.

Her dad was still in his pajamas. He gave a nod. "I'm getting in the shower. I'll see you when I get out."

This couldn't be easier. Cassie waited until he'd shut the door to his room. Then she went into the kitchen, a change of clothes and a book tucked under one arm. Sitting down at the table, she read her book, keeping an eye on the clock. When ten minutes had passed, she took her bundle to the bathroom. She waited another minute or two before turning on the shower.

This was what she'd done all last week, too. Her dad seemed pleased that on top of running, she'd taken a greater interest in hygiene.

When she stepped out, dressed and showered, her dad

was putting his bowl of cereal in the sink.

"How did it go today?"

"Great," Cassie lied, feeling a finger of guilt worm its way into her chest. "It's getting easier."

"I'm proud of you, Cassie." He watched her pull out the bread and toaster. "You should eat some protein after running. Maybe cook up an egg."

She didn't cook. Didn't he know that? She popped her bread into the toaster. "No, thanks." Butter had protein in it, right?

"Well, I'm off to work. Don't forget to wake everyone up."

Not like she could forget. That was her job. "Okay."

Mr. Jones left, and Cassie heaved a sigh of relief, only now completely relaxing. But still, she wondered. How long would she have to keep this ruse up? In a few months it would be too cold, but she had weeks until then. She had to be vigilant, or he'd catch on.

~

Andrea was already in the classroom when Cassie stepped inside. They greeted each other with a hug, and then Andrea followed her to the backpack cubbies.

"How was your weekend?" Andrea asked.

"Boring," Cassie said, her standard response these days. "I didn't go anywhere or do anything."

"Too bad your mom wouldn't let you come over."

Cassie shook her head, irritated again at the memory. The Joneses lived twenty minutes out of town, and the distance kept Cassie from meeting up with friends whenever she wanted. "She said I can some other time."

"Maybe this weekend?"

"That would be awesome." Cassie pulled her reading

time snack from the front pocket of her backpack. Crackers and cheese. "Oh." She frowned as she remembered something. "I think I have a campout this weekend with the Girls Club."

"Oh, that's right. What is that, anyway? What do you do there?"

Cassie joined Andrea at her desk, since the other students hadn't come in and taken their spots yet. Though she and Andrea had become quite close in the past few weeks since school started, there was still a lot they didn't know about each other. "It's the after school club I go to every Tuesday. They organize activities and things. This weekend we're going camping."

"Oh, that sounds fun! Can I come?"

"I don't think so," Cassie said, wishing she didn't have to tell Andrea no. "I think it's only for people in Girls Club."

"Is that the club you go to with Riley?"

"Yes."

"So she'll be on the campout with you?"

Cassie nodded.

Andrea fell silent, looking up at the ceiling tiles while she considered this. "I don't think Riley likes me."

Riley didn't like most of Cassie's other friends. "Sure, she does," Cassie said. "Why wouldn't she like you?"

Andrea perked up, a smile lighting her face. "Can you ask if I can come?"

"Sure." Cassie shrugged. "The meeting's tomorrow. I'll ask then."

"Thanks! I hope they say yes!"

The bell rang, and the students still in the hallway meandered into the classroom. Cassie went to her seat, glad to end the conversation about the campout.

~

"She wants to come on our campout?" Riley stopped walking. Cassie took a few more steps down the hallway before she realized it, then she turned around and backtracked to Riley.

"Yes. I told her I'd ask—"

"She can't come," Riley interrupted.

Cassie bobbed her head, trying to maintain patience. "I didn't think she could, and I told her that. But I promised her I'd ask today."

Riley scowled. "They won't let her. Andrea's not in Girls Club."

Cassie didn't bother explaining again. She just knew she had to ask, or Andrea might get her feelings hurt. They walked the rest of the way to the cafeteria in silence.

All the other girls were in agreement with Riley: since Andrea wasn't in Girls Club, she couldn't come.

"Does she want to be in Girls Club?" Margaret, Maureen's mom and the Girls Club leader, asked when Cassie brought it up.

Cassie shook her head. "I don't think so. She didn't say it, anyway."

"Tell her she can't come," Riley said, narrowing her greenish-blue eyes.

Margaret tapped her chin, considering the question. "We would love to have another girl in our group. Cassie, if she really wants to come, have her mom call me. Maybe I can talk her in to joining."

Riley crossed her arms over her chest and stomped away. She sat down at one of the cafeteria tables and kicked her feet at the table legs.

"I didn't mean to make her angry," Cassie said uneasily, her eyes still on Riley.

"She's just jealous. She has to learn to share her friends." Margaret raised her voice, speaking to the other girls who were in little clusters in the cafeteria. "Okay, girls! We're going to finish planning our campout today. Decide who will be your tent partner and then figure out who will bring what supplies."

Cassie hesitated, watching the other girls pair up. Though she liked them, she always spent her time with Riley. But with Riley over in the corner pouting, Cassie wasn't sure she should partner up with her. She was likely to get her head bitten off.

"Are you sharing a tent with Riley?" Leigh Ann asked, spotting Cassie still sitting at the table.

"I think so," Cassie said. "I haven't asked her yet."

"You can be in our tent," Leigh Ann said, nodding at Jaiden. "We can all three share."

"Thanks," Cassie said, but she didn't want to be with Jaiden, and she knew Jaiden didn't want to be with her. Though they didn't fight, they didn't really care for each other. Not since last year when Cassie insulted Jaiden's mom. She stood up and walked toward the table where Riley sat, arms crossed on the laminate, chin resting on her arms.

"What?" she said in a surly voice when Cassie sat down. "Aren't you going to share a tent with your best friend Andrea?"

A flash of anger unfurled in Cassie's belly. "That's exactly part of the problem. I'm never sure if you're going to be nice to me or treat me like someone you don't like."

"I'm always nice. You're the one inviting other people on

our camping trip."

Cassie rolled her eyes. "I can have more than one friend."

Riley didn't answer.

"Besides," Cassie went on, "she's probably not going to come. Which means I'm sharing a tent with you. If you can be nice, anyway."

"Maybe I don't want you to share a tent with me."

"Fine with me." Cassie stood up, hot with anger. "Leigh Ann and Jaiden said I could be in their tent. You can have the tent all to yourself."

"Wait!"

Cassie stopped mid-stride, though she didn't bother turning around.

"I'm sorry," Riley said, and she sounded like she meant it. "I just thought that Girls Club was our thing. It's supposed to be our campout."

Cassie turned to face Riley, letting out a big sigh. "You're my best friend, Riley. That should be enough."

"But you spend so much time with Andrea." Huge tears welled up in Riley's eyes. "It's like you've forgotten me."

Cassie came back and sat by her. "Don't worry about it. We'll share a tent, and everything will be fine."

"Okay." Riley gave a weak smile.

But inside, Cassie didn't know if everything would be fine. Andrea never made her feel like she had to choose who her friends would be.

~

"What did they say?" Andrea asked through the telephone that evening.

Cassie had put off calling her as long as she could once she got home, but she knew her friend was waiting. "They said no," Cassie said. "I'm so sorry, Andrea."

Andrea sighed. "Yeah, I kind of figured that would happen. But I have an idea! Let's go camping at my house!"

"Or mine," Cassie said, warming to the idea. She glanced out the bay window in the kitchen, looking out over the seven acres behind the house. She could see her mother in the garden below, grabbing a few late-season tomatoes for dinner. Chicken and rice simmered in pots and pans behind her. "We have lots of land here!"

"Yeah! How about next weekend?"

"Sure!" Cassie bounced on the balls of her feet, excited. "I'll tell my mom!"

A strangled noise in the living room distracted her. Cassie moved around the kitchen table, not really listening to Andrea anymore as she followed the sound. Then she gasped out loud. Pioneer, the family dog, lay on the living room floor, his entire body jerking and shaking. Strange grunts and whines escaped his mouth, his teeth bared, his head knocking against the wall behind him.

"What is it?" Andrea asked. "What's wrong?"

"I have to go! Something's wrong with my dog!" Cassie hung up the phone and tossed it on the floor, all while running to Pioneer's side. "Mom!" she screamed. "Mom!"

Scott and Annette appeared in their bedroom doorway first, summoned by Cassie's screams. Cassie crouched next to Pioneer, cradling his head in her lap.

"Get Mom!" she shouted at Scott. "She's in the garden!"

Scott threw some shoes on and ran out the door. The last bedroom door opened, and Emily ran down the hall.

"What's wrong?" she said. "What's going on?"

"Pioneer," Cassie said, trying not to cry. She wanted to

stroke the dog's long black fur, but the way his body shook and trembled, she worried she'd hurt him.

She heard the thundering of footsteps on the deck stairs moments before the back door opened and Mrs. Jones stepped inside, Scott right behind her. She ran over to Cassie and knelt next to Pioneer.

"There now," she said to him in a soothing voice, her hands caressing his snout, "it's okay. We're here with you."

"Is he dying?" Cassie asked, her throat tight and sore. Annette and Emily began to cry.

"I don't know," her mom whispered.

Abruptly, the shaking stopped. Pioneer's mouth opened and he panted, his chest heaving as he gasped. Then his body gave a final spasm, and he vomited all over Cassie's lap.

"Ew!" Scott said.

Cassie wrinkled her nose at the foul smell.

"Let me get you a towel, Cassie," her mom said.

Pioneer lifted his head. He panted, but looked more like himself. Slowly, he got to his feet, though he seemed a bit wobbly.

Mrs. Jones returned with a towel. Cassie used it to get herself up without getting the floor any dirtier, then she went straight to the bathroom to change her clothes. Time for her second shower of the day.

~

They took Pioneer to the vet on Wednesday. By the time Cassie got home from school, he had a diagnosis: epilepsy.

"What is that?" Cassie asked as her mom wiped down the counter.

"It's when someone has seizures from time to time.

Apparently Pioneer has this condition."

"Is he going to die?" Her throat tightened just like it had the day before during his attack.

"No. But if he starts to have them frequently, he'll need medication for it." Mrs. Jones put the rag down. "Get your things and let's go to voice lessons.

Epilepsy. Something else for her to research in computer lab.

Cassie stayed up late Thursday night getting everything together for her camping trip. So when Friday morning came along and her dad woke her up at six to go running, she had to force herself out of bed. He disappeared back into his room, and she dragged her feet to the kitchen.

Cassie sat down at the kitchen table and opened her book. But the words blurred before her face, and she had a hard time remembering the storyline. Finally, she laid the book face-down on the table and rested her head next to it, her cheek on the table.

The next thing she knew, someone was shaking her shoulder.

"Cassandra. Cassandra, wake up."

Cassie's eyes flew open with a sense of panic that she'd been caught somewhere she shouldn't be. She sat up and found her dad standing there in front of her, fully dressed.

"What, what time is it?" she fumbled. She wiped a line of drool from her face.

"You were sleeping," he said, a faint note of disbelief in his voice. "Did you even run today?"

She considered lying. But as she stared back at her father, clearly still in her pajamas, a book on the table in front of her, she knew the answer was obvious. "No."

Understanding and disappointment swept over his

features, lifting his brows and turning down the corners of his mouth. "Did you run yesterday?"

"No," she whispered.

"When was the last time you ran?"

Cassie wanted to lower her eyes, but she couldn't move them. Her body gave a slight tremble. She hated to disappoint him so much. "Last week," she said. It wasn't exactly true; it had been two weeks. But she figured in this situation, he didn't need to know that.

"You've been lying to me."

This time she didn't even answer.

"Why?"

She exhaled and finally managed to lower her eyes. "It was too hard."

"You told me it was getting easier."

"It was . . ." As far as she could tell, anyway. "But it was still too hard. I hated it." Now tears pricked her eyes, as much out of guilt as unhappiness at the thought of running again.

"What about soccer? How are you going to play if you can't even run?"

"It's different on the field," she said, and now she was in truthful territory. "I'm chasing a ball. I have a purpose. I'm with my teammates. By myself, just running, it seems too pointless."

"All right." He heaved a sigh. "You may as well go shower and get ready for the day. Don't lie to me like that again, Cassandra."

She nodded and shot away from the table, locking herself in the bathroom to avoid meeting her dad's eyes again.

~

"You've seemed sad today," Andrea said at lunch as she unwrapped her Turkey and cheese sandwich. "What's going on?"

Cassie shrugged. "It's just my dad. I got in a fight with him."

"I hate it when I fight with my parents. What happened?"

"I've been pretending to go running every morning. He just found out today that I haven't been."

"You've been pretending?" Andrea giggled. "That's pretty clever. How did you manage that?"

Cassie gave a small smile. "I hid in the kitchen when he thought I was running, and then took a shower right after so he never knew."

Andrea laughed out loud. "Pretty sneaky, Cassie. I didn't know you had that in you."

"Yeah, well." She shrugged. "I feel bad I didn't tell him. He was disappointed in me."

"So next time don't get caught." Andrea winked and took a bite of her sandwich. "You're funny."

Cassie cheered up a bit and put the incident behind her. Now all she could think about was the campout. Just two more hours.

"Cassie?" Ms. Timber called her name after recess. "Will you come here, please?"

Cassie shot a glance at Andrea, who raised an eyebrow and shrugged. Fighting down the panic that rose anytime a teacher called on her, Cassie pushed her chair back and went up to the desk.

"Yes, Ms. Timber?" she said meekly.

Her teacher shuffled papers around on the desk for another minute, Cassie anxiety growing by the second.

Finally Ms. Timber lifted her head and smiled.

"Cassie, I've been very pleased with your work so far this year. Not just the way you apply yourself with your schooling, but the way you interact with your peers. The school counselor agreed with my assessment, and you've been named the sixth grade ambassador for our class."

Cassie's eyebrows shot up. Holy cow. She hadn't expected this. "That's awesome! What will I do?"

"You're the student who will help any new students we have. You'll gather homework for kids who are sick and be friendly to those who seem lonely. Make people feel welcome and do whatever else I need you to do. Can you do that?"

Cassie nodded, pride swelling in her chest. "Yes, Ms. Timber."

"Good. Congratulations, Cassie."

Cassie turned around, unable to wipe the grin from her face. The morning might have started out bad, but it was on an upward trend now.

Episode 3: Camping Blues

CHAPTER EIGHTEEN
Sunshine and Friendship

Cassandra Jones waited with her best friend Riley after school. Riley's mom was picking them up, and they were riding up to Camp Splendor for their first Girls Club campout of the school year.

The other girls in the club waved good-bye as they got into separate vehicles. Leigh Ann and Jaiden were riding together, as were Maureen, Ciera, and Janice.

Cassie waved back, excited. "See you when we get there!" she called.

Cassie had been to Camp Splendor before, over the summer. But after an emergency snake bite and week-long stay in the hospital, she'd been forced to use crutches. She hadn't been able to participate like the other girls. This time, she would do it all.

Riley's mom pulled up to the curb, and the girls climbed in. Camp Splendor was an hour away, and Ms. Isabel had loaded the van up with snacks.

"Do you have my things?" Cassie asked, getting comfortable in the back. For once, Riley joined her, not sitting up front with her mom.

"Yes," Ms. Isabel answered. "I picked them up from your house this morning. Are you girls ready?"

"Yes!" Riley and Cassie squealed at the same time. They looked at each other and laughed, and Cassie couldn't remember why she and Riley sometimes didn't get along. Lately their friendship seemed rather tumultuous, and Cassie hoped this was a sign that things were looking up.

Instead of staying at the campsites with the platform tents, the ones Cassie had stayed in over the summer, Ms. Isabel drove them all the way through Camp Splendor to a large grassy meadow. Maureen, Ciera, and Janice had already arrived. Leigh Ann and Jaiden had probably stopped at each other's houses to get their overnight gear.

Maureen's mom, Margaret, beckoned to them as they got out of the car.

"Pick a site for your tents, girls," she said cheerfully. "I'll set up the fire pit." Margaret Hemming was the Girls Club leader, and usually very kind and friendly. Cassie liked her a lot more than she liked Trisha, the other leader.

"Bye, girls," Ms. Isabel said. She dropped Riley's sleeping bag and the tent on the ground before giving Riley a hug and a kiss on the forehead. "Have a nice time!"

"Bye!" both girls chorused, and then Ms. Isabel got in the van and drove away.

Riley found a smooth section of flattened grass, away from the road but not too far from where Mrs. Hemming was setting up the fire pit. "How about right here?"

"Looks good to me." Cassie helped her pull the tent poles from the bag.

"Let's put the poles together first," Riley said.

Cassie didn't really know much about putting a tent together. "Sure."

They took their time sorting the poles, and then Cassie picked up the limp tent canvas. "How do we put this up?"

"We have to find one of the loops and string the poles through it."

Cassie watched Riley find a series of loops, then select a pole and start pushing it through. It got stuck halfway, and Riley grunted, trying to shove it in. She caught Cassie's eye and snapped, "Well, don't just stand there. Start stringing it in on your side!"

Cassie knelt down and pulled at the tent, searching for another set of loops. Finding one, she picked up one of the longer poles. She compared it to a shorter pole, wondering how she'd know which one went where. With a shrug, she decided on the longer one.

"There," Riley said, succeeding in getting her pole all the way through. She brushed her hands together and stepped back, satisfaction on her face.

Cassie pushed on her pole. It slithered up the tent through the loops, but came to a halt about halfway in. "I can't get it anymore."

"Just keep trying." Riley picked up another pole. "It took awhile for me, too."

Cassie shoved again, but the tent resisted, pushing back at her. "I'm afraid I'm going to rip it."

"You won't."

Trisha's four-door sedan pulled into the meadow with a loud honk, and Jaiden and Leigh Ann tumbled out, followed by Trisha's four-year-old son, Ryan.

"Hey!" Maureen waved as the girls stepped out of the car. Jaiden and Leigh Ann joined her, and the three of them giggled and held hands and jumped around like they hadn't seen each other in years.

Riley dropped her pole and ran over to them. "You made it!"

They welcomed her into their circle, and Cassie set her jaw in annoyance. Now it was only her trying to put this tent up.

"You're doing that all wrong."

Cassie's heart sank, and she turned her body as Trisha approached, a large box of supplies in her arms.

"Look at this one." She nudged the pole Riley had shoved through the tent. "It obviously doesn't go here. Look how it's making the tent bow over. You need to take it out and start again. Hold your tent up and match it up to the poles, don't just guess at it."

She walked away, and Cassie felt as big as one of the blades of grass under her feet. How was she supposed to know? She was only doing what she'd been told. She pulled Riley's pole out and tried to straighten the tent enough to know what went where.

"You still don't have the tent up?"

This time it was Riley's voice, and Cassie made no attempt to hide her irritation as she spun toward her. "You're supposed to be helping me!"

Riley shrugged nonchalantly. "Actually, Janice and Ciera and Maureen offered to let me stay in their tent. They have a huge one." She pointed, and Cassie followed her finger. Sure enough, not only did they have a tent the size of a small living room, but they already had it up. "So this one's yours now."

Riley turned and walked away, and Cassie's mouth dropped open. After all that talk, everything about how this was their campout and their time and their tent, and Riley just ditched her? Cassie closed her mouth and shook her head, determined not to let Riley get to her. But still, her throat closed up, a dull ache making it hard to swallow. She lifted her chin and concentrated on her tent.

She managed to get the longest pole in through the middle set of loops, and the tent began to look more—tent-like. Her chest hurt, and sweat beaded on her brow, but she knew she could do this.

Soft footsteps approached on the grass, and she cocked her head to see Janice. She and Janice had never had a class together, but Janice had been really nice to her last year when Cassie thought about doing Odyssey of the Mind.

"Hey," Janice said. She wore a flashlight on a lanyard around her neck, and her gray t-shirt proclaimed her a spoiled rotten princess. "Need help with your tent?"

"I'm getting it," Cassie said. She turned away from Janice, a bit angered Janice, Ciera, and Maureen had invited Riley to stay in their tent. Hadn't they thought about how Cassie might feel about that?

"Yeah, but it's hard by yourself. We had four people helping us, and one was an adult." Janice took hold of the edge of the fabric and held it up, giving it more shape. "Now you can see where to put the poles."

Cassie picked up the other long pole and threaded it on. It was much easier with another person. "Thanks," she said, a bit sheepishly.

Janice helped her get the rest of the tent put together, her short brown hair swaying around her chin as she bent over. "Who's staying in your tent with you?"

"No one," Cassie said. "It's all mine."

Janice frowned. "Is that a good thing? Did you want to be by yourself?"

She wanted to say yes, to act like Riley had done her a

favor in walking away. But the truth was— "No. But Riley decided not to stay in my tent. Didn't you know?"

"Oh, well, I didn't know the details," Janice said uncertainly. "She just asked if there was room in our tent. And yeah, of course there is."

Some of the tension left Cassie's shoulders. "You didn't invite her to your tent?"

"No. Why would we?"

Then it was only Riley. At least she knew who to target her anger at. "I don't know."

"Well." Janice hesitated. "Do you want me to stay here with you?"

Cassie shrugged. She wasn't asking for any favors. "If you want."

"Sure. It'll be fun. I'll get my stuff." Janice walked away, and Cassie breathed a sigh of relief. Sleeping alone on the Girls Club campout made her feel like a friendless, rejected person. She was really glad Janice offered.

CHAPTER NINETEEN

Water Front

Margaret and Trisha, the two leaders, walked around the makeshift campsite to see how the tents were set up. Janice and Cassie stood proudly outside their tent, pleased with the results. Ryan, Trisha's little boy, circled it as if inspecting it.

"This tent was hard to put up, wasn't it?" Margaret asked, shaking her head. "It has such a funny shape to it."

"Yeah," Cassie said. "But we got it."

"Together." Janice held out her hand for a high-five, and Cassie slapped it.

"You forgot the tarp," Trisha said.

"Tarp?" Cassie echoed. What the heck was that?

"Yes. You should always use a tarp."

Janice looked at Cassie, who shrugged.

"Check the car," Trisha said. "Come on, Ryan!"

He scampered after his mother, and the two of them moved on.

"We have a tarp," Margaret said. "You can use it." Her brow furrowed. "Where's Riley? I thought the two of you were sharing a tent."

"She changed her mind," Cassie said, and left it at that. She actually didn't mind now. Janice was funny and nice.

"Oh." Margaret hesitated. "Okay, then. I'll get the tarp for you."

She walked away, and Cassie looked at Janice. "Do we really need the tarp?"

Janice shrugged. "I don't really know why we would. We didn't put one under our tent." She pointed at the big house-tent on the other side of the meadow.

"Then let's not worry about it."

~

Cassie spent the rest of the evening with Janice, except when Janice sat by Ciera and Maureen at dinner. Then Cassie sat with Leigh Ann and Jaiden. No way was she sitting by Riley, as if she had no one else to hang out with.

The foil dinners burned a little bit in the fire, and no amount of salt or ketchup made the charcoal taste better, but everyone just laughed about it and ate it anyway.

Trisha took a sleepy Ryan to her tent and laid him down. She returned with a bag of jumbo-sized marshmallows. "Who wants to roast marshmallows?"

"Me!" they cried in a slightly unharmonious chorus.

"Find green sticks so they won't burn."

When they sat back down with their sticks and starting threading the marshmallows, Margaret asked, "Riley and Cassie, will you lead us in some songs?"

Riley and Cassie knew all the songs because they'd gone to sleep away camp at Camp Splendor over the summer. The two girls looked at each other, and Riley said, "No one wants to sing songs."

"Riley," Margaret said, a warning note in her voice.

Riley heaved a sigh, the campfire clearly showing the

annoyance on her face. "I don't remember the words."

"I can do it," Cassie said. "I haven't forgotten the songs."

"Thank you, Cassie," Margaret said.

Cassie cleared her throat and started to lead the girls in a song they all knew, one they'd learned during their after-school activities.

"That's not how it goes," Riley interrupted in the middle of the second verse.

Cassie swiveled her head to look at Riley, sitting on a log on the other side of Maureen. "Yes, it is."

"No, it's not."

"Yes, it is," Leigh Ann said, taking Cassie's side. "You forgot the words, remember?"

Riley fell silent, and Cassie bit back a smile. She began the second verse again, and everyone except Riley joined in.

After several songs, Margaret stood up. "Girls, it's bedtime. Trisha and I will be in our tent over there." She pointed into the darkness. "Remember to use the buddy system. Don't go anywhere by yourselves. Use your flashlights."

"Can we stay up and tell ghost stories?" Ciera asked.

"That might not be appropriate for sleeping out in the woods," Trisha said. "Someone will get scared."

"Mom, that's what people do on campouts!" Jaiden exclaimed.

"Please?" Maureen echoed. "Just a few?"

Trisha threw her arms up. "Fine. But if you get scared, don't blame me." She followed after Margaret.

"Oo, ghost stories!" squealed Maureen. "Who has one?"

"I do, I do," Janice said. She turned on her flashlight and shone it on her face. The girls crowded around her, and she proceeded to tell a story about a man with a golden arm who came back from the dead to take other people's arms.

"Freaky!" Ciera said, shuddering.

"I've got one," Cassie said, leaning forward. She loved scary stories, and her mom told the best ones on Halloween. She cleared her throat, lowered her voice, and began her story. "A man worked the graveyard shift in a factory. One day, he came across a body. He called the police, but by the time they got there, the body was gone." She continued, weaving a tale of soul-snatching zombies with white eyes. She finished up with, "The man breathed a huge sigh of relief as the boat pulled away from the mainland, leaving behind the mob of white eyes who had chased him. 'Where to?' the ferry master asked him. And when the man turned around, he saw in the light of the moonlight that the ferry master had white eyes!"

The girls shrieked, leaning away from Cassie and covering their faces. She grinned, pleased at their reactions.

"Girls!" Trisha's voice carried across the empty night. "No more! Everyone go to bed!"

Cassie and Janice exchanged a grin as they gathered up their things and headed to their tents.

"Good night," the girls murmured to each other.

Janice came in last and zipped up the tent while Cassie buried herself deep in her sleeping bag.

"Thanks for not leaving me all alone," Cassie said, rolling up in her bag to keep warm.

"Thanks for letting me join you," Janice replied.

Cassie turned out her flashlight and closed her eyes.

She woke up freezing cold, trembling, a sensation like cold water rushing over her body. She shook in her sleeping bag and finally forced herself to poke her head out. Sunlight streamed into the tent, indicating it was morning. But the brisk air, coupled with the dampness in her bag, raised goosebumps on her arms, and she couldn't stop trembling.

In the other sleeping bag, Janice groaned. "It's so cold."

"Yeah," Cassie agreed. "Freezing."

"Are you wet?"

Cassie frowned. "Yeah," she admitted. "Everything kind of feels wet."

Janice sat up, and water dripped from her short brown hair. "Cassie! We're laying in water!"

"What?" Cassie sat up too, holding her sleeping bag around her.

Janice was right. Two inches of dirty water swirled around the bottom of their tent, circling their bags of clothing and soaking their things.

"No way!" Cassie exclaimed, jumping up. The air hit her wet, bare skin, but she ignored it as she grabbed up her clothes. Quickly she lifted them out of the water.

The shirt was dry, but the pants were soaked. Soaked!

"No," Janice moaned, assessing her own clothing.

"What happened?" Cassie exclaimed.

"I don't know. Let's go tell Margaret."

Cassie desperately wanted to put on a warm pair of clothes. She shoved everything back in her bag and followed after Janice.

Stepping outside, they soon saw why the tent was wet. Water dripped from the trees and off the canvas, evidence of a rain the night before. Cassie put her feet in her wet shoes, which squished and leaked water with every step. The wet ground under the grass sucked at her feet, trying to hold her shoes in the mud. She and Janice exchanged a grim look.

Margaret and Trisha were already up, getting the campfire going for breakfast. Trying to, anyway. Cassie saw the way the smoke wormed away from the wood, but no flames leapt in the fire pit.

"Ms. Margaret," Janice said, "I guess it rained last night." She held out her duffel bag. "All of our things got wet. The tent is soaked."

"Oh, no," Margaret said. She took the bag and riffled through it.

"How did everything get wet?" Trisha asked. "Didn't you use the tarp?"

Cassie pressed her lips together.

"Well, no," Janice said. "We didn't want to lift the tent and put one under it."

"I don't see how that would have kept us dry, anyway," Cassie said.

Trisha's lip twisted as if it took all her power not to sneer at them. "The tarp goes over the tent."

Dummy.

The unspoken word hung in the air, but Trisha wasn't done talking. "It's supposed to block the rain. For these exact situations."

"Oh," Janice said in a small voice.

Cassie looked around at the other tents and realized now that all of them had some sort of covering over the top. A matching canopy, an extra canvas, a tarp. . . . "We didn't know," she said.

"Yes, well, I told you."

But you didn't tell us what to do with it! Cassie kept her scream of frustration to herself. She knew it would do no good.

"Let's hang your clothes up to dry, girls," Margaret said. "I have some extra sweatshirts you can wear."

Trisha went to her sedan and returned with a mixing bowl and a box of biscuit mix. "Hurry back. It's good you two are up. You have breakfast duty. These will go in the dutch oven as soon as the fire is ready."

Cassie and Janice draped their wet items over a few tree branches. Then Cassie put on Margaret's sweatshirt and took the bowl from Trisha without a word. She motioned her head at Janice, and they trooped over to the picnic table to mix up the food.

By ten a.m., the sun decided to make an appearance. It came out slowly, a mild warmth heating the air, and Cassie finally stopped shivering inside Margaret's large sweatshirt. Then it gained strength, drying up the droplets of water and sucking the moisture out of their damp clothes. Cassie shrugged out of her sweatshirt and checked on her clothes drying on the picnic table bench.

"Time for some exercise!" Trisha said. "We're going to hike to the rec center. Line up with your buddies!"

Cassie hesitated as her friends grabbed hands and lined up two-by-two. Riley was her normal go-to, but so were tentmates. Usually, for Cassie, that was the same person. Today, she hadn't spoken to Riley at all, and last night had been prickly at best.

As if sensing her dilemma, Margaret came over and hooked an arm through hers. "I'll be your buddy. Since we have an odd number of girls, someone has to be with a leader. You don't mind, do you?"

"No, that's fine," Cassie said, shaking off any disappointment she might feel.

They found a well-worn path through the woods, and

Cassie found herself enjoying the walk. Over the summer at camp, she'd been on crutches and hadn't been able to hike through the forest. The camp nurse had picked her up at the campsite in a car and taken her to the mess hall for meals or the pool for swimming time.

They came out of the woods next to some tennis courts.

"This looks like fun," Ciera said. "Where do we get rackets?"

"Try that shed over there." Janice pointed.

Ciera and Maureen ran over to the shed and tried to open it. Ciera turned to face everyone.

"It's locked!" she shouted.

"So how are we supposed to play tennis?" Jaiden asked.

There was no answer to her question. Riley kicked at the ground under her feet and Cassie fidgeted.

"What do we do here if we can't play?" Janice asked, voicing the question everyone was thinking.

"I'm sure there's something fun to do," Margaret said.

They stood in silence, waiting for something to appear. The sun had grown quite hot, and it beat down on the girls now. Cassie shielded her eyes and wished she'd brought along a bottle of water, at least.

"I've got it!" Maureen said, lifting her face. "Mom, we have all those empty water balloons in the back of the car. Let's fill them up!"

"Oo!" Ciera said. "There's a water spigot right here! We can fill them up!"

"Great idea!" Leigh Ann said.

"Okay," Margaret said. "Maureen, take a buddy and run back to the van." She held out the keys to Maureen.

Maureen took them. Her eyes scanned over the group of girls. "Riley," she said.

Cassie exhaled as Maureen and Riley sprinted away.

"We can play Red Rover while we wait," Trisha suggested. "Instead of playing two teams, we'll have everyone line up as one team and one person can run into the line."

Sounded like a pretty lame version of Red Rover. But what else could they do besides stand around? Cassie joined her friends as they started a half-hearted game.

Just when Cassie started to worry something had happened to Riley and they'd be stuck playing Red Rover forever, the two girls returned, flushed and out of breath. Riley carried under her arm a plastic bag full of empty water balloons.

They immediately abandoned their game of Red Rover and crowded around Riley. At first Riley tried to fill the balloons by herself, but she took too long, so soon she was handing filled balloons to the girls, who tied them off. They made a pile on the black top, careful not to step on them. Trisha had to hold Ryan back, who whined and pulled on her arm, desperate to get to the balloons.

"How many do we need?" Leigh Ann asked.

Riley shrugged. "Probably just fifty."

Cassie raised an eyebrow. "Have you ever done this before?" With four younger siblings, she knew how fast water balloons would go. "We should fill them all up."

Ciera groaned. "No way! This is taking forever. We'll be here all day!"

"I think we're good." Riley gestured at the pile at their feet.

"Now can I? Now can I?" Ryan begged.

"Ryan gets to throw the first balloon," Trisha said. "Ryan, just one."

She released him, and he raced forward. Quick as he could, Ryan scooped up an armful of balloons.

"Just one!" Trisha shouted.

The warning came too late. Ryan took one step and lost his grip on the balloons. His arms opened, and half a dozen balloons crashed to the blacktop, exploding on impact. Ryan looked down at them and burst into tears.

Leigh Ann dashed around him and grabbed a balloon. "Incoming!" she shouted, tossing it at Maureen.

CHAPTER TWENTY

Balloonist

"Ah!" Maureen shrieked and ducked, then darted forward to grab her own. Instantly the girls converged on the balloons, moving around a hysterical Ryan as they bashed them against each other.

"Girls!" Trisha shouted. "Girls!"

No one reacted to her. Five minutes later it was all over. Every balloon was spent. They stood or crouched in a semi-circle, half-laughing, half-gasping, all dripping with water.

Trisha stepped into the midst of them, her face contorted and red. "How many times did I yell at you girls to stop? How could you do that? Frighten a little boy to death, throwing balloons around him?"

Cassie glanced at Ryan. He still stood on the blacktop, whimpering now instead of bawling, a mess of broken balloons at his feet.

"What were we supposed to do?" Leigh Ann asked. Cassie shuddered at her brazenness. She'd never speak that way to Trisha.

"Wait till he moved!" Trisha glowered.

"Mom," Jaiden said, "he took six balloons and busted them. We had to hurry and grab some before he broke them all."

Trisha's nostrils flared. She took Ryan by the hand and yanked him to her side. "He's your little brother, Jaiden. I expect you to at least watch out for him."

Jaiden rolled her eyes and turned away. Trisha jerked Ryan off the blacktop, pulling him along behind her down the trail.

"Why did he have to come along anyway?" Ciera grumbled.

"Yeah, isn't this supposed to be our campout?" Maureen said.

"Let's pick up the trash pieces," Margaret said in her normal, pleasant tone. "Then we'll head back to camp. Hopefully by then everyone will have cooled off."

Cassie knelt with her friends and picked up the pieces, but the cheerful mood was gone. Once again, Trisha had produced a storm cloud.

Trisha and Ryan didn't come out of their tent for the sandwiches the girls prepared for lunch. Margaret checked on her.

"They're taking a nap," she said when she returned.

"They need it," Leigh Ann muttered. Jaiden scowled at her but didn't say anything else.

Cassie checked on the tent she and Janice shared. The inside had dried out significantly. As had their sleeping bags, hanging over a branch in the sunshine.

"We should be dry tonight," Janice joked.

"As long as we don't forget the tarp."

They exchanged a smile, and Cassie was glad neither of them took the situation too seriously.

Someone let out a cry behind them, and both girls turned around. Maureen crouched on the ground next to her tent, holding her head. She shrieked and lowered her face to the grass.

"Oh, no!" Janice took off running toward her. Ciera and Riley already knelt beside her, and Margaret was fast approaching. Cassie followed slower, not wanting to get in the way.

"What happened?" Margaret asked.

Maureen was too busy sobbing to respond.

"I think she hit her head on this spike," Ciera said, bending to touch the tip of a tent stake with her finger. "She said she was going to put her shoes outside and lay down for a bit."

Janice gasped and pressed her hands over her mouth.

"Maureen, I need to see," Margaret said.

"Girls, get out of the way." Trisha's voice broke through the gathering just as she did, striding inside the circle and shooing everyone else back. "How can we help Maureen if you're all blocking the light?"

Cassie took a step back, as did the others, and the circle grew slightly bigger. No one dispersed, however.

"Move your hand," Trisha ordered.

Maureen whimpered.

"I'm going to move your hand now," Margaret murmured, slowly prying Maureen's hand from her face.

Cassie stood on tiptoes, holding her breath. Would there be a bloody gash? Would they have to rush Maureen to the hospital?

Maureen's hand fell away, revealing a large, pink bump swelling out of the side of her head.

"Oh," Cassie said, eyes widening.

"Is it bad?" Maureen asked Margaret, tears brimming in her eyes.

"No, honey, you're all right," Margaret said, squeezing her shoulders.

"You're not even bleeding," Trisha huffed, moving away. The seas parted to let her walk away.

"You got lucky," Margaret said. "I have some ice in the cooler. We're going to put it on there, okay?"

"Okay."

"Show's over, girls!" Trisha yelled as she headed back to her tent. "It's quiet time!"

Cassie lingered a moment, waiting for Janice. But Janice crouched next to Maureen, rubbing her back while Margaret got her ice. For a moment Cassie pictured herself in Maureen's shoes, injured, upset, hurt. Would Riley stand behind her and rub her back, hold her hand while she cried?

No. She already knew she wouldn't. When Cassie was on crutches from a snake bite, Riley was one of the first people to ditch her because she couldn't keep up with the other activities.

Cassie stopped by the table where her things were nearly dry and pulled out a book. At least it hadn't been ruined in the water. She grabbed her sleeping bag and lay down by herself in the tent, feeling the warm sunshine beat down on her, her slightly damp sleeping bag beneath her. She read a few pages, then closed her eyes and went to sleep.

She woke up after what felt like a very short time later to the sound of water hitting the side of the tent. She opened her eyes and saw Janice sitting in the tent next to her, writing in a notebook.

"Do you hear that?" Cassie asked.

"Yes."

Both girls shot up and scurried for the tent opening. Cassie poked her head outside.

"Ryan!" she exclaimed.

Janice peeped over Cassie's shoulder.

The little boy jumped from where he stood outside the tent, his pants down around his ankles as he peed—endlessly—on the girls' tent.

"You stop that right now!" Janice exclaimed.

He scowled at her. "I'm just doin' my business."

"Not on our tent, you're not!" Cassie said.

"I just did." He started to pull his pants up.

"Hold on," Janice said, climbing out of the tent. She put her hands on her hips and stared down at him. "You can't treat us with that kind of disrespect. You need to apologize, and then I'm going to march you right up to your mom and tell her what you did."

He looked up at Janice, his big blue eyes wide and his little mouth pressed together. And then he opened it and let out a string of some of the worst cuss words Cassie knew.

Janice's eyes narrowed. Her own lips pressed together. Then she marched forward and grabbed his shoulder. "You're coming with me," she said.

Cassie put her hand to her mouth, amused in spite of herself. Looked like the little troublemaker had met his match.

She watched from the safety of the tent, feeling like a coward as Janice marched Ryan right up to Trisha. She handed him over and explained what had happened. Her hands gesticulated with emphasis, but Trisha didn't move. When Janice finished, Trisha turned to Ryan and asked him a few questions. He shrugged, and Trisha sent him off, then straightened and said a few more things to Janice.

Janice crossed her arms over her chest and marched back to the tent, but Cassie could see the fire hadn't left her eyes.

"What happened?" she asked, ducking inside as Janice climbed back in.

"She didn't care," Janice said, practically breathing fire. "She said when someone has to go, they have to go. She lets him get away with everything!"

Cassie nodded, in complete agreement, but too afraid to speak out loud against Trisha. She remembered all too well the confrontation they'd had last year. "I'm sorry."

"I don't even know why she's our leader. She's always mad at us."

Cassie smiled and nodded. Then she pressed a finger to her lips and whispered, "Don't let Jaiden hear you. She'll tell on you."

Janice snorted and rolled her eyes. "She needs to get over herself. She and her mom are not the queens of the world."

Cassie reached over and hugged Janice, never feeling so close to her as she did in that moment. "I couldn't agree more."

CHAPTER TWENTY-ONE

Fire Fire Fire

Margaret and Trisha called the girls together again before dinner.

"We're going to show you the best way to make a fire," Trisha said. "This is one of your requirements, so you'll be able to check off in your book that you accomplished this." She knelt down in the dirt, beckoning for the girls to do so also. "This little pile of twigs is my kindling. You all need your own pile. Go gather about two handfuls."

Cassie wandered off with her friends. She knelt in the grass and foraged for small branches and tiny twigs. When she had a good amount, she brought it back to her leaders.

"Cassie, you set up over here," Trisha said, directing Cassie to a small section of dirt in the grass. "Now, before you light a fire, you need to make sure you have your water bucket nearby. There are buckets behind my car. Go fill one up and bring it here."

Cassie obeyed, using the spigot by the outhouses to fill the bucket. She grunted as she hefted it, always surprised at the weight of water.

Trisha had moved on to direct another girl. Cassie set

her bucket down and waited.

"You got your kindling?" This time it was Margaret asking.

"Yep," Cassie said. "And my water bucket."

"Perfect. Now what you need are bigger branches, again, about two handfuls."

This time Cassie had to go deeper into the treeline, but it only took about three minutes to gather up the required wood.

Margaret had waited for her, and she knelt next to Cassie in the dirt. "We're going to set up an A-frame for the fire. Then when you light the kindling on the bottom, it will work its way up to the top. The goal is to be able to start your fire with just one match, and this frame is the best for that."

Together they arranged the kindling and branches, and then Margaret said, "Now we need the bigger logs. Bring three pieces from the woodpile."

Ciera was at the woodpile too, picking up her logs. "These are heavy," she said.

"It's the spiders that scare me," Leigh Ann said, grabbing one also.

Spiders! Cassie hadn't even considered them. She examined the woodpile, poking at the disintegrating bark.

"Just pick one and go," Leigh Ann said, laughing at her.

"Okay," Cassie said, exhaling. She wrapped her hands around one and hobbled back to her fire pit. Two more trips, and she had all three pieces of wood.

Margaret was helping another girl. Cassie sat down and waited. Unfortunately, it was Trisha who came back.

"Good, you've got all your wood," she said. "Now take those three logs and set them up like a t-pee. Yep, that's right, so they lean on each other at the top."

Cassie touched the wood as little as possible, though she didn't want to look like a baby in front of Trisha.

"Great. Now wait for us to show you how to light it."

Cassie watched as Trisha and Margaret helped the other girls finish setting up their a-frames. Then they walked back to the fire pit.

"All right!" Trisha called, getting everyone's attention. "Now you all have your little fire frames. I'm going to show you how to light it, but when you light yours, you're only going to let the fire get started before you practice putting it out with your bucket of water. Only ours will we use as a cook fire." She pulled out the matches and crouched by her own A-frame. "Strike a match. Hold the match to your kindling. Wait for it to catch, then let the match go." Trisha went through the actions as she spoke. The tiny flame from the match smoked, grew larger, and went out. Trisha dropped the spent matchstick in her kindling pile. "It might take more than one match," she said.

Cassie shifted her weight from one foot to the other, the silence and expectation growing more awkward by the time Trisha moved on to her eighth match.

"It must be because the wood is wet," Trisha said, striking her match again. "Usually it doesn't take this long."

"That must be it," Margaret said.

The flame of the newest match grew in height, then tapered down and went out. Trisha uttered a low growl. "Get me a fire starter," she snapped, holding a hand out behind her.

Margaret jumped, then scampered back to the camping

supplies at the picnic table. She returned with what looked like a pine cone doused in candle wax in her hand.

"Sometimes," Trisha said, "you have to use a little help. That's why we have fire starters."

She lit the pine cone on fire. Cassie watched as the tiny pieces of wood finally caught, and then the branches, yielding to the flickering flame as it licked the underside of the logs.

"Finally," Leigh Ann muttered, just loud enough that those around her could hear.

"Well, now it's your turn." Trisha stepped back, brushing the palms of her hands on her jeans. "See if you can light your fire with just one match."

Just one match. Cassie took the tiny matchbook and knelt beside her A-frame. She checked to make sure the kindling was stacked and touching the smaller branches, which in turn were directly under her three logs. Everything looked ready to go. She tore a match out of the matchbook and uttered a silent prayer. She didn't dare glance around at her peers for fear one of them had already succeeded in starting the fire with only one match.

She lit the match. Here it went. Cassie reached her hand out, holding the tiny match to the underside of the kindling. A piece caught on fire, but the fire consumed the branch, curling it into a black ribbon of charcoal before crumbling to nothing.

The heat of the flame neared her finger, and Cassie dropped the match on the kindling. She held her breath as her last hope of lighting a one-match fire extinguished.

She rocked back on her heels and stole a look at the other girls. She felt some relief that every one of them was still trying to light their fire. Oh, well. Maybe she'd get it with

two matches.

She lit another and tried again. The same thing happened. Frustrated, she lit a third.

"All the wood's still a little damp." Margaret knelt next to Cassie and held out a wax-coated pine cone. "We made fire starters in case something like this happened. Here's one for you."

Cassie looked at it hesitantly. "I really want to make this work without one."

"Sure." Margaret shrugged and put the pine cone in the grass. "Just in case, here's one for you."

Cassie turned back to her pile of wood, determined to light this fire without help. She lit another match, holding it steady under the kindling, willing some part of it to catch on fire.

"Yes!" came an excited squeal from down the line of potential fires.

Cassie sat up as Jaiden jumped to her feet, throwing her fists in the air and doing a little dance. In front of her, her A-frame burned, the growing fire chewing hungrily at her logs.

"Great job, Jaiden!" Trisha said, clapping. "The first one to get a fire built! Not much of a surprise, right?" She beamed at her daughter. "Now, get your water bucket and put it out."

Jaiden hefted her bucket with a grunt, then turned it upside down over her fire. It hissed and smoked, and the bright yellow flame vanished.

"Who's next?" Trisha said, looking around. "Anyone else going to start a fire?"

Cassie heaved a sigh. She picked up the pine cone, examined it, then slipped it under the kindling. One more time, she lit a match and pressed it under the pine cone. Within seconds, the pine cone burst into flames. It burned far longer than the match had, and before it burned out, the kindling had caught. Cassie watched with a mixture of fascination and disappointment as the smaller branches caught fire. A moment later, the first log began to burn. To her left, Ciera cheered as her fire got going, and then Maureen did her own happy dance.

"You got it, Cassie!" Margaret came to stand next to her, a pleased smile on her face.

"Yeah." Next time she'd try and do it with just one match.

~

Janice and Cassie were very meticulous as they pulled the tarp tight across the top of the tent that night. A thunderstorm could come and it wouldn't affect them at all.

Not that one came. The morning dawned bright and sunny, a lingering warmth from the day before coloring the air.

"It didn't even rain," Cassie said to Janice as she rolled up her sleeping bag.

"I know," Janice said with a laugh. "We just had bad luck our first night."

Riley's mom arrived while the girls took down their tents, and soon everyone had their things loaded into the correct vehicle. Cassie hesitated as she watched Riley toss her bags into the back of Mrs. Isabel's van. Cassie turned to Janice, wanting to ask if she could get a ride home with her, but not sure how. It wasn't even Janice's car. And besides, they already had three girls in it.

"Thanks for sharing my tent," she said instead. "I had so much fun with you."

Janice leaned over and hugged her. "I did, too. We should hang out more often."

"I would love that," Cassie said.

Tearing down the campsite was much easier than putting it up. In ten minutes everyone was packed up and ready to go. Cassie said bye to her friends and reluctantly climbed into Mrs. Isabel's van. To her relief, Riley got into the passenger seat up front.

"Why don't you sit in the back with Cassie?" Mrs. Isabel said, putting her keys into the ignition.

"That's all right," Cassie said, pulling out her book and opening it. "I'm fine by myself back here."

Mrs. Isabel didn't say anything more, but somehow Cassie knew from the silence that she wasn't pleased. Cassie pushed it out of her mind. It wasn't her fault Riley ditched her at the campsite and didn't say more than two words to her all weekend. Cassie could hardly wait to see Andrea and plan their own campout.

CHAPTER TWENTY-TWO
With Friends Like This

Cassie stepped off the bus Monday morning, her friend Betsy at her elbow. Betsy was telling her a story about tipping their canoe while fishing over the weekend. Cassie nodded along, half-listening, half-watching for Riley.

She drew up short when she saw Riley get off the bus behind them. Riley shouldered her backpack and glanced around, her short blond hair bobbing at her shoulders.

"Wait," Cassie said, putting a hand out to stop Betsy from going forward.

Betsy followed Cassie's eyes. "Oh. Are you two still fighting? Or should I say, again?"

Cassie furrowed her brow, feeling her lip twist. Again. She and Riley had done nothing but fight since becoming best friends the year before. She missed her best friend in Texas. They hadn't ever fought. Was it too much to expect her best friend to be fun, supportive, kind, and loyal?

"Yeah," Cassie said, answering Betsy's question. "We're still fighting. Again."

Riley stepped into the school, and Cassie and Betsy continued forward, moving down the hallway to the sixth grade classrooms.

"Are you still fighting about the campout?" Betsy asked.

The campout had been a week ago. Cassie shook her head. "No. I got over that. It's something else."

"What this time?" Betsy asked, a note of curious hunger in her voice.

"Probably the note she sent me Friday telling me I'm fat and ugly and she hates me." Cassie kept her voice controlled, but a slight tremor crept in. She swallowed it back. She'd gone home and cried yesterday, cried until her mom demanded she not let Riley rule her life.

"She's not your friend," her mom had said. "No friend would treat you this way."

And she was right, Cassie realized. Riley wasn't her friend.

Betsy's green eyes grew wide. "Wow," she said, "I can't believe she said that."

"Yeah. She did."

The two girls parted in the sixth grade hall, going into their separate classes. Andrea hadn't arrived in the classroom yet when Cassie stepped inside, so she went to her cubby and hung up her backpack. She turned around just as Andrea came in.

"Hey!" the other girl squealed, her reddish-brown hair falling over her shoulders in soft curls. She gave Cassie a hug. "How was your weekend?" Andrea pulled back, pushing her glasses up on her nose.

"So boring," Cassie said. "Sorry my mom wouldn't let me come over." Cassie and Andrea had been trying to plan a campout in one of their backyards for over a week, but so far neither mother had agreed to it.

"That's okay." Andrea took her hand and pulled Cassie

closer. "Did you talk to Riley?" she whispered.

"Not yet," Cassie said. "But I will."

Andrea narrowed her eyes and clenched her jaw. "You have to. Or I will."

A surge of warmth flooded Cassie's chest. This was what she wanted in a friend. Someone loyal, who stood beside her and defended her. Cassie had shown Andrea the note from Riley, and Andrea had been furious enough to want to confront Riley at recess. Cassie had convinced her not to, but only after she promised to talk to her herself.

"Tonight," Cassie said. "I'll call her."

~

Cassie finished up her homework at the kitchen table, completing the math questions with only half her mind on the assignment. The other half was on Riley. They hadn't spoken all day, mostly because Cassie had been very successful at avoiding her.

But she knew Andrea was right. Cassie wasn't the one in the wrong here. She shouldn't be cowering or hiding.

She closed her math book and stared at the wall in front of her, chewing on the end of her pencil.

"Cassie?"

She looked up at her mother peeling potatoes over the trashcan. Cassie had forgotten she wasn't alone. "Yes?"

"Are you still doing homework? I could use some help with these."

"Yeah, I'm done." Cassie joined her mother, taking one of the other potato peelers.

"How was Riley today?" Mrs. Jones asked, her voice a little tight.

"I didn't talk to her."

"Are you going to leave it like that?"

Cassie shrugged. "What am I supposed to say, exactly?"

"That if she's really your friend, she'll stop treating you that way. That you don't need her. That she doesn't deserve to have you as a friend."

Cassie laughed, recognizing the protectiveness of a mother. "I'm not going to say all that."

"Then just say what you need to to make her realize she's crossed a line."

"Yeah," Cassie murmured.

Her mom began chopping the peeled potatoes and tossing them into the pot of boiling water on the stove. "Will you ask Emily to set the table?"

Cassie put down her peeler and headed down the hall to the room she shared with her younger sister. "Mom wants you to set the table," she said to Emily, who lay on her bed reading a book.

"Okay." Emily got up, and they both heard the sound of their father's car pulling into the driveway.

Their youngest sister, Annette, heard it too. She shot out of her room and ran down the hall. "Daddy!" she shouted, waiting in the entryway to pounce on him the moment he came in.

Cassie no longer jumped at her dad when he got home—she was too old for that—but she couldn't help the stirrings of excitement she felt when he got home. Of course, she'd felt a little stiff around him since two weeks ago when he'd discovered she was lying about exercising every morning. Even though she'd confessed and apologized, the guilt simmered in her chest whenever she thought of it.

She and Annette made their way down the hall where Mr. Jones gave them both a hug.

"I'm home," he said, letting them go and walking into

the kitchen.

"Did you bring the cream?" Mrs. Jones asked, backing away when Mr. Jones bent to kiss her. Cassie picked up her peeler and started on the potatoes again while Emily got out the plates and cups.

"Cream?" He reared back. "What cream?"

"The cream for dinner." Mrs. Jones gestured at the potatoes and the pot of water. "I asked you to bring some home. You said you would. I kind of need it for the soup."

"Oh." He shook his head. "I forgot."

Cassie glanced at her mom to see her purse her lips together.

"I'm sorry," Mr. Jones said.

"It's fine." Mrs. Jones put her knife down. "I'll figure something out." She turned around and opened the cupboard, then let it slam shut as she moved onto the refrigerator.

"I said I'm sorry," her dad said.

"And I said it's fine." She yanked out a carton of milk.

"But it's clearly not."

Cassie met Emily's eyes uneasily. They were arguing. It didn't happen often, but when it did, the yelling and shouting left Cassie insecure and uncertain.

"I'll just use milk instead. It will be fine."

"I've had a long day at work, Karen. I come home and don't expect to be given a guilt trip because I didn't get something you need for dinner."

"And yet you said you'd get it, didn't you?" Mrs. Jones put the milk down and faced her husband, one hand leaning on the counter.

"I'll just go get the cream, then. I didn't want to come home anyway!" He stomped out of the kitchen.

"Jim!" Mrs. Jones shouted.

The only response was the slamming of the front door.

Mrs. Jones whipped out her cell phone and typed out a quick text. She stared at it, obviously hoping for an answer. When none came, she tossed it on the counter. Then she leaned forward and pressed her forehead into the palm of her hand.

"Do you still want us to set the table?" Emily asked meekly.

Mrs. Jones looked up, her nose pink. "No. I'll do it. I'll call you girls when it's time for dinner."

Cassie and Emily went back to their room, neither saying a word until Cassie closed the door behind them.

"Was Mom crying?" Emily whispered.

Cassie nodded, feeling both like the wise older sister and the confused daughter. "Daddy hurt her feelings."

"Why did he leave?"

Cassie wasn't exactly sure. "I think Mom upset him. I think he just wanted to come home and relax but instead he got yelled at."

"Mom wasn't yelling."

Cassie shrugged. "Yeah, well . . ."

They fell into silence, and then Emily said, "I hate it when they fight."

"Me too." Cassie bit at the edges of her fingers, a habit she'd picked up years ago when she gave up biting her nails. "I'm sure they're okay, though."

CHAPTER TWENTY-THREE
Love At Home

"No, I didn't call her," Cassie said to Andrea during P.E. Their teacher had gotten it into her head that running two laps around the field was a good way to start every class. Cassie hated running. The only thing that made this even slightly tolerable was that she and Andrea could talk the entire time. Especially since both girls usually started walking as soon as Mrs. Walters wasn't watching.

"But you promised you would!" Andrea huffed.

"I know." Cassie cast a quick look over her shoulder. "She's gone inside." Mrs. Walters was nowhere in sight.

Both girls slowed down, letting their classmates run past them as they walked along the fence.

"My parents got in a big fight last night," Cassie said. "My dad walked out. My mom sent me and Emily to our room. There wasn't a chance to get to the phone."

"Oh, I'm so sorry! Is everything okay?"

"Yeah, I think so. My dad came home, anyway. It was kind of stupid." By the time her dad came home with the cream, her mom had made the soup with milk and everyone had eaten. Which didn't seem to make Mr. Jones

168

too happy, either. "But I'll talk to Riley today. I'll see her at Girls Club."

"Right." Andrea nodded.

They reached the edge of the field now and joined everyone else as if they'd run two laps instead of walked one.

"Call me after," Andrea said. "I want to know how it goes."

~

Ms. Timber watched as everyone got their snacks and books out for reading time. Cassie set out her bag of cheese squares and slipped her finger between the book pages.

"Before you get started," she said, just as Cassie opened her book, "I want to tell you guys about the science projects we'll be doing for the next two weeks." She beamed at the class, probably expecting excitement or anticipation. Cassie only felt her heart rate quicken. She hated projects. They made her nervous, and no matter how hard she tried to get it perfect, it never was.

When nobody said anything, Ms. Timber continued. "We'll be making inventions. Well, not really, but a pretend invention. I'll give you all the rubrics later, but keep that in the back of your mind while you're reading. Maybe something you read will trigger an idea of what you can invent."

Cassie turned to her book, already putting the project from her mind. But to her annoyance, now she couldn't concentrate on the novel. She kept trying to think of something she could invent, something that didn't already exist. Every idea that came to her was so ridiculous that she rejected it outright. Why couldn't she think of something cool? She just wasn't creative like that.

Her hand reached inside her plastic baggie, searching for one more cheese square. She scowled when she realized she'd consumed all of her snack. What she needed was a little box in her desk that would make food at will, whatever she wanted. Like the food replicators on Star Trek.

Her hand froze inside her baggie, her eyes widening. That was it! She could invent a replicator!

~

Walking down the hall to Girls Club after school felt long and awkward without Riley. Cassie knew she could've tried to walk with one of the other girls from the group, but instead she hung around the classroom until she felt certain Riley had left. Perhaps that moment of walking down the hall together would have been the perfect time to talk, but Cassie lost her nerve. Because now she knew what she wanted to say, and she didn't want to have to face Riley at Girls club for a whole hour after that.

Trisha was already explaining the activity to the girls when Cassie arrived at the cafeteria. She slipped into a spot next to Maureen. She wanted to know what she'd missed but didn't dare ask while Trisha was talking.

"So what are we doing?" she asked Maureen as soon as Trisha sat down.

"We're identifying plants today." Maureen opened her club book to a page with several plants on it. "We get to go outside and try and find the real thing."

"Oh." Cassie frowned. "I forgot my book. Can I share with you?"

"Sure."

They huddled over Maureen's book, memorizing the characteristics of each plant.

"Look." Cassie pointed to the highlighted map next to one of the plants. "This one grows in the wild in Arkansas."

"Perfect!" Maureen stood up, tossing her shoulder-length brown hair behind her. "Let's see if it grows in the field outside."

The late afternoon sun beat down on them, warm enough that Cassie took her sweater off and tied it around her waist. "What are you doing this weekend?" she asked as they sifted through plants.

Maureen shrugged. "It's my dad's turn to have us, so my sister and I will go to his house for the weekend."

She'd forgotten Maureen's parents were divorced. That had to be awful. "I'm sorry."

"I'm used to it. They've been divorced for three years now."

Cassie hesitated, but a burning question had formed in her mind, and she doubted she'd be able forget it now. "Did you know your parents were going to get divorced?"

"No. I mean, I guess the signs were there. They said they weren't happy, that they didn't love each other anymore, blah blah blah. But I thought we were fine. I liked my family the way it was." For a moment, Maureen paused in her foraging and looked toward the sky, a forlorn look in her eyes. "No one does what the kids want, though."

"Did they fight?"

"Oh, all the time."

"So . . . is it better now?"

Maureen gave her a sour smile. "It's supposed to be, right? That was what they said. They still fight, but I guess it's not as often. But mostly they just seem sad. And lonely. Or maybe that's just me."

A knot formed in Cassie's stomach, and she had a hard time swallowing. "I'm afraid my parents are going to get divorced."

Maureen turned and faced her. "Why do you say that?"

"They fight," Cassie whispered. "Sometimes yelling at each other. I think it's getting worse."

Maureen nodded, her expression somber and wise. "They don't like each other anymore."

"No," Cassie protested. "They still do. They're just disagreeing. A lot."

"They'll get divorced one day. That's how it starts."

Cassie's throat clenched. It was true, Maureen had experience. She'd been through this. But all people were different. It didn't mean her parents would get divorced, too.

She hoped.

The other girls came out of the cafeteria in groups of two, also identifying plants. Cassie watched for Riley and felt her shoulders tense when Riley and Ciera walked out together.

"I have to go talk to Riley for a second," she said to Maureen.

Maureen glanced toward Riley and looked at Cassie. "Uh-oh. Everything okay?"

Cassie wanted to tell Maureen, but she knew she shouldn't blab. She needed to talk to Riley first. "Yeah." Breaking away from Maureen, she approached Riley and Ciera. She tapped Riley on the shoulder.

Riley turned around, one eyebrow lifting when she saw Cassie. "Oh. It's you."

Cassie narrowed her eyes, her confidence growing in the face of Riley's attitude. "I need to talk to you for a minute."

She looked at Ciera. "That okay?"

Ciera only nodded, her blue eyes wide.

Riley sniffed. "I don't feel like talking."

Cassie crossed her arms over her chest. "Fine. I'll say it in front of Ciera. You're a lousy best friend. In fact, you're a lousy friend. I'm tired of you ignoring me when other people are around and calling me names. You're not my friend anymore. I want my best friend necklace back." Cassie lifted her chin and held her hand out, palm up, extremely proud of herself for delivering all those lines without breaking down.

Ciera's eyes bugged out of her head, and Riley's mouth dropped open. When she said nothing, Cassie wiggled her fingers.

"The necklace," she prompted.

Riley closed her mouth. "I don't have it on me," she said. "I don't wear it anymore. You're not my best friend, either."

"Great," Cassie said. "Be sure and bring it to me tomorrow."

"Fine. I will."

"Don't forget."

"I won't!"

Cassie marched back to Maureen, who had watched the interchange from a distance.

"You guys fighting?" she asked.

"Not anymore," Cassie said. And she smiled, amazed at how much lighter she felt.

Episode 4: Holding It Together

CHAPTER TWENTY-FOUR
Matchmaker Matchmaker

"What are you working on?" Emily Jones leaned over her sister Cassandra's headboard on the bed, watching with interest as Cassie measured and cut out pieces of cardboard boxes.

"A replicator," Cassie said. Sometimes she did her homework at the kitchen table, but lately the tension had been high between her parents, so she'd opted to do it in her room.

"A replicator?" Emily repeated. She wrinkled her nose. "Like, from Star Trek?"

"Like, exactly," Cassie replied.

"But those aren't real." Emily sounded a cross between condescending and confused.

"Neither is this, dummy," Cassie said. She cut out a fourth side and taped it to the other three, making a three-dimensional rectangle.

"So what does it do?"

"Nothing." Cassie faced her sister and held up the rubrics sheet her sixth-grade teacher, Ms. Timber, had given. "I have to pretend to invent something. It doesn't have to actually work, but I have to pretend like it does, present it to my class, and demonstrate it. It's supposed to be like a commercial."

"How can you demonstrate something that doesn't work?"

Cassie had already thought of this. She had it all worked out in her head. "Okay. See right there? It's a little keyboard." She showed Emily the tiny keyboard with her best handwriting on the letters. "It will go right here, on the base of the replicator." She placed it against a cube she'd already cut out and taped together. "This long thing —" she held up the rectangle she'd just put together, "is the machine. I'll cut out an opening here at the bottom where the food is supposed to appear, but I'll leave the opening attached like a swinging door so you can't see inside."

"But it's not really going to make any food. So how will you demonstrate it?"

Cassie turned back to her replicator, beginning to cut out her swinging door. "Ms. Timber already told us when we're presenting, and I'm on Friday. So Thursday night, I'll buy a hamburger and stick it inside the replicator when I get to school. When it's my turn, I'll type it in, pull it out, and wha-la! I have a hamburger."

"That's cool." Emily watched Cassie a bit longer. "If only it were real."

"Yeah," Cassie agreed. "Chocolate milkshakes whenever we want them."

"Or spaghettios."

"Or ice-cream." Cassie lowered her voice, glancing toward the bedroom door to make sure it was closed. "Do you think our parents are fighting more than usual?"

"I don't know." Emily shrugged. "They're definitely fighting."

"You don't think that they could be . . ." Cassie chewed on the side of her finger. She had to force herself to say the words out loud. "Falling out of love?"

Emily didn't say anything for a moment. "How could they be?" she finally said. "They have us."

"Maybe we're not enough."

"Well . . . what can we do if they are?"

All kinds of romantic notions of candle-lit dinners and roses and holding hands along the beach jogged through Cassie's mind. "Maybe there's a way we can help them."

"How?"

"I don't know yet. I'll think of something."

~

When Cassie got off the bus at school, she spun her body around, searching for Riley Isabel. Sure enough, she saw the other girl—her former best friend—getting off the bus behind hers.

Cassie strode right up to her, waiting until she was closer so she wouldn't have to yell. "Riley."

Riley turned around. Her features pinched together when she saw Cassie.

"Well?" Cassie said. "Did you bring it?"

"Yes," Riley said stiffly. "You thought I'd forget, didn't you?"

"Or keep it," Cassie agreed.

Riley reached into her pocket and pulled out the chain of their best friend necklace. "I don't want it. I wouldn't keep it."

Cassie held out a hand, and Riley dropped the necklace into her palm. A small rock fell into Cassie's heart, a tiny ache at losing her friend. But she brushed it off. Everything she'd said yesterday when she asked for the necklace back was true. "Thanks."

Riley shrugged, then turned around and continued into the school.

Cassie unrolled the necklace and examined the half of heart. *Best.* She already knew she wanted to give it to Andrea Wall. She planned out how she would ask her while they ran, role-playing the conversation in her mind.

"Do you have a best friend, Andrea?" she would ask.

"No," Andrea would say.

Cassie would pull out the necklace, hold it out to Andrea. "Will you be my best friend?"

"Of course," Andrea would say, and they'd hug, and Andrea would put it on, and they'd be best friends.

There was just one thing Cassie needed to do first: switch which piece of the necklace she had. Andrea could have the *Friends* half. Tonight she'd make the switch.

~

"I got an idea," Cassie said to Emily as they walked down the road toward their house after the bus dropped them off.

"Yes?" Emily said.

"We can offer to babysit. Without pay. Every weekend so they can go out on a date."

"Without pay?" Emily widened her eyes and kicked at a rock.

"Yeah. Otherwise they won't go. They're always worrying about money."

"Well, okay. It's for a good cause."

"Yep," Cassie agreed. "Besides, you're only ten. I'll be doing most of the work."

"You're offering to babysit for no reason?" Mrs. Jones said when the girls told her. She sat at the sewing machine in her office, but she kept glancing up at them in her doorway, as if she couldn't quite believe what they were saying.

"Not just this weekend, either," Cassie said, proud of herself for being so philanthropic. "We want you and Daddy to go out on a date every weekend. To have some time for yourselves."

Mrs. Jones tied off the end of a string and gave them another suspicious look. "Or is this about you having time for yourselves?"

Cassie rolled her eyes. "Right. What would we do? Read more books?"

Her mom laughed. "I guess I don't have the rebel-type kids yet."

"Yet?" Emily protested.

"Give it a few years," Mrs. Jones promised. "I'll talk to your dad. If he wants to go out this weekend, I'll take you up on your offer."

~

Cassie put on the side of the necklace that said *Best* on Thursday morning, and then rummaged through her jewelry drawer until she found the other half. She folded it up and stuck it in her jeans pocket, then went in the bathroom and examined her reflection, her large pink glasses, the long, straight dark hair. She smiled at herself, then grabbed her backpack and the completed cardboard replicator.

"Bus, everyone!" she called to her siblings. She held the door open as they all raced out, Scott last, of course.

"Come on, come on, come on!" she said as he tried on

one pair of shoes, then tossed them aside for another.

Finally ready, he ran out the door, and Cassie charged out, closing the door behind her. Her heart pumped harder all the way to the bus stop. Her mom hated it when they missed because it meant she had to get up and drive them into town.

But today they were fine. The bus was just coming up the hill when they arrived.

Cassie couldn't shake the antsy feeling all morning, though. As soon as she got to the classroom, she deposited her food replicator with the other projects on the long table under the chalkboard. She smiled at Andrea but didn't have time to talk to her before the bell rang and she had to sit at her desk.

"Thank you for bringing your projects in on time!" Ms. Timber said. "All of you already earned half your points by having it here this morning. How many you earn on the other half depends on how well your presentation goes."

Cassie clasped her hands together and glanced at her replicator, painted bright colors to hide the duct tape holding it together. There was no way her presentation wouldn't be wonderful.

"We'll start presentations tomorrow with Andrew, Cole, Monica, Nick, and Cassie, in that order."

She nodded, even though no one had addressed her directly. She hated being last, but at least by tomorrow afternoon, it would be all over.

Mrs. Walters came and got the class for P.E., and Cassie's anticipation ratcheted up a notch. She fingered the necklace in her pocket. Now was the time.

Andrea waited for her in the doorway, and then they stepped out onto the field and started their half-hearted jog together.

"How are your parents?" Andrea asked. "Still fighting?"

"I don't know," Cassie said, momentarily distracted. "They're not yelling at each other. But they seem kind of distant. Like they're just not paying attention to the other."

"Sounds awful, Cass. What are you going to do about it?"

"Well, Emily and I offered them a date night every weekend," Cassie said. "So they can go out and be alone, you know?"

"Ahh. That's so nice of you."

"Yeah." They huffed along in silence, and Cassie wondered how to turn the conversation back around where she wanted it. She ran through her rehearsed conversation one more time, then blurted, "Do you have a best friend?"

"Yes," Andrea said.

The answer caught Cassie completely off-guard, and her heart sank. She pictured her classmates in her head, wondering who else Andrea spent lots of time with. "Oh," she said. Then, because curiosity had the best of her, she asked, "Who is it?"

"You," Andrea said, and she gave her the widest smile.

"Oh," Cassie said again. Then she laughed, feeling stupid for planning out her silly little speech. "Well, I had this thing planned where I was going to ask you to be my best friend, but I guess you already are."

"Yep," Andrea said.

"And you're mine, so—here." Cassie pulled the chain necklace from her pocket and handed it to Andrea. "I have the other half."

"I've always wanted one of these!" Andrea exclaimed,

accepting the necklace. She looped it around her neck and admired the broken heart. "Friends."

Cassie pulled out her half and held it out. "Best."

They pressed the two halves together to complete the heart.

CHAPTER TWENTY-FIVE
To Boldly Go

"So your mom says you offered to babysit for us tomorrow night," Mr. Jones said that evening after dinner as he drove Cassie to McDonald's.

"Yeah." She fingered the dollar bills in her hand, anxious to buy her hamburger for tomorrow's presentation.

"Any certain reason why?"

She shrugged, conscious of her dad's eyes on her in her peripheral vision. "Just want to be nice. You guys always do nice things for us. Like drive us around to help us out with our presentations." She hoped she sounded convincing enough.

"Hmm." He pulled into the drive-thru. "Which burger did you want?"

"The cheapest one."

He placed the order, and Cassie handed over the money. She didn't even like McDonald's, but when he handed her the bag with the hot hamburger inside, her stomach rumbled, and she sniffed appreciatively. This would be fun tomorrow.

"Well, it's very nice of you and your sister to volunteer.

Your mom and I will enjoy a night out."

"Good." Cassie put the burger down by her feet. "That's what we want."

~

Cassie greeted her friends quickly Friday morning, evading any long conversations so she could slip into the classroom. She took out her hamburger and glanced around. No one was watching. She covertly put it inside the swinging door of the replicator.

"What's that?" a voice at her elbow said.

Cassie jumped. She turned and came face-to-face with Todd Wilcox, a kid from her class.

"Nothing," she lied, trying to move away from the replicator.

Todd was not deterred. He moved around her and opened the flap.

"Don't!" Cassie cried.

"A hamburger?" He stepped back and cocked his head at her. "You brought a hamburger? Why?"

Her face burned and she took a deep breath, trying to keep calm. "You'll see during my presentation."

"This should be interesting."

The bell rang, and the kids sat down at their desks. Cassie tried to concentrate on her other assignments during the day, but all she could think about was her presentation. Finally, after recess, Ms. Timber cleared her throat.

"The last thing we'll do today our are five presenters. Before we start, on Monday we'll have Andrea, Miles, Jessica, Michael, and Emmett. Now, let's see what our first group has invented. Everyone give a hand for Andrew!"

The class clapped, and Ms. Timber pulled out a tiny

video recorder. Andrew, a tall and lanky boy, walked to the table and pulled off a soda bottle and what looked like a giant syringe. "I've invented a way to refizz your soda." He put the soda bottle on the desk in front of him. "So you have your soda." He uncapped it. "And in a moment of irresponsible forgetfulness," the class giggled, "you forget to put the lid back on. The next day you pour a cup, but your soda went flat." He poured a little of the soda into a Styrofoam cup, took a sip, and made a sad face. "Oh! My soda is so awful!"

Cassie laughed with everyone else. Her shoulders relaxed, and she quit worrying so much about her own presentation.

Andrew proceeded to demonstrate how his "refizzer" worked, and Ms. Timber videotaped him drinking his renewed soda.

"Excellent job!" she exclaimed. "Cole, you're up!"

Cole stood up and demonstrated his body-heat sensing headphones that would turn off whenever they were pulled away from the head. He then launched into a ten-minute scientific explanation of how this was possible. Cassie glanced at the clock on the wall, starting to get nervous again. It had to be almost her turn. School would be out soon.

"Is this an infomercial or what?" Todd muttered, and the kids chuckled. Ms. Timber sent them a dirty look.

Cole finished and returned his headset to the project table.

"All right, Monica," Ms. Timber said. "Go as quickly as you can, okay? We only have ten more minutes before the bell rings."

"Sure," Monica said. She picked up two plastic rulers

that had been rubberbanded together. "This is my transparent hole punch. Never punch a hole in the wrong spot again!"

Monica talked quickly, and in a moment Nick was up. His low monotone put most of the class to sleep, but not Cassie. She sat up straighter and clasped her hands together on her desk. She rehearsed in her head her replicator commercial. She'd smile and act engaged and be more interesting than Nick's performance.

The bell rang, and the bus riders shot up from their desks. Ms. Timber pressed a finger to her lips and motioned at Nick to finish up. As soon as he did, she put down her video recorder.

"Okay, bus riders, go! We'll continue on Monday!"

"But." Cassie stood by her desk, her heart pounding in her throat. "I didn't get to go yet."

"Don't worry, Cassie, you can go on Monday."

"But—" she cut herself off. There really wasn't anything that could be done, was there? School was out for the day. If she didn't hurry, she'd miss her bus.

She considered grabbing her hamburger and bringing a new one on Monday, but decided not to. She certainly hadn't planned on spending all her money on hamburgers.

~

"Do you guys want ramen noodles or macaroni and cheese for dinner?" Cassie asked her younger brother and sisters. She'd put off making dinner as long as she could, but now at seven o'clock, everyone was whining at her about being hungry.

"Can't we have pizza?" Scott asked.

"No," Cassie said, losing her patience. "I just told you what we could have." Those were the only two things she knew how to make.

"I want cereal," Scott said.

"Cereal!" Annette cried.

Cassie looked at Emily to back her up. Emily shrugged.

"Cereal's easy," she said. "Then we can let them get back to their movie."

True. "Okay. Sure." Cassie closed the cupboard. "Go ahead and have cereal." It would make this babysitting job super easy, anyway.

Cassie and Emily set out the blankets in the living room, expecting Scott and Annette to fall asleep during the movie. It wasn't even nine o'clock, however, when a car pulled into the driveway.

"Who's here?" Emily asked, sending Cassie a panicked look.

Cassie frowned. They definitely weren't expecting anyone to come over. She stood up and moved to the window, peeking out of the curtain.

"It's Mom and Daddy," she said, but the explanation was needless. Barely had the words left her mouth when the sound of her parents' raised voices came down the sidewalk. The words were muffled, but Mrs. Jones jerked her hand in angry gestures while speaking to their father. He shook his head at her and opened the front door.

"It's always this way, Jim," her mom was saying. "You don't listen to me, there's no compromise, it's—"

"That's not true," he interrupted as they both stepped into the house. "You always manage to turn this around on me, like I'm the bad guy."

"If the shoe fits!"

Abruptly her mom stopped talking, her eyes landing on the four children huddling around the living room. Cassie hadn't moved from her spot next to the window. Emily stood by the couch, an arm around Annette. Scott sat on the couch, his eyes peering over the top at their parents. Mrs. Jones pasted a smile on her face.

"Time for bed, kids!"

They scattered without saying another word. Cassie followed Emily to their room, working hard to swallow the lump in her throat.

She closed the bedroom door behind her and Emily and sat down hard on Emily's bed. "They're not even trying," she hissed.

"What were they fighting about?" Emily whispered.

Cassie shook her head. "Doesn't even matter. They're just fighting. About anything. We set up a time for them to go out and have a nice time, and what do they do? Argue!"

"It's like they don't even like each other," Emily said.

The words stabbed Cassie in the heart. Wasn't that what Maureen had said?

"What else can we do?" Emily asked.

Cassie sat, considering the words. She didn't know. But she was the older sister. "Let's make dinner for them next week. Mom can take a break. Then she won't be so stressed when Daddy comes home and they'll be nice to each other."

"What should we make?"

"I don't know." Cassie shrugged. "Tomorrow, we'll go through Mom's cookbooks and find something."

"Okay," Emily said, her face brightening.

Cassie got off the bed and crawled into her own, pulling the blankets up around her chin and rolling over. Emily turned off the light, and Cassie wished she felt the same relief and hope that showed on her sister's face. Instead, a dismal black pit grew in her stomach and ate away at her insides. Cassie let the tears roll down her cheeks and over her nose in silence.

CHAPTER TWENTY-SIX
Dinner Bell

"How was babysitting?" Andrea asked Monday morning as Cassandra Jones unloaded her backpack in her sixth grade classroom.

Cassie shook her head, willing herself not to cry again. "They came home early because they had a fight."

Lately, her parents had disagreed more than they agreed. In an effort to help them "fall in love again," Cassie and her younger sister Emily volunteered to babysit every weekend. Unfortunately, it hadn't worked.

"Oh no!" Andrea said.

The tears came anyway. Cassie put her face in her hands, unable to look at her best friend another second, and sobbed. Andrea wrapped an arm around her shoulders and pulled her against her.

Other kids came behind the cubby wall. "What's wrong with Cassie?" several of them asked.

Cassie heard their stage whispers but didn't look up.

"She's just sad about her parents," Andrea said, one hand rubbing Cassie's shoulder soothingly. "They're not getting along."

Cassie could tell by the gathering of shoes under her nose that half the class was with them now.

"Are they getting divorced?" someone asked.

Another hand touched her shoulder. "I'm sorry, Cassie." Cassie recognized Maureen's voice, one of her friends from Girls Club. "I knew this would happen."

Cassie pulled away. "I'm going to the bathroom."

"Want me to come?" Andrea asked.

"No. I just want to be alone for a minute." She hurried off, eager to escape the prying questions and curious stares of her classmates. This was none of their business.

She washed her face in the bathroom and patted it dry with the paper towels, but no matter how hard she tried, the puffy redness under her eyes and the pink nose wouldn't go away. She heard the bell ring and gave up. She needed to get back to class.

Her classmates had their journals out and were writing when Cassie walked in. Ms. Timber glanced at her.

"Are you all right, Cassie?"

Cassie forced her lips upward into a smile. "Yeah. I'm fine." She sat down at her desk and pulled out her notebook. She swallowed hard as she started to write about the weekend, her parents, her fears. She didn't want to cry again.

Her classmates seemed extra-sensitive around her all day, though Cassie wished they'd just act normal. "My parents aren't getting divorced!" she wanted to shout at them. Andrea stayed glued to her side, brushing off people's questions and keeping constant contact with Cassie.

There was only half an hour left of school when Ms. Timber said, "Okay, it's time for those presentations.

Tomorrow we'll have Kyle, Todd, Allison, Matthew, and Maureen."

Cassie slapped her forehead. She'd completely forgotten about those! She ran her lines through her head again, hoping she'd remember everything she planned to say. She was supposed to go on Friday, but they'd run out of time, so now her turn would be today.

Ms. Timber set up her video recorder. "First up is Andrea. Everyone clap for Andrea!"

Cassie breathed out a sigh of relief. Looked like Ms. Timber was going to have the Monday presenters go first. Cassie gave Andrea an encouraging smile and settled back to watch her best friend show off her invention. Andrea pulled out a giant dirty clothes hamper and proceeded to explain how it was also a washing machine and a dryer.

"For when you don't have space for it all, you have it all in one space!" She finished with a smile, and everyone clapped for her.

Miles went next, and Cassie scribbled a quick note to Andrea: *"Yours was the best."* She passed it down the desks and watched Andrea read it. Andrea turned around and gave her a thumbs up sign.

Cassie tried to pay attention to the next presenters, but by the time Emmett went, she was a bundle of nerves. She kept replaying her commercial lines in her head, over and over. And then the hamburger. Take a bite. That, at least, would be fun.

The bell rang, and kids shot from their desks to grab their backpacks. Wait. Had Emmett finished?

"Have a good day, I'll see everyone tomorrow!" Ms. Timber called over the sudden increase of noise.

"But I didn't go yet, Ms. Timber!" Cassie shouted.

"What?" Ms. Timber asked.

"My presentation." Cassie pushed away from her desk and went closer to her teacher. "I still haven't gone."

"Oh. No problem. You can go tomorrow."

Cassie nodded and ran to get her backpack.

"What about your hamburger?" Todd asked her as she stuffed her books inside. "Isn't it going to go bad?"

She hadn't even thought of that. She'd purchased the hamburger on Thursday and stuffed it inside her presentation, expecting to present on Friday. "I'm sure it's fine."

~

Cassie heard Mrs. Jones in the basement office, her sewing machine rattling, when the four kids walked in the door after school. Scott and Annette immediately scattered to their rooms, though whether for homework or playtime, Cassie didn't know.

"Come on," she said, taking Emily's arm and pulling her into the dining room. One entire shelf was lined with cookbooks. "I'll do dinner, you do dessert," she said.

"But I don't really know how to cook," Emily said.

"Pick something easy. I'll help you." How hard could it be? Just follow the directions.

A few minutes later, Cassie picked a dish. "There. This will be easy."

Emily leaned over and looked at the picture. "What is it?"

"Toast with mushrooms and eggs. Except, I don't like mushrooms, so I'll just make it with eggs. It has tomato too. See?"

"Okay." Emily nodded and held out her own cookbook. "I found this custard recipe. It's mostly just milk and sugar and eggs. Shouldn't be hard, right?"

"That's perfect." Cassie carried both cookbooks into the kitchen. She checked the kitchen clock. Just after four. "You get started on the custard. Just read what it says, okay? I'll help if you need it." She put her book on the counter. "I'll tell Mom we're making dinner."

Cassie took the stairs two at a time and skidded to a stop outside her mom's office door. "Hey, Mom," she said, slightly out of breath.

"Slow down, Cassie. You're always running through the house."

"I just wanted to tell you you can keep working on that. Emily and I are making dinner tonight."

Her mom glanced at her before turning back to the seam she was ripping out. "You are? Why?"

She opened her mouth to say, "For fun," but realized that might make her mom suspicious. So instead she said, "It's for school."

"Oh. Okay. Well, let me know if you need help. And tell your teacher thank you."

"Sure." Cassie grinned, then turned around and charged back up the stairs.

"All right, we're a go," she said, panting as she came into the kitchen.

"I got the milk and sugar in the pan." Emily stirred the contents of a small saucepan. "And the butter. When it gets hot, I'm supposed to stir a little into the eggs before pouring them into the pan. Does that make sense?"

"Not really." Cassie pulled out a loaf of bread and laid out eight pieces on a baking sheet. "You stir some of the hot milk into the eggs and then put the whole thing back in the pan?"

"Yeah. I think it's a mistake. They put in an extra step."

"I'm sure you're right." Cassie nodded and buttered each piece of bread. "Just put the eggs in the hot milk and stir."

"Okay."

They worked in silence, Emily stirring the milk and Cassie slicing the tomato.

"All right, I added the eggs," Emily said. "It says to keep stirring until it gets thick."

"Sounds good, then. Pretty easy."

"Really easy," Emily agreed, looking quite pleased with herself.

Cassie put two slices of tomato on each piece of bread and read the next part of instructions. "Fry up the sliced mushrooms with the butter, then add the eggs to the mushrooms and scramble them," she murmured. She could skip that step, at least. "Pile the mushrooms and eggs onto the slices of bread." The eggs were already out, since Emily had used them. Cassie cracked open one for each slice of bread and dumped the egg on top of the tomato. "Broil for two minutes."

"When is this thick?" Emily asked.

Cassie paused with her bread and examined Emily's pot of custard. Bubbles popped out of the surface, and the creamy mixture looked thick with some lumps in it. "I think it's pretty thick. What else does it say to do?"

"Take it off the heat and let it cool before serving."

"Push it to the side. You're done." Cassie turned on the oven and waited for it to preheat.

"I'll get the plates," Emily volunteered.

"I'll get everything else." Cassie checked the time. Almost five. "Perfect. When Daddy gets home, everything will be ready." The oven beeped, indicating that it was hot. She opened it and stuck the baking sheet with the bread inside. She consulted the recipe one more time and set the

timer for ten minutes.

Cassie finished setting the table while Emily called everyone to dinner. Mr. Jones pulled into the driveway just as Cassie put the sheet of eggs and toast on the table.

"Oh, this looks . . . great," her mom said, pausing to examine the table. "Did you want a salad or anything to go with the bread?"

"Salad! Yeah. That's a good idea." Sheepishly Cassie opened the fridge and pulled out the bag of salad mix. She dumped it in a bowl and added salad tongs, wishing she'd thought of this before her mom said something.

The front door opened. "I'm home!" Mr. Jones called.

"We're in here." Mrs. Jones walked through the dining room to greet him. Cassie peeked her head around the corner to watch.

"The girls made dinner for us," Mrs. Jones said, giving him a kiss on the cheek. He squeezed her in a sideways hug.

"That was nice."

"Yes. Wait till you see it." She smiled at him, and Cassie's heart swelled. It seemed to be working.

"All right, let's pray!" Cassie said, clapping her hands and ushering everyone to sit down.

Mr. Jones led everyone in a blessing on the food, and then Cassie put a piece of toast on each plate while her mom served out the salad.

"I don't want salad," Scott said.

"You have to have some," Mrs. Jones said.

"There's something squishy on my bread," Annette said.

"What do you mean, squishy?" Cassie said stiffly.

"It's like, slimy. Look." Annette poked at a clear gel on top of her tomato. It wiggled away from her finger.

Everyone else examined their toast now, poking at the surface of the tomato.

"Cassie, did you cook the egg?" Mrs. Jones asked.

"Of course!" Cassie exclaimed. "I put it in the oven for ten minutes."

"This is raw egg," Mr. Jones said, pushing his fork into the yolk.

Cassie's face began to burn, and she felt the hot sting in her eyes. "I followed the recipe." They couldn't be raw. Could they? She picked up her own toast and held it up. The edges of the egg were white and held tight to the tomato, but the rest of it jiggled and slid down with the pull of gravity. "I must've done something wrong." She blinked rapidly to keep from crying. She'd ruined dinner.

"Did you change anything in the recipe?"

"I just left out the mushroom," she said. "I didn't think it would make a difference."

Mrs. Jones got up and checked the cookbook. "You were supposed to cook the mushrooms with the eggs, right?"

"Right."

"So when you left out that step, you also left out cooking the eggs."

"Oh." Cassie understood. Even though she hadn't used mushrooms, the eggs still needed to be scrambled in the frying pan. "I'm so sorry."

Mr. Jones chuckled, his eyes twinkling. "That's all right. At least we've got salad."

"I can cook some spaghetti real quickly, too," Mrs. Jones said.

"I made dessert," Emily said, fairly bobbing out of her chair with anticipation. "Custard."

"That will be lovely. Let me cook some food first. Cassie,

will you open a can of spaghetti sauce for me?"

"Yes," she said faintly. This meal was not going as planned.

Emily opened the fridge and pulled out her custard as soon as she finished with her spaghetti. "Here it is," she said proudly, setting it on the table with a serving spoon.

"And here are clean plates for everyone," Cassie said, glad they could still salvage this meal somehow. She handed out the plates, and Emily gave everyone a scoop of custard.

"This looks good," Annette said.

The custard on Cassie's plate spread out, revealing several small lumps. She stuck a spoonful in her mouth and frowned. Though sweet, it didn't have the texture she expected.

"Mm, yum," Emily said, looking at everyone hopefully.

"What's in this?" Mrs. Jones asked.

"Just the basics," Emily said. "Milk, sugar, eggs."

"Oh, that's what this is," Scott said, nodding. "An egg." He held up one of the lumps resting on his spoon.

Cassie picked up one of her own lumps. She licked it, revealing a yellow yolk beneath. She put it back on her plate.

Mrs. Jones chewed on her lower lip. "I don't think the eggs are supposed to be whole still."

"No." Emily stared at her plate, her expression downcast. "I guess I didn't mix them right."

"Do we have to eat this?" Scott asked.

Mrs. Jones bit harder on her lip, and then a giggle escaped her mouth. She pressed a hand to her forehead and looked at the table, her shoulders shaking as she laughed.

"We blew it, huh," Cassie said miserably.

"Oh, girls," she said. "It was a lovely sentiment. And I sure appreciate the effort. Cooking gets easier every time, I promise."

"So this was just a practice?" Scott looked relieved. "We don't have to eat this?"

"No." Mrs. Jones took Cassie and Emily's hands. "You don't have to eat it. But next time, it will be amazing."

CHAPTER TWENTY-SEVEN

Flower Girl

"Well," Cassie said as she and Emily put their pajamas on, "dinner was a total fail."

"But not completely," Emily said, buttoning up her flannels. "They were in good moods. No one fought."

"I guess that's true," Cassie said. And she'd seen her mom kiss her dad, which had to be a good sign. "We need to make sure they're okay, though. Really cement their relationship while they're on this good path right now."

"How do we do that?" Emily asked.

Cassie snapped her fingers. "Mom needs to write a love note to Daddy. Then he'll be all happy with her and feeling loving too. And he can send her flowers."

"But . . ." Emily wrinkled her nose. "We'd have to tell them about our plan."

"Or." Cassie leaned forward, grinning conspiratorially. "We can do it for them, and they'll just think it's from each other."

"That's awesome! How will get flowers?"

"I'll handle the flowers." Cassie still had a few dollars in her piggy bank. "You write the note."

"For tomorrow?"

Cassie nodded. "Yeah. Let's do this."

~

Cassie walked up to Ms. Timber's desk on Tuesday morning, anxious to remind her about the presentations.

"I know," Ms. Timber said when she saw her. "You're going first. Don't even worry about it."

Cassie smiled in relief and went to her desk.

"I checked on your hamburger," Todd said. "It's still there."

Cassie spun around to face him. "You didn't tell anyone about it, did you?"

"No." He shrugged. "Why not? Is it a secret?"

She took a deep breath, telling herself to calm down. He'd ruin her whole presentation if he told everyone. "I just want it to be a surprise, that's all. Everyone will see it today when I present."

"Okay."

He went back to his desk, and Cassie slipped her hand into her pocket, making sure she still had her money. She'd have to act quickly after school if she was going to make it to the flower shop across the street and back before the buses left. It would be her only chance to get flowers for her mom, though. She had to try.

The day ticked slowly by, and finally it was almost over.

"All right, class, let's clear your desks," Ms. Timber said. "Put away your math assignments, and let's hear some presentations."

Cassie took a deep breath and put her math binder away, glad she'd finished her homework in class. One less thing to worry about at home.

"Cassandra, I believe you've been waiting. You're up

first." Ms. Timber smiled at her and got her video recorder out.

Cassie stood up, her heart already doing a little jig in her throat. She took a step toward the desk to pick up her replicator—

—and the fire alarm went off.

Ms. Timber frowned. "Hang on." She stuck her head out in the hall and conferred with the other teachers, then came back in. "All right, fire drill. Everyone line up by the door."

The students did so, Cassie more agitated than she wanted to admit. Her fingers twitched with nervous energy.

They went outside and lined up at their usual spot against the fence.

"I keep waiting to see what that little box of yours does."

Cassie turned around at the whisper behind her and found Miles grinning at her. She grinned back. "If I ever get to give my presentation, you'll find out."

"I hear there's a hamburger in there."

Todd! Cassie forced her grin to stay in place. "Maybe."

"Quiet out here!" Ms. Roxi, the other sixth grade teacher, said.

Cassie fell silent, but she exchanged another smile with Miles. His words warmed her heart. She hoped he'd be impressed by her invention.

The teachers walked through the rows of students, checking heads, talking with each other, and glancing around. Then they huddled up and murmured together, looking back at the school from time to time.

Cassie fidgeted. "How long will they make us stand here?" she whispered to Miles.

"We should have grabbed our backpacks. Look." He

nodded toward the pick-up line.

Was it already time? Cassie followed his gaze and saw the line of cars forming around the front of the school. The first bus pulled into the bus lot, pulling all the way to the front to make room for the other buses.

"Oh no." Her heart sank. How would she find the time to buy flowers?

"What's wrong?" Miles asked.

She shook her head. "Nothing. It's just—no, it's nothing."

He nudged her with his elbow. "No, come on. What is it?"

"Flowers," she blurted, and then blushed. When he only stared at her, she explained, "I'm supposed to buy flowers for my mom. As a gift from my dad."

"That's good, then!" Miles said. "You're parents are getting along?"

She'd forgotten that the whole class knew her family issues. "Yeah, I guess," she said. That was all he needed to know.

A shrill blast came from the school building, followed by two short ones. Immediately, the teachers began hussling their lines forward.

"Get your backpacks as soon as we get inside," Ms. Timber said. "Don't forget your homework. We'll do the presentations tomorrow."

"What about Cassie's hamburger?" Todd asked.

Ugh! Did everyone know? Cassie turned around, anxious to hear her teacher's answer.

"We'll worry about it tomorrow. Hurry, bus riders! The buses are here!"

Cassie grabbed her backpack with a sigh of frustration.

No presentation, and no flowers. Emily should fare better, at least.

Cassie sank into the seat next to Emily on the bus. "Did you write the note?" she murmured.

"Yes." Emily pulled it from her backpack. "Want to read it?"

"No, that's okay." She exhaled, her shoulders relaxing slightly. "At least something's going right."

"Where are the flowers?" Emily peered around Cassie as if she expected to see flowers hiding behind her.

"I had no chance to buy them." Cassie scowled. "The fire drill messed everything up."

"Well, maybe you'll find something on the way home."

"Where?" Cassie said, irritated. "There's not a flower shop between the bus stop and our house."

Emily shrugged and opened her book, already tuning Cassie out.

Cassie sighed and looked down the aisle, some of her irritation fading as she mulled over Emily's words. There were wild flowers growing along the side of the road. If she could find enough big pretty ones, she could pick a bouquet for her mother. Somewhat cheered, she imagined the kinds of flowers she would look for her bouquet.

They hopped off the bus at their stop, and Cassie wandered over to the side of the road.

"What are you doing?" Scott asked.

"None of your business," Cassie said, not wanting to explain to him. He might accidentally let it slip. Instead, she pushed aside the weeds and thorns, looking for flowers.

"Did you lose something?" Emily asked, joining her.

"No," Cassie said, rolling her eyes. "Just take everyone

to the house. I won't be long."

With a shrug, Emily gathered Annette and Scott around her. Cassie continued searching. At first she looked for the tall, bright, and colorful flowers she'd pictured in her mind. With none of those were forthcoming, she began picking whatever colored flowers she could find. After a few minutes, she opened her hand to see what she'd gathered.

Dandelions. That's all she'd found. She lifted her eyes, discouraged, and spotted some Queen Anne's Lace. The wispy white flowers didn't have the typical petals, but neither did dandelions. Cassie picked a few, and her path led her to some Black-eyed Susans. Satisfied now with her find, she tromped through the grass up to the house.

She poked her head in the front door and listened. She heard the murmurer of little voices, but her mom didn't appear to be in the kitchen. Cassie stepped inside, holding her flowers behind her back as she walked onto the tile.

Emily looked up from unloading the dishwasher. "What did you do?"

"Picked flowers." With a smile, Cassie brandished her bouquet. "Aren't they lovely?"

"Oh, they're great!" Emily opened a cupboard and pulled out a tall cup. "Put them in here. I'll add some water."

Cassie arranged the stems, frowning as most of the dandelions slipped between them and fell into the cup of water. She should've picked them longer.

"What about the note?" Cassie asked her.

"I stuck it on Daddy's pillow. He'll see it when he gets home."

"Where's Mom?"

"Downstairs. She didn't even see me when I went in her room."

"Perfect," Cassie breathed. She took the plastic cup down the hall and into her parents' master bathroom. She had to clear a spot on the cluttered counter, but she set the flowers down. Taking a step back, she surveyed her work. Some of the flowers already drooped, but the others held upright, bright and perky. She nodded. It looked great. Certainly her mom would think it was from her dad.

Just in case . . . she looked around for something she could write on. Nothing except tissue paper. She grabbed a sheet and set it on the counter. She found a pencil in her mom's make-up case and wrote, "Love, Daddy." No, no, no, her dad wouldn't say that. She took a new sheet of tissue paper and tried again. "Love, Jim."

There. She smiled at her own cleverness and skipped out of the room.

CHAPTER TWENTY-EIGHT
True Love

Mr. Jones came home right before dinner time. Cassie and Emily exchanged a secret smile, even though they knew their parents hadn't seen the gifts yet.

"How was work today?" Mrs. Jones asked. She ladled the soup into bowls for the family.

"Long day." He heaved a huge sigh and loosened his tie. "But we finished up that project. From here to the end of the year should be smooth sailing."

"Good for you, Jim!" She put the last bowl down and held out her hands. "Shall we pray?"

Cassie bowed her head as her father blessed the food. Barely had he said "amen" before he pushed back his chair and stood up.

"I need a different shirt," he said. "This one's uncomfortable."

He left the table, and Cassie felt a squirm of anxiety. What if he went in the bathroom? He'd see the flowers. And the note. And he'd know he hadn't given them to her mother.

He returned moments later, and Cassie let out a breath

of relief. There hadn't been enough time to go to the bathroom.

"Did you give your presentation today, Cassie?" he asked.

"No." She shook her head with a grimace. "There was a fire drill that interrupted class. I guess I'll give it tomorrow."

"Maybe you won't have to give it," her mom said.

"It kind of feels that way," Cassie admitted. "But after all that work and all this waiting, I'll be disappointed if I don't get my chance."

"Tomorrow will be your day, then," Mr. Jones said.

"I'll clear the table," Cassie said when everyone finished eating.

"It's not your job," her mom said. "It's Scott's."

"I'll do it for him. Emily will help. Right?" she looked at Emily.

"Yep." Emily nodded. "I'll help."

"You're volunteering to do someone else's job?" Mr. Jones shook his head and put his plate in the sink. "I must be at the wrong house."

"I help out sometimes!" Emily protested.

"All the time," Cassie added.

"Well, since you're helping," Mr. Jones said, "if you girls get the table, cleared I'll do the dishes."

"Looks like you guys have it under control." Mrs. Jones stood up. "I have more laundry to fold, so I'll be in the bedroom."

Cassie had hoped to talk to Emily, but she couldn't really do that with their dad there. She couldn't decline his offer to help, either, or he would think something was wrong. Instead she just shrugged at Emily and started putting the leftovers into containers.

Mrs. Jones wandered back into the kitchen, her lips pursed together and her brow creased. She stood at the counter staring into space.

"You okay, Karen?" Mr. Jones asked.

She turned to face him, a smile creasing her expression. "Yes, Jim. It seems that someone left me flowers."

Cassie caught her breath. She froze, a plate in one hand, her fingers almost touching the rim of another.

"Flowers?" Mr. Jones said. His own expression morphed into a frown. "Who would do that?"

Cassie shot a wide-eyed look at Emily. That wasn't how this conversation was supposed to go.

"Well, apparently you did," Mrs. Jones said, her smile widening.

Cassie groaned internally. Why hadn't she considered the fact that her parents would talk to each other about this? She stared at her dad, willing him to just go with it.

"I did?" he repeated.

"Yes." Mrs. Jones stepped up to him and wrapped her arms around the back of his neck. "And you signed your name with my eyebrow pencil on tissue paper in the bathroom."

Mr. Jones blinked rapidly, an expression of absolute confusion on his face. "What?"

"Don't you remember, dear? You left me some flowers on the counter. And signed a tissue?"

He continued to look at her blankly.

Mrs. Jones tugged on his arms. "And you signed the tissue in Cassie's handwriting?"

Cassie gasped. Was she that obvious?

He still just stared at her mom, and Mrs. Jones kissed his

cheek. "It was very sweet of you."

"But I didn't—" he began.

"No, no," she said, shushing him with one finger to his lips. "I think we need a moment to ourselves." She took his hand and pulled him out of the kitchen.

Cassie didn't realize she was holding her breath until she exhaled. Emily leaned toward her, two plates in her hands. "Did we just . . ."

"I think so," Cassie whispered back. Her lifted her chin, pride swelling in her chest. "We did."

The two girls giggled and clutched hands, and Cassie returned to clearing the table, immensely pleased with herself. They'd managed to save their parents' marriage.

Heavy footsteps thumped on the carpeted floor, announcing Mr. Jones' approach before he stepped into the kitchen.

"Oh, you don't have to do the dishes, Daddy," Cassie said. "We'll take care of them."

"Thanks," he said, the corners of his mouth pushing upward. "I wanted to ask, though, why Emily wrote me a love note."

"What?" Emily gasped. She stopped where she stood at the sink, rinsing the bowls before loading the dishwasher.

Her dad held up the wide-ruled piece of notebook paper. "This is your handwriting, Emily. But you wrote me all these nice things . . ." He opened it up, cleared his throat, and read, "I love you so much, Jim. You are my soulmate. You make my heart sing. I am so glad we will be married forever."

Cassie glanced at Emily, whose face was turning bright red, all the way up to her ears. "I didn't say those things. Why would I say that?"

He looked at her over the sheet of paper and raised an eyebrow. "That's my question."

Mrs. Jones came up behind him and hooked an arm around his waist. "Cassie, you want to tell us what's going on?"

Now Cassie's face flamed up, and she imagined the color matched Emily's. "Well, um." What should she say? Her mind raced, trying to come up with a feasible story that wouldn't be a huge lie.

What was the point? They were already on to her. Cassie heaved a sigh. "We were worried about you guys. Because you've been fighting so much. We just wanted to make sure you feel loved. By each other." Each word stuck in her throat, and she had to force it out.

Mrs. Jones turned her face into Mr. Jones' shoulder. A strange sound, muffled by his shirt, erupted from her.

"Did we do something wrong?" Cassie whispered, horrified. Or was it too late? She couldn't bring herself to ask that question out loud.

Mrs. Jones straightened up, and Cassie realized she was laughing. Laughing so hard she could hardly catch her breath. Mr. Jones started chuckling also.

"I think you girls are very, very sweet to worry about us that way," Mrs. Jones said. "But girls, you have to understand. Sometimes in marriage, people fight. Sometimes they fight ugly, and sometimes the fight lasts weeks, even months."

"But your mom and me, we're forever," Mr. Jones said. "We might get mad at each other, but you don't have to worry about us. I'd never let this woman get away from me."

Mrs. Jones gave him a smile.

"You were fighting so much," Cassie said, bewildered. "Always arguing. It was like—like you didn't even like each other."

Her parents sobered up. Mrs. Jones cast her eyes down, and Mr. Jones said, "That's my fault, Cassie. I've been dealing with some hard things at work, and I've been bringing my problems home. I need to be better about that. I will be better about that."

"So—you guys are okay?" Cassie blinked up at her parents, tears welling in her eyes. She'd had nothing to worry about, after all.

"Yes." Mr. Jones pulled both girls to him in a hug. "We are okay."

~

"Cassandra." Ms. Timber smiled at her Wednesday afternoon. "It's your turn for your presentation."

Finally. Cassie stood up, holding her chin high as she walked across the room. She could feel the other kids' eyes on her, waiting to see how this would go. She picked up her cardboard replicator and turned around, flashing a huge smile at Ms. Timber's video recorder.

"Welcome to the Xenob, home of the future, where every house has its own replicator!" She brandished her hand in front of it, showing off the metallic tape. "Whatever you want to eat, simply type it into the keypad, and immediately the food will appear. For example. Let's say you have a craving for a hamburger." Cassie bent over the replicator and spoke the letters as she touched them. "H-A-M-B-U-R-G-E-R. Hamburger. Ding." She imitated the sound of a bell, then opened the little flap and pulled out her hamburger. Turning around, she waved it at the class. "Just like that, your food appears!" She unwrapped it, sank her teeth into the meaty bun, and took a bite. "Yum!"

"Ew!" Todd shrieked.

Ms. Timber turned off the video recorder and joined in the laughter with the rest of the class. "Cassie, spit that out! That burger's been in there for nearly a week!"

And it tasted fine to Cassie. If it were up to her, she'd just eat it. But with her classmates looking at her and laughing, she didn't have much choice. With a shrug, she walked to the trashcan and threw it away.

"Quiet down," Ms. Timber said. "It's time for another presentation."

Cassie ducked into her chair and scooted closer to Andrea.

"Good job," Andrea giggled. "You did fantastic."

Miles leaned back from his desk and whispered, "Even with that nasty burger."

Cassie laughed too. She hooked her arm through Andrea's and leaned into her, more content in that moment than she could remember being in quite sometime.

CHAPTER TWENTY-NINE

Class Ambassador

"Did you see the new girl?" Andrea asked in a hushed voice on Thursday morning.

Cassie glanced at her best friend. The two of them had just walked into the classroom and were hanging up their coats and backpacks in the cubbies.

"No," Cassie said. "What new girl?"

"She's talking to Ms. Timber."

Cassie felt her heart squeeze in sympathy. Last year, she'd been the new girl. At least she had moved in over the summer and not November, almost the middle of the school year. "Where'd she move from?"

"I don't know. I just saw her. Hey, what should I bring for our campout this weekend?"

Cassie smiled, glad Andrea had brought that up. For weeks the two of them had been begging their moms to let them have a campout in one of their backyards, and finally their moms had agreed. "Just bring a pillow and a sleeping bag. I have the tent and everything else."

"I wish I could just ride home with you."

"I know." Cassie nodded. "But then you'd have to lug

your sleeping bag around the classroom and the bus."

"Yeah, and that would look funny."

They both giggled. They walked around the cubbies, separating to go to their individual desks. Cassie stole a glance toward Ms. Timber. Sure enough, a girl with wavy white-blond hair stood by the desk, her arms laden down with books and school supplies. Ms. Timber put an arm around the girl's shoulder and directed her to the cubby.

The morning bell rang, and Cassie pulled out her journaling notebook. The class knew the routine by now; every morning, as soon as the bell rang, they spent fifteen minutes writing in their journals. Wednesday had been a quiet day for Cassie, and she didn't have much to say. So she talked about how pretty the trees looked around her house as the leaves turned different colors.

"Cassie."

She looked up when Ms. Timber bent over her desk.

"This is Esther," Ms. Timber said, moving the new girl toward her. "She just moved here. Since you're the sixth grade ambassador, I'm putting her next to you. You'll help her for her first week of school until she feels comfortable with our routine."

"Oh. Sure." Cassie had forgotten that she was the ambassador. No one new had moved in, and she hadn't really had the chance to use her role.

Ms. Timber moved a desk next to Cassie, and Esther sat down.

"Hi," Cassie said, giving her a smile. Esther didn't smile back, but turned her eyes down toward her desk. Cassie shrugged it off. She was probably shy, maybe even scared. "I know what it's like to be new. Last year it was me. I didn't know anyone. You'll make friends quickly."

Esther cast a sideways glance at Cassie. "Where did you move from?"

"Texas. I lost all my friends when we moved here."

Esther nodded and returned to staring at her desk.

"Well . . ." Cassie searched for something more to say. But with a silent partner, the conversation just kind of died. "We'll have recess after math. You can hang out with me and my friends if you want."

Esther gave a brief nod but said nothing.

When they lined up for recess, Cassie introduced Esther to Andrea.

"We always walk around the playground," Cassie said.

"Sometimes I walk with them," Miles said, poking his head into the group.

"When we invite him," Cassie said, elbowing him back out. Her skin tingled at the contact, and a warmth spread over her face.

They walked outside together, and Cassie turned around to say something to Esther. But she was gone.

Cassie spun around, searching for her, and then she saw her. Esther had stopped walking and stood against the brick exterior of the school, studying her fingernails. Cassie looked at Andrea, perplexed.

"Am I supposed to stay and talk to her?" she asked.

"No." Andrea shook her head. "She wants to be alone. Let her."

She didn't have to work hard to convince Cassie. Shrugging off any nagging doubts, Cassie followed Andrea out to the playground.

Esther didn't say more than two words the rest of the day. Usually Cassie loved the opportunity to make a new friend, but now she felt a huge relief to leave the classroom and escape her ominous presence for a few hours. She said bye to her friends and headed out to the bus.

She stepped on and searched the seats for Betsy. Before she spotted her, she spotted someone else: Esther.

Cassie jolted to a stop. Esther sat alone, staring out the window. Kids pushed past Cassie, already finding a spot. Betsy waved from the back, and Cassie bit her lip, an internal war raging within her. She knew she should sit by Esther. But Esther had not been friendly, and Cassie had another friend here. But it was her job as sixth grade ambassador.

Before she could change her mind, Cassie forced her feet forward and plopped into the seat next to Esther.

"Hi," she said. "Looks like we're on the same bus."

Esther looked at her, blue eyes widening in momentary surprise. "Oh," she said, relaxing. "Yeah, I guess so."

"So what did you think of school today?" Cassie asked, giving the whole conversation thing one more try.

Esther picked at a tear in the back of the seat in front of her, poking her finger in it until it got bigger. "It's different."

Again, Cassie felt her heart squeeze in sympathy. "Yeah. I know. But you'll get used to it."

"Everyone says that," Esther murmured. "I don't really want to, though."

They fell into silence, but this time Cassie didn't think it felt so ominous. She watched the scenery pass by as the bus drove out of town and into the countryside. "Where's your house?"

"I have no idea." Esther gave half-hearted laugh. "Way out in the middle of nowhere."

"I felt that way when we moved here," Cassie said. "One

time, my teacher tried to give me a ride home from school, but I got us lost. I couldn't remember where I lived."

This time Esther's laugh was more genuine. "That's funny. How long did it take you to feel like this was—I don't know, home?"

"Home?" Cassie squinted, analyzing the question. "Sometimes I still miss Texas. I miss my friends. I miss the heat. But I've made friends here. I like it here. I guess it took about a year."

"A year." Esther mouthed the words to herself.

They turned onto Cassie's road, and she pointed through the trees. "Look. You can just barely see my house in there. When the leaves fall off all the trees, you'll be able to see it

better."

"Oh, it's pretty," Esther said.

"Thanks." Cassie smiled, more to herself than Esther. Who would have thought? Apparently she really did just need to warm up.

~

Esther wasn't on the bus in the morning. Cassie put away her backpack and chatted with Andrea and Miles, all the while watching for Esther to walk in. She did, just moments before the bell rang.

"I didn't see you on the bus today," Cassie said, scooting into her desk as Esther sat down.

"I don't ride in the mornings," Esther said.

"Oh, okay. So, the first thing we do is journaling. Pick one of your notebooks and just kind of write down your thoughts, your feelings, anything important that happened yesterday."

"You told me yesterday," Esther said.

Cassie pursed her lips together, put off by the abrasive tone in Esther's voice. "Well, Ms. Timber does read these from time to time, so don't write anything you wouldn't want her to read."

Esther didn't respond. She opened her notebook, took out a pen, and started writing.

CHAPTER THIRTY
Front Yard Adventures

"She hasn't said a word to me all day," Cassie said to Andrea as she unwrapped her ham-and-cheese sandwich at lunch. "Well, except to tell me that she knows how to do everything because I already told her."

"I wouldn't expect anything from her," Andrea said. "She wasn't exactly nice and friendly yesterday."

"Yeah, but see, that's the thing," Cassie said. "The whole bus ride home, we were like, talking. She was nice."

"Really?" Andrea looked doubtful. "Are you sure she wasn't just being polite?"

"No!" Cassie shook her head. "She was actually friendly. Like she wanted to talk to me." But even now, she wasn't so sure. Maybe she'd imagined the friendliness.

"Well, I wouldn't worry about her," Andrea said. "Because tonight we're having a campout!"

Cassie squealed along with her. "What time are you coming over?"

"In time for dinner, of course." Andrea grinned. "Wouldn't miss cooking on the campfire."

Esther didn't ride the bus that afternoon, and Cassie was

relieved. She couldn't bear the suspense of wondering whether they would talk.

Mr. Jones helped Cassie find a flat, smooth section of ground in the front yard. She stopped her dad when he started to put up the tent.

"Andrea wants to do that," Cassie said. "She's never been camping. She wants the full experience."

"Sounds like fun," he said. "Make sure you build your fire in the fire pit."

Cassie rolled her eyes. "Don't worry, Daddy. I know all about fire safety. I'm a Girls Club girl, remember?

"Of course," her dad said, but Cassie saw him hide a smile. "Just remember, we're right inside if you need something."

"We won't need anything," Cassie said cheerfully.

Andrea arrived half an hour later. She hugged Cassie and set her sleeping gear on the patio next to Cassie's. "What first?"

"We need to put up our tent. We also need to start our fire so we can cook dinner."

"Great! Let's do the fire. What's dinner?"

"Hot dogs." Cassie held up the package of processed meat. "And marshmallows for dessert. Real campfire food."

"So how do we build the fire?"

"Well." Cassie knew how to do this—in theory. They'd learned how at the last Girls Club campout she'd been on. She hadn't been able to start hers without the fire starter, though. "I'll show you." She told Andrea how to gather the smaller wood sticks, or kindling, and then they put on the bigger sticks, followed by the logs her dad had stacked up for her.

223

"This is a lot of work," Andrea commented once they had the basic A-frame set up.

"Yes," Cassie agreed.

"Wouldn't it be easier to pour lighter fluid on a bunch of wood and light it up?"

Cassie had to admit that sounded easier, and faster. "Maybe. But this is cooler, right?"

Andrea arched an eyebrow. "Sure. Cooler."

Cool might not be the right word. "More challenging."

"Definitely."

Lighting an A-frame fire with one match would be a major accomplishment. Unfortunately, Cassie didn't have any more luck with it today than she had last time. After twenty minutes, she tossed down the match box, frustrated.

Andrea laughed. "It's harder than it looks, huh?"

"Yeah. It doesn't really work." She glared at the troublesome A-frame.

"So." Andrea picked up the matches. "Let's make it work. Have any lighter fluid?"

"My dad might," Cassie grumbled.

"Then let's light this up."

Andrea's idea worked. In less than five minutes, the fire began to grow, quickly consuming the kindling and chomping down on the bigger pieces of wood with hungry snaps and crackles. The girls set about putting the tent up while the fire grew.

"This is so much fun," Andrea said, threading a hot dog on a skewer. She settled herself in front of the fire, propping up her feet. "What a great idea, Cassie."

"It took two," Cassie said, holding up her soda to Andrea. "Thanks for wanting to."

"Thanks for being my best friend," Andrea replied, grinning.

Cassie swallowed past a sudden ache in her throat. "Thank you. For being the best friend ever."

After the marshmallows, Andrea and Cassie crawled into the tent. The temperature was dropping, and Cassie buried herself in her sleeping bag, shivering and curling her body around itself.

"So do you still like Miles?" Andrea asked.

Cassie's face warmed, even though she knew she didn't have to be embarrassed around Andrea. "Yeah. I guess so."

"Does he like you?"

"I don't know. How would I know?"

"Well, the way he talks to you. The way he looks at you. It would be like, romantic."

Cassie considered their friendship, the way he teased her, how they hung out. "No. I don't think he likes me."

"That's too bad. Maybe later."

"Maybe."

The conversation dwindled, and Cassie shivered compulsively, unable to get warm even in her sleeping bag. "What about you? Do you still like Connor?"

"Yes. And I think he likes me. Whenever I look at him at lunch, he smiles at me."

Did that mean he liked her? "That's good." Not really. Cassie didn't like Connor. He was on her soccer team, and the one time Cassie had gone to practice, Connor had called her fat and made fun of her the whole time. It didn't help that Cassie hated running and was the slowest one on the team.

"Yeah. I think he might ask me out."

"What would you say?" Cassie asked, a mixture of awed

and horrified. She wasn't allowed to date until she was sixteen. She didn't understand the whole "going out" thing, when kids would say they were boyfriend and girlfriend but not do anything. Except maybe smile at each other across the lunch room.

"Yes, of course. Wouldn't you?"

Cassie wasn't sure she would. She wasn't sure her parents would approve.

The silence went longer this time, but Cassie didn't sleep. Her body kept up a steady rhythm of shivering. She heard Andrea roll over and heave a sigh.

"Are you okay?" Cassie asked.

"It's just a bit cold."

"I'm freezing," Cassie said, relieved it wasn't just her.

"I thought the fire would keep us warm."

"The fire's almost out," Cassie said. "And it's not close to the tent."

"Oh." After a moment, Andrea said, "Do you think we could get another blanket from the house?"

"Yes." Cassie braced herself and climbed out of the sleeping bag. The night air was even colder than she expected, and goosebumps popped up all over her flesh.

"I'll come with you." Andrea scurried out, too. They hooked their arms together and scrambled across the front yard.

Her dad had left the front door unlocked, and Cassie closed her eyes when the blast of warm air from the house hit them. "Come on." She went down the hall to the closet with the blankets. She pulled two down and held one out. "Here's one for you." When Andrea didn't take it, Cassie looked at her. She wasn't there. "Andrea?"

A quick glance around showed Andrea wasn't in the

hall. Cassie retraced her steps toward the front door. "Andrea?"

"Here," came a soft voice.

Cassie followed it and peered over the top of the couch. Andrea had curled up on top, her arm around a pillow.

"I got you a blanket," Cassie said, holding it out.

"Thank you." Andrea took it and wrapped it around herself. Then she closed her eyes.

Cassie looked at the clock on the television. It was almost midnight. "Are you coming back out to the tent?"

"Are you?" Andrea whispered.

Cassie lay down on the floor next to the couch and wrapped her blanket around her. The instant warmth enveloped her, and she closed her eyes, already feeling her heart rate slow as her body melted into the soft blanket. "No," Cassie whispered. "Here is just fine."

~

Cassie woke up when Scott turned the television on. The sound blared through the living room, and Andrea groaned, pulling the throw pillow over her head.

"Scott!" Cassie murmured. "We're still sleeping."

He didn't even answer, his eyes already glued to the TV.

Mr. Jones stepped out of the kitchen, his Saturday grubbies on. He smirked at Cassie. "Guess you girls didn't last long outside."

"We did!" Cassie protested. She stretched and sat up, twisting her head to work out the kink in her neck. Her fingers searched the carpet beside her until they closed around her glasses. "It just got cold. So we came in."

"But it was a lot of fun," Andrea added, sitting up as well. "Thanks for letting us do it."

"Just remember to take your tent down. Are you still

cooking breakfast on the fire?"

Cassie remembered the dutch oven pancakes she had wanted to cook. First she'd have to make the fire, then let it cool so there were some coals. Then she'd put the dutch oven full of pancake batter in the coals and let it cook for half an hour. She discarded the whole process with a shrug. "No. We'll just eat in here. What do you want, Andrea?"

"I think cereal sounds great." Andrea slipped her glasses on and gave a huge yawn.

"Cereal sounds perfect."

CHAPTER THIRTY-ONE

Ms. Nice

Esther didn't say more than five words all day in school Monday. When Cassie saw her on the bus after school, she told herself to just walk on by. Whatever pretense of friendship she thought she'd imagined last week had obviously faded.

But Esther looked so alone, staring out the window, her hand twisting and untwisting a fabric bracelet on her wrist.

It's my job, Cassie told herself. *I'm supposed to befriend her.* With that, she plopped into the seat next to her.

"Hi," Cassie said.

"Hi," Esther murmured, picking up her backpack and pulling it closer to her.

"How was your weekend?" Cassie asked, pretending like they hadn't just spent an awkward, wordless day together in school.

"It was fine," Esther said, her attention returning to the view outside.

She didn't ask how Cassie's weekend was, but Cassie expected that. "Mine was great," she said. "Andrea came over, and we had a campout."

"Who's Andrea?"

"My best friend. I introduced you to her. She's got long reddish-brown hair, wears glasses."

"She's kind of chubby like you?"

Cassie shut her mouth, startled. "I'm not chubby," she said finally.

"Oh. So you're just large-boned."

Something stung Cassie's chest, and she worked hard to swallow and not react. "Andrea's not chubby, either."

Esther looked at her, a shrewd, calculating look in her eyes. "I guess you have different definitions in Arkansas."

Cassie just blinked, caught so off-guard that she wasn't sure how to respond. Was Esther insulting her? Or was she unintentionally rude? "Anyway," Cassie said, "she's the best person I know. She's really nice. She spent the night and—"

"What about that boy you talk to every day?" Esther interrupted.

"What boy?"

Now there was a definite eye roll. "You don't talk to a lot of boys every day."

Cassie's face burned. "You mean Miles?" she stammered.

"Yes. Miles." Esther nodded. "He seems nice."

"He is," Cassie said, defensive for some unknown reason.

"How long have you known him?"

"Well, I just moved here last year. That's how long I've known everyone."

"But you like him."

"Of course," Cassie said. "I like most people."

"You look at him different. You like him." The words

230

were accusatory.

Cassie regretted sitting here. "I don't know what you mean."

Esther shrugged and turned her face back to the window. She didn't say anything else, and Cassie had never been so happy to see the bus pulling up to her stop.

"Well, I'll see you tomorrow," she said, standing up.

Esther nodded without looking at her.

"Yikes," Cassie muttered, getting off the bus. Definitely not her friend.

~

Cassie didn't try to talk to Esther in school the next day. At lunch she told Andrea all about their horrible bus conversation, leaving out the part where Esther called both girls chubby.

"I don't like her," Andrea said. "She's not very nice."

"She doesn't like me," Cassie replied. "I don't know why. But she seemed very annoyed and irritated with everything I said."

"She's jealous."

"Of what?" Cassie had to laugh. She had absolutely nothing anyone should envy.

"Of you and Miles."

"Me and Miles?" Cassie glanced down the table to where Miles and Jeffrey goofed off, poking their straws into their pickles and jiggling them at each other. One of the pickles flew off, and both boys cracked up. "But we're just friends."

"Exactly. And she doesn't have any. You'll see." Andrea nodded knowingly and took a sip of her chocolate milk. "I'm right."

Cassie and Andrea had just started their walk around

the play yard during recess when Andrea seized Cassie's arm.

"Look," she breathed, nodding her head. "Look at Esther."

Cassie followed Andrea's gaze. Esther stood on the sidewalk, one hand on Miles' forearm, the other giving a girly wave while she laughed. She leaned her body into Miles, saying something that Cassie couldn't hear.

"What is she doing?" Cassie said.

"Flirting with Miles! Obviously. Cassie. You can't just let this happen." Andrea tugged on Cassie's arm, trying to drag her forward.

Cassie didn't budge. "What am I supposed to do about it?"

"Interrupt them! Flirt with Miles!" Andrea stopped moving and turned to face Cassie. She put both hands on Cassie's shoulders. "Cassie, you've never even let Miles know you're interested. And now she comes along, and she's clearly interested. If you don't say something, do something now, she's the one he's going to notice."

Still Cassie didn't move. "What am I supposed to do? Fight her? Interrupt her?"

"No, just join her. Talk to Miles too!"

Cassie could see the logic in Andrea's words, but she couldn't do it. She wasn't going to cause an issue right there in front of Esther. "I will," she promised. "But not right now. Not with her standing there." Watching her, judging her.

"You better hurry, Cass. She's going to dig her claws into him."

~

Cassie's pulse quickened as she approached the bus,

already nervously anticipating Esther's presence. She wouldn't sit by her again. But how was she supposed to act? Just walk on past without making eye contact? Pretend she wasn't there? Or smile, say hi, and act like nothing Esther did bothered her?

She still hadn't decided when she reached the top step and turned to face the aisle. Her eyes scanned the seats, and then her heart rate began to slow down when she didn't see Esther. She sat down next to Betsy, still watching outside to see if Esther would get on.

"What, your new friend's not here, so you thought you'd sit with me again?" Betsy said with a sniff.

"She's not my new friend," Cassie said. The bus doors closed, and Cassie's shoulders relaxed as the vehicle started forward. "She's the new girl. But I'm the ambassador, so I had to sit by her and be nice for a few days."

"Oh. Well, you're a good person for it."

"She's not nice, though." Cassie settled into her seat, moving her backpack around to her lap. "I'm really glad she's not here. I was getting tired of trying to be nice."

"You, Cassie?" Betsy's eyes widened. "You're the nicest person I know! If you don't like her, she must be pretty awful."

"Well." Cassie shifted uncomfortably. She didn't like to call someone names. "She and I just don't get along. That's all."

"But we're still friends?"

"Of course!" She reached over and hugged Betsy. "I missed sitting by you."

~

Cassie watched Esther come into the classroom

Wednesday morning. She hoped today was the last day they'd have to sit by each other. After watching Esther and Miles yesterday, Cassie didn't want to talk to her at all.

Esther sat down at her desk and pulled out her journaling notebook. She opened it and started writing without even glancing at Cassie.

Cassie opened her own notebook and told herself not to say anything. But the bell hadn't rung yet, and the class was a dull roar of laughter and talking. Cassie couldn't just ignore Esther.

"Good morning," she said.

Esther arched one eyebrow and spared her a glance. "Good morning."

At least she'd been acknowledged. Encouraged, Cassie said, "You weren't on the bus yesterday."

"I'm not going to ride it anymore." Esther continued writing, not looking up from her notebook. "My mom thinks it's not a good environment."

Cassie felt the jab even if none had been intended, though she suspected it had. "Then I guess it's good you are getting out of it."

"Yeah." Esther lifted one shoulder. "Oh, do you have Miles' number?"

"As in, his phone number?" Cassie shook her head. "No." She'd never even considered calling him.

"Yeah, I didn't think so. He gave it to me yesterday."

Cassie looked at her, the word "why" on the tip of her tongue. But she bit it back. She knew instinctively that Esther's game was to bruise her ego. "That was nice of him," she said instead, as if she didn't care. Inside, though, she wondered. Why hadn't he ever given it to her?

Esther smirked. "Yep. Nice. Anyway, after today, I'm

sure I can ask for a new seat. I've learned my way around and don't need a babysitter anymore."

The bell rang, and the students dispersed to their desks.

"Journals out, everyone!" Ms. Timber called, clapping her hands to silence the last-minute conversations.

Cassie wrote the date across the top, and then wrote the first line that came to her head: *I sure hope Esther is right. I don't want to babysit her anymore, either.*

She looked up from her paper, frustration seeping at the edges of her mind, wanting to crumple it up and hurl it at Esther.

Miles was looking at her from his desk. When she met his gaze, he smiled and showed her a paper airplane on his desk. He stole a glance at Ms. Timber. She had her back to the class as she wrote on the whiteboard, and he threw it at Cassie. She caught it, feeling the heat of Esther's eyes on her as she did.

"Miles is throwing paper airplanes at Cassie!" Todd yelled.

Ms. Timber turned around, and Miles muttered, "Tattler!"

Cassie quickly opened the airplane even as Ms. Timber approached.

"Cassie, give me the plane. Miles, that's five minutes off recess."

Cassie handed it over, but not before she'd read what it said.

I bet I still throw a better airplane than you.

Her heart warmed at the memory. She and Miles had met at a paper airplane competition that Cassie had accidentally signed up for. When her first airplane failed dismally, he helped her build her next one. She looked up and mouthed at him, "You're on."

He just grinned, and she knew that her airplane skills hadn't improved in the least. But that didn't matter. What mattered was that Miles considered her a friend, even if he'd never given her his phone number. Cassie picked up her pencil and wrote in her journal again.

Esther can do her worst, but she can't take my friends away.

Episode 5: Birthday Goals

CHAPTER THIRTY-TWO

Plus One

Cassandra Jones hopped impatiently from foot to foot in front of the bus, waiting for her younger siblings to get on in front of her. Early December in Arkansas wasn't as cold as some of the northern states, but the mornings were frosty and nippy. She shivered in her jacket, her hands trembling in her pockets. Finally there was room for her on the steps, and she hurried onto the bus.

Immediately the warm air fogged up her glasses. For a moment Cassie couldn't see anything, and then the fog dissipated. A quick scan revealed the usual crowd. She settled into the seat next to her friend Betsy Walker.

Betsy lifted her head from the back of the seat in front of them, her greenish eyes sleepy. "Good morning," she yawned.

"Yeah," Cassie said. She rubbed her gloved hands together. "Just two more weeks."

"Two more weeks," Betsy agreed.

All the kids at school were saying the mantra. Two more weeks, and then Christmas break would start.

"Oh, that reminds me!" Betsy brightened a bit,

straightening her shoulders. "I'm having a Christmas party next Friday. I want you to come."

"I love parties!" Cassie said. "That sounds awesome!"

"Great! Talk to your parents and let me know. You can try and call me, but the phone doesn't always work." Betsy scribbled her phone number on a piece of paper and handed it to Cassie. "Oh, and you're supposed to bring a friend."

"Like, I can invite Andrea?" Having her best friend Andrea at a party would make it that much more fun.

"No, silly." Betsy giggled. "It's a couples' party."

She wiggled her eyebrows and grinned, and Cassie suspected she should understand what that meant, but she didn't. "Couples' party?" she echoed.

"You know."

When Cassie didn't say anything, Betsy waved a hand and said, "Like boy/girl? A date? There's going to be dancing and games and stuff!"

"Oh." *Oh.* That kind of party. Cassie's shoulders drooped, and her excitement diminished. "Yeah, I don't think my parents would let me go to a party with boys." They definitely wouldn't let her take a date. No dating until she was sixteen. They had made that clear over and over again.

"Really? Why? My parents will be there. Nothing bad will happen, I promise."

Cassie shrugged. "I'll ask them." But she knew what they'd say.

It was almost bedtime before Cassie worked up the nerve to ask her parents. Her younger brother and sister Scott and Annette had already gone to bed. Cassie and her other sister, Emily, sat at the kitchen table working on assignments while her parents looked at something on her dad's computer. Cassie chewed on the eraser of her pencil and then put it down.

"Mom, Daddy?" she said. "Can I go to Betsy's Christmas party?"

Her mom looked up, resting one arm on the table. "When is it?"

"This Friday."

Mrs. Jones shrugged. "That should be fine. We don't have anything else that night."

Cassie braced herself. She had to tell them the rest of it. "There will be boys there."

That got her dad's interest. He lifted his eyes from the computer screen, adjusting his glasses. "What kind of party is this?"

"A Christmas party," Cassie said. "With boys."

"Like a dance?"

She shrugged. "There might be dancing."

He shook his head. "No dancing until you're fourteen."

"Jim." Her mom put a hand on his shoulder. "It's not a real dance. It's a group of kids getting together to celebrate Christmas. She's around boys all day in school. This won't be that different."

Cassie looked at her mother in surprise. She hadn't expected anyone to stand up for her.

"Well." Mr. Jones hesitated. "How well do we know this family?"

Mrs. Jones shook her head. "Not well. We know Betsy; she's spent the night here before."

"I want to talk to her parents, then."

"I have her phone number." Cassie went to her backpack and retrieved the paper. "Betsy says it doesn't aways work, though." She handed it to her dad.

"Well, let's give it a try." Her dad picked up the cordless phone and dialed the number. "Hello? Yes, this is Jim Jones, I'm Cassandra's father. Doing great, thank you. I just had a few questions about the Christmas party Betsy is throwing. Uh-huh. Sure. How many adults will be present? Okay. And do you know what kids will be there? Oh, okay. Sure, makes sense. Yes, I think so. Yes, thank you. Okay. Bye."

He hung up and turned to face Cassie and Mrs. Jones' expectant expressions, and even Emily had looked up from her homework to watch.

"Well, it sounds like it will be well-supervised, both parents will be there. And Betsy's keeping it small, she's only invited four people."

And their dates, Cassie thought, but that part she didn't dare say out loud. "So I can go?" Cassie hardly dared believe it.

"Yes, you can go. But I'll take you. And I'm going to stay at the party."

Cassie nodded eagerly. "Sure! That's fine!"

~

Betsy threw her arms around Cassie as soon as she got on the bus the next morning. "I"m so happy you're coming to my Christmas party!"

"Yeah," Cassie said, grinning. "I didn't think my parents would say yes. But they did. My dad's going to stay at the party too, but he's fine with it."

Betsy shrugged. "My parents won't mind if he stays. Now, which boy are you going to invite?"

That again. Cassie frowned. "I don't think I'll invite anyone."

"Oh, you have to!" Betsy exclaimed. "We need boys and girls there!"

Cassie pictured herself trying to explain to her dad that they needed to pick up a boy before going to Betsy's house. So not happening. "You just invite what boys you want there."

"I already invited my boyfriend Chris."

"Who's Chris?"

"Chris Anthony? He's in my class. I'm sure you know him."

The name was familiar, but Cassie couldn't picture him. "So invite a few others."

"*You're* supposed to invite one, Cassie!"

"Yeah, okay." Cassie nodded like she'd decided to do it. "I'll think of someone to invite."

"You could invite me," Andrea said when Cassie told her her conundrum during PE.

The two girls were running their laps, a requirement before they could start the other, slightly less painful PE exercises. The only thing that made running these laps halfway bearable, in Cassie's opinion, was that she got to run next to Andrea and talk to the whole time.

"Yeah, I thought of that," Cassie said with a sigh. "I even asked. But no, I have to invite a boy."

"Oh." Andrea shrugged. "Well, you already know what boy you like. Just ask him."

Miles Hansen. Cassie's mind flashed to her friend, with his brown hair that he sometimes wore parted on the side, sometimes spiked up, his brown eyes and wire-frame glasses, and most of all, his easy, friendly smile. Her chest tingled at the thought of asking him, and her heart warmed at the idea of holding his hand, dancing with him.

But she couldn't ask him. "We're just friends."

Andrea clucked her tongue. "Maybe Miles wants to be more than just friends, too."

Which brought Cassie back around to the question that had plagued her these last few weeks: How would she know? Andrea was convinced Miles liked Cassie. He smiled at her a lot, teased her, threw airplanes at her, and sometimes joined her and Andrea on the playground at recess.

But Miles did this with other girls, too, particularly Cassie's nemesis, Esther Vanguard.

"He doesn't," Cassie said.

"Except you don't actually know that," Andrea said. "And you won't unless you ask him."

Which, Cassie decided, she wasn't going to do.

~

"So, did you decide who to invite to my party?" Betsy asked on the bus ride home. "It's in four days! Time's running out!"

"No," Cassie said, playing with the zipper on her backpack. She opened it, closed it, did it again. "I don't think I'm going to ask anyone."

"What?" Betsy exclaimed. "Come on! It's the perfect opportunity!" She lowered her voice. "You like someone, don't you?"

Cassie didn't answer. She was afraid to say. The more people who knew, the more likely it was that Miles would find out.

"So just ask him, Cassie. Don't you want to know if he likes you? Besides, think how much fun it would be if he came!"

Cassie thought about that. She thought about being at a

party with Miles. How they'd be able to talk together, sit next to each other and laugh. He might hold her hand.

"Okay," she said. "I'll ask him tomorrow."

"You could just call him," Betsy said. "Tomorrow is pretty last-minute."

Betsy had a point, but no way was Cassie asking him over the phone. "I'll do it tomorrow."

CHAPTER THIRTY-THREE
Boys and Girls

Cassie waited all day Wednesday for the perfect opportunity to ask Miles. She wanted to do it when they were alone, so no one could ridicule her if he said no. She watched for him in the morning before class started. He came in and put his backpack away, then stood by his desk sorting his box of colored pencils. Cassie got up from her desk and made her way toward him.

"Hey, Miles," Michael said, coming in and sitting down next to him.

Miles glanced at him and gave a nod. "Hey."

Cassie turned and went back to her desk. She wasn't saying anything now.

She thought maybe during laps at PE she'd get a chance. "I've decided to ask Miles to the party," she told Andrea as they lined up to go outside. "So I'm going to run a little faster and catch up to him."

Andrea nodded, eyes wide. "Go! Good luck!"

Cassie dashed out the door. She saw Miles up ahead, running by himself. For the moment. She knew it wouldn't be long before someone else caught up to him. She urged her legs to run faster, and for a moment her body obeyed. She sprinted forward. Within minutes, though, the burst of energy faded. That, coupled with the cold air rushing in and out of her lungs, slowed her down. She tried to make her gait wider, but her side started cramping, her lungs hurt, and her throat burned. She came to a complete stop, holding her side and bending over.

An arm hooked through hers, and she looked up to see Andrea holding her up.

"Come on," she whispered.

Cassie nodded. Encouraged, she forced herself to jog again with Andrea. But her stamina had left her. They finished up their laps slower than normal, and she never caught up to Miles.

"I have a plan," Andrea said at lunch. "When it's time for recess, I'll distract Miles. Ask him for help with something and make him stay behind. You wait in the hallway. When he finally comes out of the classroom, you ask him. It will just be the two of you."

"Yes," Cassie said. "Okay." This would work. It had to. Her palms got clammy at the mere idea, but she could do this.

"Recess!" Ms. Timber said at a quarter after two. "Get your jackets, it's cold outside!"

Andrea caught Cassie's eye and nodded. Cassie returned the gesture. Cassie joined her class, her heart beating too fast as she tried to imagine what Andrea would do. What if Andrea couldn't make him stay? What if Cassie got in trouble for waiting in the hall?

She slowed down, bending over as if to tie her shoe. The line parted around her and continued out the door, heading to the playground for recess.

Behind her in the classroom, she could hear Andrea's cheerful chatter. Cassie straightened up and looked around. She was alone.

Barely had she thought that before Miles stepped out of the classroom, slipping his arms into his puffy jacket sleeves.

"Cassie," he said, spotting her loitering in the hallway.

"Oh, hi," she said, trying to play it cool. "I stopped to tie my shoe."

"Okay. Coming outside?"

"Yes." Her heart pounded away. This was the perfect moment. It was just the two of them, and she didn't know when she'd get another chance. Why was it so hard to ask?

Miles opened the door to the playground. "Brr," he said as a blast of cold air hit them.

"Want to go to a party Friday night?" Cassie blurted.

He paused, the door still wide open. "Um, what?"

She took a deep breath and slowed down. "My friend Betsy is having a Christmas party Friday night. She said I could ask someone to come with me. So, I just thought maybe you'd like to."

"Oh." Miles let go of the door. It closed with a whoosh, and he shoved his hands into his pockets. "That sounds like a lot of fun, but I can't."

"You . . . can't?" Cassie echoed.

"Yeah." He shrugged. "Have something else going on Friday. Sorry."

Her face flamed, and she nodded. She forced herself to smile and say, "Sure."

"Well." Miles opened the door again. "Have fun, though." He stepped outside.

She waited until he'd gone down the sidewalk, then

leaned her hot cheeks against the cold glass with a groan.

"What happened?"

She turned as Andrea came over, an expectant expression on her face. "Did you ask him?" she asked.

Cassie nodded. "Yes. And he said no." The humiliation hit her between the eyes now, and she buried her face in her hands.

Andrea reached over and rubbed her shoulder. "Oh, I'm so sorry! Was he mean?"

"No, of course not." Miles would never be mean. But that was part of what made it so confusing. "I just don't know why he said no."

"He didn't give a reason?"

"He said he has plans already or something."

"So, okay. Maybe he really wanted to go."

"Or maybe he didn't and that was just his excuse."

Andrea smiled, her eyes sympathetic. "There's really no way to tell."

~

Betsy was disappointed when Cassie told her she wasn't bringing a boy, but she cheered herself up by saying she'd just invite a few extras. Cassie tried to be excited by the idea of meeting other boys, but she wasn't even looking forward to the Christmas party anymore.

That changed Friday evening as Mrs. Jones pulled her into her bathroom to do her hair.

"You don't seem all that excited, Cassie," her mom said. "I thought you were really looking forward to this party."

Cassie shrugged and lowered her eyes. "Miles isn't going."

"Ah." Her mom tsked. "And these sorts of parties aren't nearly as much fun without the boy you like in attendance."

"Exactly," Cassie sighed.

Her mom swooped the long hair off Cassie's shoulders. She loosened a few pieces in the front, then wrapped the rest into a twist in the back. "Just because the boy you like won't be there doesn't mean you can't look pretty. We don't dress up for boys, you know. We do it for ourselves." She met Cassie's eyes in the mirror and smiled.

A spark of interest lit in Cassie's chest. "Does that mean I can wear make-up?"

Now her mom laughed. "You know your dad's rule on that. Not until you're sixteen."

Well, it had been worth a try. "Do I wear a dress?"

"Nah. Just your best jeans and a pretty sweater."

Her hair done up, Cassie went to her closet. She pulled out her prettiest black jeans, a pair she hadn't worn since last February. She'd gotten taller, she realized as she hitched them over her hips, but they weren't too short. The problem came when she tried to button them. She couldn't get the two sides together, no matter how much she tried. She sucked in her gut, held her breath, and pulled. She lay down on her back on the bed and wiggled, but she still couldn't button them. With one final effort, she took a deep breath, squinted, and forced the button into the hole.

There. She'd done it. Cassie stood up, breathing shallowly. The jeans pinched her skin. She pulled up her shirt and winced. The belly flesh wrinkled and puckered where she'd forced it into the waistline of the pants. "Ouch," she murmured. She walked to her closet, looking for a nice sweater to go with her pants. She found a red glittery one and slid it on, relieved when it wasn't tight. She hurried to the bathroom to check out her reflection.

The sweater looked nice, but . . . It bunched up oddly around her waist, making it look like she was hiding a halo under her shirt or something. Cassie lifted the sweater and frowned at her belly. The excess flesh created the ring around her body. And the tight jeans were starting to burn where they rubbed against her skin.

"I don't think I can wear these pants," she whispered. She had outgrown them. That was a good thing, right? She was a growing girl.

Cassie removed her black jeans, laying them on Emily's bed so her sister could have them. She didn't have anything quite as nice, but she chose a pair of blue jeans that at least she could button.

"I'm ready," she announced, coming out of her room. The rest of her family was just sitting down to dinner, but Betsy had assured Cassie there would be plenty of food at the party.

"I like your sweater," her mom said. "Don't you have any red earrings to wear with it?"

"Oh, sure." Cassie ran back to her room and grabbed them. "I think I need new clothes, Mom," she said as she forced one earring into her ear. "My pants were too small."

"Hmm," her mom said, her tone noncommittal.

"Well, let's go." Mr. Jones pushed back from the table.

Betsy lived even farther out than Cassie, heading toward the chicken farms that dotted the countryside of Springdale, Arkansas. Cassie always knew when they were close to one of the farms because the stench of the chickens reached all the way to the road. Even with the windows closed, there was no escaping it. Betsy's house was a small mobile home in front of a series of long chicken houses. The front door had blinking red and green lights on it.

"I guess we'll get used to the smell," her dad said, parking the car.

"Aren't you coming in?" Cassie asked, undoing her seatbelt.

"I changed my mind," he said, pulling out a paperback book from somewhere. "I'll just sit out here. But you come straight out if there's any trouble."

Cassie rolled her eyes. "There won't be any trouble."

"I believe you. That's why I'm staying here instead of coming inside."

"Thanks." Cassie waved and climbed out of the car.

It turned out Cassie was the first one to arrive. Betsy greeted her with an enthusiastic hug. She wore a pretty white dress with a pink pinafore and white Mary Jane's. Cassie suddenly wished she'd worn a dress. Betsy put Cassie to work setting up food and drinks. One table had a dry-ice machine going, so the living room floor was coated in a layer of smoky fog.

"Who all is coming?" Cassie asked.

"My boyfriend, of course. A few other people from my class."

"Anyone I know?"

The doorbell rang, and Betsy ran to answer it. "Hey!" she exclaimed, throwing her arms around the boy who stood there. "Come on in!" She clung to his hand and pulled him into the room, her face pink and excited. Cassie glanced down at their clutched hands with a pang of jealousy. She wished Miles had come. If only he showed some kind of interest in her.

Betsy stopped in front of her. "Chris, this is Cassie. She rides my bus. Cassie, this is Chris. He's my—" she giggled. "Boyfriend."

He looked so normal. Cassie had expected a boyfriend to seem older, more mature, more sophisticated. He waved a hand, his curly blond hair poking out in odd places against his head. "Hi."

"Hi," she replied.

The doorbell rang again, and Betsy released him to let someone else in.

"Would you like a drink?" Cassie said, remembering her role to help serve people.

Chris followed her to the drink table, and Cassie handed him a cup.

"What is this?" he asked, taking a sip.

"Some kind of punch." Cassie took a sip as well. She'd watched Betsy make it. "It's got orange juice, sprite, and pineapple juice."

"Wow. It's really good."

A few other kids joined them, and Cassie handed out punch to everyone. She recognized them, but no one she was really friends with. She wandered over to the food table and picked up a tiny hot dog wrapped in dough and baked. Chris followed her.

"So did you help Betsy set all this up?" he asked.

"No. I just got here first, so she asked for my help. Where is she, anyway?" She peered through the half a dozen kids, looking for Betsy.

"Over there." Chris pointed. Betsy stood next to her dad, handing him several CDs.

"Oh, looks like we're going to start the dancing part soon."

"Do you dance?"

"I don't know." Cassie shrugged. "I've never really tried it before."

252

"I'll dance with you."

Cassie finally turned to him, studying his features. His round face was open and inviting, his blue eyes clear. "Won't you be dancing with Betsy?"

He shrugged. "Sure. But not the whole time."

"Well, if it's okay with her."

The music started up, too loud at first. Everyone covered their ears while Betsy's dad turned it down. Upbeat, loud, and traditional Christmas music piped out of the speakers.

"Okay, everyone!" Betsy called, clapping her hands to get her guests' attention. "Time to dance!" Beaming, she stepped into the small living room and held a hand out to Chris. He stepped forward and took it. They started dancing. A few other kids joined them, but the rest, like Cassie, found a comfortable spot on the couch or next to the food table.

Cassie fought off a yawn. Watching other people dance was kind of boring. She wondered what time it was. Her dad was just outside in the car. Would Betsy really care if she left early?

Chris and Betsy finished dancing, and Betsy started mingling with her guests. Chris sat down in a chair next to Cassie.

"Need some more punch?" he asked her.

She checked her cup. "Maybe just a bit."

He got up and filled her cup, then brought it back to her with a cookie. "In case you're hungry."

"Thanks." She took it and nibbled at the edges. She'd already eaten half a dozen hot dog things.

"Want to dance now?"

"Did you ask Betsy?"

"She won't mind."

Cassie looked for her friend. Somehow she didn't think Betsy would be that okay with it. "Actually I'm only staying for a little while. My dad's here."

"Oh. But you're in Ms. Timber's class, right?"

"Yes."

"Then I'll look for you at school on Monday."

"Okay." Cassie stood up and made her way to Betsy. She tapped her on the shoulder, and Betsy swiveled toward her.

"Hi Cassie!" she exclaimed. "Have you danced yet? Are you having fun?"

Cassie smiled and nodded. "Yeah, it's been great. But my dad's here. Sorry I have to go early."

"Oh. But you had fun?"

"Of course." Cassie gave her a hug. "Thanks so much for inviting me."

Betsy hugged her back. "Thanks for coming! See you Monday!"

Cassie stepped out the front door and shivered in the night air. She spotted her dad's car and made her way across the yard to it.

"That was fast," he said when she climbed in. "Is everything okay?"

"Yep." Cassie handed him a cookie. "It was just rather boring."

CHAPTER THIRTY-FOUR

Dashing Starts

Cassandra tried to focus on the cheering coming from the sidelines as she chased the soccer ball down the field. But her side was cramping, and the hot sun beat down on her, and she really wanted a drink of water. . . .

Before she realized it, she was slowing down. She heard her dad's voice above the others, hollering at her to move again, but it was too late. The other team had the ball—passed the ball—and they scored. Cassie drew to a halt, dropping her hands to her knees and panting. She didn't meet any of her teammates' eyes as they moved past her toward the goalpost behind her. She knew she'd see disappointment in them.

Straightening up, she turned around and walked back as well. She hoped Coach would see how slowly she walked. Maybe he would sub her out.

"Cassie!" Coach Price shouted.

Sure enough. Cassie exhaled in relief and hurried to the sidelines, grateful for the chance to drink water and rest. She grabbed her water bottle and dumped the contents across her neck.

"You're not such a bad player," Landon, the coach's son, said. He also sat at the sidelines, waiting to sub back in. "But you don't run quick enough."

Cassie eyed him and guzzled her water. Easy for him to say. With short blond hair and long, long legs, one of Landon's strides carried him across the field twice as fast as Cassie's. "Yeah," she sighed, then turned around and watched the game. With any luck, Coach wouldn't play her for the rest of the day.

She lined up with everyone again when the game ended, trooping past the opposite team with her hand extended, batting their hands and muttering, "Good game, good game."

Her team lost, and she couldn't help wondering if it was her fault. Cassie had wanted to play soccer since last fall, but she'd only officially joined up with the team last month. After a few weeks of practices, the games had started. All of her expectations that she'd enjoy running more when there was a purpose were dashed the first time Coach played her on offense.

"What happened out there, Cassie?" her dad said as they walked back toward the van. "You kind of just stopped."

"It's too hot today," she said, and it kind of was. March weather in Arkansas yo-yoed back and forth from snowing to sweltering, and today was one of the hot ones. After two weeks of rain, the warmth took her breath away. Even now sweat dripped into her eyes, and she wished for an ice-cream cone. "Can we go to Braum's?"

"When your team wins we can go out for ice-cream. Not if you lose."

If you lose. Cassie scowled. He made it sound so personal. Maybe it was.

She turned the AC on full blast in the van, shooting the vent at her face. Soccer had sounded like so much fun in theory. In truth, she just wasn't very good at it.

~

By Monday, Cassie had mostly put the game behind her. The weekend heat diminished somewhat, leaving cooler, sweater-appropriate temperatures. Cassie took a deep breath as she stepped outside for recess. She closed her eyes, relishing the feel of the early spring sunshine on her skin. Although the air still carried a biting chill to it, the whisper of warmth from the overhead sun warmed her soul.

"Finally, some sun." Her best friend, Andrea, echoed the sentiment as she jogged next to Cassie. "I didn't think it would ever stop raining."

Cassie nodded. At least jogging was more tolerable in the cold. This year, the PE teacher had devised the plan to make every student run two laps every day. Nine months into the school year, and Cassie despised running more than she ever had.

"You know what's my favorite thing about March?" she asked, shooting a sly grin at Andrea.

"What?" Andrea asked.

"My birthday."

"Oh!" Andrea's eyes went wide. Last year, when Cassie turned eleven, all of the friends she'd invited to her birthday party ended up not being able to come. Andrea and another girl, Betsy, had come at the last minute, saving Cassie's party.

Andrea grinned. "Do I get a real invitation this time?"

"You get an invitation to every party I have for the rest of my life," Cassie said.

"Yes!" Andrea said, pumping her fist. "Who else will you invite?"

"This is a special year," Cassie said. "I get to have a real party. With boys."

"Oo, wow," Andrea said.

That might not seem like a big deal to other kids, but Cassie's parents had only let her have one or two friends over for as long as she could remember. Twelve meant she crossed the bridge from childhood into adolescence, however. To celebrate, she got to have twelve friends over, in any combination of boys and girls she wanted.

"I'm inviting you, of course. You can spend the night. No one else is invited to do that."

"I won't miss it."

"And maybe Andrew. He's funny."

"Yeah," Andrea agreed.

"Betsy and Emmett, for sure. Maybe Riley."

"You still talk to Riley?" Andrea asked.

"I see her every Tuesday at Girls Club. We talk." Not like they used to, though. They'd had a bit of a falling out, though they still tried to be friendly with each other.

"Okay, so that's five people," Andrea said. "What about Miles?"

Cassie pressed her lips together, her face warming. "Last time I asked Miles to something, he said no."

"Because he had other plans, Cassie. He's one of your best friends."

He was a lot more than a friend, but Miles didn't seem to know it. "I don't think I could take it if he said no again."

Andrea elbowed her as they neared the end of their second lap. "You've got to at least ask. He might get his feelings hurt if you don't."

Cassie considered that and nodded. "Yeah, okay. I can ask."

~

"If you're staying after school to help with the service project, make sure I have your permission slip," Ms. Timber, Cassie's sixth grade teacher, said. Last week, students had brought in shoes and jackets for the children's shelter. Today, those who could stay would be organizing them into age groups.

Cassie took out her permission slip and walked it to the front of the classroom, placing it on the desk with the other permission slips.

When the bell rang for school to get out, only a small handful of students gathered their backpacks and left. Cassie watched them go with sympathy, glad that she was among the students staying behind to help.

"Those of you staying," Ms. Timber said, "we need to move these desks into groups. Let's make four groups of five."

Cassie hopped up and began pulling on her desk, grunting as it scraped across the linoleum. She tried pushing it, but instead it almost tipped over.

"I can help," Miles said, coming to the side of her desk.

Cassie had known he'd come. Whenever she needed something, Miles seemed to know it. He always appeared, ready to help her or make her feel better. "Thank you," she said, watching him out of the corner of her eye as they pulled the desk into a bigger group. Like Cassie, Miles wore glasses, only his were wire frames while Cassie had huge pink frames. His eyes were a lighter brown than Cassie's, which were nearly black, and he wore his brown hair shorter, sometimes combed down and other times spiked up. He was, in Cassie's opinion, so cute. But even more than that, he was so nice.

"There we go," he said, sliding her desk into position.

Cassie stepped back to see if anyone else needed help, but the other students had also finished.

"Okay," Ms. Timber said. "For once, I'm not going to tell you where to sit. This table will be the sorting table." She put a hand on a collection of desks. "Here all the donated goods will be placed. The other three groups will represent ages. Babies, kids, and teenagers."

Cassie listened to the rest of the instructions and decided the sorting table would be the most fun.

Miles leaned toward her. "Which table are you going to work at?" he whispered.

Cassie whispered back, "I was thinking the sorting table. It would be fun to see everything."

"Yeah. That's where I'm going."

Ms. Timber finished explaining, and Andrea grabbed Cassie's hand.

"Come on," she said.

Cassie resisted as Andrea pulled her forward. "Where are we going?"

"The baby table. I want to make the little piles of baby shoes and baby clothes," she cooed. "Babies are just so darling!"

Cassie didn't have any certain affinity to babies. What was more, she already knew Miles would be at the sorting table. "Don't you think it would be more fun to sort through everything?"

"No way!"

Cassie cast another glance toward the sorting table, where Miles had already found a chair and sat down.

Andrea was still tugging, and Cassie reluctantly gave in. She shouldn't choose Miles over her best friend. Even if it was tempting.

Even as she watched, Esther Vanguard, Cassie's nemesis, pulled her chair up to the sorting table. She sidled in right next to Miles, peeping at him from under her lashes and giving a smile.

Cassie rolled her eyes and sat down with Andrea. Good thing she hadn't sat with Miles. She couldn't bear to be next to Esther for more than a few seconds at a time.

They spent the next hour folding little baby clothes and putting them together into bundles with shoes. The time passed quickly, and then Ms. Timber said, "All right, it's time to wrap things up. Thanks for staying and helping! It made this event go so much faster!"

Cassie glanced at the clock. She still had another twenty minutes before her mother would be here, based on the time she'd expected the activity to end. The other kids gathered their backpacks and filed out, but Miles stayed back, moving the chairs and desks to their original positions.

"Coming?" Andrea asked her, removing her backpack from the cubbies.

"I think I'll stay." Cassie inclined her head toward Miles meaningfully. "Help clean up for a bit."

Andrea broke into a face-splitting grin. "Sure. See you tomorrow."

Ms. Timber glanced around the room. "I'll be next door talking to Ms. Roxi for a moment. Don't burn anything down." She walked out, her heels clipping neatly against the floor.

Cassie joined Miles at the desk he tugged on. "Need

help?"

"If it's you helping," he responded. He gave a weak pull. "Oh, this desk is so heavy!"

"You need some real muscles behind it." Cassie pushed from her side, nearly toppling it and spilling the contents.

"Whoa, now!" Miles threw both hands in the air and jumped backward. "You gotta warn me before you throw your whole body into it! Sheesh!"

Cassie couldn't help laughing. "I've got some man-power."

"You got some she-power." A piece of paper jostled out of the desk, and Miles picked it up, flicking it at her. "Take that, she-power."

"Oh, oh." Cassie unwrapped the wad of paper. "Let me see if I can make a paper airplane."

"Oh, yes, your skills are legendary." He put on a thick accent and leaned closer, watching as she smoothed the paper. "Go on. Let's see the masterpiece."

Cassie bit her lip, giggling. "I've improved so much since the last time you saw this." Which was a complete lie, and he had to know it. She folded the paper in half and paused.

"Yes, yes," he said, still in the accent. "That's good. Now what?"

Hesitantly, Cassie folded one side over to make a wing.

"Oh," he said, his voice dramatically sad.

"What? Is that wrong?" Cassie unfolded it.

"No, keep going. I want to see you try and fly that." Now he grinned at her, his eyes gleaming with mischief.

Cassie threw her folded paper at him, and it fluttered to the ground two inches in front of her.

"Good job," he said, laughter in his voice as he struggled to maintain his fake accent. "You almost hit me. And I'm right in front of you."

"Shut up!" Cassie laughed, whacking him on the arm.

"Ah, ah, she-power strikes again!" Miles howled, hopping away while clutching his arm.

Something moved in the corner of Cassie's eye, and she turned her head. She nearly gasped in fright when she realized someone was watching them, but she caught herself before she did. It was only Esther.

Not that that was a good thing. And judging from the angry glare on Esther's face, she didn't like what she saw.

Miles noticed her too. He stopped hopping around, the grin fading from his face. "Oh, hi, Esther," he said. "I didn't know you were still here."

"I was getting my backpack from the cubbies." Esther turned her attention to Cassie. "You can go. I'll help Miles finish cleaning up."

Cassie had been about to go, actually. Her mom was probably here now. But Esther's commanding dismissal of her rubbed her totally wrong. "I've got it under control here, Esther. Miles and I are almost done."

Esther sneered. "Doesn't look like you've accomplished much of anything."

Miles glanced at the clock. "Actually, I should go. I bet my mom's waiting." Without meeting the eyes of either girl, he grabbed his backpack and walked out.

Cassie went around the cubbies to get her own bag. She had to step past Esther, who blocked the way as if she meant to prevent Cassie from passing. But she didn't stop her.

"I guess I'll go now, too," Cassie said. "You can finish up if you want."

"Yeah, now that Miles is gone, you're leaving too," Esther snapped, her eyes flashing angrily.

Cassie shrugged. "He's my friend."

"You *like* him!" Esther exclaimed. "And your flirting is ridiculous! Everyone can see how much you like him, including Miles. And if he were interested, he would have done something by now. Stop embarrassing yourself and leave him alone. He doesn't like you."

The words hit Cassie hard. They echoed some of her innermost thoughts, the fears she never dared voice.

Cassie turned around and strode from the classroom, but shame burned her face and brought tears to her eyes. Esther was right. If Miles liked her, he would have made it known.

CHAPTER THIRTY-FIVE
RSVP

Mrs. Jones liked to be official. She stayed up with Cassie on Monday night and helped her design invitations for her birthday party.

"Who are you inviting?" she asked.

"Andrew, Emmett, Miles, Riley, Andrea, Betsy, Chris, and Maureen," Cassie said, ticking off the names on her fingers.

"I told you you could have twelve people, right?"

"Yes." Cassie nodded. "But I'm not that close to a lot of people. I'd rather just have my good friends."

"Well, all right." Mrs. Jones hit "print" on the computer, and the invitations began spewing out. "Don't forget to hand these out tomorrow."

"I won't."

In school the next morning, Cassie handed out the invitations to Andrew, Emmett, Andrea, Betsy, and Maureen. She gave Chris's invitation to Betsy, since they were in the same class. She held onto Riley's until Girls Club. And Miles'—Cassie hesitated with his invitation, holding the envelope close to her chest. She stood by the backpack cubby and peeked around the corner, watching him get settled into his desk. He'd already walked past her and said good morning, but Esther's words kept ringing through her head: "If he were interested, he would have done something. Everyone knows you like him. He doesn't like you."

Now he was laughing with Michael, drawing funny faces on Michael's paper. Cassie couldn't do it. She couldn't bring herself to walk up to him and hand him the invitation. Instead, she ducked into the cubbies and put the invitation in his backpack. She'd ask him tomorrow what he thought.

~

Every Tuesday Cassie had Girls Club, an after-school club aimed at helping girls learn social, life, and preparedness skills. Though she didn't really hang out with any of the girls during school, she considered all of them her friends.

The club leader, Margaret, fairly burst with excitement as she showed the girls their activity today: cross-stitching. Cassie had done it before, but with yarn on a plastic loom. This time, there was no loom, just a piece of fabric with lots of tiny holes in it.

"You girls will love this," Margaret said. "It's therapeutic. I've got all the colors you could possibly need." She opened up a plastic holder and displayed row after row of colors.

"Wow," the girls said, admiring the string.

"I'll show you how to thread your needles and make the stitch. In the meantime, I brought several patterns. So we'll have two stations. Four of you go pick your patterns. The other four, come here and I'll show you how to get started."

Cassie sat down next to Maureen and Leigh Ann at the pattern table.

"What do you think of this one?" Maureen asked, holding up a complex flower.

"Pretty," Cassie said.

"But it looks hard, right?"

Cassie shrugged. They all looked hard.

Riley joined their group, focusing off in the distance with a nonchalant attitude.

"Hi, Riley," Cassie greeted, breaking the constant ice barrier between them.

"Oh, hi," Riley said, turning and looking at her as if she'd just noticed her.

Cassie gestured at the patterns. "Go ahead."

Maureen and Leigh Ann moved to the other station, their patterns picked. For a moment, it was just Riley and Cassie.

"So," Cassie said, "I'm having a birthday party this Friday. You're invited."

Riley's eyes widened briefly. "Really? After—" She cut herself off.

After last year. Cassie gave a tight smile, knowing that's what Riley meant. Last year Riley had ditched Cassie's birthday party for another girl's party—without even telling her. The betrayal still stung. "You're not the only one invited this year. If you can't make it, that's fine. Just let me know."

Riley looked down, her short blond hair falling around her face. "I'm sorry about that," she said in a small voice.

The apology surprised Cassie, mostly because it was a year after the fact and Riley had always pretended like nothing happened. Cassie shrugged it off. "It's okay. Thanks to you, I got to be better friends with Andrea."

"I'll see if I can come." Riley still didn't lift her face.

"Sure. Just let me know. I have your invitation in my backpack." Cassie picked a pattern and moved to the other station. She'd invited Riley, and she felt good about that. But if she didn't come, Cassie knew it wouldn't bother her.

~

"I need to know how many people are coming to your party," Mrs. Jones said to Cassie at dinner. She sniffed, then took a sip of water. "Did you hand out all the invitations?"

Cassie nodded. "Yes. And I already know for sure Andrea's coming. She'll stay the night Friday."

"Can I have a friend spend the night?" Cassie's younger sister Emily asked.

Of course the other two children had to pipe up after that.

"And me!" Annette said.

"No," Mrs. Jones said with a shake of her head. "This is Cassie's birthday. Her twelfth birthday." She bestowed a proud smile on Cassie.

"What's so special about twelve?" Scott asked, looking more annoyed that curious.

"This is the age where Cassie crosses the threshold from child to adult," Mrs. Jones said. "She'll join the youth group at church and start going to the weekly meetings."

"Wow," Cassie said. She hadn't really thought about the youth group. "What night is that?"

"Wednesday."

"So I'll have Girls Club on Tuesday, voice lessons on Wednesday, and youth group after that?"

Mrs. Jones rubbed her temples. "Yes."

"Be grateful to your mother," Mr. Jones said. "She sacrifices a lot of her time for you kids."

"So Cassie will be an adult now?" Annette asked.

"Not quite," Mrs. Jones chuckled.

"But practically," Cassie added.

"Well, the first task you need to do in your budding adulthood is find out how many people are coming to your party. Did you decide on a cake theme?"

"Yes." Cassie hesitated, afraid of hurting her mom's feelings. "Can I just have a plain cake with icing that says 'Happy Birthday Cassie'?"

Her mom furrowed her brow in confusion, and then her expression cleared. "You don't want me to decorate one for you all fancy?"

Cassie shook her head. "Not this year." She just felt too old for a silly designed cake like that.

Mrs. Jones smiled, but Cassie thought she detected a hint of sadness on her face. "Sure, Cassie. If that's what you want."

~

Cassie tracked down her friends one by one Wednesday morning to see who was coming to her party. Betsy was easy, since they rode the bus together.

"I'll definitely be there," Betsy said. "Is it a slumber party?"

Cassie shook her head. "Not this year." She didn't mention that Andrea was spending the night.

"Cool. Wouldn't miss it!"

"And Chris?"

"I'll ask him and let you know after school. I think he's planning on it."

Cassie found Riley on the sidewalk as they walked toward the school.

"So?" Cassie said, joining her. "Are you coming to my party?"

"My mom said I could, so I think so. Do I need to bring my sleeping bag?"

"No. It's not that kind of party."

"Oh." Riley looked disappointed, but she nodded. "Okay. I should be there."

Two down. In class, Cassie got yeses from Maureen, Michael, and Andrew. Emmett couldn't make it. Now she had to get up the nerve to ask Miles.

She stopped by his desk after turning in her homework. "Hey, Miles."

He glanced up at her, and then returned to the sketch he was making. "Hey, Cassie."

Cassie shot furtive looks around, then leaned closer. "Are you coming to my party?"

He lifted his eyes again, this time giving her his full attention. "Party?"

Cassie's heart sank. He hadn't seen the invitation! She should have just handed it to him. "Yes. I put an invitation in your backpack. For this Friday?"

"Oh." Miles blinked, both eyebrows raising. "I didn't know. I'll check with my mom and tell you tomorrow."

"Sure." Cassie worked hard to keep the smile on her face as she went back to her desk, but she had the sneaking suspicion that Miles wouldn't be able to come.

Cassie was almost back to her desk when she saw a familiar green book cover. She paused to get a better look at the book in Esther's hands, recognizing it as one from a horror series she also enjoyed.

"Oh, I have that book!" she said. "And the ones after it. Which one's your favorite?"

Esther lifted her eyes from the book with obvious effort. "I haven't read all of them."

"But you like them, right?"

"Yes." Esther lowered her eyes.

"Do you have the others?" Cassie pressed on.

"No."

"Do you want to borrow mine?"

Esther heaved a sigh. "If I need the next books, I'll buy them myself. All right?"

Cassie's excitement diminished as she remembered who she was talking to. "Right. Of course."

CHAPTER THIRTY-SIX

Viral Attack

Chris and Emmet were both a no's, but everyone else had been a yes.

"What did Miles say?" Andrea asked at recess. The two girls took advantage of the sunshine to sit on the sidewalk and pick flowers. Cassie especially liked the little yellow ones.

"He didn't see my invitation yesterday," she said with a sigh. "He has to ask his mom."

"That's all right. I'm so excited. What are we going to do?"

"Well, we got a pinata. So we'll probably do that first. Then eat, and cake and ice-cream, of course."

"Nice. And then?"

"Presents!"

Cassie and Andrea both giggled.

"Once everyone leaves, we'll put on a movie," Cassie continued. "Sleep out in the living room, like last year."

"Wait," a voice said behind them, interrupting. "She's spending the night?"

Both girls looked over their shoulder to see Riley

standing on the sidewalk.

"Were you just standing there listening to us?" Andrea said.

Riley's face reddened. "I was coming over to say something. Then I heard you. So is she spending the night?"

"Yes," Cassie said, defeated.

Riley huffed, her chest puffing out. "I thought you said this wasn't a slumber party!"

"I only get to have one friend spend the night," Cassie said, resenting that she needed to explain this. "What were you going to say?"

"It was about your party," Riley said. "But it doesn't matter now."

"Why is that?" Cassie asked, though she already had a sneaking suspicion.

"Because I'm not going!" Riley turned and stomped away.

Cassie looked at Andrea, who tried to look serious, then burst into giggles. She buried her head in her arms and mimicked, "Because I'm not going!"

Cassie had to smile too. For a moment, Riley had made her feel guilty for not asking her to spend the night. Now, Cassie just felt grateful for Andrea.

~

Miles didn't say anything about the party on Thursday, and Cassie didn't want to ask. Finally on Friday, she broke down. She had to know.

She trailed him after lunch, staying close enough to him that she could snag him before he went into the classroom.

"Miles," she said, clutching at his sleeve. She let go as soon as he turned to her.

"Yeah?" he said, looking at her expectantly.

Didn't he remember? Her fingers lace and unlaced. "I was just wondering about my party. If you can come."

"Oh, I forgot to tell you." He faced her now. "My mom says we have some church thing to go to. I'm sorry I can't make it."

"Sure." Cassie nodded, her shoulders sagging. Once again, he turned her down. "It's no problem."

Andrea was watching her when she came into the classroom. Cassie shook her head and sat at her desk. Andrea winced and mouthed, "Sorry."

Cassie tried to let the disappointment go and focus on her upcoming party. When the bell rang to let school out, Maureen called, "I'll see you at your party, Cassie!"

"Yes!" she said, brightening.

"Me too," Andrew said with a wave.

"Cassie, I'm sorry I can't come," Miles said, grabbing his backpack and hesitating next to her. "It does sound like fun."

"I'm sure you'd come if you could," Cassie said sweetly.

He nodded, his expression downtrodden. He seemed genuinely sad, and it warmed her heart.

"Well, I'll see you Monday," she said.

Andrea met her at the door and took Cassie's hands. "I'll be over in an hour," she said. "Just as soon as I get home and get my stuff together."

Cassie squeezed her hands. "I'll be watching for you."

~

Cassie was immediately greeted by the delicious aroma of baked cake when she stepped through the front door. "We're home!" she called.

There was no response from the kitchen, so she ran

downstairs to see if her mom was in the sewing room. No one there, either. "Mom!" she called. She ran back up the stairs, taking them two at a time. "Mom!"

Emily appeared in the hallway. "She's in her room."

"Okay." Cassie went down the hall and stepped into her mom's room. "Mom! I'm home!"

She stopped short when she saw her mother lying in a ball on the bed, the blankets bundled up over her body. "Mom?" Cassie said, approaching carefully.

Her mom rolled over, her hair tangled and disheveled, dark shadows under her eyes. "Hi, honey," she whispered. "I baked your cake."

Cassie stared down at her mom and felt her throat tighten. "You're sick."

"I'm so sorry," her mom responded, holding out a hand.

Cassie took it, feeling how cold and weak it was. She couldn't be angry at her mom for being sick. But this was her birthday. How was she supposed to do it alone?

"Your dad will be home soon," her mom continued. "He'll help you with whatever you need."

Cassie nodded, withdrawing her hand. She swallowed past the lump in her throat. "Thanks for making my cake." She tried hard to keep the resentment out of her voice. "I'll see what I can do to help."

Cassie tried to keep calm as she closed the door to her mom's room. She hurried to the kitchen, checking the clock anxiously. Andrea would be here soon. People would arrive. She picked up the phone and called her dad.

"Hello!" he said cheerfully.

"Daddy," Cassie said, her voice catching. "When will you be home? Mom's sick. I need help getting ready for the party."

"I'm on my way home, Cass," he said, his tone becoming more serious. "Did she bake the cake?"

Cassie's eyes darted around the kitchen. She spotted the oblong shape, un-iced, on the stove top. "Yes, but it doesn't have icing yet."

"I'll bring some home. You make sure the house is clean. Get all the toys into the bedrooms and vacuum the living room. Then sweep the kitchen floor and put away everything on the counter."

"Okay," Cassie said, breathing out a sigh of relief. Having orders helped.

Cassie had just put the broom away in the laundry room when the doorbell rang. Her heart immediately jumped into her throat, and all the nerves she'd managed to calm down moments ago flared into excitement. Where was her dad? She rushed to the door, relieved to see the outline of Andrea's red-gold hair.

"Andrea," she said, grabbing her friend up in a hug.

Andrea turned around and waved goodbye to her mother, then faced Cassie. "What's wrong? You seem nervous."

Cassie pulled Andrea into the house. "My mom's sick. Northing's ready for the party. I cleaned the house but we don't have anything decorated, nothing's set up."

"That's okay." Andrea went down the hall to Cassie's room and dumped her duffel bag. "What do we need to do? I'll help."

"Of course you will." Cassie could already feel herself relaxing. "We need to blow up the balloons and set up the pinata. Then set the table. My dad is bringing the food."

"Oh, easy." Andrea waved a hand. "Let's start on those balloons. Where's your sister? She can help us."

"I'll find her." Cassie found the balloons and candy in the pantry. She put the plastic bag on the couch, then ran down the stairs. "Emily!"

Emily had the TV on and was watching a show with the younger kids. "What?" she said without turning away from the screen.

"I need your help. Can you come blow up balloons with me?"

Now Emily looked up. "You need help? Yeah!"

"Come on." Cassie beckoned, and Emily followed her up the stairs.

"Hey," Andrea greeted from the dining room. She already had a pile of three balloons rolling around her feet. She handed the bag of colored latex to Cassie.

"What's that noise?" Emily asked.

"What noise?" Cassie said, and then she heard it too. A rustling sound came from the living room, like someone shaking a plastic bag or crumpling tissue paper. "Scott?" she called. "Annette?" No one answered, so Cassie put down the balloons and went to the living room to investigate. "Pioneer!" she exclaimed when she saw the family dog. He had his nose in the bag of candy, one paw scratching at the opening. Half-eaten candies and torn wrappers littered the ground around him.

"No!" she groaned, wrestling the bag away from him. "This is for the pinata!"

Not anymore. While the dog had only actually eating maybe a quarter of the candy, he'd managed to mangle and drool on almost all of it. Cassie swallowed hard. This party was going downhill fast.

"What is it?" Andrea asked, coming out of the dining room. She tied up the balloon she'd blown up and let it fall to the floor.

Cassie sighed and waved at the candy bag. "The dog ate the candy." She looked down at Pioneer, who lowered his head shamefully.

"Well . . ." Even Andrea looked exasperated. Then she shrugged. "Emily can blow up the balloons. Let's clean this up."

"Yeah," Cassie said. She knelt down and began picking up the slobbery, wet pieces of candy.

"Is your dog okay?" Andrea asked.

"He's fine." Cassie put the trash pieces in the grocery bag. "He just gets into everything."

"No, I mean—have you looked at him?"

"What? Why?" Cassie finally turned her eyes toward Pioneer. The dog lay on his side, his legs trembling and his head bobbing with tiny convulsions. Soft whimpering noises escaped his clamped jaw.

"Oh no." Cassie dropped the bag and huddled next to him. "He's having a seizure."

"What do we do?" Andrea's eyes went wide.

"Emily!" Cassie called. "Get me a towel!"

"What is it?" Emily came into the room and saw the commotion. "I'll get Mom!"

"No, Mom's sick!" Cassie shushed the dog and rubbed behind his ears, trying to keep him calm. "Just get me a towel!" Drool collected around his mouth, and Cassie kept one hand out, waiting expectantly for the towel. As soon as Emily dropped it into her hand, she sopped up the slobbery mess.

"How often does he do this?" Andrea asked.

"Not often," Cassie said. But often enough. She knew the drill.

"How long does the seizure last?"

"Only a minute or two."

"And then what?"

As if on cue, Pioneer hunched his back, made a retching sound in the back of his throat, and vomited all over the towel in Cassie's lap. She took a deep breath and tried not to breathe through her nose.

"That," she said, head lifted.

"He throws up?"

"Every time." Cassie folded the towel carefully. Pioneer pushed to his feet, still a bit shaky, but he managed to walk himself over to a corner of the room. Then he sat down and put his head on his paws.

Cassie carried the soiled towel to the laundry room, where she dumped it in the sink. "It's how we know he's done," she said to Andrea, who had followed.

Andrea looked a little green. "That's pretty sick."

"Yeah." Cassie sighed, exhausted now. "Maybe we should just cancel the party and watch a movie."

Despite using the towel to catch most of the vomit, Cassie's clothes stank. She hurried to her room to change just as another car pulled up outside. By the time she got a clean shirt on and hurried out, the doorbell was ringing, and another car had driven into the circle driveway.

"Hi!" Emily said cheerfully, playing hostess to the arriving guests. "Come on in. We're putting presents over here."

Cassie surveyed the living room. It was clean, at least, with no sign of vomit, and hardly any stench. And also no sign of an impending party, other than the three balloons rolling around by the couch. She turned to Andrea. "Go put on a movie downstairs and I'll shepherd everyone your direction."

"Which movie?"

"Anything that looks fun. Hi!" She joined Emily in the entry way, accepting gifts, giving hugs, and wondering where on earth her father was. "Just go on downstairs! We're going to watch a movie before we eat!"

"At least people are coming on time," Emily commented after the third person headed downstairs.

"Better than last year," Cassie said with a wan smile.

"Yeah," Emily agreed, and they both laughed.

More car tires rolled over the gravel outside, and Cassie straightened up. "Someone else."

The door opened, and Mr. Jones walked in.

"Daddy!" Cassie exclaimed, throwing her arms around him. "You made it!"

"I did. Did you keep it under control?" He handed her a grocery sack and carried several pizza boxes into the kitchen.

Cassie checked the bag and saw a can of icing. Then she looked at Emily and winked. "Yep. We had it all under control."

CHAPTER THIRTY-SEVEN
Book Mania

Esther Vanguard wasn't in school on Monday.

She wasn't there again on Tuesday or Wednesday.

Normally, Cassie didn't pay much attention to Esther. But after three days of absences, Cassie began to worry. She was the sixth grade ambassador, and if a student got sick or needed something, Cassie was supposed to help.

So when Ms. Timber called Cassie up to her desk Wednesday afternoon, Cassie had a suspicion of what it was about.

"Yes, Ms. Timber?" she said, pushing her pink glasses up on her nose. She clutched her hands in front of her and tried to look confident.

"You've probably noticed Esther's been sick for a few days," Ms. Timber said.

Cassie blinked. "Um, yes." Then she held her breath. What would she be expected to do?

"Esther has pneumonia. She might be out for quite some time."

Pneumonia. She had heard of the disease. From what she remembered, it could be very dangerous. "Is she all right?"

"She was in the hospital for a few days, but she's home now." Ms. Timber smiled at her. "I need you to collect Esther's assignments and take them to the office after school. Her mom will pick them up."

"Oh." Cassie smiled back and felt her shoulders relax. That wasn't so bad. "Sure. I can do that."

"You'll need to take two sets of notes, one for you and one for Esther."

Again Cassie nodded. "Okay."

"And I need you to call Esther every day and see how she's feeling."

A rock dropped into the pit of Cassie's stomach. "Call her?" She didn't even call Andrea every day.

"Yes. Just a quick phone call. Make sure she understood the assignment, see if she needs help, and ask her how she feels."

Now Cassie had to work hard to keep the smile on her face. She didn't think it would go over well if she told Ms. Timber they weren't actually friends.

"Can you do that?" Ms. Timber asked, focusing squarely on Cassie now.

"Of course." Cassie forced her head to nod. "Yeah. Not a problem."

After recess, Ms. Timber had Andrew pass out a colorful flier to everyone.

"The book fair will be here on Friday," she said. "This is a great chance for you to stock up on new books. Every purchase will donate a little bit of money to the school, so it's beneficial for everyone."

"Thank you," Cassie murmured when Andrew handed her the flier.

At her desk across from Cassie, Maureen asked, "What

books are you going to get, Cassie?" Maureen already had her pen out and was circling the ones she liked.

Cassie stared down at the images, trying to concentrate. There had to be a dozen books here she wanted, but all she could think about was having to call Esther later. "I don't know. I'm sure I'll pick a few."

Ms. Timber let her leave the classroom early so she could walk Esther's assignments to the office before it was time to board the buses. Cassie wrote out detailed instructions with the homework packet, hoping it would make her phone call with Esther that much shorter.

The bus bell rang right after Cassie left the office, and she tightened her backpack strap. Delivering Esther's homework had been the easy part. Cassie's heart rate quickened at the very thought of what came next: calling her.

"Hey, Cassie!"

She turned around at the male voice calling her name, for a split second hoping it was Miles. But no, she chided herself, Miles was a car rider. He lived close to the school.

Instead she saw Will Harris, a boy from another class who she knew but not that well. "Hi, Will," she said.

He caught up with her, his shaggy, dark hair falling in his face. "You left class early."

"Yeah. I had to deliver something to the office."

"Oh. Which bus is yours?" He joined Cassie, walking in step with her.

"The first one." She nodded to the first bus waiting against the curb. "Yours?"

"The last one." He pointed to the very back. "I always wanted to walk with you, but you're usually gone so quickly after class. Lucky I saw you today."

She wasn't sure what to say to that. "Yeah. Lucky."

"Want me to carry your backpack?"

"To the bus?" Another two steps and they'd have to part directions. Besides, Cassie's bus was right here.

"Oh, I guess that's kind of silly, huh. You don't have far to go."

"Yeah." Cassie shot him a sideways look. He was acting strangely. "Well, I'll see you tomorrow."

"Bye." He waved and jogged toward his bus.

As soon as Cassie got inside the house, she sat down on the stool and stared at the telephone. "Just do it," she told herself.

"What are you doing?" Emily asked.

"I have to call a girl from school," Cassie said.

"So?"

Cassie shrugged, not feeling like explaining. She picked up the phone, checked the number on the assignment sheet, and dialed.

The phone rang twice before a woman answered. "Hello?" the mature, female voice asked.

"Oh, hi," Cassie said, trying to sound sure of herself. "Is Esther there? This is Cassie from school."

"Sure." The woman sounded pleasant enough. "Hold on one minute."

A moment later, Esther's voice, sounding lower and groggier than usual, said, "Hello?"

"Hi, Esther, it's Cassie." She waited, heart pounding hard, for Esther's response.

"Hi," Esther said.

So far, so good. "I just wanted to make sure you got your homework. And that you know how to do it."

There was a pause, and then Esther said, her voice

slightly distanced, "Mom, did you pick up my homework?"

Cassie couldn't make out the response, but then Esther said into the mouthpiece, "Yeah, I got it."

"If you need help, you can call me," Cassie said as politely as possible.

"Okay," Esther said.

"I hope you feel better."

"Okay."

Cassie hung up. "Oh!" she cried, grabbing the phone again. "I forgot to say bye." Too late. She pressed it to her ear, but all she heard was the dial tone. Oh, well. It hadn't gone as bad as she feared.

~

"Is your homework done, Cassandra?" Mr. Jones asked at dinner.

Cassie put a pile of rice on her plate, then added another spoonful. She was about to add a third when her mother cleared her throat.

"Other people might want some rice, also, Cassie."

"Right." Cassie passed the rice to her sister, then answered her dad. "Almost done. I just have one more page of math. I'll get it done before bed."

"You need to get it done before we leave for voice lessons. And we have church after that."

She paused with a forkful of food almost to her mouth. "Church?" she echoed.

"Since when do we go to church on Wednesdays?" Emily asked, mirroring Cassie's confusion.

"Not you," Mr. Jones said, "only Cassie. She turned twelve last week. Now she gets to go to the youth group."

Cassie let out a little gasp of surprise. She'd completely

forgotten.

Emily exclaimed, "That's not fair!"

"Of course it is," Mrs. Jones said. "When you turn twelve, you'll get to also."

"I don't know why you'd want to," Scott grumbled. "Going to church on Sundays is boring enough."

"What do I need to bring?" Cassie asked, pushing away from the table. "Should I change my clothes?" She glanced down at her t-shirt and jeans.

"You can finish your food, first of all," her dad said. "And your clothes are fine. But you do need to finish your homework first."

CHAPTER THIRTY-EIGHT

Boys and Basketballs

"Hi, Ms. Malcolm," Cassie said, depositing her songbook bag by the foot of the piano. She positioned herself in front of the mirror, feet the proper distance apart, and put her hands at her side. She shifted her weight, impatient to start the warm-up.

"You seem energetic today," Ms. Malcolm said, the bright red lipstick around her mouth catching Cassie's eyes. "Having a good day?"

"I get to go to youth group tonight," Cassie said. "Since I turned twelve last week."

"Oh, how exciting. That reminds me." Ms. Malcolm turned to her bookshelf and thumbed through it, then pulled off a short paperback. "I have this book for you."

"Really?" Cassie said, eyes widening as she accepted the gift. *The Phantom of the Opera.* "Thank you, Ms. Malcolm! I never knew this was a book too!"

"And someday I'm sure you'll learn the songs," Ms. Malcolm said, smiling at Cassie's reflection in the mirror. "Now, get your mouth shaped right."

Cassie put the book away and focused on the warm-up.

When she'd first met Ms. Malcolm, the woman had frightened her. Now, just a few short months later, she knew that although her voice teacher was strict, rigid, and extremely professional, she was also a kind woman with a thoughtful heart. And when it came to music, she was the best teacher.

~

As soon as lessons were over, Cassie's dad drove her to church, and she fidgeted excitedly. While she realized these were the same kids she saw every Sunday, she wondered if they'd treat her differently. She was twelve now, after all. That meant she wasn't a kid anymore.

Mr. Jones parked the small green car at the same time as the Reeves' giant white van pulled into a parking spot. The Reeves boys, Jason and Tyler, quickly climbed out, a basketball under Jason's arm.

"There's Tyler!" Cassie squealed, pitching forward in her seat. Tyler went to a different school but was in sixth grade also.

Mr. Jones rolled the window down. "Hey, boys," he called.

"Hey, Mr. Jones!" They called back, then came over to the car.

"You know my daughter Cassie, right?"

Both of them peered in at her, two pairs of blue-eyes with short brown hair.

"Yeah," Jason, the older one said. "We know her."

Cassie warmed under his gaze. She ducked her head.

"Tonight's her first night. Make sure she finds her way around, okay?"

"Sure," Jason said, switching the basketball to the other arm. "We'll take her to the girls' side."

The girls' side? Something inside Cassie wilted in disappointment. She'd hoped to hang out with the boys.

They started down the hallway inside the building. "When did you turn twelve?" Cassie asked Tyler, who hadn't said a word to her yet.

"A few months ago," he replied. He stopped at the doors to the gym. "I'll be in here, Jason."

"See ya." Jason saluted, then led Cassie to a classroom. "The girls meet in here."

"Thanks," Cassie said. She pushed the door open and went inside.

"You must be the girl who just turned twelve," a woman greeted her. "I'm Cindy."

"I'm Cassie." She glanced around at the other girls. They sat in a circle on the floor, laughing and talking together. They were a year or two older than her, and she didn't know them.

"Oh," Cindy said. "This is Jessica, Michelle, and Sue. And my daughter Lily."

The girls swiveled in their circle long enough to say hello, then closed it again, their backs to Cassie.

The door behind them opened, and a man poked his head in. "The boys are ready for you."

The girls jumped up, their chatter jumping up a notch.

"Boys?" Cassie said, following everyone out of the room.

"Tonight we're playing basketball with the boys," Cindy said. "We do activities with them sometimes. I hope you're good at sports." She winked.

Cassie's steps faltered, and she swallowed. Good at sports? Not hardly. She'd nearly given up on soccer because she hated to run. But this was just for fun. Hopefully no one would notice her.

A few more girls from different classes joined them, and by the time they gathered in the gym, they had about forty boys and girls. The same guy who'd stuck his head in the room cleared his throat.

"Okay!" he said, "we've already split into two teams. My team captains here will choose one at a time until there's no one left."

Cassie crossed her fingers and toes, a familiar anxious feeling forming in her gut. She hated when they chose. She was always picked last. *No one here knows me*, she reminded herself. *They have no reason to pick me last.* Still, she held her breath with the captains began choosing girls. Her heart rate quickened each time she wasn't chosen. But then, when there were still a handful of girls left, one of the team captains said, "The new girl. What's her name? Yeah, you."

"She's Cassie Jones," Tyler said.

Cassie smiled at him, elated. Not only was she not last, but she was on Tyler's team!

The team captains took charge, organizing who was on the court and who was watching. Cassie wasn't up first, and she was glad. She stood on the sidelines and tried to figure out the rules of the game. Move the ball down the court—don't drop it—throw it—don't let anyone take it—catch it—too many rules! She pushed her glasses up on her nose, nervous again.

"It's Cassie, right?" the team captain, a tall blond boy, asked.

Cassie nodded, her stomach all a flutter again.

"You're up."

"Okay." Her heart flip-flopped in her chest, and her tongue lodged itself in her dry mouth. What was she supposed to do here? She couldn't even fake this.

She entered the yellow-stained wood court and hesitated at the sidelines. Kids rushed by her with the ball, shoes squeaking as they patted it away from each other, bouncing it around her. Cassie put her hands out in an attempt to touch the ball, but another kid already had it.

"Cassie!" the tall blond yelled. "Follow the ball to the basket!"

She nodded, glad for direction. She jogged after her teammates just as Tyler thew the ball at the basket. He missed. Someone else got the ball, and they did a little dance on the wood floor, bobbing up and down with the ball between them until Tyler got it back somehow. Then they danced again, swiveling around each other, only this time the other kid had his arms out while Tyler held onto the ball. Tyler glanced over his shoulder, and his eyes met Cassie's where she stood a few feet behind him.

"Catch!" he shouted, and lobbed the ball at her.

She saw the orange orb arcing through the air, coming at her, and she envisioned herself jumping up, grabbing it with both arms, and throwing it into the basket. She held her breath and tensed her muscles to jump. Almost. Closer. Now!

But she didn't jump. Instead, she bounced on her feet, and before she could try again, the ball smacked her in the face, knocking her glasses off. A few kids murmured sympathetically while others tittered with laughter.

None of that was as bad as Tyler's reaction, though. His face turned red, and he yelled, "All you had to do was catch the ball, dummy!"

Cassie stood stock-still, the blood freezing in her veins.

"Tyler, it's just a game," she heard Jason say. Someone put her glasses in her hand. But all she noticed was the

stinging sensation in her eyes and her numb face. She swallowed hard, a pounding starting up in her head.

"Are you okay?" someone asked.

Without a word, Cassie turned around and walked off the court. She stumbled until she got her glasses on, and then she let herself into the hall. *Don't cry*, she told herself. *Don't cry.*

She managed to the get the bathroom door open. Only then did she let herself cry.

~

"How was your first youth group night?" Mr. Jones asked when he picked Cassie up outside.

"Fine," she said, glad the darkness hid her pink nose. She'd stayed in the bathroom the rest of the time, even locking herself in a stall when other girls came in. Someone called her name once, but she didn't respond, and they went away.

"Were the girls friendly?" her dad asked, putting on his blinker as they pulled onto the highway.

"We played basketball," Cassie answered.

"Oh." A pause. "How was that?"

"Awful." Cassie sighed. "I hate basketball."

Mr. Jones chuckled. "I didn't think that was your thing. Don't worry, Cassie. You won't be the best at everything. But you excel at other things."

She kept her mouth shut, wishing she knew what exactly she was good at.

Episode 6: Coming of Age

CHAPTER THIRTY-NINE
Going Together

Esther Vanguard was still absent on Thursday. As the sixth-grade class ambassador, it was Cassandra Jones' job to collect the homework assignments for all sick kids.

Never mind that Esther detested Cassie and had made that clear from the first day they met. Cassie had a job to do.

She copied down the homework assignments, knowing this was the easy part. The hard part was having to call the student every day.

Cassie held the cordless phone in her hands after dinner, trying to talk herself into making the phone call. *It went okay yesterday*, she reminded herself. *Just do it.* Bracing herself, she dialed the number.

Esther's mom put Esther on the phone.

"Hi, Esther, it's Cassie," she said, feeling foolish.

"Hi."

With that one word, they drifted into silence. Cassie listened to the ragged breathing on the other line. "Is your pneumonia better?"

"No."

"When will you be back in school?"

"I don't know." Esther coughed loudly.

"Tomorrow's the book fair," Cassie said. "I hate for you to miss it."

"Yeah," Esther said. "That's too bad."

Cassie had run out of things to say. "I'll make sure you get your homework."

"Thanks."

"Bye," Cassie said, remembering to say it before she hung up this time.

~

"Esther must really be sick," Andrea Wall, Cassie's best friend, commented the next day as she watched Cassie copying two sets of notes, yet again.

"Yeah," Cassie said. "She's got pneumonia. It could be awhile before she comes back."

"Is she being nice to you?"

Cassie shrugged and put the homework assignment in a neat pile. "It would be hard to be rude on the phone."

"All right, class," Ms. Timber, their teacher, said. "It's time to go to the book fair. If you brought money, please get it now. If you didn't, you're welcome to peruse the books and check something out."

Cassie went to the backpack cubbies with the rest of her class. She had money. She planned to buy three books.

"Are you getting anything?" she whispered to Andrea as they walked down the hall, even though she knew Andrea didn't like to read.

"I'll probably get one of those cool light-up pencils they usually have."

"I like those," Cassie agreed.

Her heart fluttered with excitement when they walked

into the library, and she smiled to see the shelves spread out and open with brand new books on them. If she ended up working in a library or bookstore for the rest of her life, she would be content.

The buzz of excited chatter filled the small room as kids looked over the books they wanted. Right away, Cassie found the three she'd circled in the flier. She started toward the cash register and paused. A nagging thought entered her mind, and once it set root, she couldn't get it out.

Esther.

Esther would miss the book fair, and Cassie knew she liked to read. She even knew what kind of books Esther liked to read, since she'd seen Esther reading them. They were the same kind Cassie liked.

Hesitantly, she turned around and went back to the bookshelves. She picked up the sequel she knew Esther didn't own and held it in her hands. If she bought this, she'd have to put back one of her own.

She was still standing there thinking and staring when Andrea joined her.

"Did you find what you wanted?" she asked.

Cassie nodded without looking at her best friend. "But I think I need to get this book for Esther."

"For Esther?" Andrea scoffed. "Why would you do that? She doesn't even like you."

That was true. "Because she's missing this. She'd want a book." Cassie heaved a sigh. There was no other option. She put back one of her books and carried the book for Esther to the cash register.

"You don't have to do this," Andrea said, following her.

"I know." But truthfully, she did have to. She would feel bad if she didn't.

Cassie put her newly purchased books in a plastic bag while Andrea examined the light-up pencil toppers and pens with invisible ink. Michael slid up next to them. He was one of Miles' friends, a funny blond-headed boy who was really good at math.

"Hi, Cassie," he said, then turned his back on her to face Andrea. "Andrea, can I talk to you for a second?"

Andrea glanced at Cassie and put down the pencil topper. "Sure?"

Cassie stood up straighter, her curiosity piqued. "What is it?" she mouthed.

Andrea shrugged and followed Michael over to the Reading Corner of the library, complete with beanbags and a desk. Cassie watched them, trying to interpret their conversation. Michael scratched his eyebrow, spread his hands out wide, lifted his shoulders. Andrea nodded several times without saying a word. Then she also shrugged. They waved, and Michael went back to his friends, his face bright red.

"What was that?" Cassie asked as soon as Andrea reached her.

"He asked me out," Andrea said, picking up the pen with invisible ink. She laid down some money. "I'll take this."

"Wait, he did what?" Cassie asked, confused.

Andrea pocketed her pen and turned back to Cassie. "We're going out now. He's my boyfriend." Andrea started toward the library doors where kids were beginning to gather. Cassie followed, her mind trying to wrap around the idea.

"How can he be your boyfriend?" Cassie asked. "You're only twelve."

"So? I had my first boyfriend when I was seven."

"But you can't like, kiss him or anything." Cassie's face warmed at the very idea.

"Sure I can. If I want."

"Are you going to?" Cassie breathed.

"I don't know." Andrea shrugged. "Maybe."

"But I didn't know you even like Michael. I thought you liked Connor." Not that Cassie minded. Connor was on her soccer team and a total jerk.

"Well, I do." Andrea glanced around. "But he doesn't pay me any attention. I may as well go out with Michael, since he asked."

Cassie couldn't think of what else to say. The whole concept was kind of odd.

"Don't worry," Andrea said. "I'm sure someone will ask you out soon."

Cassie hadn't been thinking about that at all. But now that Andrea said it, it made her wonder. Were there any guys that liked her? Did someone want to be her boyfriend? Something shivered in her chest, and she realized she hoped someone did.

~

"Hey, Cassie!" Will caught up to Cassie before they made it outside to the buses this time.

"Hi," she said, not surprised this time to see him.

"Ready for the weekend?"

"Of course." While Cassie enjoyed school, getting away from the homework and the tests and waking up early for a few days was heaven.

"What are your plans?"

She shrugged, pausing on the sidewalk. Kids shuffled past her, and Cassie inched closer to her bus. "Probably read. I bought a few new books today."

"Oh yeah, you like reading."

She nodded. "Like" was an understatement.

"Do you think I could call you?"

She felt one eyebrow lift of its own accord. She couldn't think of why Will would want to call her. "Sure, I guess."

"Awesome." He pulled out a small phone. "What's your number?"

"I don't have my own phone," she said, eyeing his device. "It's the house phone."

"Sure, sure." He waved her off. "Just tell it to me, I'll put it in."

Cassie cleared her throat and rattled off the phone number, watching as Will's fingers typed in the numbers.

"Great," he said, looking up. "I'll call you." With a wave, he ran off toward his bus.

"That was weird," Cassie said as she sat down next to Betsy.

"What was weird?" Betsy asked, looking up from the book she was reading.

Cassie shook her head. "Will Harris just asked for my phone number."

Betsy stood up, leaning across the aisle to peer out the window. "From my class? Where'd he go?"

Cassie grabbed her arm and pulled her back down. "He's already gone to his bus."

Betsy's green eyes widened. "He must like you!"

"Why would you say that?" Cassie blinked at her, confused.

"Because that's why guys get girls' phone numbers! Because they like them!" Betsy grabbed Cassie's arm and yanked it. "He's going to call you!"

Cassie couldn't imagine why, and she wasn't sure what they'd talk about. But Betsy ought to know. She'd had a boyfriend for three months now. Cassie pressed the back of her head into the vinyl seat and stared up at the bus ceiling, waiting to feel some kind of excitement about a boy liking her. Nothing happened.

~

Cassie didn't know why, but when Monday rolled around and Will hadn't called all weekend, she felt a little disappointed. It didn't really matter . . . but it felt kind of nice to think someone wanted to talk to her.

All thoughts of Will completely fled her mind when she walked into class and saw Esther sitting at her desk.

Cassie's mind flashed back to Friday, and she groaned inwardly. She'd forgotten to call Esther! Esther probably would have told her she'd be back in school today. At least she'd remembered to turn the homework packet into the office.

But the book!

"Why are you just standing there?" Andrea murmured, coming up behind her.

"Esther's back," Cassie said, her throat clenching nervously. "I was going to leave the book on the desk for her. What do I do now?"

Andrea glanced toward the other girl. "Just go give it to her. It's not big deal."

But it was a big deal. Esther had showed nothing but scorn and disdain for Cassie ever since they'd met. What if she rejected the book?

Cassie finally forced her feet to move. She deposited her backpack at the cubbies and pulled Esther's book from the plastic bag. She held it to her chest, trying to calm her pounding heart. Then she walked out to the row of desks, dropped the book in front of Esther, and hurried to her own desk. She sat down and opened the journal, pretending to be absorbed in the first assignment of the day. Even from where she sat, she could hear Esther's puzzled comments to her neighbors.

Andrea scooted her chair out, walked over to Esther, and said, "Cassie got that for you. She felt bad that you missed the book fair, so she bought you a book." Then Andrea turned around and went back to her seat.

Cassie's face flamed, but she felt a rush of gratitude toward Andrea. Ms. Timber called the class to order and told everyone to start their journaling, and Cassie allowed herself to relax. The deed was done.

And then a white piece of notebook paper, folded in half, landed on her desk.

Cassie stared at it, then reached out and very slowly opened it.

In scrawling print it, read, *Thank you!!! I love the book. Thank you so much. Esther.*

Cassie couldn't even believe it. She leaned forward and saw Esther smiling at her. Cassie sat back, a warmth starting in her chest and moving up to her eyes. She'd definitely made the right decision.

CHAPTER FORTY

K-I-S-S-I-N-G

Cassie wasn't surprised when Michael joined her and Andrea at lunch, sitting across the table from them. He didn't say anything, just ate his food and talked to his friends. When lunch ended, he went off with the boys.

"I don't understand how he's your boyfriend," Cassie said to Andrea, her best friend, as they ran their required laps for PE. "You don't do anything."

"We eat lunch together," Andrea said, as if that were the most important thing in the whole world. "And sometimes we hold hands."

"You hold hands?" Cassie sputtered. "When?" She was quite certain she would've seen this happen.

"Whenever we feel like it," Andrea replied, a bit defensively. "We don't have lots of opportunities."

Cassie waited for Andrea to clarify, maybe give an example, but Andrea didn't.

They finished up their laps, and Cassie spotted Michael heading for the blacktop. "There's Michael," she said, pointing him out. "Did you want to say hi?"

Andrea looked his direction. "No, he looks busy. I'll

catch him later."

Cassie glanced at Michael. He was sitting on the blacktop now, hands balancing behind him. He didn't seem busy.

She shrugged off Andrea's response. Maybe in sixth grade, boyfriends were just boring.

~

"Hey, Cassie!"

Cassie turned around as she stepped off the bus the next morning, surprised to hear someone calling her name from the doorway.

"It's Will," her friend Betsy murmured, coming up behind her and giving a little giggle. "Told you he likes you."

"Shush," Cassie said, shoving Betsy off. "Hi, Will," she said with a brief smile.

He slowed down beside her, forcing Cassie to walk slower.

"I'll see you after school," Betsy said, giving her a knowing look. Cassie rolled her eyes.

"Hey, I want to ask you something," Will said.

"Sure," Cassie replied. She wondered if Andrea was already in the classroom. The bus riders usually arrived first, but sometimes Andrea's mom dropped her off early.

"Will you go with me?"

"What?" Cassie swiveled her head to stare at him, her mental gears whirling to catch up with the subject change.

Will's face turned bright red, clashing with the mop of brown hair on his head. "I said, will you go with me?"

"I—uh—" She knew her mouth was opening and closing like a fish, and she forced herself to say something coherent. "I don't know. I need to ask my mom." As soon as she said the words, she winced. Ask her mom? Now he would think she was a baby who couldn't do anything without talking to mommy! "I mean, I have to think about it."

He looked a lot less certain. "When will you know?"

Cassie shoved her glasses up on her nose, even though they weren't falling off. "By tomorrow."

"Okay, then." He hesitated, then moved past her and continued into the school.

Cassie blinked and stared after him. Betsy had been right, after all!

~

"He asked you out?" Andrea breathed during morning recess.

Cassie had fidgeted all morning and written several notes to her best friend, so anxious to tell her the news and get her advice. In the end, she hadn't sent any of the notes, but held onto the information until she could tell her in person.

"Yep," Cassie said, rather proud of that fact now.

"What did you tell him?" Andrea stole a glance at Cassie as they walked around the perimeter of the play yard. It's what they did during every recess.

"I haven't told him anything yet."

"But you're going to say yes, right?"

"Well . . ." Now Cassie hesitated. "I don't know."

"Cassie." Andrea took her arm and pulled her over to the outside wall, away from prying ears. "It's kind of a big thing. If you have a boyfriend, I mean. It means you're— well, you're—"

Cool. Andrea didn't have to say it; Cassie already knew. It was a status thing, and she couldn't deny the longing she felt to have that status. But her heart wasn't in it. Shouldn't it be? "But he's not who I like," she said slowly.

"I know." Andrea patted her on the arm. "You like Miles. But Cassie, he's not asking you out."

No, he wasn't. Cassie looked away. "I have to ask my parents, anyway."

"Your parents?" Andrea sounded skeptical. "What do they have to do with this?"

Well, they were kind of in charge. But somehow Cassie didn't think that would go over well. "I like to know their thoughts," she said instead.

"That's nice of you ," Andrea said. "Just remember it's your decision."

"Yeah. Okay."

~

That night, Cassie waited until everyone was eating dinner before turning to her mom.

"Will Harris asked me to go with him today," she said, as casually as she could.

The instant she'd said it, she knew she'd chosen the wrong moment. All mouths stopped chewing and forks paused in midair. Except her dad's, whose fork clattered to the table. Cassie winced. She should have cornered her mom and asked her.

"Asked you to go with him?" her mom repeated. "Go with him where?"

Cassie rolled her eyes, irritated even though she'd had the same reaction the first time she'd heard the term. "It's just what they call it, Mom."

"What's it mean?" her dad asked. "He wants to take you on a date? Absolutely not. You're only twelve."

"So's he," Cassie defended. "And it's not like that. He

would just get to sit by me at lunch and stuff."

"Then why did he ask?" Mrs. Jones said. "Why doesn't he just sit with you?"

"It doesn't work that way." Cassie felt her frustration rising. "It has to be official."

"So he can call you his girlfriend?" Mr. Jones picked up his fork and pointed it at her. "No. You can't have any boyfriends until you're sixteen."

"But—" Cassie shut her mouth. She saw the way her younger siblings watched the conversation, eyes wide. She couldn't make her parents understand that this wasn't a big deal. Besides, why did she want to? She didn't like Will that way. She didn't want to go with him. "Okay."

Her dad seemed caught off-guard by her acceptance, but her mom went straight back to eating.

"No dating until you're sixteen," Mr. Jones said, as if to clarify the matter.

Cassie shoveled food into her mouth without answering.

She thought the matter was over until her mom knocked on the open bedroom door that Cassie shared with her sister Emily. Both girls looked up from their beds, each absorbed in a book.

"Emily," her mom said, "do you mind if I talk to Cassie alone for a bit?"

"Sure," Emily said. She closed her book, tucked it under one arm, and scurried out of the room.

Mrs. Jones closed the bedroom door and sat next to Cassie. "Tell me about Will."

"Well." Cassie pushed herself up and sat against the wall. "He's a boy in the other sixth-grade class. He's taller than me, with brown hair."

"Is he nice?"

"Sure." Cassie shrugged. "He walks with me to the bus. Offers to carry my backpack."

"Do you like him?"

"As a friend." She shrugged again. "I'm really not interested in him as a boyfriend. But he asked, so, I did too."

Her mom let out a breath. "You understand, Cassie, why we said no?"

"I guess. I'm not supposed to date yet."

"But do you really understand why?"

Cassie supposed she did. This all boiled down to the big three-letter word: SEX. And by not dating, she wouldn't be faced with that option. She didn't want to say all that, though, so she just said, "Yeah."

"And why is that?"

Her face warmed as she realized her mom wanted her to spell it out. "So I won't—you know."

Mrs. Jones laughed. "Something like that. The thing is Cassie, you're only twelve. And the first thing that's going to happen when you like a boy is you're going to hold his hand. And you'll have the most delicious, wonderful feeling when you do. But after awhile, it won't be enough. You'll want to be closer to him. So you might hug him. A lot. Maybe even kiss him."

A first kiss. Cassie's heart gave a little tremor.

"And then there will be more kisses, and at some point, Cassie, the kissing won't be enough. You'll want more."

Cassie stared at her toes.

"If you start holding hands now, when you're only twelve, those feelings are going to come sooner. Way too soon. And we don't want this to be harder on you than it already will be."

Cassie blinked, not fully comprehending what her mom meant. What would be hard? She didn't want to ask, though.

"So just wait, sweetie. The time will come for dating, for holding hands, even for kissing. But not yet. Do you understand?"

Cassie nodded. She might not understand everything, but she got it. She knew what her mom meant.

"Does it make sense?"

"Yes," Cassie said.

Her mom hugged her shoulders and planted a kiss on her forehead. "You're a smart girl. Be wise."

Be wise. Those words echoed in her mind after her mom left her alone in the room.

CHAPTER FORTY-ONE
Oh Wise One

Cassie stayed on the bus as long as she could the next morning, not at all anxious to let Will know her decision. Believing it was the right thing was one thing, having the courage to tell him was quite another. Only after she saw him go inside did she venture from her seat.

Andrea cornered her by the cubbies before Cassie even hung up her backpack.

"Did you talk to Will yet?" she whispered.

"No." Cassie pulled out her homework and hugged it to her chest. "I saw him when I got off the bus. I'll find him at recess."

"And what are you going to say?" Andrea held her breath, staring at Cassie with wide eyes.

"I'm telling him no. Just like I said I would." She wasn't sure she'd put it exactly like that, but even yesterday it was the decision she'd been leaning toward.

Andrea exhaled with a whoosh. "Why? Your parents wouldn't let you?"

Cassie hesitated. In truth, she could say that. But it was more than that. "My mom explained to me why I shouldn't have a boyfriend yet. I believe her. I don't want to get serious right now."

"But this isn't serious," Andrea said, blinking at her with obvious confusion. "You're not in the same class. Michael and I are, and we hardly even hold hands."

"Yes, but—" Cassie shook her head. There wasn't much point explaining. "That's my answer."

Cassie knew she'd have to face Will at recess. She could only hope his reaction was more understanding than Andrea's.

She found him at the soccer field, leaning with one arm against the goal post. Every time the ball wandered out of bounds, he was quick to kick it back in.

"Hey, Will," she said, trying to smile while her heart did somersaults in her throat.

He turned around, his face lighting up when he saw her. "Hi, Cassie."

They stood there for a moment saying nothing, then Cassie coughed.

"So, about what you asked me yesterday," she said.

"Yes?" He straightened up.

Cassie lowered her eyes. She couldn't face him right now. "I have to say no."

"You do?" He sounded confused. "Why?"

She shrugged and decided to keep it simple. "I'm too young to date. I have to wait till I'm sixteen."

"But I'm not asking you on a date. You would just be my girlfriend. Mostly at school, ya know."

"I know. I know." Cassie sighed, her face burning. This was worse than she'd expected. "But I can't."

"Okay," Will said. Then he turned around, his back to her as he watched the soccer game.

Cassie wrung her hands, her stomach still knotted. "We can be friends, though."

Will didn't answer. After a moment, Cassie walked back to the school building.

~

Cassie spotted Will after school as he moved down the hall in front of her. "Will!" she called out.

He paused at the sound of his name and glanced over his shoulder. When he saw her, his face darkened, and he continued forward, faster this time.

Cassie halted until someone walked into her. Was he mad at her?

She continued to the bus in a bit of a daze, trying to sort through her feelings at his reaction. She slid into her spot next to Betsy. "Hey, Betsy," she began, and then she took a good look at her friend.

Betsy sat with her forehead against the window, her shoulders trembling, soft sounds coming from her mouth.

Cassie leaned toward her and put a hand on her thigh. "Betsy? Are you okay?"

Betsy hunched her shoulders around her ears and cried a little harder.

Cassie didn't know what to do. She wasn't sure how to help. So she just rubbed Betsy's shoulders and said, "It's okay. It'll be okay."

Betsy didn't turn around, and she didn't say a word. Finally the bus reached Cassie's stop, and she got off. Her thoughts stayed with Betsy all the way home, though. She hoped everything really was okay.

~

Betsy wasn't on the bus in the morning, but Cassie couldn't dwell on that for long. She'd barely taken two steps into the school building when a fifth grader she didn't know stopped her. Two other boys flanked him on either side.

"You're Cassie, right?" he said.

She looked him up and down, not recognizing him. "Yes. Who are you?"

"You're the prude who won't go with Will," he said, scoffing.

The heat exploded in her cheeks, wrapping around her head. "I just think we're too young . . ."

"Yeah, he told us." All three boys laughed, and the leader spoke again. "He said your mommy wouldn't let you. Because you're saving yourself."

All of that was true, but the way he said it, in that mocking, belittling tone, stung. Cassie wanted to deny his words, but how could she? "Will wouldn't say that. We're friends."

"Not what he said on the bus. He said he only asked you out because he thought you'd be desperate. He doesn't actually like you. Doesn't even think you're cute."

She couldn't stop the tears that sprang to her eyes, so instead she pushed past the boys and hurried to the bathroom. She shut herself in a stall and cried. Was that really what Will thought of her?

She stayed in the bathroom until the warning bell rang. Then she hurried to class. With any luck, all the people on Will's bus would be in other classes, in other grades.

She felt Andrea's eyes on her as soon as she walked in, but she didn't meet them. Cassie hurriedly put her stuff away and slipped into her chair just in time to get out her morning journal. Ms. Timber called the class to order, and Cassie focused on expelling her thoughts with a stiff, halted hand. She pressed the pen into the paper and scribbled her anger at Will's words.

A note appeared in front of her nose, and Cassie pulled it under the desk to open it. It was from Andrea.

Cass—

Will's talking about you. Are you okay?

Cassie swallowed hard, her stomach turning over. So other people had heard. She scribbled back, *No. What did you hear?* She passed the note back and tried to concentrate on her journaling, but she watched out of the corner of her eye for the reply. Finally it came, shuffling between hands until it plopped onto her desk. Again, Cassie pulled it under and read it.

Talk during P.E.

Cassie crumpled it up and shoved it into her desk. Not a good sign.

~

As soon as the class let out for P.E., Cassie started her lap. She ran far enough away to be out of speaking range of her classmates, hugging the perimeters of the fence. Andrea caught up with her.

"What happened?" she breathed. "Did he get mad when you told him?"

Cassie shook her head. "He didn't say much at all! I don't understand what's happening now."

Andrea jogged beside her in silence for a bit, chewing on her lower lip.

Cassie hesitated, almost afraid to ask, and then she said, "What did you hear?"

Andrea took a moment to respond. "That you asked him to kiss you and he turned you down."

Cassie lost her balance and pitched forward. She felt the

tears stinging her eyes again even as Andrea grabbed her arm and helped her up.

"I never did," Cassie sobbed out. "I never did that."

"I know."

They slowed to a walk, Andrea putting an arm around

Cassie's shoulders. Cassie shook her head.

"If this was supposed to make me feel bad for saying no, it's doing the opposite. I'm so glad I didn't say yes!"

"Yeah," Andrea agreed. "He's a total jerk."

The teacher separated all the students during PE, making them go through their own routine of push-ups and burpees. Cassie kept her eyes down, afraid to make contact with any of her classmates. She could feel them looking at her, whispering, giggling.

Class ended, and Cassie immediately searched out Andrea. She saw her talking to Michael, and then she walked away from him.

"You okay?" Andrea asked her when she got closer.

"I think so," Cassie said. "As long as I don't talk to anyone."

They went to the classroom long enough to grab their lunch boxes, then headed for the cafeteria. Cassie sat down by Andrea and glanced around.

"Where's Michael?" she asked when he didn't sit down in front of them.

Andrea shrugged, keeping her eyes on her lunch as she peeled off the plastic wrap from her sandwich. "Who knows? Probably sitting with his friends."

Cassie furrowed her brow. "But he's been sitting with us for like a week."

"Yeah, well." Andrea shrugged and took a bite. "That was when we were going together."

Her words were jumbled by the food, so it took Cassie a second to work them out. "Wait. Are you not now?"

"Nope." Andrea took a drink, still very calm and nonchalant. "We broke up at PE."

Cassie felt her jaw drop open. "You did? Why didn't you tell me? Why?"

"I didn't want you to worry." She put down her food and looked directly at Cassie. "You're right. Guys are jerks."

Something tightened in Cassie's stomach. "He said something about me, didn't he?"

"Well . . . more like he believed Will."

Cassie stared at her best friend. "You broke up with him because he believed Will?"

"I told him it wasn't true. He didn't believe me. So I told him we were done." Andrea's lip curled up. "It's okay. I didn't really like him anyway."

CHAPTER FORTY-TWO

Cassie the Prude

Cassie remembered Betsy when she got on the bus after school and her friend wasn't there. Suddenly Will and his antics seemed utterly ridiculous. Something was wrong with Betsy, and she wasn't sure how to find out what it was.

When she got home, she pulled open the phone book on the counter and flipped through it until she found Betsy's number. Betsy had given it to her in December, before her Christmas party. Cassie dialed the number and held her breath.

The error tone chimed seconds before the message, "The number you have reached has been disconnected or is no longer in service. If you believe—"

Cassie hung up, not waiting for the end of the message. "Mom?" She wandered down the hall to her parents' room but didn't see her. "Mom?"

"Downstairs!" the voice floated faintly from the basement.

Cassie skipped down the stairs to her mom's sewing office. "Can you drive me out to Betsy's house?"

Her mom put down the fabric and looked at Cassie over the machine. "Drive you over? Why?"

Cassie scratched at the wood in the door. "I'm kind of worried about her. Yesterday she wasn't doing so good and today she missed school."

"Why don't you just call her and ask?"

"Well, I tried, but her number's been disconnected." For like the hundredth time that day, tears pricked her eyes. "I'm afraid something's wrong."

"I'm sure she's okay. Sometimes people get sick or have bad days. She'll probably be in school tomorrow." Mrs. Jones put the fabric down on the machine again.

"And if she's not?"

Her mom met her eyes, and Cassie sensed her impatience. "Then ask her teacher. Someone's probably collecting homework or something."

"Yeah. Okay." Cassie started to leave, then turned around and blurted, "I told Will today that I wouldn't be his girlfriend. And he started spreading lies about me."

Now Mrs. Jones put the cloth down and focused on Cassie. "What kind of lies?"

Cassie shrugged. Maybe she shouldn't have said anything. "That I asked him out. That he only talked to me because he felt sorry for me." She didn't feel like telling her mom what else he'd said.

Mrs. Jones studied her, and Cassie shifted slightly under the scrutiny.

"Do I need to call the school?" her mom finally asked.

"No!" Cassie shook her head. "No, it's okay."

"Cassie, you defend yourself. Make sure people know the truth. And no matter what this Will says, deep down, I promise you he respects your decision. Maybe that's why he's acting out. Maybe he feels bad for even asking you."

He definitely did. But not for the reasons her mom thought.

"Get ready for soccer," her mom said, turning back to the sewing machine. "Your dad will take you to your game."

~

Cassie huffed and puffed through the third-quarter of her soccer game, the hot sun beating down on her. The ball passed in front of her feet, and she swiveled enough to land a kick on it. It shot down the field, and the sidelines broke into cheers.

"Go after it, Cassie! Go!" her coach shouted.

Cassie groaned and forced her legs to move forward. Her side ached and her lungs seemed to be constricting in her chest. *Run faster*, she told herself.

But someone on the other team had already intercepted the ball, and she slowly came to a stop.

"Sub!" Coach Price shouted, and Cassie found the energy to jog off the field.

Connor Lane caught her eye as she sat down and sneered at her. Then the game resumed, and Cassie didn't have to look at him anymore.

"Good game, team," Coach Price said when it was over, and they sat around drinking their juice boxes. "That's our first win of the season."

"That's because some of us actually chase the ball," Connor said, and several giggles erupted from the group.

Heat rushed to Cassie's face. She kept quiet, hoping no one else knew he meant her.

"Who do you think doesn't chase the ball?" Nicole Bass, the other girl on the team, asked. She sounded defensive.

320

"Some of us are running harder than you out there."

"Some of us," Connor agreed. "Others are standing still waiting for the ball to do all the work."

"Hey, we're a team," Coach said. "We all work together."

"Not Cassie," Connor said. "She stops in the middle of the field and lets the other team get the ball."

"I do not!" Cassie exclaimed, unable to keep silent any longer.

"You do too. Every game. If you weren't so fat you could keep up."

"Connor!" Coach barked. "Two laps around the field, now."

"Why?" he grumbled, pushing to his feet. "I'm just—"

"Now!"

Cassie stumbled up, her drink trembling in her hands.

"Are you okay?" Coach asked.

"I'm not fat!" she burst out. Her eyes stung, and she couldn't prevent the tears that fell. "I have breathing problems. It's hard for me to run, that's all!" Then she stomped away, not even caring if they didn't believe her. For all she knew, it might be true. Maybe she should get tested.

Or maybe she should just quit soccer.

~

Cassie woke up Friday morning with her stomach in knots. She lay in bed, wondering if she'd forgotten an assignment or something, before remembering Will and his tormenting comments yesterday. She groaned and pulled the blankets over her head, wishing she didn't have to go to school. But staying in bed wouldn't make it go away. She kicked the covers off and dragged herself out of the room.

She wore a hoodie to the bus, managing to hide her face behind the hood. Betsy wasn't on the bus again. It took all Cassie's courage to walk into Ms. Roxi's class and ask about her. She avoided looking at Will's desk or any of this friends, knowing they'd be glaring at her.

"Hi, Ms. Roxi," she said, stopping at the teacher's desk.

Ms. Roxi glanced up from her grade book. "Oh, hello, Cassandra. Can I help you?"

"Well, I ride the bus with Betsy," she began.

Ms. Roxi's eyes brightened. "Oh, are you here to collect her homework? I was wondering when someone would come. Let me get it."

"No, wait," Cassie said, putting a hand out. Her heart fluttered anxiously in her chest. "I'm just trying to figure out where she is. So no one's picking up her homework?"

Ms. Roxi's shoulders sagged. "Oh. No."

"Is she sick or something?"

"Well, I don't really know." Ms. Roxi hesitated. "I haven't heard anything."

Cassie wanted to ask more questions, press for answers, but she knew the teacher wasn't going to tell her any more. She put on a smile. "Okay. Thanks."

The murmurs started as soon as Cassie turned her back on Ms. Roxi. She stiffened her shoulders and hurried out. The looks and whispers continued throughout the day, and Cassie did her best to ignore them. She told herself she was imagining it, that not everyone in her class was talking about her.

She went to the cubbies during reading time and searched in her backpack for a new book. If only she could hide back here and read.

Miles stepped into the cubby area, heading for his backpack. Cassie took one look at him and wished she could shrink. Had he heard the rumors too? What did he think of her now?

"Hi, Cassie," he said, glancing at her and then turning back to his bag.

"Hi," Cassie murmured, clutching her book to her chest. Should she try and sneak past him? Or wait for him to leave?

He got his book and straightened, facing her. "Cassie." He hesitated. "I want to ask you something."

She couldn't breathe. "Go ahead," she choked out.

Again he took his time, not quite meeting her eyes. "What happened with you and Will?"

She felt the sting of tears and blinked several times to keep them from falling. Her hands shook around her book. "Nothing," she whispered. "He asked me to go with him. And I said no."

Miles' brow furrowed. "That's all?"

She nodded vigorously, wondering which rumor Miles had heard. "That's all. Nothing else happened."

"So why is he—?" Miles stopped.

"I don't know," Cassie said, anxious to explain herself. "I think he's mad at me for saying no."

"Why'd you say no?"

"I didn't want to go with him."

"Because you don't like him?"

"That's part of it," Cassie admitted. "I'm not interested in him that way. I like someone else." And then her cheeks flamed, and she had to look at the wall, the ground, anywhere but Miles. "But also, I don't think it's the right time. We're just kids." The words sounded so stupid coming out of her mouth, Cassie wished she could take them back. Why couldn't she sound mature and wise?

"So even if you liked him—you would have said no."

She nodded, still not looking at him. "Yeah."

"Okay." Miles swiveled on his feet, then turned back. "I'm glad he's lying. I mean, I'm not glad he's lying about you. But I'm glad what he's saying isn't true." Then he turned around and walked away.

Cassie stayed there a second longer, finally able to breathe. But she spent the rest of the day trying to interpret Miles' words.

~

Cassie remembered about Betsy as soon as she got on the school bus. She burst into her house, determined to make her mom drive up to Betsy's house.

Her mom was at the dining room table, putting stamps on envelopes.

"Mom," Cassie began, all fired up, "Betsy wasn't in school again today. But it's more than that. I talked to her teacher, and Ms. Roxi doesn't know where she is. No one's coming to get her homework. Something's wrong. We have to go out to her house."

Her mom didn't look up from the envelopes the whole time Cassie talked. Cassie waited a moment.

"Mom?" she said again.

Finally Mrs. Jones looked up, and Cassie was startled to see that her eyes were red.

A warning bell went off in Cassie's mind. "Is everything okay?" she said slowly. Her mom crying was never a good thing.

"Cassie, I got a call today." Mrs. Jones took a deep breath and exhaled. "It's about your friend."

"Betsy?" Cassie asked, her chest constricting.

"Yes. She's in trouble."

CHAPTER FORTY-THREE
Ward of the State

"What does that even mean, she's in trouble?" Cassie asked. She could already feel the tears threatening. "What happened?"

"Her parents—" Mrs. Jones shook her head. "Cassie, her dad was physically abusive. Mostly to her mother, I think, but children aren't allowed to live in homes where abuse is happening, so the state took her away. She's going to live somewhere else."

Cassie stared at her mother, and then the world tilted and she had to grab the table. She knew what abuse was. Ever since the first grade she'd gone to the seminars talking about avoiding strangers, not keeping secrets, knowing what was appropriate and inappropriate touching. But she'd never known someone that was abused. "But she never said anything," Cassie said, her voice trembling. "She spent the night over here. I've been to her house."

"I know," her mom said softly, her own eyes watering.

"Is she going to be okay?" Cassie's eyebrows lifted seconds before the tears spilled down her cheeks. "Is she hurt? Is she coming back?"

"I don't know, sweetie." Her mom stood up and hugged her. "Betsy listed you as a contact, and her social worker called me. Betsy can call and write letters, but for now you can't see her. I don't know if she'll ever be back."

"Can I call her?" Cassie asked, her tears soaking her mom's shirt.

"No. We don't have her number. But she'll call you. I'm sure of it."

"Where is she going to live?"

"Right now she's with a foster family. But I think her social worker is getting it set up where she can live with her aunt."

"I want to see her," Cassie sobbed.

"I know, sweetheart. You will. Just not right now."

Cassie didn't have any appetite at dinner. All she could think about was Betsy. What had her home life been like? Was it perfectly miserable? Why hadn't Betsy ever told her? She'd always seemed so normal, happy.

She helped set the table but cried so much that her mom said she could be excused. Instead, Cassie went to her room and wrote Betsy a letter, wishing she could talk to her friend.

~

Getting on the bus Monday morning and not seeing Betsy just upset Cassie all over again. She holed up in the corner of her seat and stared out the window, pretending not to hear or notice anyone else. She was so wrapped up in her own misery that she completely forgot about the whole Will fiasco—until she stepped off the bus and he was standing there.

She drew up short, her eyebrows pulling together. He

looked at her, and his face reddened. People bumped into her getting off the bus, and Cassie urged her feet forward. She started around him, but Will reached out and grabbed her sleeve.

"Cassie," he said, and she halted.

"What?" she asked.

"I—I just wanted to say sorry. For what I said about you."

An apology? Cassie hardly dared believe it. A million retorts ran through her mind, the desire to demand an explanation. But in the end, she realized, it didn't matter. She wasn't interested in Will. She didn't need to guilt-trip him. Cassie nodded. "Okay. Thanks for telling me."

Will let go of her sleeve. "We can be friends, still, right?"

They were never friends to begin with. But she just bobbed her head again. "Sure."

By lunchtime the rumors had died down, and Cassie could almost put the whole thing behind her.

Right before school let out, Ms. Timber brought in a television and set it in front of the class.

"I have a surprise for you guys," she said.

Cassie pressed her hands together and sat up straighter. She loved movie days.

Ms. Timber held up a small electronic device. "I have on here all of your invention presentations you did in October. I thought they would be fun to watch."

That wasn't as exciting as a movie, but Cassie couldn't complain, since it didn't involve school work or taking notes. Besides, the inventions had been fun, and it had been so long ago she couldn't remember what everyone did. She remembered Andrea's dirty clothes/washing machine, but that was about it.

Ms. Timber made everyone put their books away and get their backpacks, and then they settled in to watch the presentations. Cassie rested her head on her backpack, feeling a little sleepy as she watched again as Andrew demonstrated how to add carbonation back to a soda. Her eyes closed, lulled into a warm contentedness by the monotonous voice on the television screen.

And then she heard her own voice, and Cassie's eyes shot open. For a moment, she had completely forgotten her replicator. She sat up straighter, watching herself on the screen as she pressed fake buttons on her invention. She opened the little door and pulled out the tiny hamburger, still wrapped in paper from the fast food restaurant.

With a big smile, the television-Cassie unwrapped the hamburger and took a bite. "Yum!" she cried around a mouthful of week-old hamburger, just as Todd Wilcox's recorded voice shouted, "Ew!"

Immediately the class burst into laughter. Cassie's face grew hot, and she wished she could disappear under her desk.

"Great job, Cassie," Ms. Timber said, also laughing as she turned off the television. "I'll never forget that moment when you bit into that rotten hamburger."

The bell rang, and everyone stood up, making a beeline for the door.

"It was great, Cassie," Miles said, elbowing his way past other kids to join her. "Now if you can make fresh hamburgers appear, you might just have a winner."

"I can," she said, flashing a smile. "I just haven't shared that power with anyone yet."

He cast her a sideways glance. "Well, when you decide to share, be sure and let me know."

The crowd came between them, and Miles let himself get pulled toward the car riders. Cassie slowed, sweeping along toward the buses.

"I will," she said softly, her chest warm for a reason she didn't understand.

~

By the time May rolled around, the warm sunshine and sweltering humidity promised a hot, lengthy summer just around the corner. Along with the promise of summer came the expectation of sixth grade graduation.

"I know you are all ready for summer vacation," Ms. Timber said, quieting down her students after recess. "But we still have one more month of school. Try to stay focused."

Try to stay focused. Even Cassie recognized the futility in that statement. The desire for long days at the pool and no alarm clocks was quickly overtaking her love of learning.

"Everyone get out your math workbook and do pages one-twelve and one-thirteen. As soon as that's done, I'll tell you what we'll be doing for social studies for the rest of the year." Ms. Timber smiled as if she had a wonderful secret she could hardly wait to tell.

"What could possibly be fun about social studies?" Andrea whispered, leaning close to Cassie.

Cassie nodded but didn't answer. Just yesterday, Ms. Timber had let them rearrange their desks so they sat by who they wanted, for the first time all year. Cassie worried that talking too much with Andrea would take away the privilege.

Ms. Timber walked around the class, watching as they finished up the math assignment. Each student placed their workbook on her desk for grading, and when the last workbook was set down, Ms. Timber returned to the front.

"This will be the biggest project you do all year," she said, beaming. "It will be the most important, one that you will remember for the rest of your lives. You will cherish it forever. Therefore, you need to do your very best."

Cassie exchanged a look with Andrea. This project sounded daunting and overwhelming, not in the least bit fun.

"I'm going to give each of you a sheet of paper. On this paper, you'll see all of your classmates' names, followed by a date. It's in alphabetical order. For example, today is Cara Barnes. Here on my desk I have two stacks of paper. One is a blank white sheet, while the other is lined." Ms. Timber held them up, her smile growing bigger. "On the blank sheet, you'll draw a picture of Cara. The very best you can. Some of you are artistic, and some of you aren't, but it doesn't matter. On the lined sheet, you'll write about Cara. Things you like about her, things you remember about her, hopes you have for her future, whatever you want. As long as it's nice." She fixed them all with a stern look.

The class began to fidget and murmur, and a rush of anticipation ran through Cassie. She wasn't as good an artist as some of the other kids, but she enjoyed drawing, especially from photos. She could draw a nice image of her classmates.

It was the writing part that excited her, though. She excelled at getting her thoughts down on paper. And she could think of no better way to let some of her classmates know how much they'd meant to her this year.

CHAPTER FORTY-FOUR

Lovingly Drawn

"Cassie," Ms. King said in music time as they all got into their assigned seats, "will you stay after class a moment? I want to talk to you about something."

"Sure," Cassie answered, pulling out her songbook and trying not to sound too curious. She liked Ms. King, but they hadn't spent a lot of time together since last year when Mr. Jones ran the school band. Now that he'd given it up, Cassie only saw her teacher once a week, during music time. The paranoid part of her whispered that she might be in trouble, but she cast it aside. She hadn't done anything wrong.

Class ended and everyone lined up at the door, waiting for Ms. Timber, but Cassie put her book on the shelf and walked over to the piano. She was surprised to notice Andrew Simpson, a friendly kid from her class, also walking to the piano.

"Yes, Ms. King?" she asked, arriving at the same time as Andrew.

"Oh, good." Ms. King smiled at both of them. "I have some very exciting news for you."

Cassie waited. It had to do with music, which she loved, so it must be good.

"I've been informed that the community is creating a children's choir. They've asked me to select four students, two sixth graders and two fifth graders, to be in their choir. I've chosen you two. Are you interested?"

Cassie gaped, stunned, and Andrew said, "Yeah, that sounds like it would be fun."

"Cassie?" Ms. King asked, and they both looked at her.

"Of course!" Cassie sputtered, finding her voice. She beamed at her teacher. "I would love to." She couldn't believe the honor.

"Great." Ms. King handed them both an envelope. "Take this home, I need your parents to sign it. If you can stay late after school on Thursday, we'll do a little singing exercise with all four of you. Then the community director will reach out to you about more practices."

"Sure," Cassie said, taking her envelope. She hoped her mom wouldn't mind.

"Your class is gone." Ms. King nodded to where the line of kids had stood only minutes ago. "Better catch up with them. And let me know if you have any questions, my number's on the form."

Cassie clutched her envelope to her chest as she walked with Andrew back to class. "Isn't this cool?" she breathed.

"Yeah. It's pretty neat."

Cassie hesitated, then blurted, "It's like Ms. King thinks we're really good singers—like maybe, the best."

"That's why she asked us." He turned and grinned at her, a piece of his longish blond hair falling in his face.

"Yeah." Cassie couldn't hold back her own smile. "Must be."

Every day for the next few days, Cassie rushed through her math assignment so she could work on the class caricatures, as Ms. Timber called them. So far they hadn't been any of her close friends. Andrea's last name was Wall, so she would be near the end. Miles would be in a week and a half, though, just a few days before her. His would be special. Cassie needed her skills to be up to par before his turn came around.

Today was Michael Cox. A few months ago, Cassie had considered him a friend. She'd even invited him over to her twelfth birthday party. But last month, Michael had helped spread rumors about Cassie when she wouldn't be Will's girlfriend. Even though everyone had apologized and the situation was mostly behind them, Cassie hadn't really talked to Michael since.

She hesitated on his narrative. She wanted it to sound kind while still being genuine. So she wrote about her birthday, and how fun it had been to have him there. She mentioned the times they ate lunch together when Michael liked Andrea. Then she added, truthfully, that Michael had been an impactful part of her sixth grade year, and he had helped her become the person she was.

For better or worse. She didn't add that, of course, but Michael would know.

She finished up the narrative and started on the picture. She'd start it here in school, but she really needed last year's yearbook. She drew the basic outline of a person from the torso up.

"How's your drawing coming along?" Andrea asked, leaning in. She had a set of colored pencils out and was already shading Michael's face.

334

"Pretty good. I'll do most of it at home."

"Yeah." Andrea nodded. "That's a good head shape."

Cassie scowled, and Andrea giggled. "Thanks a lot," Cassie growled. "Let's see yours."

Andrea moved her elbow out of the way, and Cassie studied the clean, precise pencil marks on Andrea's paper. She'd done a fantastic job capitalizing on Michael's features, making it recognizably him while still having a whimsical, cartoonish feel. Cassie felt a pang of jealousy.

"You're a much better artist than me," she said, turning back to her own paper.

"Not true," Andrea protested. "Yours will be just as good when you're done."

Cassie didn't bother objecting. She put her paper inside her folder, determined to finish it at home where no one would see it.

~

Cassie walked with Andrew to Ms. King's classroom after school Thursday.

"Welcome!" Ms. King said, ushering them over to the piano. "I'm so glad your parents gave you permission!"

"Me, too," Cassie said. It had taken some pleading and cajoling to convince her mother, especially since she had soccer right after this. "I"m glad too."

Two fifth grade girls already waited by the piano. Ms. King introduced the students to each other, then sat down behind the keys.

"All right, we'll be quick," she said. "I'm just going to play an ascending and descending scale to get your range. Sing along on an 'ah' until you can't anymore."

The piano notes started, and the four of them started singing. At first they all sang together. Andrew was the first to drop out as the notes climbed. Then one of the fifth grade girls. The other one sang along with Cassie for several more notes before she, too, dropped out. Ms. King shot Cassie an indecipherable look as Cassie continued to sing, hitting the notes as they rose higher and higher.

"All right," Ms. King said, her hands stilling on the piano keys. "You hit a high C. I'm very surprised you can go that high." She took out a notebook and wrote in it. "Definitely a soprano." Her hands went back to the keys. "All right, let's go back down!"

Cassie sang along, her mind lingering on Ms. King's words. What did it mean, exactly? Was it unusual to be able to sing so high? Her body tingled at the idea that she might have some sort of special talent.

Not for singing low, though. She frowned as the scale descended, dropping into her lower register and struggling to get the notes out. With a shake of her head, she shut her mouth, the first to drop out. The other girls continued singing until finally only Andrew was left.

"Very nice!" Ms. King said, retrieving her notebook again. "I think I chose very well." She beamed at them. "Cassie, you'll be a soprano, Lindsey a soprano, Courtney an alto, and Andrew, you can sing whatever you're asked to sing." She put down her pencil. "Your first practice is Saturday. Good luck, guys!"

~

Cassie hurried outside, pleased to see her mother already waiting at the curb.

"How was it?" Mrs. Jones asked.

"Great," Cassie said, opening her lunch box to see if she had any food left. Nothing. She'd eaten it all. "We didn't do much, just sang so Ms. King could hear our range."

"And what was yours?"

"Soprano." Cassie put her backpack at her feet and looked out the window, watching the tall trees go by. The constant rain and the bright sunshine left a bright shade of green across the foliage. The grass fairly shimmered with it, the leaves seeming to swell with pride at the fine color. "I'm not really surprised. Ms. Malcolm says I have the potential to be a lyric soprano." Ms. Malcolm was her voice teacher, and she heard Cassie sing more than anyone. Although what exactly that was, Cassie wasn't sure.

"Well, good. I'm glad to see you participating in something you enjoy."

"Yeah."

"Your soccer clothes are in the back. Go ahead and get changed, and I have dinner in the plastic bag by your chair."

By the time Cassie got home from soccer, her bruised ego just wanted to curl up with a good book. But she wasn't done with Michael's caricature. Her mom made her shower and get ready for bed, and then she sat at the kitchen table with her fifth grade yearbook open in front of her, examining Michael's picture. She figured it didn't have to be perfect, since he wasn't one of her best friends, but she wanted it to be good.

The phone rang, and Cassie glanced at the clock above the stove top while her mom answered it. Almost eight.

"Um-hum." Mrs. Jones said. "I see. Yes, thank you." She hung up the phone and leaned against the counter, arms folded across her chest.

Cassie frowned. Was she in trouble? "What?"

"That was Betsy's social worker," Mrs. Jones said.

Cassie's breath caught. It had been a few weeks since

Betsy disappeared. Cassie had been waiting so long to hear from her she'd almost thought it wouldn't happen.

"And?" Cassie said, finding her voice again. "What did they say?"

"It's all arranged for her to live with her aunt. She'll be moving to Mountain Home next week."

"Where's that?" Cassie asked, her throat closing up.

"It's a city about three hours from here."

Three hours. So far away. Cassie's eyes blurred with tears. "I'll never see her."

"Not very often," her mom agreed. "But Betsy wants to see you. If you can, the social worker has arranged for you to visit Betsy at her hotel room this Saturday, before she leaves for Mountain Home."

This Saturday. Cassie's heart soared, and then it nose-dived as she remembered something. "Saturday is my practice with the community children's choir. And then I have my last soccer game."

"What's more important?"

Betsy. Without a doubt. She didn't really mind missing soccer, but the thought of not being in the choir made Cassie's stomach tighten. "I'll tell Ms. King tomorrow that I can't make it," she whispered.

Mrs. Jones put her hands on Cassie's shoulders and looked her in the eyes. "How about this. You tell Ms. King that you'll be there, but you'll have to leave early because of a family situation. That way, you can do both."

Cassie sucked in a breath, excitement returning. "Okay!" She pulled away from her mom and headed to the cupboard for the dishes, already jittery with anticipation at seeing her friend again.

CHAPTER FORTY-FIVE

Family Situation

Saturday morning couldn't come soon enough, and yet when it finally arrived and Cassie's mom pulled her up to the front of the junior high where the practices would be, Cassie suddenly doubted her ability to walk up to the doors.

"The only person I'll know here is Andrew," she said, just realizing that.

"Then go make new friends."

Still Cassie didn't move. Her fingers fumbled with the door handle. She watched the other kids walking in, almost all of them older than her, taller, skinnier, prettier. Cassie glanced down and frowned at her tummy bulging over the lip of her blue jeans. She was short, chubby, and still in elementary school.

"Cassie?" her mom said, and Cassie shook herself. None of that mattered. She was here to sing.

"I'll be back in an hour," her mom said. "Be out here waiting."

"Of course," Cassie said, pushing the door open. She followed behind the other kids, continuing into the school building.

A woman ushered them into the room, asking their names as they stepped inside.

"Harrison Larkin," the boy in front of her said.

The woman consulted her list and pointed him in another direction.

"RyAnne Spencer," a girl said, tossing her wavy, raven-colored hair over her shoulder. Tall, with olive skin and a sculpted nose, she radiated beauty and self-confidence. Cassie tried not to stare.

"That corner, with the first sopranos," the woman said.

A few more kids stepped up, and then it was Cassie's turn.

"Cassandra Jones."

A quick glance at her list, and the woman pointed to the left. "First soprano."

Cassie breathed a sigh of relief and climbed up to that section. She found a chair next to a pretty blond and flashed a smile.

"I'm Cassie," she said.

"Kenya," the girl replied. She folded her hands in her lap and looked straight ahead.

"What grade are you in?" Cassie asked.

"Sixth," Kenya said.

"Me too!" At least she wasn't the only sixth grader here. "A lot of the kids seem older."

"My school sent in two sixth graders. Me and RyAnne. She's a soprano, also." Kenya pointed to the stunning brunette Cassie had noticed earlier.

"No way," Cassie said, her eyes widening. "She's in sixth grade?" With her refined features and tall figure, Cassie would've guessed eighth.

"Yeah. She's a really good singer, too." Kenya looked at her then, pointedly, as if she doubted Cassie's ability.

"Oh," was all she could think to say. She looked toward her hands, wishing she'd brought a book to hide in.

The woman patted her hands on the piano, silencing the talking. Cassie gladly focused on her. She had curly strawberry-blond hair, a sharp nose, and a pointed chin. She smiled, and it softened the harsh lines of her face. "Welcome to the new children's community choir! It's time we got started, but first I want to introduce myself. I'm Vanessa Vanderwood, and this has been a dream of mine for years. I've been conducting choirs in school but always wanted to put something like this together, something for, well, kids. I'm so pleased each one of you decided to join me! Without further discussion, let me hand out the music."

Cassie accepted her sheet music and didn't attempt to make conversation with any of the kids around her again. Despite the fact they were all singers, this didn't seem like her crowd.

As the minute hand crept closer to the hour, she became more and more anxious. She would have to step down and walk across the room in front of everyone to get out They would all see her leave early. Would Ms. Vanderwood say anything? Try to stop her?

The minute hand paused on the hour, and Cassie didn't move. They were in the middle of a song. She couldn't just get up and go.

Ms. Vanderwood cut them off. She called on the altos and began pointing out their mistakes, all while Cassie fidgeted. The clock kept ticking, and Cassie knew her mom would be in the parking lot, waiting.

Just do this, she told herself. She took a deep breath and stood up—just as Ms. Vanderwood turned to the sopranos.

She made eye contact with Cassie. "Do you need something?"

"Yes," Cassie said, saying the first thing that came to her mind. "Can I use the bathroom?"

The students tittered, and her face warmed, though she wasn't sure if it was her improper grammar or her excuse that made them laugh at her.

Ms. Vanderwood pursed her lips together and gave a quick nod. "Hurry back."

Exhaling and keeping her eyes down, Cassie walked down the steps, past the rows of staring kids. She made her way across the room, feeling the eyes on her back.

"All right," Ms. Vanderwood said, and Cassie closed the door behind her.

She was out, at least. She might be in trouble later, but for now she had escaped.

Sure enough, the blue van was parked out front, waiting for her.

"Cassie," her mom said when she opened the door, "what took so long? It's ten after."

"Sorry," Cassie said. "I had a hard time getting away." She didn't explain what had gone down. It was too embarrassing.

"Well," Mrs. Jones said, pulling the car out of the parking lot and heading for the main road, "how was it?"

Agonizing. Humiliating. Humbling. "She put me in first soprano. I like the songs we're learning."

"That's good! Is she nice? What did she say about you leaving early?"

"Yeah, she's nice. And she didn't say anything." She

hadn't, after all.

Betsy was staying with her social worker at a motel in downtown Springdale. It only took fifteen minutes to get there. The motel wrapped around the outdoor pool, all of the room numbers facing toward the courtyard. Mrs. Jones parked her car directly in front of Betsy's room number. As Cassie got out, her stomach suddenly twisted with nerves. What if they had nothing to say to each other? What if Betsy was different? She followed behind her mother and let her mom take the lead.

Mrs. Jones knocked on the door. After a brief moment, the door cracked open, still barricaded by a small metal chain.

"Hi," her mom said. "I'm Karen Jones, Cassandra's mom. We're here to visit with Betsy."

The door closed, and Cassie's eyes widened. Was that it? Were they not welcome? Or did they have the wrong information?

But then it opened again, without the chain, and Betsy flew out the door.

"Cassie!" she cried, her light brown hair blowing behind her as she threw her arms around Cassie. And then her shoulders shook, and Cassie realized she was crying.

Cassie hugged her back, her throat tightening. "It's okay. I'm here."

The social worker ("Jenn," Betsy said) left them alone in the room while she and Mrs. Jones went to the lobby. Now that they were alone, Cassie was less sure of herself.

"How are you?" she asked tentatively, feeling foolish for the question.

"I'm good," Betsy said, and then she hesitated, her eyes turning down and her mouth dropping its smile. "It's been really hard, Cassie. Really awful, actually."

"I don't understand what happened," Cassie said, measuring her words carefully. She wanted Betsy to talk, but she didn't want to seem as though she were prying. "Everything seemed fine when I was there."

Betsy let out a deep breath, her shoulders sagging. "It was. Sometimes it was. But other times, it wasn't."

"What wasn't?"

"My parents. My dad, actually. He—would drink. And when he did, he'd get mean and angry." Tears pricked Betsy's eyes. "My mom would lock me in my room, but I'd still hear. I'd hear it all."

"What did you do?" Cassie whispered, horrified.

"Nothing. But one time, the last time, I had the phone with me. And I called the police. They came out to the house and arrested my dad. They took him away and told my mom they were filing a report with childcare services. When I came to school, I was so sad because my dad was in jail."

Cassie took Betsy's hand and squeezed it. "You should have said something."

"I couldn't," Betsy whispered. "I was so ashamed. I thought no one would ever look at me the same again."

"I'm so sorry."

"Child protection services were waiting for me when I got off the bus. They waited while I packed a bag and then took me away."

Cassie waited a moment to digest the information, willing herself not to cry. Betsy was holding it together. Cassie couldn't fall apart. "And now? What happens next?"

"I'm going to live with my aunt. She'll take care of me.

My parents are supposed to get their lives back in order if they want me back, but—" and now tears welled up in Betsy's eyes. She blinked, and they spilled over. "My dad said they don't want me back. My mom said I'll be better off with my aunt. I don't know if I'll ever go home."

"Betsy." Cassie reached over and hugged her. Betsy's tears seemed to be permission for her own, and they cried together.

~

"I just don't understand," Cassie said to her mom in the car as they drove home. "How can someone's parents decide they don't want them?"

"I don't know, sweetheart," Mrs. Jones said, slowing

down for a red light. "Drugs do crazy things to people. They lose track of what they really love. The things that used to be important seem less so."

"I still don't get it." Cassie remembered Betsy's mom driving her to Cassie's house for her birthday party last year. She'd been so nice, giving Betsy a five-dollar bill so she could have a gift for Cassie. And her dad acted so normal at the Christmas party, just a few months ago.

"Betsy's lucky she has an aunt to go live with," Mrs. Jones said. "Otherwise she might be put into foster care."

"What's that?" Cassie asked.

"Foster care is run by the state. It's like adoption, but it's temporary. Children stay with a family for a few months, maybe longer, until they go somewhere else."

"Somewhere else?" Cassie tried to picture a child getting comfortable in a home, only to be moved away from it. "Like where?"

"Well, sometimes back to their parents, if the problem is gone. Other times, though, they just go to another family."

"And then they're adopted?"

"Sometimes, sweetie. If it works out that way."

Cassie didn't say much the rest of the way home. She hoped Betsy would be happy with her new family. At least she wouldn't be shuffled around from one family to another.

Episode 7: Endings

CHAPTER FORTY-SIX
Class Study

The last weeks of sixth grade flew by, and Cassandra Jones found herself absorbed in one thing only: the class caricatures. As the grand finale to the sixth-grade year, her teacher Ms. Timber had assigned them the task of writing an essay about each classmate. Not only that, but they had to draw a portrait of their classmate.

During the school day, Cassie would write the page of praise and compliments for her fellow classmates. Then at night, she'd come home and carefully draw their portrait, using the yearbook as a model. They were fun, and none of them were so important that she worried about getting it perfect.

Until it was Miles Hansen's turn, that was.

Just looking at the lined paper with Miles' name at the top made Cassie's heart beat harder. She was afraid to put her pencil to the paper, certain that somehow anyone watching would see her emotions written on her sleeve. She rehearsed in her head what she would say: "We've been friends for a year now. I'll never forget the way you showed me how to make a paper airplane so I wouldn't feel so stupid in that competition. You are the kindest, most thoughtful boy I've ever met." She cringed and mentally erased the words. Boy? She couldn't call him a boy! And he probably didn't want to be the kindest, most thoughtful, either. Those words belonged to sissies.

How could she possibly tell him how she felt? That she admired him like no one else? That something inside of her warmed whenever he looked at her, that she melted whenever he laughed?

She couldn't say that. She couldn't say any of it.

There was no one to talk to on the bus anymore, so Cassie drafted out her page on another sheet of paper. She mentioned their friendship, how grateful she was for it, how he made each day a little better. She touched lightly on his more charming characteristics, hoping she didn't sound too gushy.

That sounded good. Satisfied, she copied her draft onto the official paper, using her best handwriting as the bus jolted up and down over the bumps and holes.

She read back over it when she finished, expecting to feel pleased. But it didn't feel like quite enough. Something was missing, and she knew what it was: her true feelings. Cassie tapped the pencil on the paper, trying to figure out how to properly word this. After some hesitation, she added one more line: "I won't ever forget what you mean to me."

She settled back in her seat and studied the sentence. Was it too much? Sudden fear seized her. What if she ruined their friendship? She considered erasing the sentence, but she'd have to get a new paper. He'd still be able to see it.

Stop worrying, she told herself. *It's just a nice sentiment. It will be fine.* She pushed it from her head and put the paper away.

As soon as dinner was over, Cassie pulled out the yearbook and started stenciling Miles' face. This one she had to have just right. She got his eyes, the face shape, the tilt of his glasses. But when she got to the smile, she just couldn't seem to get it right. She drew it, erased it, tried again, but it just got worse.

Frustrated, Cassie ignored his face for now and started on his shoulders, his posture, the way he sat in the chair and smiled at the camera. She drew with soft lines, ready to erase at any moment. Then she got out the colored pencils and filled in the shirt, the hair color, even his brown eyes, everything except his mouth.

Her mom came in with a pile of papers and settled into the chair next to her at the kitchen table. "That one looks really good. Who is it?"

"Miles," Cassie said, not looking up.

"Ah. Miles."

The yearbook background was a dull gray, but Cassie had been adding colored lines behind her classmates, just to add some pizazz to the portraits. She did this now with Miles, then settled back to examine it.

It looked pretty good, if she could just get his smile right. She tried again, then heaved an angry sigh.

Mrs. Jones looked up. "What's wrong?"

"His smile is."

"His smile's what?"

"Wrong!" Cassie sucked in a breath before she got too emotional.

Mrs. Jones cocked her head and examined the paper. "Looks good to me."

"No." Cassie shook her head. "It doesn't capture it."

"Want me to try?"

Mrs. Jones was pretty artistic and could probably do it, but that rubbed Cassie the wrong way. She wanted this to be from her. It was her gift to Miles, even if he didn't know it. "I have to do this."

"Then take a break from it. Finish up the rest of the portrait and come back to the smile later. Maybe tomorrow morning."

"Why will that make a difference?" Cassie grumbled.

"I don't know, but it does. Sometimes you have memory of what you already drew and it influences what you're trying to do."

"Fine," Cassie sighed, willing to give in if for no other reason that she didn't want to try again right now. Instead, she focused on the background. She added a few more lines criss-crossing with the other colored ones, using a ruler to make sure they were straight. Then, just because, she added smaller lines at the intersections, almost like a star. She added a few more and pulled her head back to study the effect. She liked it. Almost as if the paper sparkled.

"I can tell this one means a lot to you."

Cassie had forgotten her mother still sat there. "It's Miles," she said, her face burning with the admission behind those two words. She put her pencils away and returned the almost-completed portrait to her binder. "Good night, Mom." She moved her binder to the counter, away from the breakfast crowd that would take over the table in the morning.

"Night, Cassie."

The moment Cassie got up in the morning, she

remembered the unfinished portrait. She brushed her teeth, combed her hair, and dressed quickly, then hurried to the kitchen. While her siblings ate breakfast, she pulled out the paper. She laid it out on the counter and gave it a good look before carefully taking her pencil. She didn't even glance at the yearbook picture; instead, she closed her eyes and imagined Miles' smile. Then she lifted her pencil and tried one last time.

It worked. Cassie's lips drew upward in her own smile when she saw the paper. Now it was right.

When Ms. Timber called for the portraits and essays, Cassie joined the line of students placing their drawings on the desk. She held hers close to her chest. She didn't want anyone to see it; not before Miles did. She laid her papers down quickly. She'd barely set them down before another student covered them up with their own set.

She exhaled, feeling her heart rate slow as she returned to her seat. She put the portrait out of her head and focused on her school work.

"Cassie!" Ms. Timber called out to her just before she exited the classroom when school let out.

Cassie paused in the doorway, her classmates bumping her as they rushed past. "Yes, Ms. Timber?"

Her teacher joined her, her expression unreadable. "You've been doing a fantastic job on these class studies, Cassie."

"Thank you," Cassie said, not sure what else to say.

"I hope you continue to pursue your skills. You are the best author and artist I've ever had. No other student has poured so much emotion into this project. I'm very pleased."

Cassie's face warmed under the praise. "Thank you, Ms.

Timber."

"Don't you forget that, Cassie."

"I won't."

~

On Saturday Cassie had another children's choir practice. She walked in nervously, not quite sure what the director would say.

As it turned out, she didn't say anything. Cassie found her spot on the risers. Nobody asked her why she'd left early, and she realized no one had even noticed. She almost laughed with relief. Sometimes it was good to be invisible.

After an hour of practice, Ms. Vanderwool held up a hand.

"I think we've got it, gang! Next Friday, come an hour early before our performance so we can run through this one more time."

Andrew waited for Cassie outside the practice room. "What do you think?"

Cassie shot him a smile, unable to hide her enthusiasm. "It's great! I love the songs. You?"

"Sure. They're great." Andrew shoved his hands in his pockets and shrugged. "You really like singing?"

"Love it," Cassie sighed. "I've been taking voice lessons all year. I think it might be, I don't know, my talent. What I'm really good at."

"What about the clarinet? You played that in the talent show last year."

"Yeah. But I was never very good at it."

"Ms. Timber thinks you're a great writer."

Cassie squinted at him as they passed beneath the doors leading outside. How did he know that? "Just for fun. I don't think I could write all the time."

"I guess authors don't make any money, anyway."

Cassie had never even considered that; she'd never considered making any money, really. "Guess that's a good reason not to be one. Musicians make money."

"Tons."

She spotted her mom's van parked in the lot with the other parent vehicles. "I'll see you Monday."

Andrew waved, and she hurried to the car.

~

"I have an announcement to make," Ms. Timber said on Monday as the students began to pack up their school things for dismissal.

"We already know," Todd said. "Saturday is graduation."

The class erupted with cheers, eager and excited voices. Cassie straightened in her seat, wiggling her legs in anticipation. Sixth grade graduation. The end of elementary school. Next year they'd all move on to junior high, a whole new sphere of existence.

"Quiet down, please," Ms. Timber said, lowering her hand. When the kids stopped talking so loudly, she said, a slight smile on her face, "Yes, next Saturday is graduation. And we'll spend all of this week getting ready for it. But that's not my announcement. Three weeks after that, at the end of June—" She took a deep breath, her face flushing, and said, "I'm getting married."

A hush fell over the room. Cassie blinked in surprise, looking up at her teacher. That wasn't what she'd expected, and judging from the reactions, or lack thereof, of her classmates, no one else had, either.

"I didn't even know you have a boyfriend," Maureen said.

Her statement broke the silence, and then all at once the kids were asking questions. "When?" "How long have you been dating?" "Why did you keep this a secret?" "Can we come?" "What will your name be?" "Are you moving?"

Ms. Timber chuckled. "I didn't feel it was appropriate to discuss my personal life with my students. But now that school's almost out, I figured I should tell you. Especially since you're all invited to my wedding."

The boys continued to sit in stunned silence, but the girls broke into little squeals, high-pitched voices thrumming with excitement.

"A wedding!" Andrea said, her eyes sparkling as she leaned close to Cassie. "We'll get to dress up! Maybe we can help throw a bridal shower!"

Cassie nodded, though she wasn't even sure what all those words meant. "Yeah. Fun."

"One more thing," Ms. Timber said loudly. She waited until the eager voices died down. "I have your character books nicely bound. I think you'll be quite pleased with how they turned out, the things your classmates said about you. These books should be something you'll treasure for years to come. If you'll stay seated, I'll bring them to you."

Cassie's heart began to pound in anticipation as Ms. Timber wandered the room, placing the colorful, laminated books on each desk. She could hardly breathe as she wondered what Miles might have said about her. What if he said something amazing? Should she talk to him about it?

What if he said nothing at all?

She shook off that thought. Everyone had to say something.

Her book landed on her desk, the big typed header that

read "Cassandra Jones: Sixth grade" beaming up at her. Her fingers trembled as she gripped the edge of the page.

Don't turn it, she told herself. *Wait till you get on the bus.*

Somehow, that pacified her. She would read this in the privacy of her bus seat, all by herself now that Betsy didn't ride also.

As soon as the bell rang, she bolted from her seat, throwing her backpack over one arm and making a beeline for the bus. Her hands shook as she settled herself into the seat. She took a deep breath and forced herself to open to the first page. She wouldn't skip ahead. She would read these through, very calmly—

No, she couldn't. She had to know.

Cassie skipped through until she found Miles' contribution. She smiled at his drawing of her, more fun than accurate, a big smile with white teeth and huge pink glasses. Then she turned her head and read his essay.

Cassie is one of the sweetest, most fun people I've ever met. She's the kind of person you can talk to for hours about nothing. She's kind to everyone, always trying to be a good friend. She's smart, and talented, and I'm pretty sure she'd win America's Got Talent *if they held a show here. As long as the competition didn't involve paper airplanes. She hasn't mastered those yet. But she's a nice girl and a good friend. I'm glad I got to know Cassie even more this year.*

She exhaled, feeling her heart pump just a little harder even though the adrenaline rush was fading. A smile pulled itself across her face. It didn't say too much, it didn't say everything, but it said enough.

CHAPTER FORTY-SEVEN
Wedding Planners

"Can you believe Ms. Timber is getting married?" Andrea Wall asked.

Cassandra Jones watched as her best friend jumped higher and higher on the trampoline. Each jump jostled Cassie just a bit from her vantage point on the edge, and she held on tighter, feeling the springs lengthen and compress beside her fingers.

"It's so cool," Cassie said with a sigh. She pictured their sixth-grade teacher with her short brown hair, pixie nose, and big smile. "I wonder what he's like?"

Andrea dropped down beside Cassie. "I wonder why she never said anything about him."

"Why we never met him," Cassie agreed, echoing Andrea's thoughts.

Andrea threw herself back on the trampoline. Cassie lay next to her, and they stared up at the blue sky, the clouds floating delicately by. It was Monday of the last week of school, and they had no homework, no assignments, nothing to do except prepare for graduation. Mrs. Jones had agreed to let Cassie come over after school, though she still said no to a slumber party.

"I bet he's cute," Andrea said.

"Of course he's cute," Cassie scoffed. "She wouldn't marry him if he weren't."

"As cute as Miles?" Andrea giggled.

Cassie felt her face burn. She pushed up on the edge of her glasses even though they weren't falling—how could they be when she lay flat on her back? She hadn't showed Andrea yet what Miles wrote in her memory book, even though Andrea had been begging to see. The words were too close to Cassie's heart, and too ambiguous. She couldn't take the chance that Andrea would make light of them. "Miles is different."

"Yeah, because he's twelve."

Now Andrea laughed, and Cassie joined her. But she pictured Miles, with his wire-framed glasses and dark hair and brown eyes. As cute as he was, it was his kindness that got to her.

"Someday you and I will get married," Cassie said, the words just slipping out.

"To who?" Andrea whispered.

Cassie didn't answer. She couldn't even joke about this.

Maybe Andrea felt that too. "What kind of dress will you wear?" she asked. "Old-fashioned white or something more modern?"

"You mean traditional white?" Cassie said. "Of course. White and long with a veil and a long, long train."

"And sequins," Andrea said. "All around the waist and chest."

"And a big white gathered bow," Cassie said, picking up steam. "A v-neck with puffed sleeves."

"Puffed sleeves? Big white bow?" Andrea poked her,

laughing again. "I think you mean my mom's wedding dress."

Cassie flushed. How should she know what kind of dress she'd wear? She'd never really thought about it before.

"Hey, I know." Andrea sat up, her blue-green eyes lighting with an idea. "Let's throw Ms. Timber a party."

"What kind of party?" Cassie asked.

"A bridal party! It's 'traditional.'" She winked at the last word. "Usually the bride's friends do it, but wouldn't she be surprised if her students did it?"

"Oh, yeah!" Cassie pushed up on her elbows. "We'd have to get to school early to set it up."

"No! We could sneak in during recess when she's on duty. Set everything up, and when she comes in, surprise!"

"I love the idea!"

The girls went to Andrea's room and spent the next hour planning who they would ask to help set up, what decorations they would have, and what treats, if any. Cassie volunteered her mom to make a cake.

"Hearts," Andrea said. "We need lots of hearts." She wrote it down on her yellow notepad and tapped the pen against her lips. "Can you come back over tomorrow?"

"No," Cassie said. "I have Girls Club." They met every week on Tuesdays.

"How about Wednesday?"

"I have voice lessons."

Andrea made a face. "Why are you so busy? Fine. How about Thursday? Has to be, because then we only have Friday for the party!"

"I don't know," Cassie said. At least soccer was over. Could still be iffy, though. Two days in one week?

"Ask your mom. Tell her it's for Ms. Timber. I'll invite the other girls from class over, too."

Mrs. Jones might say yes, if she knew what it was for. "Okay."

~

"Cassandra." Mrs. Jones burst into Cassie's room Wednesday after school. "I've been calling you for ten minutes. Why haven't you answered?"

Cassie looked up from her notebook, immensely irritated with her mother. She'd been trying to draft the perfect letter for Ms. Timber ever since she got home. She wanted it to express her love and appreciation without sounding too cheesy or syrupy. Every time her mom called her name, she lost her train of though. "I'm right here." *Duh.*

Mrs. Jones looked at her watch. "Cassie, it's almost five. You'll be late for voice lessons."

Voice lessons! "Oh crapola."

"Don't say that," her mom said, scowling.

"Why?" Cassie pushed herself to her feet and shoved her shoes on. "It's not bad."

"It is the way you say it. Your dad will pick you up and take you to church after."

Cassie groaned. "When will I get this letter done?"

"Take it with you. You can do it while you wait for your dad."

"What about dinner? I'm hungry!"

"I packed you some rice to eat in the car."

Cassie stood there staring at her mom, tears pricking her eyes. "I have too much to do!" she wailed.

"What homework can you possibly have? There's only two days of school left."

"It's something for Ms. Timber. I really need to finish it!"

Mrs. Jones blinked. "Honestly, Cassie. It's the same schedule every Wednesday."

"I don't want to go." The tears leaked over.

"Don't start this. We're leaving now."

Cassie picked up her notebook and shoved it into her backpack. How unfair. She didn't feel like singing or hanging out with the kids at church who didn't talk to her. She didn't want stupid rice for dinner.

Her mom left Emily in charge and backed out of the driveway. Cassie kept her eyes on the trees as they drove into the city, refusing to look at her mother.

"You're being ridiculous. It's like I'm forcing you to do voice lessons. You asked for this, remember?"

"But I haven't practiced." Cassie finally faced her mother. "Ms. Malcolm's just going to yell at me."

Mrs. Jones shrugged. "Well, again, Cassie, this is nothing new. You know when you have voice. There's no one to blame but yourself."

Cassie returned her gaze out the window, the tears pricking again. Of course her mom wouldn't understand.

Mrs. Jones pulled up at the music center and put the car in park. "All right, Cassie, pile out. And stop crying before she wonders what's wrong with you."

Cassie reached under her glasses and wiped at her eyes. "I'm not crying."

Her mom didn't answer, and Cassie slammed the door shut. The van pulled away as Cassie let herself in.

Ms. Malcolm looked up from the piano as Cassie entered the studio.

"Cassandra," she said, "you're late."

"Sorry," Cassie mumbled.

"Well, let's not waste any time. Pull out your vocal book,

please."

Cassie squatted beside her backpack and unzipped it. Just as she did, she realized something: this was her school bag, not her music bag. Her hands continued searching for the vocal book, unwilling to accept the fact that it wasn't here. Finally she stopped, staring at her bag, a lump in her throat.

"Cassie?" Ms. Malcolm said.

"I don't have it," she whispered. "I brought the wrong bag."

Tears pricked her eyes in the silence that followed. Why was today going so horribly wrong?

"I guess we'll have to use my copy, then," Ms. Malcolm said.

Cassie exhaled. "Okay."

Her teacher put her fingers on the piano keys and met Cassie's eyes in the mirror. "Posture, Cassie. And don't look so upset. It's just music."

Cassie nodded and straightened up, pushing her shoulders back to open her chest as she'd been taught. Ms. Malcolm always seemed so stern, so rigid, yet sometimes she seemed quite gentle, also. At least she wasn't angry.

"You all right?" her dad asked when she got in the car after voice.

Cassie flipped down the mirror in the visor and examined her red eyes. An hour later, and she still looked like she'd been crying. "Yeah."

"Your mom said you were in a mood."

Cassie scowled at her reflection and shut the mirror. Why would her mom say that? "I'm not."

"It's normal, you know. When kids get older they get moody. Goes along with all the body changes."

Cassie folded her arms over her chest. She knew all about the body changes, and she did not want to talk about them with her dad. "I wasn't moody."

"Next you'll start to hate your parents. The moment you turn thirteen, you'll think you know everything and we know nothing."

She swiveled in her seat and frowned at him. "What are you talking about? I'd never hate you guys."

"Oh, you just wait. All teenagers go through it. You'll think we're evil."

She blinked, caught off-guard by the idea. Hate her parents? She had good parents. "Whatever, Daddy. That won't happen."

"We'll see." He shot her a grin, and she harrumphed. She'd prove him wrong.

CHAPTER FORTY-EIGHT

Big Ideas

The next day, seven girls gathered in Andrea's living room. She put colored construction paper on the coffee table and beamed at everyone.

"Okay, girls. The goal is to cut out thirty hearts. That's only like five each."

"Are we cutting out anything besides hearts?" Maureen, a girl Cassie knew from Girls Club as well as school, asked.

"Like what?" Andrea asked.

"Like, I don't know, wedding cakes," she said. "Or candles."

"Shoes!" Cara Barnes said. Cassie was surprised Cara had come, since she usually seemed too engrossed in boys and looking cool to appear at a function like this.

"Shoes?" Several girls gave Cara a strange look.

A pink tint crept over the bridge of Cara's nose. Her brows lifted above the soft brown eyes, her perfectly curled hair falling down her back. She looked fifteen, not twelve. "Yes. When my sister got married, she shopped for hours looking for the right shoes to go with her dress."

"Kind of makes sense," Andrea said, nodding. "Okay.

Thirty hearts, and then some shoes and cakes!"

Cassie picked up a pair of scissors and knelt next to Andrea. She cut in silence, listening to the chatter and giggles of the other girls. After two hearts, her wrist started cramping. She put the scissors down and shook it out. She cut out another heart before Andrea got out a bag of chips. She started on another heart, but realized her greasy fingers were leaving streaks on the construction paper, so she put it aside.

"Does anyone know what her wedding dress looks like?" Maureen asked. Her long brown hair slid over a shoulder as she reached for more chips.

"Oh, I hope we'll get to see it!" Andrea said.

"Maybe she'll invite us," Kendra said.

"Yeah, right," Maureen scoffed. "Like she'd want to have a bunch of sixth-graders at her wedding."

"Seventh-graders," Cara corrected. She alone continued cutting, her hearts perfect and symmetrical as she laid them down on the carpet. She didn't look up from her task. "We'll be considered seventh-graders by then."

"She already said we're invited," Cassie said. "Right?" Had she heard that wrong? She thought Ms. Timber invited them all when she made the announcement.

Silence met her statement, no one confirming her words.

"I have an idea!" Andrea turned around and booted up the computer at the desk behind her. "Let's look at dresses and try to guess what hers looks like!"

That sounded way more fun than cutting. Cassie and the other girls gathered around Andrea, the cutting forgotten.

"Where do you think they'll go on their honeymoon?" Monica asked.

"Somewhere exotic," Jessica said. "Like Hawaii."

"Or somewhere fun like Branson," Maureen said.

"Branson?" Allison laughed. "That's just across the border in Missouri. How fun would that be?"

Maureen's face flushed pink. "We go all the time. I love it."

The other girls all laughed.

"I've never been," Cassie said, trying to take the spotlight off Maureen. "Sounds fun to me." She remembered her family's trip to Disney World last year and added, "I want to go to Disney World on my honeymoon."

That just brought on more laughter, though Cassie couldn't imagine why.

"You and Maureen are so boring," Allison said. "I want to go to France."

Cassie looked at Andrea, who shrugged. She leaned over and whispered, "I'd go to Disney World too."

~

The last day of sixth grade arrived, and as Cassie selected a long blue t-shirt and black jeans to wear to school, her stomach tightened. Not just because it was the last day of school, either, but because of Ms. Timber's surprise party.

Her mom usually stayed in bed while Cassie got all the kids on the bus, but today she was up.

"Last day of school!" she said cheerfully when Cassie walked into the kitchen. She swiveled a white cake on the round pedestal, carefully dotting it with the icing bag in her hand.

"Is that for Ms. Timber?" Cassie asked, unable to tear her eyes off the white confection. It looked as beautiful as anything in a store.

"And it's not done yet." Mrs. Jones took a step back and beamed at the cake.

"You remember what time to come?"

"Of course. Now go on before you miss the bus."

Cassie shepherded her siblings out the door. Her mom had the cake almost ready. Now as long as Andrea remembered the decorations, the party should be good.

Nearly every student arrived in the classroom before Andrea. Cassie tried to start her morning journaling just to keep her mind occupied, but every two seconds her eyes flicked to the doorway. Finally, just as the final bell rang,

Andrea slipped inside. She threw her backpack into the cubbies and ducked into the desk next to Cassie, her cheeks pink and her breathing fast.

Ms. Timber stood up, welcoming the class and talking about the day's activities.

"Where were you?" Cassie hissed out one side of her mouth. "I was starting to think you weren't coming."

"Sorry," Andrea whispered back. "I forgot everything."

"What?" Cassie gasped, and then clamped a hand to her mouth. No one had noticed her, though. They were busy cheering along to everything Ms. Timber said.

"Don't worry," Andrea whispered, scooting her chair forward and bending closer to Cassie. "We went home and got it all. What about you? Is your mom bringing the cake?"

"Yes." Cassie's muscles relaxed. This really was going to work out. "Wait till you see it."

~

Andrea caught Cassie's eye as Ms. Timber lined them up for recess. Each hour had been filled with one activity after the other. But the best one, in Cassie's opinion, was about to happen. Andrea gave Cassie a long, slow nod, which Cassie returned. She then turned around, caught Maureen's eye, and gave the same nod. Maureen did it back. Cassie smiled and faced the front. The plan was in motion.

The girls filed out with the rest of the sixth grade class, but one by one dropped to the back of the line. When Ms. Timber turned the corner of the building, the seven of them ran back inside the classroom.

"Quickly, quickly, quickly!" Andrea said, pulling out the cut-out hearts and shoes. (No one ever got around to cutting out cakes.)

"Isn't your mom bringing food?" Jessica asked Cassie.

"She'll be here any minute," Cassie said, her pulse racing. She'd been very specific about the time. Now would be a very bad time for her mom to be late.

They taped their cutouts to the desks, the windows, even hung a few to the ceiling.

Then Mrs. Jones came in carrying a cake concealed beneath a crystal dome. "Hello, girls," she said, setting the cake on the desk. She lifted the dome, and they crowded around to "oo" and "aw" over it. Mrs. Jones had looped white ribbons of icing around the cake, accented with little silver balls. Glorious pink roses sat on top.

"It looks great," Cassie said, beaming at her mother. Not that Cassie expected anything less. Her mom was gifted with cakes, always making the most amazing ones for birthdays.

"Oh!" Andrea exclaimed, looking at the time. "We have to get outside. If we're not there at line-up, she'll miss us!"

"I'll just hide behind the backpacks," Mrs. Jones said.

The girls scurried out, hurrying to rejoin their classmates before Ms. Timber noticed they'd been gone. When she blew the whistle to line up, Cassie jostled into place next to Andrea. They looked at each other, and Cassie couldn't resist the grin that spread across her face. Her fingers nudged Andrea's.

"She'll be so surprised!" Andrea whispered, gripping her hand. They put their heads together and giggled, then acted solemn just as Ms. Timber walked by.

Each step toward the building dragged on, and Cassie held her breath as Ms. Timber grabbed the door.

"Hey!" Todd said loudly as he walked into the

classroom. "What's this?"

"What?" someone else said. Loud voices and exclamations burst into the hall.

Ms. Timber furrowed her brow, pulling the exterior door closed and hurrying inside.

Cassie stepped inside right before her teacher and looked up to see her reaction.

"What—?" Ms. Timber gasped. Her eyes went wide, and she pressed a hand to her chest.

"Surprise!" Maureen shouted, and the rest of the class joined in, even though only a handful of them had known about the party.

"We wanted to surprise you," Andrea said, coming up. She looped an arm through Cassie's. "We planned this."

"Did you see your cake?" Maureen gestured to the beautiful white cake on the desk.

Ms. Timber swallowed, and moisture pooled in her eyes. "I don't even know what to say. I'm touched."

Cassie and Andrea grinned at each other.

CHAPTER FORTY-NINE
Community Show

"There."

Mrs. Jones stepped back to examine her daughter's reflection in the mirror. "How does it look? Do you like it?"

Cassie swiveled her head one way and then the other, noting the way her mother had swooped the dark hair into a braid before wrapping half of it into a delicate bun. The other half of her long hair hung down her back, straight as matchsticks. She looked at herself again, blinking brown eyes behind her pink glasses. Did she look older? Thirteen, maybe, instead of twelve? She was almost a seventh-grader now.

"Well?" her mom prompted.

"I love it," Cassie said. "I look so grown up."

Mrs. Jones laughed. "Yes, you do. All right. Go put your dress on."

Cassie went to her room and selected the soft blue dress with the white belt. It was one of her favorites, and she hadn't worn it since last summer. Tonight's choir concert would be the perfect time to put it back on. She smiled at her reflection and pulled the dress on over head. It got stuck around her chest, and she had to yank to get it down. It didn't fit her quite like it had a year ago, and the smile faltered. She couldn't even put the belt buckle in the hole she'd used last year.

"Mom, is my dress too small?" She returned to the bathroom and twirled for her mom.

"No! You look lovely."

"Are you sure?" Now she examined herself in her mom's mirror. The dress looked a bit pinched around her waist, even with the looser buckle hole. She pulled down a strand of hair, suddenly noticing how pudgy her face seemed. "Am I getting fat?"

"Absolutely not." Her mom's tone was firm. "You're getting bigger. You're growing. You can't expect everything to fit you the way it did last year. You're twelve now."

"Okay," she said, slightly reassured but still uncertain. Hadn't she noticed for the past few months that her clothes were tighter? She didn't even like to wear pants anymore because of the way they bit into her stomach.

"Here." Her mother slipped a silver chain with a blue medallion over Cassie's neck. "You have to be there an hour early, and it's all the way in Bentonville, so we better go."

Cassie nodded and followed her mother out to the car. She grabbed her choir book and studied the music on the drive. Ms. Vanderwood wouldn't want her using the binder for the actual performance, but Cassie just wanted to brush up on the words. She had them memorized, and singing in a choir didn't make her nervous like singing a solo. Still, it never hurt to be sure.

"Look, there's Andrew," her mom said, pulling up to the

curb of the performance center.

Andrew was the only other sixth grader from Cassie's school asked to be in the choir, and he was her friend.

"Hey, Andrew!" she called, hopping out the door.

He was already halfway up the steps. He stopped and waited for her.

"Hi, Cassie," he said.

"Hi," she replied, slightly out of breath from running to join him. She reached a hand out. Andrew's hand came out too, but Cassie already had hers lifted and tucking back a piece of hair before Andrew's movement registered to her. Oh! Was he reaching for her? By the time she brought her hand down, though, he'd already tucked his safely in his pocket.

She wasn't quite sure what to say. So she didn't say anything, and neither did he.

~

The children's choir performance went smoothly, and Cassie's heart soared with the applause that came from the audience with each song. A few of them brought tears to her eyes. She felt the music in her body, in her soul.

Ms. Vanderwood beamed at them after the last song. She pressed her hands together and mouthed to them, the words barely audible on the stage: "Thank you. Thank you so much for all you did. I would love for all of you to join the chorus again in the fall. I'll be in touch." Then she turned around and bowed to the audience, stepped back, and held her hand out to the children.

Cassie was on a definite high as they filed off the stage. She spotted Andrew and hurried over to him. Though she'd learned the names of several of the kids in the chorus with her, she didn't think any of them were very friendly.

"We did awesome," she said to him, smiling.

"Yeah," he said, grabbing a cup of water from the little refreshment tables.

They stood there watching people exit the big doors.

"Well," Cassie said, "are you going to join in the fall?"

Andrew hesitated. "It was fun. But I don't know if it was that fun."

"Oh." She shrugged, her heart sinking a bit. What if she signed up and didn't know anyone? Maybe it wouldn't be as much fun, either.

"What about you?" Andrew asked.

"Still deciding." She smiled, letting the euphoria from the performance wash over her again. "I loved it."

"There he is!"

Cassie recognized Andrew's mom, with her coiffed blond hair and sparkly sweater. Almost everything she wore had sparkles on it. She threw her arms around Andrew and hugged him.

"Such a great singer you are!"

Someone tapped Cassie's shoulder, and she turned away from the scene to see her father. Now it was her turn to get squished into a big hug, but she welcomed it.

"Good job, Cass," he said. "I'm glad to see you've found something you enjoy so much."

Her mom joined them, followed by Cassie's three younger siblings, Annette, Emily, and Scott.

"I want to do it too," Emily said, which didn't surprise Cassie at all. Two years younger than Cassie, Emily wanted to try everything Cassie did.

"Well, what did you think?" Cassie asked. "Did we sound good?"

"It was boring," Scott said. All of eight years old, he

found life incredibly dull.

Mrs. Jones gave him a small shove. "No, you were fantastic. The music was beautiful. And I could see you being very expressive up there."

"Just like Ms. Malcolm taught me." Cassie had been taking private voice lessons for almost a year, and she knew she was a better performer now.

"Can we go to Kikiberri now?" Annette asked, slipping her small hand into Mr. Jones'.

"Kikiberri?" Cassie perked up. The self-serve frozen yogurt place was a family favorite, but the forty-minute drive to Bentonville from Springdale made it an infrequent stop. If Annette wanted Kikiberri, they were likely to get it. The youngest Jones child got most of the things she wanted.

"I don't know." Mr. Jones looked at his wife and arched an eyebrow. "Do you think they earned it?"

Her eyes sparkled, and a smile teased her lips. "We may as well. Another day, and we'll officially have a seventh grader."

Me! Cassie stood straighter, feeling immediately more mature. Tomorrow was her elementary school graduation, and then it was over. She wouldn't be a child anymore.

CHAPTER FIFTY

Growing Girl

For the second day in a row, Cassie stood in her mother's bathroom while her mother pulled and tugged at her hair.

"My big girl," Mrs. Jones said.

Cassie glanced down at the white dress she'd borrowed from her mother, complete with a purple sash and little purple flowers. She smoothed her hands over the stomach area. Her mom wasn't joking. Sometime in the past year, Cassie had gotten bigger. It had mostly escaped her notice until now, but she didn't like it. "I can't even fit in my clothes anymore."

"We went over this yesterday. You're not a kid anymore. Soon you'll be a woman."

Cassie just frowned at her reflection. She still looked like a kid. Big round cheeks, long brown hair, thick pink glasses. Some of the girls in her class already wore make-up. Others had their hair cut and styled in cute, trendy ways. "I've had the same hair since I was in first grade."

"Well, did you think it would change?"

Cassie rolled her eyes. "That's not what I mean. I mean, it's the same style. Long and straight and boring."

"We could try something different. Do you want to perm it?"

"No!" She couldn't imagine her long, straight brown hair in kinky curls. "I'd look like a poodle." She pictured herself with bangs, with hair that hung in a bob around her shoulders. "Can we cut it?"

"Cut it?" her mom echoed, pulling back to study her. "Your beautiful hair?"

Cassie remembered asking four years ago if she could cut her hair, and how her mom had told her once it got cut, it wouldn't grow back. At the time that scared her enough to make her stop asking. She didn't believe it anymore. "It's not beautiful. It's long and scraggly."

"How about we just give it a trim?"

Cassie exhaled in frustration. That's all her mom ever did. Cassie didn't want this hair anymore. She wanted to be stylish and cute. She plucked at the fabric pulled tight across her stomach. "Am I fat?"

Her mom drew in a breath. "No, of course not!" She turned Cassie around and hugged her. "Sweetheart, you are perfect. Quit worrying so much about your looks."

"Okay." Cassie pasted on a smile and tried to focus on her upcoming graduation.

Her mom left the bathroom, and Cassie trailed behind her.

"Jim!" Mrs. Jones poked her head in the kitchen, where the rest of the family calmly ate dinner. Cassie had shoved a muffin into her mouth half an hour ago; the aroma of grilled hot dogs made her stomach growl.

"We're leaving," her mom said. "See you there?"

"Of course," Mr. Jones said, looking up from the table. "Good luck, Cassie!"

She smiled, feeling how the skin around her eyes stretched unwillingly.

The beautiful spring sunshine from yesterday had vanished. Now a torrential downfall peltered her and her mother as they ran out to the van. Cassie slammed the door closed and shook off droplets of water from her arms and hair.

"What rain!" her mom exclaimed. "Can you even believe this weather?"

Mrs. Jones turned the windshield wipers on full blast, and they started down the country road leading into town. The closer they got to the school, the more her stomach tied itself in knots. This was it. The end of elementary school. Her leg bounced up and down in jittery expectation.

The rain hadn't let up when they arrived, and Mrs. Jones pulled into the drop-off zone.

"I'll go park the car," she said. "You go on in. No reason for both of us to get soaked."

Cassie looked down at her white dress and had to agree. "Okay."

"Go find your class. I'll be in the cafeteria."

Cassie opened the car door and flinched when the side-blowing rain slapped her in the face. She jumped out of the car, holding her dress close around her and running for the door. She shuddered as she stepped inside, heart hammering in her chest.

Ms. Frats, the school principal, stood in the entryway. "Welcome!" she said, putting an arm around Cassie's shoulder and moving her into the cafeteria. "Quite a rainstorm out there! Go find your teacher and sit with your class."

Cassie moved out of her embrace and scanned the

cafeteria. She spotted Ms. Timber talking to the other sixth-grade teacher, Ms. Roxi. She saw her friend Riley hitting Connor Lane on the nose. Behind her was Emmett talking to Andrea. And next to Andrea, laughing at something Todd said, was Miles. Her eyes took in his dark suit and tie, his plastered hair, and warmth crept to her cheeks.

"Cassie!" Ms. Timber stepped over to her with a clipboard in her hand. She marked something on the paper, and then handed Cassie an envelope. "Find a seat anywhere. We'll move to the music room in a minute."

"Okay." Cassie turned her gaze to Andrea and hurried over as gracefully as she could in her dress.

"Hi!" Andrea said, spinning away from Emmett to hug her. "Ew, you're wet!"

"It's raining," Cassie returned, wishing she had a sweater. "How are you not?"

Andrea raised an eyebrow, her lip quirking upward also. "My dad let me use his umbrella."

An umbrella. What a novel idea. "Well, that was nice. What's in this envelope?" She pulled out the thick, cream paper Ms. Timber had given her.

"Oh, you haven't opened it yet? Do it now!" Andrea's eyes sparkled, and she clasped her hands together.

Cassie shot a suspicious look at her friend, then looped her finger under the seal and pulled it open.

"A wedding invitation!" she gasped out.

"Ms. Timber invited the whole class!" Andrea squealed. "Won't it be so exciting?"

"Oh, yes!" Cassie exclaimed. She started to say something more when Ms. Timber clapped her hands, and Ms. Roxi shouted, "Hey!"

Everyone quieted down, the excited chatter dulling to a

murmur as all eyes focused on their teachers.

"We're going to move to the music room," Ms. Timber said in a soft voice that required silence. "Ms. King will run you through your song again, and then we'll lead you on stage. You must be very quiet because your family and friends will be able to hear you out here. When the curtains open, it's show time. Come on, Wildcats!"

Instantly the noise level rose as voices joined the scraping chairs on the cafeteria linoleum.

"This is it!" Andrea squealed in Cassie's ear. "After this, we're seventh graders!"

It took a good five minutes for Ms. King to get everyone serious enough to sing, but she didn't seem to mind. They sang through the song three times before she cut them off.

"You're ready. Good luck, sixth graders."

They lined up in their prearranged order, no longer by class but by last name. Cassie did not know the kids on either side of her, which was probably a good thing because she wasn't tempted to whisper or giggle as they filed out of the music room, down the hall, and up the back stairway to the stage. She glanced behind her once for Andrea and spotted her way in the back. Then she took her spot on the risers.

The heat on the stage was oppressive. The footsteps echoed in the small area as students climbed the ascending steps. Ms. King stood in front, guiding them with her fingers. When everyone stood in place, she silenced them with a look.

Just beyond the curtain, Cassie heard Ms. Frats welcome the parents to the graduation ceremony. She congratulated all the kids and launched into a speech that nearly put Cassie to sleep. Then the clicking noise began, the one that indicated the curtain was rising, and Cassie straightened, eyes wide open.

The thunder boomed just as the curtains reached the top, and for a moment the cafeteria was backlit by lightning. Cassie blinked, then the image returned to normal. She scanned the rows and rows of people, searching for her family.

There. She spotted her mom off to the left, and her dad, grinning like a clown and waving. She smiled back.

Ms. King's arms went up, and the piano started. Cassie pulled her eyes away from her family and joined in the song. Her heart swelled, the music seeming to beam right out of her chest like little rays of sunshine.

They had almost finished the second verse when a loud wail broke through the auditorium. Ms. King's arms faltered, but she didn't stop. The wailing came again, rising in pitch and volume and then falling away, only to begin again.

Behind Ms. King, parents were getting to their feet. Cassie broke off her singing as Ms. Frats ran to the microphone.

"Students and parents," she said, her voice strained, "we are under a tornado warning."

CHAPTER FIFTY-ONE
The Tempest

"Parents," Ms. Frats continued, almost yelling into the microphone to be heard over the voices and thunder, "please follow me to the south hallway to take cover. Don't worry about your students. Teachers, please lead the students to the north hallway."

Tornado warning! Cassie turned wide eyes to the boy next to her. Then Ms. King ushered them off the stage, her normally placid expression pale and agitated.

"Quickly, quickly," she shouted, waving them past her.

Cassie hurried down the stairs, following the other kids to the hall. Her heart pounded in her throat, a nervous patter. What would happen if the tornado hit the school? She wanted to be with her parents. Were they okay? Around her, she heard someone crying, and another kid asked the same questions she was thinking.

Ms. Timber was already in the hall, seating them against the wall. "Silence!" she roared in a voice most unlike her calm classroom voice.

Immediately everyone hushed. Cassie pressed up against the white-washed bricks behind her, blinking at her teacher, waiting for further instruction.

"Tornado drill positions," Ms. Timber said, her voice much calmer. "You know what to do. Head between your knees, arms over her head."

Cassie ducked her head down just as she had during drills for the past few years. Tornado drills weren't a new thing for her; even when they lived in Texas, they had frequent drills. But being in a tornado, this was new. Her arms shook as she clasped her fingers over her head. She tried not to listen to the wrenching, shrieking wind that could tear the roof right off the school. She doubted the soft flesh of her hands would be any sort of protection if flying debris came through, or if the wall collapsed.

Ms. Timber and Ms. Roxi walked around the students, whispering to them, calming some of the more hysterical

ones. After what seemed like an eternity, the wailing outside stopped. The two teachers stood together, glancing down the hall and murmuring. Rain still pelted the school outside, hard drops drumming against the ceiling. But the wind wasn't screaming anymore, just blowing and sometimes howling.

High heels clicked across the linoleum, and Cassie turned her face, pressing her cheek against her knee. Ms. Frats rounded the corner, her perfectly curled hair in slight disarray, her clothing speckled with water.

"It's safe now," she said. "The radar shows the danger has passed."

Ms. Roxi frowned and plucked at the principal's blouse. "Did you go outside?"

"Just to make sure it was all clear." She rolled her shoulders back. "Shall we go back?"

"Are we still doing the graduation?" Ms. Timber asked.

"There's no reason not to. The storm is dying, and we have both parents and students here. Let's finish this."

Looking rather uncertain, Ms. Timber and Ms. Roxi urged the kids to their feet.

As soon as Cassie stood up, she felt the blood rushing back into her legs. With it came the aftermath of her adrenaline rush, a warm excitement that she'd been through a tornado warning and survived it.

"Did anyone see the tornado?" Todd was asking.

"There might not have been one—" Emmett started to say, but the chatter went right over him.

"I can't believe we went through that!" Leigh Ann squealed.

"We're alive!" Jaiden threw her arms around Janice and sobbed.

"That was more excitement than I was expecting."

Cassie turned her head at the sound of Miles' voice. He was talking to Andrew, but he caught her eye and smiled when he saw her.

She smiled back. "Yeah. But it was kind of fun."

The rest of the ceremony was rather dull in comparison to the adventure of the tornado warning. When Ms. Frats called Cassie's name, she walked across the stage to receive her certificate from Ms. Timber. For a moment, she turned and smiled at the auditorium, and at least two cameras flashed her direction.

When it was over, Mrs. Jones hugged Cassie tightly. Cassie saw tears in her eyes when she pulled away.

"Did the tornado warning scare you?" Cassie asked.

Mrs. Jones laughed and wiped her eyes. "No. I knew you were safe. Sure scared Annette, though."

Cassie glanced toward her six-year-old sister. At least she seemed fine now.

"Cassie," her mom said, "get your friends together for a picture."

"Sure!" Cassie spun around, spotting Andrea right away. "Andrea!" She beckoned to her, and the other girl ran over. Cassie scanned the crowd for her other friends, noticing Maureen and Janice. They came when she called them, and Cassie put her arms around them both.

Just as Mrs. Jones started to count down for the picture, Cassie saw Riley. Something tugged in her heart. Though they hadn't been good friends this year, Riley had been one of her best friends in fifth grade. Cassie still liked her. "Riley!" she called out.

Riley turned, and when she saw them posed for a picture, she approached uncertainly.

"Come join us!" Cassie said.

"Yeah," Janice said, holding a hand out. "There's room."

"Okay," Riley said, and she smiled with them for the camera.

Cassie and her friends hugged, promising to see each other at Ms. Timber's wedding. They dissipated, and Cassie fiddled with the belt on her dress.

"We ready to go?" Mr. Jones said, tossing his camera bag over one shoulder.

"Is there someone else you're looking for?" Mrs. Jones asked, her eyes on Cassie.

She started to respond when she spotted him. Instantly Cassie stood on tiptoes and waved over the crowd. "Miles!" she shouted.

He and his family were moving toward the other exit. He turned when she called his name, his eyes moving over the heads of other students until he spotted her. He smiled and waved back.

Cassie motioned for him to come. Miles said something to his mom, then wove through the crowd until he got to Cassie.

"Hi, Cassie," he said. "I guess we've graduated."

Cassie beamed at him, practically swelling with joy. "Take a picture with me."

His eyebrows bounced upward in surprise. "Oh—okay."

"Ready?" Mrs. Jones steadied the camera.

Cassie stood next to Miles and smiled at her mom. His elbow was close enough to hers that she felt the fabric of his jacket brush her skin. She clasped her hands together. "Ready."

Don't miss Cassandra's adventures in seventh grade! Coming soon!

Tamara Hart Heiner

Southwest Cougars Year 1

Other years in Cassandra's life include her fifth grade year!

Walker Wildcats Year 1

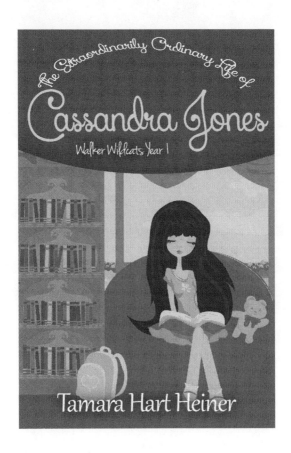

About the Author

Tamara Hart Heiner is a mom, wife, baker, editor, and author. She lives in Arkansas with her husband, four children, a cat, and a rabbit. She would love to add a macaw and a sugar glider to the family. She's the author of several young adult suspense novels and one nonfiction book about the Joplin Tornado, *Tornado Warning.*

Connect with Tamara online!
Twitter: https://twitter.com/tamaraheiner
Facebook: https://www.facebook.com/author.tamara.heiner
blog: http://www.tamarahartheiner/blogspot.com
website: http://www.tamarahartheiner.com

Thank you for reading!

Made in the USA
Middletown, DE
03 June 2018